HOUSE OF THE RISING SUN

A NOVEL

James Lee Burke

Simon & Schuster

New York London Toronto Sydney New Delhi

Simon & Schuster
1230 Avenue of the Americas
New York, NY 10020

First Simon & Schuster hardcover edition December 2015

SIMON & SCHUSTER and colophon are registered trademarks
of Simon & Schuster, Inc.

For information about special discounts for bulk purchases,
please contact Simon & Schuster Special Sales at
1-866-506-1949 or business@simonandschuster.com.

The Simon & Schuster Speakers Bureau can bring authors
to your live event. For more information or to book an event,
contact the Simon & Schuster Speakers Bureau at
1 866-248-3049 or visit our website at www.simonspeakers.com.

Manufactured in the United States of America

1   3   5   7   9   10   8   6   4   2

Library of Congress Cataloging-in-Publication Data

Burke, James Lee.
House of the rising sun : a novel / James Lee Burke.
—First Simon & Schuster hardcover edition.
    pages ; cm
1. Texas Rangers—Fiction. 2. Fathers and sons—Fiction.
3. Voyages and travels—Fiction. 4. Grail—Fiction. I. Title.
PS3552.U723H68 2015
813'.54—dc23   2015012518

ISBN 978-1-5011-0710-8
ISBN 978-1-5011-0716-0 (ebook)

In memory of John Neihardt and A. B. Guthrie,
without whose work there would probably be no American West

Go tell my baby sister
Never do like I have done,
To shun that house in New Orleans,
They call the Rising Sun.

—From "House of the Rising Sun," as collected by Alan Lomax

Truly I say to you the tax collectors and prostitutes will get
into the kingdom of God before you.

—Matthew 21:31

In Flanders fields the poppies blow
Between the crosses, row on row,
That mark our place; and in the sky
The larks, still bravely singing, fly
Scarce heard amid the guns below.

—From "In Flanders Fields" by John McCrae

1916

Chapter 1

THE SUN HAD just crested on the horizon like a misplaced planet, swollen and molten and red, lighting a landscape that seemed sculpted out of clay and soft stone and marked by the fossilized tracks of animals with no names, when a tall barefoot man wearing little more than rags dropped his horse's reins and eased himself off the horse's back and worked his way down an embankment into a riverbed chained with pools of water that glimmered as brightly as blood in the sunrise. The sand was the color of cinnamon and spiked with green grass and felt cool on his feet, even though they were bruised and threaded with lesions that were probably infected. He got to his knees and wiped the bugs off the water and cupped it to his mouth with both hands, then washed his face in it and pushed his long hair out of his eyes. His skin was striped with dirt, his trousers streaked with salt from the dried sweat of the horse. For an instant he thought he saw his reflection in the surface of the pool. No, that was not he, he told himself. The narrow face and the shoulder-length hair and the eyes that were like cups of darkness belonged on a tray or perhaps to a crusader knight left to the mercies of Saracens.

"¡*Venga!*" he said to the horse. "You have to be instructed to drink? It is no compliment to me that the only horse I could steal is probably the dumbest in Pancho Villa's army, a horse that didn't even have the courtesy to wear a saddle."

The horse made no reply.

"Or is stupidity not the problem?" the man said. "Do you simply consider me an ogre to be feared and avoided? Either way, my sensibilities are fragile right now, and I'd appreciate it if you would get your sorry ass down here."

When the horse came down the embankment and began to drink, the man, whose name was Hackberry Holland, sat on a rock and placed his feet in a pool, shutting his eyes, breathing through his nose in the silence. It was a strange place indeed, one the Creator had shaped and beveled and backdropped with mountains that resembled sharks' teeth, then had put away for purposes he did not disclose. There was no birdsong, no willow trees swelling with wind, no tinkle of cowbells, no windmill clanking to life, the spout drumming water into a galvanized tank. This was a feral land, its energies as raw and ravenous as a giant predator that ingested the naive and incautious, a place closer to hell than to heaven.

He longed for a firearm and a canteen sloshing with water and a tall-crown hat and a pair of boots and soft socks and a clean shirt. It was not a lot to ask. Death was bad only when it was degrading, when it caught you sick and alone and lying on sheets soiled with your smell, your fears assembling around you like specters in the darkness.

"You see those two strings of smoke up on that mountain?" he said to the horse. "I suspect those are cook fires built by your former owners. Or by banditos that got no use for gringos from Texas. That means we're going to have to cross those mountains north of us, and other than the grass growing in this sand, there's probably not a cupful of feed between here and the Rio Grande. You think you're up to that?"

He rested his palms on his knees. "That's what I thought," he said. "So I guess the big question is: What are we going to do? The answer is: I got no idea."

He stared at the water rippling across the tops of his feet. A great weariness seemed to seep through his body, not unlike a pernicious opiate that told him it was time to rest and not quarrel with his fate. But death was not supposed to come like this, he told himself again. His fingernails were rimmed with dirt, his belt taken from him by his captors, his toes blackened with blood where they had been systematically stomped. He looked up at the sky. "They're already circling," he said. "They'll take me first, then they'll get to you, poor horse, whether you're breathing or not. I'm sorry it's worked out this way. You didn't do nothing wrong."

The horse lifted his head, ears forward, skin wrinkling from a blowfly that had lit on his rump.

"What is it?" Hackberry said.

Then he turned his face to a breeze blowing down a slope not more than a hundred yards away. No, it wasn't simply a breeze. It smelled of mist and trees, perhaps pines, and thunderheads forming a lid above canyon walls. It smelled of cave air and fresh water and flowers that bloomed only at night; it smelled of paradise in a mountain desert. "You reckon we found Valhalla? It's either that or I'm losing my mind, because I hear music. You think you can make the climb up there, old pal?"

This time Hackberry didn't wait for a response. He picked up the horse's reins and led him up the embankment on the far side of the riverbed, convinced that his deliverance was at hand.

HE WORKED THE horse up the incline through the entrance of the canyon and followed a trail around a bend scattered with fallen stone. A paintless one-story Victorian house, with a wide veranda and cupolas on the corners and fruit trees and two cisterns in back, was perched on a grassy bench with the voice of Enrico Caruso coming from a gramophone inside. The incongruity of the scene did not end there. A hearse, outfitted with brass carriage lamps and scrolled with paintings of white and green lilies and drawn by four white horses, was parked in front. There were red sores the size of quarters under the animals' harnesses.

At least a dozen horses were tethered to a rail, and others were picketed in the side yard. Some of the horses wore United States Army saddles. Beer and tequila bottles had been broken on the rocks along the trail that led to the yard. Just as the wind picked up, Hackberry's horse spooked sideways, walleyed, pitching his head against the reins.

"It's all right, boy," Hackberry said. "We've probably ridden into a straddle house, although I must admit that hearse is a little out of the ordinary."

The horse's nostrils were dilated, ears back. Hackberry dismounted and walked him up the grade, trying to see inside the hearse. Someone had restarted the recording. He could see no one through the windows. Directly above, the clouds had turned a shade of yellow that was almost sulfurous. The wind was cooler and blowing harder, creating a sound in the trees like water rushing through a riverbed. He seemed to have wandered into a magical place that had nothing to do with its surroundings. But he knew, just as the horse did, that sentiments of this kind about Mexico had no credibility and served no purpose. The campesinos were kept poor and uneducated; the police were corrupt; and the aristocracy was possessed of the same arrogance and cruelty that had given the world the Inquisition. Anyone who believed otherwise invited the black arts of both the savage and the imperialist into his life.

He gave up on the hearse. The trees in the rear of the house had thick, dark green, waxy leaves and were shadowed by the canyon's walls. But something was wrong with the image, something that didn't fit with the ambiance that Gauguin would have tried to catch with his oils. Hackberry closed and opened and wiped his eyes to make sure his hunger and dysentery had not impaired his vision or released images that he kept walled away in his mind. No, there was no mistaking what had transpired in the canyon lidded by yellow clouds that seemed to billow like thick curds from a chemical factory. Four black men in army uniforms, two of them with their trousers pulled to their ankles, all of them in their socks, their hands bound behind them, had been hanged from the tree limbs, each dying on a separate tree, as though someone had used their death as part of an ornamental display.

Hackberry turned the horse in a circle and began leading it back down the slope.

"Hey, *hombre! ¿A dónde vas?*" a man's voice said.

A Mexican soldier in a khaki uniform had stepped out on the porch. He was thin and sun-browned and wore a stiff cap with a black bill and a gun belt he had cinched tightly into the flaps of his jacket. He had a narrow face and pits in his skin and teeth that were long and wide-set and the color of decayed wood. "You look like a gringo, man," the soldier said. "*¿No hablas español?*"

Hackberry gazed idly around the yard. "I cain't even *habla inglés*," he said. "At least not too good."

"You are a funny man."

"Not really." Hackberry paused and squinted innocuously at the sky. "What is this place?"

"You don't know a *casa de citas* when you see one? How do you like what has been hung in the trees back there?"

"I mind my own business and don't study on other people's grief."

"You know you got a Mexican brand on your horse?"

"I found him out in the desert. If you know the owner, maybe I can give him back. Can you tell me where I am?"

"You want to know where you are? You are in a big pile of shit."

"I don't know why. I don't see myself as much of a threat to nobody."

"I saw you looking at the hearse. You bothered by corpses, man?"

"Coffins and the like make me uneasy."

"You're a big liar, man."

"Those are hurtful words, unkind and unfair, particularly to a man in my circumstances. I'd feel better if you would put that gun back in its holster."

"You want to hold my gun, man?"

"No, cain't say as I do."

"Maybe I'll give you the chance. Maybe you might beg to hold my gun. You get what I'm saying, gringo?" The officer's mouth had become lascivious.

Hackberry stared at the figures suspended in the trees up the slope, at the way the limbs creaked and the figures swayed like shadows when the wind gusted. "What'd those colored soldiers do?"

"What did they do? They cried like children. What you think, man? What would *you* do?"

"Probably the same. Tell you what. I cain't pay for food, but I'll chop wood for it. I'd like to feed my horse, too. Then I'd like to be on my way and forget anything I saw here."

The Mexican officer took a toothpick from his shirt pocket and put it in his mouth. His hair was black and thick and shiny and bunched out from under his hat. "Some Texas Rangers attacked one of our trains and killed a lot of our people. You heard about that?"

Hackberry glanced up at the clouds that were roiling like smoke. He rubbed the back of his neck as though he had a crick in it, his pale blue eyes empty. "What would provoke them to do such a thing?"

"I'd tell you to ask them. But they're all dead. Except one. He got away. A tall man. Like you."

"I still cain't figure why you hung those colored soldiers. Y'all don't let them use your cathouses?"

"You ever seen dead people tied on car fenders? Tied on like deer full of holes? Americans did that in the village I come from. I saw it, gringo." The Mexican soldier drew down the skin below his right eye to emphasize the authenticity of his statement.

"Never heard of that one."

"You're a tall gringo, even without boots. If we hang you up, you're gonna barely touch the ground. You're gonna take a long time dying."

"I guess that's my bad luck. Before you do that to me, maybe you can he'p me out on something. Those soldiers back there were members of the Tenth or Eleventh Cavalry. There's a white captain with the Tenth I've been looking for. You seen a young captain, not quite as tall as me, but with the same features?"

The Mexican removed the toothpick from his mouth and shook it playfully at Hackberry. "You're lots of fun, man. But now we're going inside and meet General Lupa. Don't talk shit to him. This is one guy you never talk shit to, you hear me?"

"You're saying he's not quite mature, even though he's a general in your army?"

"That's one way to put it, if you want to get your head blown off. The Texas Rangers I was talking about? They killed his son when they attacked the train."

Chapter 2

T HE WALLS OF the parlor were paneled with blue and magenta velvet dulled by either age or dust. The curtains were a gauzy white and embroidered on the edges, swirling and puffing with the wind, as though the decorator had wanted to create a sense of airiness and purity the house would never possess. There was a fringed rug on the floor and, in the corner, a pump organ. The settees had red cushions; old photos of nudes with Victorian proportions were framed in convex glass on the walls. Above the mantel, also encased in convex glass, was a painting of a pink and orange sunrise, with cherubs sitting on the sun's rays. A wide hallway with a series of doors led through the back, like in the shotgun houses of southern Louisiana.

Two girls in shifts who looked like Indians sat in a corner, their legs close together, their eyes lowered, their hands folded on their knees. A middle-aged woman was standing behind a small bar cluttered with beer bottles. She wore a dark blue brocade dress with a ruffled white collar. Her eyes were recessed, almost luminous, unblinking. Behind her, on a table stacked with records in paper covers, was a windup gramophone with a fluted horn that had a crimson-mouthed, heavy-breasted mermaid painted inside it.

Hackberry's attention was focused on a huge man sitting in an armchair, one leg stretched out in front of him, a blood-soaked

9

dressing showing through a rent in his khaki trousers. He wore a billed cap with a polished black brim, like his junior officer, except it was canted on his head. He held an uncorked bottle of mescal on his thigh. When he picked it up to drink, the thick white worm that was the measure of the mescal's potency drifted up from the sediment. The general's mouth was wet and glistening when he perched the bottle on his thigh again. The coat that covered his sloping girth was stiff with table droppings and spilled liquids. The general sniffed. "You must have been far from water a long time, *señor*," he said.

"If you've got a tub, I'll take advantage of it."

"You're a prospector, you say?"

"I was till some Yaquis jumped me."

"Do you know what our government has done to the Yaquis?"

"I'm not up on that."

"You never heard of the one hundred and fifty who were burned in a church? The Indians are a long-suffering people."

"Maybe that's why they were in such a bad mood."

"You do not have the eyes of a prospector. You have the eyes of a gunman. Your eyes do not match the rest of your face."

"I was prospecting south of Mexico City in 1909. I prospected in the Yucatán and Chile. I've done other things as well, none of them dishonest. I'd surely like something to eat."

"Yes, I think you should eat and build up your strength."

"I'd like some feed for my horse, too."

The general wagged his finger back and forth. "No, you don't got to worry about your horse today. Your horse is Mexican. He's gonna stay right here."

"Does that mean I'll be staying, too?"

"People go where they need to be. Under certain circumstances, people go to places inside their own minds. They find safety and comfort there. Or they try."

"What kind of circumstances are we talking about, General?"

The general replaced the cork in the bottle of mescal and squeezed it solidly inside the glass with his thumb. "I think you are either an arms vendor or a Texas Ranger. We need to determine the truth about this question. That thought saddens me."

"Not as much as it does me."

"In one hour, nothing you tell us will be believable. Why go through such an ordeal to achieve nothing?"

"You don't believe what I say now. What difference does an hour make? I heard Villa at least gave his prisoners a running chance."

"My friend General Villa did not lose a son."

"My son is an officer with the Tenth Cavalry. His name is Ishmael Holland. I came down here to find him. I don't care about y'all's revolution one way or another. You haven't seen him, have you? He's big, like me. He's got a big grin."

"Why does a father have to look for his son? Your son does not tell you where he is?"

"He gave up on his father a long time ago."

"You are indeed a sad man."

"What are you fixing to do, General?"

"Maybe you will feel better if you tell others of your sins."

Hackberry gazed out the window at the sunlight lengthening on the canyon walls. "I put John Wesley Hardin in jail. Only two lawmen ever did that. I was one of them."

"That is not a subject of interest to us. Why do you raise the subject of a Texas gunman?"

"I'd like a redeeming word or two on my marker."

"In Mexico only the rich have markers on their graves. See this wound in my leg? I have no medicine for it. In your country, the medicine that could save my leg would cost pennies. I've heard the Negroes rub garlic on their bullets. Is true?"

"Villa raided across the border, General. You're blaming the wrong people for your problem."

"Texas Rangers fired blindly into the cars on the train. My son was sixteen. Your temper is your undoing, *señor*."

"Then we'd better get to it."

Hackberry saw one of the prostitutes lift her face to his, her eyes moist and full of sorrow, a tremble working in her cheek.

It cain't be that bad. It's never as bad as you think, he told himself.

They took him outside, close by the trees where the bodies of the black soldiers were suspended, close enough to the house for him to see the faces of the Mexican enlisted men who watched his visit to the Garden of Gethsemane with the impassivity of statues.

PAIN WAS A slice of brassy light dancing off a mirror, a spray of blood flung across the tops of the grass, a smell like animal hair dissolving in an incinerator. Someone poured water into his face in order to revive him, then wrapped his head with a towel and flooded his throat and nostrils. When he passed out, he went to a place deep inside himself that he never wanted to leave, as though confirming the general's prediction about Hackberry's impending need for safe haven. It was a cool place that smelled of clover and sunshine on warm stone and rain blowing in the trees and flowers blooming in his mother's window boxes; it smelled of spring and childhood innocence and was lit by a rainbow that arched into a green meadow. He thought he saw his mother smiling at him from the kitchen doorway.

He felt himself picked up roughly by men who cared nothing for his person or his life or the dreams that took him back to his childhood. His newly acquired friends carried him inside, knocking him against a doorjamb, dropping him on a dirty mattress. Someone tied his wrists behind him with a rope, then looped the rope around his throat and ankles and snugged it tight and left the room. As the sun climbed in the sky, the room became an airless wood box that smelled of old wallpaper and mold and the activity that had taken place on the mattress. When he tried to straighten his legs, the rope cut off the flow of blood to his brain. He slipped back into a state of half-consciousness, one in which small brown men were stuffing divots of grass in his mouth and holding burning sticks to his armpits.

Then the rope binding his wrists to his neck and ankles went slack, and he found himself staring into the face of the woman in the brocade dress. She held a short dull-colored knife in one hand. "It's true Captain Holland is your son?"

At first his eyes could not focus. His throat felt filled with rust, his words coated with phlegm. "Say that again."

"Ishmael is your son?"

"Why would I lie?"

"Because I think you're a worthless man who lies with regularity."

"What is my son to you?"

"I was attacked in my carriage by some of Huerta's jackals. They accused me of working for the government. They were going to bury me alive."

"What did Ishmael do to Huerta's men?"

"He killed them. The general and his men are outside. They're going to ambush him."

"They're going to ambush my son?"

"Yes, why do you think they're still here? They've already slept with all my girls. Now they will kill your son."

"He's a customer here?"

"No, he is not. But he'll come for his men when they don't return to their camp." She began sawing through the rope on his wrists. "There's a gun under the mattress. I let one of the girls keep it there after she was beaten."

"Who are you?"

"Why do you care?"

"You have such anger toward me."

She reached into a pocket on her dress and took out a half-filled pint of whiskey. "Drink this."

He tried to get up. Then his knees caved and he sat down on the mattress, hard, his hands shaking. He drank from the bottle, then closed and opened his eyes, the room spinning. "Answer my question," he said. "You've never seen me before. Yet you judge and condemn me."

"You smell of the blood you've shed. You're a mercenary, no matter what you call yourself," she said. "Get up from the bed and go. Do what you can for your son. But leave my house."

He felt under the mattress until his fingers touched a hard object. He retrieved a nickel-plated derringer and opened the breech. Two .41-caliber cartridges were inserted in the chambers, one on top of the other. He closed the breech and rested the derringer on his thigh. "This won't cut it."

"What does that mean?"

"It means do you have a rifle or a shotgun?"

She seemed hardly able to control the animus that lived in her face. "There's one in the closet. It belongs to the Austrian who beat the girl."

"What Austrian?"

"One you do not want to meet. He's coming today."

"You have a French accent. You look like a Creole. I think you're from the Islands or New Orleans."

"Be glad I've saved your life." She opened the closet door. A .30–40 Krag rifle was propped in the corner. "The Austrian shoots coyotes with it. The shells are in the leather pouch on the floor."

"I've got a feeling all this is about the hearse."

"That's because your mind is always on personal gain. We may all be dead by the end of the day, but you think more about profit than your own survival. Your son told me what you did to him."

Hackberry felt himself swallow. "He still hates his father, does he?"

"I don't think he would go to the trouble of hating you. You're a pitiful man, Mr. Holland."

"Are you Ishmael's lover?"

"I'm his friend."

"You've hauled his ashes, too."

She slapped his face.

He waited before he spoke. "I'm sorry if I've brought my difficulties into your house. I was at the attack on the train, but I told the general the truth when I said my intention was to find my son. I'm in your debt for speaking up to the Mexicans on my behalf."

But she was looking at his feet and not listening, the disdain and anger in her face focusing on practical considerations. "They burned the soles of your feet. You won't be able to walk. Stay here."

She went out in the hallway and returned with a pan of water and a pair of socks and sheep-lined boots. She knelt and bathed his feet and rubbed them with butter, then slipped the socks over his blisters and torn nails.

"Thank you," he said.

She raised her hand, indicating for him to be silent. She stepped closer to the window, her body perfectly still. The curtains were puffing in the wind. She turned around, her eyes charged with light. "There's a wagon on the trail. It's them."

"Who?"

"American soldiers."

"How do you know they're Americans?"

"Their wagons have iron rims on the wheels. Mexican wagons do not."

"Whose boots did you give me?"

"A functionary of the government in Mexico City. I watched him executed out there among the trees. He was corrupt and served the rich and betrayed his people. They made him dig his own grave. He got on his knees and gave up the names of informers in their ranks. I suspect some of the names he gave were those of innocent men. I won't say you are like him. But you serve the same masters. You ambush and kill illiterate people who go to bed hungry every night of their lives. Does that make you proud?"

"Why is my son exempt from your scorn?"

"He's a soldier who carries out orders he doesn't like. You kill for pleasure and money. Mexico is full of Texans like you."

"What's your name?"

"Beatrice DeMolay."

"I guess that's the worst thing anybody has ever said to me, Miz DeMolay. You're not fooling me, are you?"

"Fool you about what?"

"I haven't died and gone to hell, have I?"

HE WENT OUT the back door, chambering a round in the .30–40 Krag, the derringer tucked in his back pocket. He circled behind the two cisterns that were mounted on stilts and passed a pole shed stacked with cordwood and another shed with an iron bathtub and a wood-burning water heater inside, then cut through the trees where the bodies of the black soldiers hung as crooked-necked and featureless as wax figures that had melted in the heat.

He worked his way into a circle of sandstone formations and

boulders that formed a perfect sniper's den above the general and his men, down the grade. He positioned himself between two boulders so he would not silhouette against the sky, and wrapped his right forearm in the leather sling of the Krag and aimed the iron sights at the general's back. Perhaps one hundred yards out on the hardpan, he could see a mule-drawn wagon with two black soldiers in the wagon box and a third riding a buckskin in the rear. They wore wilted campaign hats and kept glancing up into the brilliance of the sun, shading their eyes, perhaps allowing themselves a desirous thought or two about the brothel, with no awareness of the danger they were in.

Maybe Ishmael was riding behind them, Hackberry told himself, and even though the circumstances were perilous, he would see his long-lost son again. But he knew that was a lie. If Ishmael were with his men, he'd be out in front, regardless of military protocol. Even as a little boy, Ishmael never shirked a challenge; he'd swell out his chest and say, "I carry my own water, Big Bud," using Hackberry's nickname, as though the two of them were brothers-in-arms. Hackberry felt a sense of shame and remorse that was like a canker on his heart. How could he betray and fail the best little boy he had ever known? Worse, how could he betray him for a jealous woman whose only strength lay in her ability to manipulate her goddamn moral coward of a husband?

"Hey, General! It's me again," he called down the grade.

The general turned around. He was standing on crutches carved from tree limbs, the forks notched into his armpits, his round face bright with sweat. "Hey, *mi amigo*! I'm glad to see you're feeling better," he replied.

"How about telling your *muchachos* to lay down their weapons?"

"Are you joking, *señor*? We may be under attack soon."

"You have many more men in the hills. I wonder why they're not with you."

"They are guarding the country."

"Are you conducting some business affairs you don't want other people knowing about?"

"Your voice is echoing, *señor*. The glare is very bad, too. Come down so we can talk as *compañeros*. Maybe you can have that bath and we can listen to music on the gramophone of the *puta*."

"Those buffalo soldiers were flashing a heliograph," Hackberry said. "Those are General Pershing's boys. He's going to be pretty upset about what y'all have done here."

The general was straining to keep his weight off his wounded leg, the pain starting to take its toll. In the brilliance of the day, his face was shiny and yellowish-brown, like worn saddle leather, dented with scars; sweat was leaking from under his hat. "Watch and see what we can make happen with the gifts of the Germans."

He said something to a Mexican soldier squatting behind him. Then Hackberry saw the detonator box and the wire leading away from it on the hardpan. The soldier clasped the plunger with both hands and pushed it down.

The wagon exploded in a mushroom of gray and orange dirt and splintered wood and tack and mules' hooves and viscera and spoked wheels and wagon springs and shattered axles and pieces of uniform that floated down like detritus from an aerial fireworks exhibition.

The rider on the buckskin was thrown to the ground. He got up and began running, trying to free his revolver from the holster. Just as he got to the top of a rise, a fusillade from the general's soldiers seemed to freeze and impale him against the sky.

The reverberations of the dynamite rolled through the canyon.

"Now we can talk, amigo," the general called. "You like a cigar? Come down. It is not good we shout at each other like this."

While the general offered his invitation, two enlisted men on one flank and two on the other began laboring their way through the boulders and slag toward Hackberry's position. Hackberry tracked the soldier nearest him with the Krag's iron sights and squeezed the trigger. The soldier grabbed his side as through his rib cage had been struck with a hammer; he sat down heavily in the rocks, breathing with his mouth open, staring woodenly at Hackberry as though he could not understand what had happened to him.

Hackberry ejected the spent casing and sighted on the Mexican directly behind the wounded man. The Mexican was trying to aim his rifle into the glare, his eyes watering. The metal-jacketed .30–40 round cored through his forehead. His knees buckled and he went straight down, as they always did, their motors cut.

The soldiers advancing on the opposite side of the canyon were obviously stunned by the fact that the man they'd tortured had acquired a high-powered rifle. They were caught on top of a great round rock with no cover, staring directly into the sun, when he shot one of them through the chest and the other one in the face.

Hackberry swung his rifle on the general and sighted on the exposed skin between his throat and the white flash of long underwear showing at the top of his coat. Hackberry tightened his finger inside the Krag's trigger guard.

"Does this mean we're not amigos anymore?" the general said. "Tell me, killer of my son. Tell me, man who kills the poor."

The general's image seemed to blur inside the rifle's iron sights. Was it the sweat in Hackberry's eyes or the sun's glaze on the rifle barrel? Or maybe the hunger in his stomach or the drain of his energies from the pain the Mexicans had inflicted upon him? Or was the problem in the sting of the general's words?

Hackberry pulled the trigger and saw the general's coat collar jump. The general pressed his hand against the red stripe where the bullet had grazed his neck. He looked at his palm. "I think your aim is slipping, *amigo*. Bad for you but good for me, huh?"

Hackberry fed five fresh needle-nosed rounds into the rolling magazine and worked the bolt. "The next one is coming down the pipe."

"*Chinga tu madre*, old *maricón*."

"I look like a nancy?"

"Shoot me. I'm not afraid. I urinate on you. I urinate on your family. *Me cago en la puta de tu madre*."

The junior officer and the two surviving enlisted men had taken up a position behind a pile of rocks and dead cypress trees. The enlisted men carried bolt-action rifles, probably Mausers, and wore black leather bandoliers with pouches that looked stuffed with ammunition clips. Hackberry backed out of the crevice and crawled across a table rock in full sunlight, beyond the Mexicans' line of vision. Then he ran for the canyon wall, squatting low, disappearing inside the shade and a clump of willow trees next to a sandy red pool, his head swelling with a thick roar like a kettledrum's.

He could see the general and the junior officer and the two enlisted men, but they could not see him. With the echo of the rounds, he could probably pot them one at a time before they figured out where he was. There was only one problem: He could not get the words "man who kills the poor" out of his ears.

Chapter
3

THE ATTACK ON the train was payback for Villa's raid on Glenn Springs, in Brewster County, just across the Rio Grande, where a four-year-old boy was murdered. The train had been a military objective. The freight cars were filled with soldiers, some riding the spine, some in uniform, some wearing peaked straw sombreros and cartridge belts that glimmered like rows of brass teeth crisscrossed on their chests. There were .30-caliber machine guns set up behind sandbags on the flatcars. No one could say this was not a troop train, nor claim it was not under the command of Pancho Villa.

But there were others on the train as well. Hackberry saw them when the Rangers first attacked, all of them riding hard out of an arroyo, the sun no more than a dying spark among hills bare of grass and trees, the sky a chemical green. He saw the faces of children and women in the open doors of the cattle cars and behind the slats in the sides, all of them seeming to stare directly at him. Hackberry felt trapped inside a macabre oil painting depicting humanity at its worst. The air was cold and smelled of creosote and the soot and smoke blowing from the engine. The women and little girls wore scarves and blankets and coats that had no color, as though color were a luxury that had never been their due. He saw a fat woman holding her hands to her ears, as though self-imposed deafness could protect her and her children. Hackberry heard a machine gun begin

21

firing from a flatcar, then the captain drew his Peacemaker and aimed it down the line and pulled the trigger. The flame that leaped from the barrel into the gloom somehow released the rest of them from the consequences of their deeds, and at that moment each convinced himself in the quickening of his pulse that bloodlust in the service of a higher cause was no longer bloodlust.

Hackberry held his horse's reins in his teeth, at a full gallop, and fired his pistols with both hands. He heard the rounds from the Rangers' guns slapping into wood and metal, the labored huffing of the horses, the locomotive whistle screaming, the steel wheels screeching on the incline, the dull knocking of the machine gun. But those were not the sounds that would take up residence in his head for the rest of his life. The screams of the children and the women were like sounds one hears inside the wind. Or in a dream. Or in a burning building about to collapse. Or in a universe where you helped dim the stars and murder the voices of charity and pity that should have defined your soul.

Man who kills the poor.

He picked up a rock and flung it in a high arc so it struck the opposite wall of the canyon and clattered loudly down the grade. The Mexicans turned and stared at the place where the rock had landed. Hackberry stepped out on a stony plateau in the sunlight, the Krag cradled across his chest. "I'm still here," he said.

"You are a crazy man, but one who has *cojones, hombre*," the general said.

"Put away your guns and I'll set down the Krag."

"Why do you make this strange offer, one that you know is silly and stupid?"

"Because I don't like a big, fat shit-hog thinking he's my moral superior."

"You are not a killer of women and children? You did not fire indifferently into train cars filled with innocent people?"

Hackberry's face felt cold in the wind, even though he was sweating. "Maybe I did."

"So why do you feel so offended? Why put on this display?"

"Maybe I want to do business with you."

"Now we see who our brave Texan really is?"

"Read it any way you want."

"We are not laying down our weapons, *señor*."

"I'll give you mine anyway. How's that?" Hackberry loosened the sling from his left arm and placed his palm under the butt of the Krag and flung it end over end through the air. It bounced muzzle-down on a boulder next to the general and pinwheeled farther down the slope.

"*¡Que macho!*" the general said. "A man of commerce who rises above petty resentments. What business do you wish to conduct?"

"Tell me about the Austrian."

"Why would he be of concern to you?"

"I think he's probably an arms dealer. That's a subject I'm highly educated in."

"What is it you are offering, *señor*?"

"The Savage Company is manufacturing a new light machine gun called a Lewis. It's air-cooled and doesn't jam and has a ninety-seven-round drum magazine. It fires over five hundred rounds a minute. The British are already using them in the trenches. I can get you a mess of them."

The general turned to his men. "Did you hear our friend's proposal, he who has killed our comrades? What do you think we should do with this strange, unwashed gringo?"

"Invite him down here, General," the junior officer said. "This is a very entertaining man."

"Yes, please come," the general said. "We have *pulche* and roasted corn and pig. The Austrian will be very pleased to meet you."

Hackberry walked down a narrow gravelly path between two huge boulders that were round and cool and gave shade and made him think of a woman's breasts. He lifted his hands in the air to show they were empty, the sunlight full on his face, his eyes filming in the glare. "The Austrian beats women?" he said.

"When they ask for it," the junior officer said. "Sometimes that's what *puta* want. That's why they're *puta*, man."

"I could stand some of that roast pig and corn on the cob."

"Ah, the gringo is ready to eat," the general said. "Tell us what else you want. We should bring some girls up here for you? We should give you money that belongs to the people of Mexico?"

"You're hurting my feelings something awful," Hackberry said. "You wouldn't go back on your deal and try to do me in, would you?"

"We made no deal with you, *señor*. I think you have *mierda* for brains."

They were laughing, all their fear gone. The junior officer opened a flask and poured rum into a tin cup and gave it to the general.

"Could I have some of that?" Hackberry said.

"I am always amazed by you. Do you want a blindfold?"

"Sir?"

"It makes it easier. A man can concentrate on his thoughts. He can pray. He can have visions of his family."

"Those don't sound like good options."

"I am going to be your executioner, *señor*. You and your friends took my son's life. And now I will take yours. It is only fair. Don't embarrass yourself by protesting your fate."

"Isn't there some other way to do this?"

"Look to the east, *señor*. It is there where all life begins. No, do not look back at me. Concentrate on the horizon and the dust and the rain blowing in the sky. That is where you are going. It is not bad." The general moved his right hand from his crutch and lifted a heavy revolver from his holster. His eyes were recessed deep in his face, like marbles pressed inside tallow, a drop of spittle or snuff on his lip.

"You dealt it for both of us, General. Sorry, there's some people you just cain't cure of their rowdy ways," Hackberry said. "I guess that says it all for both of us." He pulled the derringer from his back pocket and fired the first barrel into the general's chest and the second barrel through the junior officer's neck. Before the enlisted men could react, Hackberry took the revolver from the general's hand. It was a Merwin Hulbert double-action .44. Both of the enlisted men were dark-skinned and sloe-eyed and had the dull-witted resentful expressions of men for whom life had always been a trap, no matter whose interests they served.

"*¡Bejan las armas!*" Hackberry said.

They stared at him, their lips parted, their teeth exposed, generations of anger sealed in their faces.

"*Suben los brazos,*" he said.

"*No entiendo,*" one said, and smiled sardonically.

Hackberry shot and killed them both, the two reports as hard as a slap on his right ear, his palm stinging with the recoil.

HE WALKED TO the front of the house, the pistol hanging from his hand. There was no movement inside. Someone had released the white horses from their harnesses, and they were eating from a trough hollowed out of a log not far away. He crossed the veranda and opened the door. Beatrice DeMolay was standing with her girls in the parlor. The girls' faces contained the empty look of people who believe the revelation of their thoughts can bring catastrophe upon them. He pushed the revolver down in his belt. "Why are y'all so afraid of me?" he said.

None of them would speak.

"Answer me," he said.

"You killed them all?" the woman said.

"My selections were limited."

"The general, too?"

"I'd say he's pretty dead. Tell these girls I won't hurt them."

"You tell them."

"They won't believe me. They'll believe you. That's the way they've been taught to think. That's not of my doing."

"You've interfered in the Austrian's business affairs. You've made a mistake."

"What time is the Austrian due here?"

"He comes when he comes," she replied.

"Does the hearse contain firearms?"

"Of course."

"I cain't figure you. How long have you been running a hot-pillow joint?"

"Don't refer to me in that fashion."

"Excuse me."

"The general stole the weapons and ammunition from Villa. He was going to sell them to the Austrian. The Austrian's name is Arnold Beckman. He will probably sell the guns back to Villa. Do not be here when he arrives."

"I wouldn't challenge your estimation of your clientele, Miz DeMolay. Give me food and let me take a bath. I'll leave."

"You have ears that do not hear and eyes that do not see."

"I know I have my shortcomings, but I'll be damned if I can explain how I wandered into an asylum that masquerades as a cathouse run by a crazy woman. Maybe I'm being punished for my misdeeds in a previous life, something on a level with original sin."

"You're as irreverent as you are arrogant. You need to shut your mouth, Mr. Holland."

"You're a handsome woman, but half a dozen like you could have men taking vows of celibacy all over the Western Hemisphere."

"Go out to the bathhouse and take off your clothes. The girls will heat water. I'll tell them not to look at you. No one deserves a fate like that."

"I thought my first wife might be the Antichrist. Shows how wrong a man can be."

"What did you say?"

"Not a thing. I'm done. I don't want no more trouble."

"You don't think you're in trouble now?"

"I've seen worse. Wes Hardin killed forty-five men. He said he was going to make me number forty-six when he got out of Huntsville."

"Why didn't he?"

"A lawman named John Selman put a ball through his eye at the Acme Saloon in El Paso. Hardin had just rolled the poker dice out of the cup. He said, 'You got four sixes to beat.' That's when Selman came up behind him and busted a cap on him. That was the only way he could get him."

"You wouldn't have done it that way?" she said.

"No, ma'am, I surely wouldn't." He let his eyes hold on hers.

"Go out back and get in the tub," she said. "We'll burn your clothes. I have other clothes you can take with you."

"Who unharnessed the white horses?"

"They were hungry and thirsty."

"You did?" She didn't answer. "I didn't mean that about the Antichrist," he said.

"Don't lie."

Through the front window he could see rain and lighting and dust devils rising off the hardpan, probably harbingers of a monsoon that would cause the desert to bloom and the creeks to swell with mud and driftwood and the willows to lift wetly in the wind like the hair of mermaids. *Ishmael, Ishmael, where have you gone? Where is my loving little boy when your father needs you most?*

Then he felt ashamed at his self-pity and went outside and did as the woman had told him.

THE GIRLS HEATED the water in buckets on a woodstove next to the tub and poured it gently over his shoulders and head while he lathered himself in the tub with a bar of Pears soap. They seemed to take no notice of his nudity, and he felt no sense of discomfort in front of them. "Do any of y'all speak English?" he asked.

They shook their heads.

"It's just as well," he said. "I have nothing of value to impart. My life has been dedicated to Pandemonium. That's a place in hell John Milton wrote about. That also means I'm an authority on chaos and confusion and messing things up. I am also guilty of the kind of prurient behavior ladies such as yourselves are secretly disgusted by. That said, would one of y'all get me a drink of whiskey or rum, and roll me a tortilla with jerky and peppers in it?"

One of the girls patted him on the head and looked him in the eye. "You sure you don't want nothing else, *viejo*?" she said.

"You ladies are full of surprises. Oh, Lordy, yes, I do want something else," he replied. "I declare, I'd like to take two or three of y'all to a dance hall and hire a band that would serenade you all night. That's the kinds of thoughts a poor, tattered, wayfaring stranger such as myself is always having. But I'm not going to succumb to temptation, no matter how beautiful and young you are.

Plus, I don't have any money, even though I know that subject would not be of importance in our relationship."

The girls were laughing among themselves, splashing water on his face and back, pouring more of it over his head. In the distance he could see the sky growing darker and a twister dropping out of a cloud and wobbling like a giant spring across the desert floor in sunlight that was as bright as gold. There was a fatal beauty at work in this cursed land that he would never be able to recapture or describe to others. Mexico was a necropolis where the quick and the dead were inextricably linked on opposite sides of the soil, one always aware of the other. It was a place where killing was lauded, and where peasants wore depressions with their knees in the stone steps of seventeenth-century cathedrals, and where the light was harsher and brighter than it should have been and the colors were so vivid they jittered when you looked at them too long.

The girls brought him unpasteurized milk and tortillas stuffed with green peppers and onions and the pork the Mexicans had cooked. As he gazed at the shade and the rain advancing across the hardpan, cooling and cleansing the land, he felt years of rage and violence seep from his body into the bottom of the tub. He closed his eyes and let the wind touch his face and anoint his brow as though he were reliving his baptism by immersion in the Guadalupe River. He heard a rumble of thunder that could have been mistaken for cannon fire. In truth, he didn't care if it was. *The earth abideth forever,* he thought.

He opened his eyes and realized the dust had transformed the sun into a reddish-purple melt, and the bathwater that rose to his chin looked as dark and thick as blood, so sticky in texture he would never be able to wipe it from his skin.

Chapter 4

HE DRESSED IN a cotton shirt and denim trousers and a canvas coat and a straw sombrero the woman sent down to the bathhouse, pulled a saddle off a dead Mexican's horse, and saddled his own. Hail was clicking on his hat when he went to the hearse and opened the side door and looked inside. He saw two Maxim machine guns and crates of Mauser rifles and ammunition. The woman was watching him from the gallery, the wind flattening her long dress against her legs. He closed the door on the hearse and walked up to the veranda.

"I'm fixing to light it up. The bullets will be popping in the heat, but they're not going anywhere. I'd keep the girls inside nevertheless."

"Beckman considers that his property. You're going to burn it?"

"The Huns are arming the Mexicans to stir up trouble so we keep our mind off Europe. I don't want my boy dying from a gun that's in that hearse."

"There is no end of problems with you."

"Tell Mr. Beckman I'm sorry I missed him. If he wants to come looking for me, I'll get directions to him."

This time she had nothing to say. He was discovering that her silence had a greater effect on him than her insults, and he found that thought deeply troubling. He took off his hat, even though hail was still dancing in a white haze on the ground. "For whatever reason, you took mercy on me, Miss Beatrice. I hope the Mexicans don't hold you accountable for the men I had to kill or the ordnance I'm fixing to set afire. You're a beautiful woman." He turned and walked toward the hearse.

"Stop," she said. She approached him, her hair flecked with ice crystals, her face sharpened by the wind. "Beckman is the most evil man I've ever known."

"All the bad ones seem that way until you punch their ticket."

"You'll always be welcome here," she said, and went back into the house.

If that woman doesn't know how to set the hook, he thought.

FROM A GULCH he snaked tangles of broken tree limbs that were as hard and smooth and pointy as deer antlers. He crushed them under his boot and stuffed them beneath the hearse, then ripped the curtains and the felt headliner from the interior and packed them inside the branches. He searched under the driver's seat for a flint striker or the matches needed to light the carriage lamps, and found a box of lucifers. As an afterthought, he decided to make use of a grease-smeared blanket he had seen wedged between a crate of rifles and the side of the hearse. When he tried to lift it, he realized it contained objects that were heavy and metallic and probably ill-suited for carrying in a makeshift sack.

He squatted down and unfolded the blanket and spread it on the ground. Inside it were seven brass candlestick holders and two candelabras and a leather bag of low-denomination Mexican coins and a hinged rosewood box. He opened the box and stared mutely. An artifact lay pressed into a hard cushion of green silk; it resembled a chalice, perhaps one stolen from a church. The impression, however, was illusory. The chalice was actually two goblets that looked made from onyx, both inverted, each base fused to the other. They were encased by a framework of gold bands encrusted with jewels that could have been glass or emeralds and sapphire. The shades of color in the goblets were the strangest he had ever seen in a mineral: dark brown with tinges of black and a subdued yellow luminosity that seemed to have no source. The top goblet was inset with a gold cup.

He picked up the artifact and turned it over in his hands but could see no markings that indicated its origins. He replaced it in the deep pocket that had been formed in the silk cushion and closed the top. On the bottom of the box, someone had carved a small cross and the word "Leon."

He knew the Mausers in the crates would be coated in packing grease and in need of thorough cleaning before being fired, so he set down the rosewood box and returned to the canyon and picked up a Mauser dropped by one of the dead Mexicans; he also stripped the bandoliers from the body. In the saddlebags of the junior officer he found a spyglass and a bowie knife in a beaded deerskin scabbard and photographs of women in corsets and bloomers, their hair piled on their heads. He found a clutch of letters probably written by family members. He threw the letters and the photographs on the ground and searched the general's body for the ammunition that went with the Merwin Hulbert. Then he slung the Mauser on his shoulder and put the bowie knife and the spyglass and the Merwin Hulbert and the ammunition and the bandoliers in the saddlebags and walked back to the hearse.

The hail had turned to rain, and the sun had slipped into a layer of cold white clouds that resembled a mythic lake. He slid the wood box and the bag of Mexican coins in the saddlebags, and tied the bags onto his saddle, and set fire to the fuel he had stuffed under the hearse.

As he rode away, he heard bullets popping like strings of Chinese firecrackers in the flames and wondered if the woman was watching him from a window. When he turned in the saddle, the windows in the house were as glossy and impenetrable as obsidian. Maybe in the morning he would find his son's encampment. Or maybe he would be found by Beckman. Or maybe neither of those events would happen and he would ride all the way to Texas by himself, left to the mercy of his thoughts, a hapless and cynical pilgrim who could neither correct the past nor live with its consequences.

THREE DAYS LATER, at dawn, he and his horse were camped on a ridge overlooking a bowl-like desert glistening with moisture from the monsoon that had swept across the countryside during the night. Hackberry peered through his spyglass at a single column of smoke rising from a campfire at the foot of a mesa where a group of eight or nine men had picketed their horses and slept under their slickers and were now boiling coffee and cooking strips of meat on the ends of sticks. As the blueness went out of the morning and the mesa grew pink around the edges, he could make out the face of each man in the group. He recognized none, but he knew their kind. They were exported from Texas on passenger cars and put to work in the Johnson County War. They ran "wets" across the border and ran them home when they were no longer needed. They were "regulators" or sometimes "range detectives." In Ludlow, Colorado, they fired machine guns from an armored vehicle into striking miners and asphyxiated women and children in a root cellar for John D. Rockefeller. A professionally charitable person might say their real enemy was modernity. The West had shut down and the party was over. Regardless, the best of them would cut you from your liver to your lights for a bottle of busthead or a roll in the hay with a black girl.

Through the glass Hackberry could see one man who was unlike the others. He was hatless, his hair silvery blond and as long as Bill Cody's, his features delicate and aquiline, his skin the color of a plant that had been systemically denied light. While the others ate, he seemed to study the outlines of the buttes and mesas and canyons that surrounded the ancient lake bed on which he had camped.

Beckman, Hackberry thought.

His identification of the Austrian arms merchant had nothing to do with a rational process. There were those among us who were made different in the womb, and you knew it the moment you looked into their eyes. They showed no remorse and had no last words before their horse was whipped out from under them beneath a cottonwood tree. They would challenge a mere boy into a saloon duel and gun him down for no other purpose than personal amusement. Their upbringing had nothing to do with the men they became. They loved evil for evil's sake, and any animal or woman or man or child who ventured into their ken was grist for the mill.

Hackberry heard a skitter in the rocks farther up the ridge. "Who's up there?" he said.

There was no sound except the wind. He set down the spyglass and walked up the incline to a cluster of boulders below a cave. "You deaf?" he said. He picked up a handful of sharp-edged rocks and began flinging them into the cave, hard, one after another.

"That hurts!" a voice said.

"Come out here and I'll stop."

A man appeared in the mouth of the cave, wearing sandals and a nappy black duster without sleeves, his eyes hollow, his head out of round and his face curved inward, like a muskmelon that had gone soft in the field. Hackberry could not remember seeing a more woebegone creature. "Mind telling me who you are and why you're spying on me?"

"I used to be Howard Glick, of San Angelo, Texas. Now I don't go by a name. Unless you count the one the Indians give me."

"What might that be?"

"Huachinango. It's not complimentary."

"They call you a redfish?"

"It's what I look like when I drink. I haven't figured out what to do about it. You want some grub?"

"What do you have?"

"Grasshoppers. I fry them in oil. I got some fresh diamondback, too." He looked at Hackberry. "I say something wrong? You're a mite pale."

"Have you been out here very long, Mr. Glick?"

"A while. I was in the Philippines, then I looked for gold in the Sierra Madre."

"Why did you quit using your name?"

"I was in the Philippines from '99 to '03. You ever hear stories about what went on there?"

"One or two. I'm not sure I believe them."

"Most people don't. That's why I don't bother telling them about the things we did in their name." Glick walked past Hackberry and raised his head just above the boulders and looked out at the mesa and the campsite that lay in its shadow. "You're aware that bunch is trailing you, aren't you?"

"How do you know it's me they're trailing?"

"They staked out an Indian yesterday and made his family watch it. They thought you'd been at his hut. They were looking for a Texan over six and a half feet. Know what their kind can do with a wadded-up shirt and a bucket of dirty water?"

"I don't study on other people's grief. Have you seen any colored cavalry? The Tenth in particular?"

"I've met up with some white soldiers, mechanized infantry and such. I'd say they were right nice boys. Why's that bunch down yonder after you?"

"I burned up a load of their guns and ammunition. What happened to the Indian?"

"He hid in the hills when they got through with him. People say Indians are savages. I'll put my money on a white man anytime."

"You're not making my morning any better, Mr. Glick."

"I'd appreciate it if you wouldn't use that name. You want some grasshoppers?"

"Not right now. What'd you do in the Philippines that made you give up your name?"

"It's what *all* of us did. In their villages, along the river where the women washed clothes, on the roads and in the fields, anyplace we found them. We wouldn't leave a stone upon a stone. It gets inside you. I woke up thirsting for it. Worse than that. I'd wake up in a male condition thinking about it."

"Does the name 'Beckman' mean anything to you?"

The man in the duster fixed his eyes on Hackberry's. "That's Beckman out there?"

"Beckman is the man whose property I destroyed," Hackberry said. "There's a fellow down below who might be him, but I couldn't swear to it. You know him?"

The man sat down on a rock, his hands cupped over the rips in the knees of his trousers. His eyes were swimming.

"I didn't mean to upset you," Hackberry said.

"There's no hiding from it."

"From what?"

"When you do certain things to others that humans aren't supposed to do, somebody is assigned to find you out. The worse you are, the worse the man that gets sent after you."

"You offered me food after I threw rocks in your cave. Not many would do that. My opinion is you're a good fellow."

The man lifted his gaze, either at the sky or at nothing. The sun was shining directly in his face; his eyes seemed as bright and empty as crystal. "Out here in the desert, I don't have to think about what I don't have. Out here, I don't have a past. I'd like to keep it that way. I've been fooling myself."

"I hate to tell you this, sir, but your words have a way of zooming right past me."

"They find you. No, *it* finds you. Always. You haven't learned that? It's out there."

"What is?"

"*It.*"

HACKBERRY SADDLED HIS horse and rode down the far side of the ridge, leaving behind the man who had no name. Within hours, he found himself talking to his horse, a habit he had seen only among prospectors and solitary travelers in the Great American Desert, many of the latter longing for a saloon or a straddle house or the tinkling sounds of a piano to forget that Cain's mark did not go away easily.

By sunset, when he saw a village on the edge of a milky-brown river, he was light-headed with hunger and aching from his injuries and the wood-slat military saddle he'd pulled off a Mexican soldier's horse. He dismounted and walked into the village, his Mauser rifle slung upside down on his shoulder. Then he realized he was witnessing one of those moments that caused people to call Mexico a magical land. The sun had dipped below the hills, but the bottom of the sky remained blue, and the rest of it was mauve-colored and sprinkled with stars. As he entered the main street, he saw people beating drums and dancing with bells on their ankles and wrists and singing in a language he didn't understand. The children carried baskets of marigolds and chrysanthemums and placed them on an altar by a stone well where the dirt streets of the village converged. Some of the adults wore death masks; others carried poles hung with skeletons made from carved sticks that were painted white and clicked like bones. The air was filled with smoke and the smell of firecrackers and hissing pinwheels and bottle rockets popping in the sky.

The Day of the Dead, he thought. *Is it that late in the season? Do I face the close of another year without the touch of my son's hand, without the forgiveness that I've purchased with years of bitterness and remorse?*

Once again, his thoughts had shifted to himself. He wanted to hide himself in a bottle of busthead and sleep for a week.

In the torchlight he saw an adobe wall pockmarked by gunfire, a jail where two uniformed soldiers with rifles lounged in a breezeway, a blind woman roasting unshucked corn in a fire, children running through pooled rainwater, a priest in a cassock watching the revelers from the entrance of a mud-walled church, a five-seat merry-go-round pulled in a slow circle by a donkey. Hackberry tilted his hat low on his brow and walked his horse past the jail, trying to keep the dancers between the soldiers and the Mexican cavalry rig on his horse.

He went down an alley and tethered his horse by an outhouse behind a cantina and untied his saddlebags from the horse's rump and entered the cantina through the back door, the rifle still on his shoulder. The light from the oil lamps was greasy and yellow, the cuspidors splattered with tobacco juice, the towels in the rings under the bar's apron grimed almost black. The prostitutes were either middle-aged fat women or teenage girls whose teeth had already gone bad and who sat demurely by the small dance floor as though they were not sure why they were there. The fat women were garrulous and loud and obscene and drunk or deranged, and openly grabbed or fondled men's genitalia as part of the entertainment. Hackberry took the leather coin pouch from his saddlebags and set it on the bar. The bartender pointed to a sign on the wall. It read NO SE PERMITEN ARMAS.

Hackberry handed the bartender his rifle. "Whiskey *con una cerveza, por favor,*" he said.

"*Un bebedor serio,*" the bartender said. He had the face of a funeral director and wore a starched white shirt buttoned at the throat without a tie and a black coat that could have been stripped from a scarecrow.

"*También quiero un filete,*" Hackberry said.

"*Como usted desee. ¿Quiere una chica?*"

Hackberry ignored the question and gazed at the three guitarists playing in the shadows.

"*¿No le gustan chicas, hombre?*" the bartender said.

"I came here for the philosophic discussion."

"*¿Que dijo?*"

"*¿Quienes son los soldados en la cárcel?*"

"*Son los protectores del país. Son los soldados de Huerta. Son los guardianes de los prisioneros.*"

"Huerta's jackals?"

The bartender shook his head in warning. "*No hables asi aquí. Los prisioneros son comunistas.*"

"You've got Karl Marx in the jail, have you?"

The bartender's eyes were pools of black ink. He set a glass of beer on the bar and poured whiskey in another. Hackberry counted out his coins and pushed four of them toward the bartender with the heel of his hand. "*Salud,*" he said.

He sat at a table and waited on his steak. As at all saloons and brothels and gambling houses he had ever visited, the mind-set and conduct of the clientele changed only in terms of degree. The meretricious nature of the enterprise and the self-delusion of the victims made him wonder at the inexhaustibility of human folly. Gandy dancers, drovers, saddle tramps, gunmen for hire, prospectors, wranglers, drummers from the East walked through the door of their own volition and allowed themselves to be fleeced until they were broke or until "old red-eye," as they called the early sun, broke on the horizon.

But what of his own history? Somehow he had always translated his sybaritic past into memories of beer gardens with brass bands and strings of Japanese lanterns under the stars, or Kansas dance halls and hurdy-gurdy saloons where the girls were young and as fresh as flowers, where a young cowboy could be forgiven for temporarily forgetting his upbringing. The alcohol that boiled in his blood was simply a means of satisfying the pagan that lived in everyone. The men who died in front of his guns were part of an Arthurian tale, not the result of a besotted and childish man's self-glorification.

Paradoxically, this kind of introspection took him to one place, a whiskey-soaked excursion into a long black tunnel lit by the fires burning inside him, where he never knew what lay beyond the next bend, where the viscera governed all his thoughts, and violence and enmity always had their way. True, his adversaries were deserving of their fate and their loss was the world's gain. That was not the problem. The problem was the secret knowledge about himself that Hackberry carried in his breast and never confessed to anyone: Had he not worn a badge, he would have ended his days like the Daltons and the Youngers and Black Jack Ketchum and Bill Kilpatrick and Frank James and all the other bad men who closed down their act on the scaffold or in a weed patch or as caricatures in sideshows.

He remembered eating the steak in the cantina, the blood mixing with the darkness of the gravy as he sliced it from the bone. He remembered draining a whole bottle of whiskey, and he remembered a girl sitting on his lap while she filled her mouth with his beer and pushed it into his. Maybe he went into a crib with her, maybe not. When he awoke in the middle of the night, he was lying in a pole shed full of manure and moldy hay, his saddlebags under his head, the Mauser rifle cradled in his arms, his throat flaming. He cupped water out of a trough and vomited, the stars blazing coldly in a black sky. He went back into the shed and passed out, too weak and sick to check or even care about the contents of his saddlebags, his coat pulled over his head.

He had a dream of a kind he had never experienced. In it, he saw the woman named Beatrice DeMolay standing outside the shed, still wearing the dark blue dress with the ruffled white collar. She knelt beside him, placing her palm on his forehead. He tried to get up, but she held him down, her eyes never leaving his.

Why are you here? he asked.

Her lips moved silently.

I don't know what you're saying. Are you in trouble?

She leaned down and placed her mouth on his. He could feel his manhood rising.

Did the army or Beckman's men hurt you? I should have driven the hearse away and not burned it in front of your house.

His words had no more influence on her than confetti blowing on her face. She stroked his hair and eyes and kissed his hand. *You're chosen,* she said.

Chosen for what? You're saying I'm a Hebrew? She didn't answer, and her silence frightened him. *What's wrong with you, woman?*

He waited, but she refused to speak.

This is a dream. I'll wake from it and you'll be gone. I won't forgive myself if someone has hurt you on my account. Brothel madam be damned, there's something mighty good in you.

See? You're kind. That's why you've been chosen. Don't be afraid.

Don't you be calling me that.

Mi amor, she said.

He sat straight up, shaking with cold in spite of his coat, the eastern sky ribbed with pink clouds. He called out her name, convinced that her lips and body were only inches from his.

He untied the flaps on his saddlebags. Everything he had placed there was undisturbed. He opened the wood box that contained the fused goblets. Were the jewels real? They could be. The chalice could have been looted from a cathedral in Monterrey, in the Mexican state of Nuevo León. Or from the home of an aristocrat who discovered that peons possessing the importance of barnyard animals were about to take everything he owned, including his life.

He stared at the sunrise, sick and nauseated, his head throbbing, the smell of beer and whiskey rising from his clothes. He had already mortgaged the day, and he had a choice of living through it dry or drinking again and mortgaging tomorrow. He rode his horse through the alleyway. The street was totally quiet, the pools of rainwater wrinkling in the wind. Four soldiers were riding their horses in single file toward the jail. The last rider was leading a prisoner on foot by a rope knotted around his neck. The prisoner wore sandals and a black duster that had no sleeves; his eyes seemed lidless, half-rolled in his head, not unlike those inside a severed head upon a platter.

"What have you got yourself into, partner?" Hack said under his breath. He didn't know if his words were addressed to himself or the unfortunate eater of fried grasshoppers.

Chapter 5

Hackberry dismounted in front of the jail. The soldiers had locked their prisoner in a cell with several other prisoners and were drinking coffee from fruit jars and eating with their fingers from tin plates in the breezeway. Hackberry's hat was slanted over his brow, his eyes downcast, the way he would approach a horse in order to avoid personal challenge. "*Muy buenas*," he said.

The soldiers looked sleepy and irritable and didn't bother to answer.

"*¿Qué pasa con el hombre que no tiene mangas?*" he said.

"*No te metas, viejo,*" replied a soldier who was leaning forward in a straw chair so he would not drop crumbs on his uniform.

"*No creo que soy viejo.*"

"Either your Spanish or your hearing is not too good, gringo," the same soldier said.

"Probably both. I think I'm still pretty *boracho*."

"That could be the problem, man. Where did you get the rifle?"

"From General Huerta. He's a friend of mine."

"That's pretty nice of him. Can I look at it?"

"He'p yourself."

The man in the straw chair was bigger than the others, his cuffs rolled neatly on his upper arms, his skin as smooth as clay, his nose thin, one nostril smaller than the other, a delicate scar at the edge

41

of one eye, like a piece of white string. He partially opened the bolt and squinted at the empty chamber and the rounds pressed into the magazine. He ran the balls of his fingers along the bolt and rubbed them with his thumb. "It's still got what-you-call-it on it."

"Cosmoline?"

"That's the word. When did General Huerta give you this?"

"Two or three months ago, I think. In El Paso."

"That's funny, 'cause he died in January. This is November."

"That's probably why the nights are getting right chilly."

"I think you'd better get out of here, gringo."

"I appreciate your advice. I just wondered about the man you brought in. I think I've talked to him before. He seemed like an ordinary fellow to me, not a *bandito*."

"He's an informer." The soldier closed the bolt and snapped the firing pin on an empty chamber. He returned the rifle, staring into Hackberry's face. "An informer for the gringos is what he is, gringos like you."

"The man lives in a cave and eats insects. I doubt he's taken a bath since Noie's flood. Why be harsh on an afflicted man?"

The soldier stood up from his chair and stretched. "Maybe we can arrange for you to take his place," he said.

HACKBERRY REMOUNTED HIS horse and crossed the river on a wood bridge that was roped together in sections and seemed about to break apart in the swollen current. The trail was lined with cactus that bloomed with red and yellow flowers; he tried to concentrate on the flowers and the grass growing from the humps of sand and not look back at the village. What good could he do there? He was not the Creator. When you ventured south of the Rio Grande, you learned to accept people as they were or you would be quickly undone by them. Mexico was not a country; it was a state of mind that never changed and was responsible for the blood on many a stone altar. The man who blinded himself to that fact deserved whatever happened to him.

He was willing to share his food with you, as paltry and stomach-churning as it was.

"Shut up," he said to himself.

His captors are jackals. You know what they're capable of.

"They'll probably turn him loose. He's of no value to them."

You know better.

"Have it your way," he said to whomever.

He turned off the trail and tethered his horse inside a grove of cottonwoods. The morning was cold and smelled of sage and pinyon trees and creosote and the fresh scat of wild animals. He removed the spyglass from his saddlebags and sighted across the top of a sandstone rock at the back of the jail. A man with shackles on his ankles was emptying two buckets of feces into an open ditch. Hackberry focused the spyglass on the barred window in the back wall but could not see into the shadows. He collapsed the spyglass and sat down with his back against the rock and shut his eyes. Then he opened them and looked at the sky. *What the hell am I supposed to do?*

His question remained unanswered. A tiny stream ran through the cottonwoods. He drank from it and sat back in the shade and listened to the wind rustling in the leaves overhead. What a grand day it was. He wanted to shed his life as a snake sheds its skin. Of all the iniquity of which human beings were capable, was not betrayal the one hardest to undo? When he experienced these thoughts, he wanted to weep.

Instead, he again aimed the spyglass at the jail. This time he had no doubt what was taking place with the prisoners. Five of them had filed out of the building, their hands bound behind them. A soldier with a hammer was clanging a large iron bell by the side of the jail to bring the villagers into the street. The last prisoner in the line was Huachinango. The prisoners were motionless, staring at the adobe wall pocked with gunfire, almost all the holes roughly at the same height.

The priest from the mud-walled church was talking with the soldier Hackberry had let examine his rifle. The priest was obviously pleading. The soldier lifted up a horse quirt and poked him in the chest with it, pushing him backward, jabbing him in the ribs and spine, herding him as he would a hog.

Hackberry swung up on his horse and leaned forward in the saddle, bringing the heels of his boots hard into the horse's ribs, the Mauser balanced across the pommel. Just as he turned down the main street, his horse heaving under him, he heard someone shout "*¡Fuego!*" and saw five Mexican soldiers fire their rifles chest-high into three prisoners who were standing blindfolded against the wall. Their faces seemed to shudder in the smoke, then they went straight down, like puppets whose strings had been cut.

THE VILLAGERS WERE bunched across the street from the adobe wall, afraid to look at the dead and afraid to look away from the soldier conducting the executions. The men held their hats in their hands; the women had covered their heads with shawls, as though they were attending Mass. The villagers' craggy, work-seamed faces resembled teakwood carvings. The soldier in charge was explaining to them why the executions were taking place and why the villagers must remember the event they were witnessing during the three-day Festival of the Dead.

The soldier assured them the prisoners were not loyal and good *campesinos*, as were the villagers; the prisoners were traitors and deserters and *marijuanistas* and informers and tools of the Americans. Had the villagers not heard of the gringo called Patton, the American officer who tied bodies on the fenders of his motorcar? The gringo about to die, Huachinango, was not a harmless drunk but a spy who spat on the cross and gave up the names of patriots to American killers. Today should be one of joy, not mourning, he said. Today these enemies of the Mexican people would be covered over in the anonymous graves they had earned.

Hackberry held his rifle aloft with one hand as he got down from the saddle. "I'm here on a peaceful mission. I have no quarrel with you," he said. "The one you call Huachinango lives in the desert because he's deranged. He's a poor man, like the *campesinos*. The last thing this fellow wants to do is hurt anybody." He repeated his statement in Spanish.

"You are a very troublesome man," the soldier said. "Would you introduce yourself? I didn't catch your name earlier."

"I didn't give it. Actually, I'm down here prospecting talent for William Cody's Wild West show and would like to interview you and others about that possibility."

"Then you are famous? A man of the people?"

"That's why Mr. Bill gave me this job," Hackberry said. "How about it, amigo? Cut this fellow loose, and you and me can talk business."

"Let me see your rifle once more."

"Yes, sir, just don't snap the firing pin on an empty chamber, if you don't mind. It tends to mess up the spring."

"I will take care not to harm your rifle, even though I suspect it was taken off a Mexican soldier. You don't have a pistol?"

"Not *on* me."

"Why did you tell me you were a friend of General Huerta? Why did you tell me such a ridiculous lie?"

"I wouldn't exactly call it a lie. I met the man. I met Emiliano Zapata, too. You can ask him."

"You tell your lies to us because you think we're stupid. You fuck our women, you buy our leaders, you take our minerals, you lay waste to our villages. You do all these things because Pancho Villa killed a handful of worthless people in New Mexico. I feel very much like killing you, gringo."

While the soldier spoke, he held Hackberry's rifle in one hand and gestured in the air with the other, his back to his men, clearly knowing they awaited his command. Hackberry watched them lead the remaining two prisoners to the wall. The American refused the blindfold.

"Don't do this," Hackberry said.

"What will you do for me if I stop it?"

"I'm at your orders, *señor*."

"Then get down on your knees."

"Sir, we shouldn't be discussing activities of a *maricón* nature here."

"Kneel down, gringo. You need to learn what it is like to be a Mexican in your country."

"I run off at the mouth sometimes. I promise Mr. Glick won't be no more trouble."

"You can do it, *hombre*," the soldier said. He shifted his stance and inserted his thumb inside his belt buckle so his fingers hung down on his fly. "It will improve your humility, your spiritual vision."

"I've got some money. I've got a couple of artifacts from a church. I've got a rare pistol in my saddlebags. I would like to make a present of them."

"You have been looting churches? You have been a very bad gringo. It's time you show humility. What you will do down there will take less than a minute or two. Then everything will be as before. You can take the crazy one out in the hills and the people will call you a saint."

The soldier was smiling, the forked white scar at the corner of his eye as tiny and thin as a snake's tongue. He began to unbutton his fly.

"You don't want me as an enemy," Hackberry said.

"You are very vain. It is too bad for your friend the crazy man." Without taking his eyes off Hackberry, the soldier shouted, "*¡Fuego!*"

The rifles fired in unison just as the soldier butt-stroked Hackberry with the Mauser, knocking him into the dirt. Then he raised the butt and drove it into Hackberry's head. In his mind's eye, Hackberry saw his horse bolting down the street, stirrups flying, the saddlebags flopping on its rump. A mariachi band began playing in front of the cantina, and a bottle rocket popped high overhead. The festival had resumed.

HACKBERRY WOKE ON a wood pallet in a dank dirt-floor room that smelled of moldy hay and water that had seeped through the walls and candles that were burning in an adjacent room. The priest who had tried to intercede on behalf of the prisoners was sitting on a chair by the pallet. He removed a damp rag from Hackberry's forehead. "We caught your horse for you, up the trail in the hills," the priest said.

"You're American?"

"I'm a Maryknoll missionary. You have to leave."

"Where's my rifle?"

"The soldier who struck you took it. His name is Miguel Ordoñez. He's drunk and in the cantina now. Don't let him get his hands on you again."

The priest couldn't have been over twenty-five. His face was lean and unshaved, his hair over his collar, his breath heavy with the smell of alcohol and cigarettes.

"What about my saddlebags?"

"They're with your horse. No one has opened them. Miguel has told the villagers you robbed a church. Is that true?"

"No, sir. I'm a Texas Ranger."

"If Ordoñez finds that out, he'll shoot you for fun."

When Hackberry sat up, he thought his head would fall in his lap. "Maybe he ought to be afraid of *me*."

"He isn't. This is Mexico. You're an outlaw and he's the government."

"I've been rode hard and put away wet, Padre. Cain't I hide here'bouts for a while?"

"Believe it or not, I'd like to stay alive. So would my friend who hid your horse."

"I had that one coming, didn't I?"

The priest made a noncommittal expression.

"On another subject, I've been looking for my son," Hackberry said. "He's a captain in command of colored cavalry. His name is Ishmael Holland. Has some nigra cavalry been through here?"

"I don't know. You use the term 'nigra'?"

"It's a pronunciation. Yes, 'nigra.' It's not like they wouldn't stand out. Have you seen any?"

"Aside from your bad sense of humor, you obviously don't understand our situation. When Americans come into a village and the villagers feed them, the villagers pay for it. The government thinks all Americans are adventurers working for Villa. The price for the villagers is very high. In the United States, you don't hear about these things. That makes it convenient for you but not for us."

"Can you give me some food to take with me?"

"Of course. But you must go. We can't bargain on that point."

"And a big canteen? I'll pay you for it."

"I have a goatskin wine bag. Anything else you need?"

"I didn't mean to provoke you, Padre."

"I asked what else you needed."

"I could use a hatchet."

"For building a campfire? The dry washes are full of fuel."

"There's nothing like splitting your own wood," Hackberry said, rising to his feet, the room tilting sideways. "Oh, Lordy, I'm getting too old for this."

THE PRIEST PUT him in the back of a wagon full of corncobs and drove him up the trail to a shack in the hills where a goatherd lived. Hackberry retrieved his horse in back and thanked the priest and the goatherd and tried to give them money, which they refused.

"It will be dark in two or three hours," the priest said. "If I were you, I'd leave now, while Miguel and his friends are in the cantina, and not rest until sunrise."

"That's good advice," Hackberry said.

"Why is it that you look away from me when you speak?"

"Because I didn't tell you the entire truth about something. I said I didn't loot churches. I have some artifacts in my saddlebags that may have come from one."

"What do you plan to do with them?"

"I haven't thought about it. Sell them, maybe."

"They're not yours."

"They're not anybody else's, either."

"I hope you have a good life, Mr. Holland."

"Your second meaning isn't lost on me. I've asked the Man Upstairs for he'p in finding my son, but all I hear is silence. Maybe it's different for you."

"Not entirely."

"I'll have to study on that one," Hackberry said.

For the first time since they met, the priest smiled.

HACKBERRY WENT NO more than five hundred yards farther up the incline, then turned the horse down an arroyo onto a flat bench that looked out upon the village and the milky-brown river and the low hills in the distance and a volcano from which a thin column of smoke rose into a turquoise sky. "You've been a loyal horse, and I know you'd like to skedaddle for Texas, but there's a mean huckleberry down there in the cantina we just cain't let slide. No, sir. What's your opinion on that?"

His horse looked at him, one ear forward and one ear back.

"Those are exactly my thoughts," Hackberry said. "It's not honorable and it's not Christian. You do not let the wicked become the example for the innocent and uninitiated. Is that the way you see it?" He patted the horse on the neck. "Forget my teasing. It's about time we give you a name. How about Traveler? That was the name of Robert E. Lee's horse. Look at that sunset, Traveler. The sky is on fire in the west, and the rest of it is as green and vast as the ocean. Don't let anybody tell you there's no God, old pal."

But he could not hold on to his ebullient mood. The curse of his family, the one that caused him to curve his palm around the grips of an imaginary revolver in his sleep, was always with him. Sometimes his eyes did not go with the rest of his face, and those who knew him well would separate themselves from him. His mother had been a loving woman, his father sometimes stern and inflexible but fair in his business dealings and protective of children. Some in the family had a bad seed, some didn't. Those who had it found or created situations that allowed them to do things others preferred not to hear about.

Hackberry hadn't simply knocked John Wesley Hardin out of the saddle and stomped his face in. He'd nailed him to the bed of a wagon with chains and kicked him between the buttocks with the point of his boot and thrown him headlong into the sheriff's office, hoping all the while that Hardin would fight back and get his hand on a weapon so Hackberry could finish the job and purge the earth of a man whose merciless glare reminded him of his own.

As the sky turned from green to purple, he peered through his spyglass and saw the executioner, Miguel Ordoñez, and his five compatriots exit the cantina and ride single-file through the revelers and along the banks of the river, which they crossed on the wood bridge held together by rope. The executioner was slumped in the saddle, half asleep, a corked bottle of greenish liquid propped between his thigh and scrotum. The line of six horses disappeared from view, in the shadows of a hill. Hackberry closed the spyglass and followed.

He watched them cross a dry lake bed that cracked under the horses' feet and left a long line of serpentine tracks entwined like a braided scar across the landscape. They camped at the foot of a hill, among brush and cottonwoods, and built a fire around which they squatted as their simian ancestors might have. One man left the firelight and went into the bushes to defecate. His friends acknowledged the event by arching dirt clods down on his head.

Hackberry tied his horse to a bush and pulled the .44 double-action revolver and the hatchet and the bowie knife from the saddlebags, and worked his way uphill in the dark, until he was above the campsite and could look down on it without silhouetting against the stars. *Six to one,* he thought. *Well, it could be worse.* Then he added, as he was wont with his thoughts, *Not really.*

Two of the soldiers had gone to sleep on bedrolls. Three others were listening to a joke Miguel the executioner was telling while he sat on a log, taking small sips from his bottle, the bottle lighting against the fire each time he raised it. The joke was not actually a joke but a story involving a prostitute and a donkey performing on a stage. The soldiers' horses were tied in a remuda between two trees; the soldiers' rifles were stacked.

Hackberry's sheathed bowie was stuck in his back pocket; he held the .44 in his left hand, the hatchet in his right.

He stepped into the firelight, his coat open, his straw sombrero pushed up on his forehead. "Top of the evening to you, boys," he said. "This is from my friend Mr. Glick."

The first two who died never knew what hit them, one of them falling into the fire. The men in the bedrolls ran for their rifles. Hackberry kept shooting, not counting rounds, hardly able to make out a target in the smoke and waving shadows, the .44 bucking in his palm. Then it snapped dryly on a fired shell. He let the revolver fall to the ground and pulled the bowie from his back pocket with his left hand and slung the scabbard from the blade and plunged his own body into the midst of those still standing. He felt the bowie embed to the hilt in a soldier's side, felt him slide off the blade as another man shot at him with a Mauser, the bullet whining into the darkness like a whipsaw. He swung the hatchet blindly behind him and struck nothing, then caught a fleeing soldier between the shoulder blades.

Just as quickly as his vendetta had begun, it ended, and he was standing in front of the executioner, who stared at him openmouthed, the bottle of mescal still in his hand, as though his possession of it could return him to that envelope of time and security just before his camp was attacked. Hackberry's sleeves were red with splatter, his ears filled with a sound like wind echoing inside a cave.

"I am only a soldier carrying out orders," Miguel said.

"Take my knife."

"No."

"I'll give you the hatchet and keep the knife."

"No."

"Pick up one of the rifles."

"I'm only a functionary, little more than a clerk. I am not one who makes decisions."

"Then drink from your bottle. All of it."

"No. Not unless you will join me. We are both soldiers."

"Look at the evening star. Right above the hills. It always winks, like a faithful girlfriend. In the summertime, on the Guadalupe, it rises into a lavender sky about nine o'clock. You can pert' near set your watch by it."

"See, you are like me, a man of intelligence. There should not be these difficulties between us. Down there in the village, the people live as ants, as *Indios*. They appreciate nothing." He pointed. "The women are good for *chingada*, but what good are the others? I am glad that—"

After it was over, Hackberry threw the hatchet in the fire and peeled off his bloody coat and wiped his face and hands on the liner, and rolled it as he would a cloak and dropped it into the flames, then walked up the slope to the place where Traveler waited for him.

LATER HE WOULD remember little of his ride back to the border. He knew he was drunk part of the time; he suspected he had an attack of food poisoning and was delirious for a night and a day; he thought he and Traveler rode in a boxcar in which the chaff spun like dust devils; he bathed in a gush of ice-cold water he released from a chute under a tower by train tracks; he saw bodies floating in a river at sunset, their clothes puffed with air. He was sure of almost all these things, at least for a few moments. Then he would remember the peyote buttons he ate in an Indian's hovel, the rum he drank for breakfast, the fear he saw in the eyes of everyone he passed, and the voice of Wes Hardin whispering, *You're mine forever, Holland, a killer like myself, odious in the sight of God and Man. How does it feel?*

Then one bright morning Hackberry found himself on the banks of a river bordered with willow trees that had turned yellow with the end of summer. The air smelled of rain and schooled-up fish and a farmer on the far side of the river plowing under his thatch with a steam tractor. In the distance he could see cattle on a hillside and a white ranch house with a red tile roof, and a single oil derrick and poplars planted along a driveway that led to a rural church.

Was it Sunday? He couldn't remember. He paid a ferryman to take him across the river. On the landing a man reading a newspaper under a pole shed set aside his paper and got up and put on his hat and walked toward Hackberry, a revolver hanging on his hip like a pocket watch swinging on the vest of a blind man. "American citizen?" he said.

"Do I look or sound like a Mexican?"

"It's just a question. You don't have to act smart."

"My name is Hackberry Holland and this is my horse, Traveler. I'm a Texas Ranger. He's not. I'm a citizen. He is not. Is there a town up there where we can get something to eat?"

"Yes, sir, about three miles."

"Can I come inside my country now?"

"It's nothing personal, Mr. Holland, but maybe somebody ought to tell you."

"What's that?"

"You don't look half human."

"That's because I'm not," Hackberry replied.

Chapter 6

Her name was Ruby Dansen. Some said her parents came from Amsterdam and died in a circus fire set by the mother. Others said she was a foundling left in a shoe box on a sidewalk in Houston. Hackberry met her in 1890 at a Texas Ranger gathering in a deluxe hotel on Galveston Island, where a drunken United States congressman tried to feel her up and she threw a cherry pie in his face.

"Do you know who that man is, dutchie?" Hackberry asked.

"A potbellied old gink who just cost me my job. Call me 'dutchie' again and I'll give you some of the same."

He looked her up and down. "Doing anything later?"

That was how it began. She was twenty-two, she said. Then she confessed she was only nineteen. After dinner in the restaurant of the massive hotel on the beach, she changed her mind again and said she wasn't sure how old she was. She was from either Germany or Denmark. She had been a waitress and a laundress since at least age thirteen. She also cleaned fish in the open-air market by the pier. What else did he want to know?

"You don't remember where you grew up?" he said.

"What difference does it make? I don't sell my cuny on Post Office Street, like some others I know."

"You're a pretty girl. Why do you want to talk rough like that?"

57

"What's being pretty got to do with it? Don't put on airs. You're not in Galveston to milk through the fence?"

He gazed out the window at the green waves cresting and breaking on the beach, the foam sliding back into the surf. "I have a ranch up on the Guadalupe. I live there by myself."

"You're not married?"

"It depends on who you talk to."

She looked sideways, then back at him. The room was filled with diners, most of them in evening dress, candles burning inside glass chimneys on their tables. "I'm sure what you just said makes sense to somebody, but it's lost on me."

"I jumped the broomstick with an Indian girl up on the Staked Plains when I was seventeen. I think I got married once in Juárez. That was about the same time I discovered peyote and talking in tongues. I also entered into a couple of common-law situations the state of Texas may not recognize. My last marriage was in front of a preacher, but later my wife said it wasn't legal because of my other marriages. I got tired of trying to sort it out and wrote the whole mess off."

"All those marriages, you wrote them off?"

"Thinking about it hurts my head. Let's go out on the beach."

"What for?"

"To talk about our possibilities. You got something else to do?"

"I don't like the way you're talking to me."

"What's wrong with it?"

"There's no 'our' between us. I'm not a possession."

"I bet you could pick up a hog and throw it over a fence. Men rate physical strength in a woman a lot higher than we let on."

She looked around at the other tables. "I think someone put you up to this."

"If I make a mess, it's usually of my own doing, Miss Ruby. Let me be honest with you. What you're looking at is what you get. Unfortunately that means you won't be getting too much."

She put down her fork, blinking. "You behave like you're not right in the head."

"That's a matter of perspective," he said. "I never use profanity in front of a woman. I don't smoke or chew tobacco in the house. What's mine, I share with the woman who can abide a pitiful wretch such as myself. On occasion I attend services at the New Hebron Baptist Church. I was baptized by immersion in the Comal River on September 8, 1879, by a minister who fought at the Battle of San Jacinto. I was friends with Susanna Dickinson, the only adult white survivor of the Alamo. I read the encyclopedia for one hour every night."

"Do you always wear a gun inside your coat?"

"No, I usually wear it on my hip, at least when I work. I'm not a full-time Ranger anymore. I'm city-marshaling right now. I suspect one day I'll go back to full-time rangering."

"Rangering? Have you killed anyone?"

"Nobody who didn't deserve it."

"I know a horny old bastard when I see one."

"Number one, I'm not old, and number two, I'm not a bastard. I cain't deny the other part. It's how human beings get born," he said. He stood up and removed several bills from his wallet and dropped them on the table. "Are you coming or not? You're one of the most beautiful creatures I ever saw, Miss Ruby. That's not a compliment. It's a natural fact."

"A 'creature'?" she said.

THEY WALKED OUT on the beach. She was an erect and tall girl, wearing a full-length dress, sleeves to the wrist, and a short-brim, flat-topped straw hat with cloth flowers sewn on it. She didn't have a coat but seemed to take no notice of the chill in the wind or the sand that stuck to her shoes and stockings. The sky was maroon and ink-stained, the waves crashing five feet high on the beach, filled with seaweed and tiny crabs and the bluish-pink sacs of Portuguese man-of-wars. In his boots, he could hardly keep up with her.

"I'd get you your own buggy and horse," he said. "We can visit San Antonio. Or take a boat to Veracruz and see Mexico."

"What would be my obligations?"

"He'p me run the ranch. Take care of the books. Shoo varmints out of the yard."

"Anything else?"

"I'd like your company. It's no fun living by myself."

"Then why didn't you keep one of your wives around?"

He seemed to study the question. "I think the problem is I've never had high regard for normalcy. I've always been drawn to women who probably left their bread in the oven too long. It's a mystery I haven't quite puzzled my way through."

She seemed to ignore his attempt at humor, if that's what it was. "Why do you want me and not somebody else?"

"Because you're young. Because you represent the next century. Look at the hotel."

It was massive, undoubtedly the biggest building in Texas, hundreds of electric lights blazing with a coppery radiance.

"The times I was born in are ending," he said. "Thomas Edison is going to change the entire country. I don't have illusions. My kind will be swept into a corner. I want somebody around who's brighter and younger than I am. You have an extraordinary carriage. You have sand, too. I think you're the one."

"Don't ever raise your hand to me."

"I would never do a thing like that, not to you, not to any woman. A man who strikes a woman is a moral and physical coward."

"Don't ever talk down to me, either."

"I won't. I'll get you your own gun. If you take a mind, you can shoot me."

"When would we leave?"

"Tomorrow morning. Have you ever ridden on a train? It's a treat."

She stared at the waves bursting on the beach and the stranded baitfish flipping on the sand. "I need to pack."

Hackberry looked at the evening star flickering in the west. He turned his face into the wind and filled his lungs with the vast density of the Gulf and all the inchoate life teeming under its surface. "Smell that?" he said.

"Smell what?"

"The salt, the rain falling on the horizon, the fish roe in the seaweed, the fragrance of the land, and the coldness of the wind, the way it all comes together like it's part of a plan. It's the first chapter in Genesis. It's the smell of creation, Miss Ruby. We're part of it, too."

"You make me a little nervous," she said.

Chapter 7

HIS HOUSE WAS on a breezy point overlooking a long serpentine stretch of the Guadalupe River and the cottonwoods and gray bluffs on the far side; he also had a grand view of his cattle pastures and the unfenced acreage where his ancestors were buried and where the grass was a deeper green in the spring and sprinkled with bluebonnets and Indian paintbrush. He had a wide front porch with a glider and lathed wood posts and latticework with vines to provide shade in summer, and a two-story red barn and roses and hydrangeas in his flower beds, and several acres dedicated to tomatoes, beans, cantaloupes, watermelons, okra, squash, and cucumbers. The house was part wood and part adobe and part brick, with a basement and a fireplace and chimney made out of river stone, cool on the hottest days and snug in a storm, the rifle loop holes from the Indian era still in the walls.

He believed it was a fine place to bring a young woman. If people wanted to talk, that was their choice. "Spit in the world's mouth," he said. "Easy for you," she answered.

"They look at me funny," she said on her third day at the house.

"Who does?"

"The grocer. A snooty woman in the milliner's. People coming out of the church."

"That's because you're beautiful and most of the ladies at the church are homelier than a boot print in a pile of horse flop," he said.

"You said you didn't use profanity in front of women."

"A truthful statement about the physiognomy of busybodies is not profanity."

"The *what*?"

"It's from the Greek. It means 'facial features.'"

"Then why not say that?"

"I just did."

"Is that why you keep encyclopedias and dictionaries all over the place, so you can use words nobody else knows?"

"Drovers were paid a dollar a day to follow a cow's flatulence through dust and hail storms and Indians all the way to Wichita. Know why?"

"They were uneducated and dumb?"

"You're sure smart."

But what he called his irreverent sense of humor was a poor remedy for the problem besetting him. He thought that somehow their age and cultural differences would disappear, and in an unplanned moment, perhaps while walking under the bluffs along the river where she picked wildflowers among the rocks, she would glance up into his face and see the man who was like her father or the father she should have had, and the thought *He's the one* would echo inside her head.

That moment did not come. She seemed vexed by roosters that crowed at dawn, hogs snuffing in the pen, the absence of neighbors and electricity, the men who wore spurs into the house or sat on the porch and poured their coffee into the saucer and blew on it before they drank. When Hackberry went to Austin on business for a week, the wind died and the air shimmered with humidity and the smell of cattle in an adjacent field became insufferable, to the point where she closed all the windows and thought she'd die of heat exhaustion. She ordered Felix, the foreman, to move the cattle into a field farther down the river. "That's all red clover down there, Miss Ruby," he said.

"I don't care what color the clover is. Get those animals downwind from the house. The inside of my head feels like a combination of hairball and dried manure."

"Yes, ma'am," he said. "I understand. Maybe you should let me explain something."

"*Do it!*"

"I'll get right on it. I knew it had been too quiet around here."

"Take the mashed potatoes out of your mouth."

"Hackberry is always saying he just wants a little peace and quiet in his life. It never works out that way. Search me as to the reason." He looked at her expression. "Yes, ma'am, as you say."

When Hackberry returned from Austin, he stared out the side window at his cattle grazing in the pasture downstream. "Felix told you about the red clover down there?"

"What is all this about clover? It's what cows eat, isn't it? Clover is clover. I hope the bees don't sting them."

"You have to ease Angus into red clover. Otherwise they get the scours."

"What are the scours?"

"The bloody shits."

"What a lovely term. Thank you for telling me that."

"The bloody shits are the bloody shits. What else are you going to call them?"

"How was I supposed to know about the intestinal problems of cattle?" she said. "Maybe I should read from some of your encyclopedias. Should I look under 'B' for 'bloody' or 'S' for 'shits'?"

"Felix should have explained. It's not your fault," he said.

"You look worn out. You want me to heat water for your tub?"

"Why don't we sit down and have a cup of coffee?" He waited, hoping she wouldn't see the need in his eyes.

"I just had some," she said.

She went into the backyard and stared into the distance, the wash flapping angrily on the line.

HE DIDN'T SLEEP that night. Maybe it was time to give up trying to alter his fate. Didn't Jesus say some were made different by a hand outside themselves? Perhaps that meant living alone, at the mercy of one's thoughts and the bloodlust that neither whiskey nor profligate women could satisfy. His dreams were often filled with the rumble of horses silhouetted against a red sky, their tails flagging, their nostrils breathing fire. There were worse images to live with, weren't there? Solitude and the role of the iconoclast had their compensations.

Then an event happened that caused him to wonder at the great folly that seemed to govern his life, namely, his attempts to plan and control his future. Most of the events that changed his life had taken place without his consent and at the time had seemed of little consequence. Our destiny didn't lie in the stars, he told himself, or even in our mettle. It lay in our ability to recognize a gift when it was placed in your hands.

The black woman's name was Ginny Prudhomme, but everyone called her Aint Ginny. She had come to Texas from Louisiana as a slave with Stephen F. Austin's colonists in 1821, and had picked cotton on the same plantation outside Natchitoches until the close of the Civil War, when she found herself destitute and without shelter or family. The grandson of her former owner was a Methodist minister who took her and several other former slaves with him to a farm he had bought on the banks of the Guadalupe. Aint Ginny lived in a cabin behind the main house and tended a vegetable garden and put up preserves in the fall and cared for the minister's children and was a happy person, even though she had reached ninety and her eyes had turned to milk.

When the minister died and his children moved to cities in the North, Aint Ginny continued to live in her cabin. The new owner of the property, a man named Cod Bishop, who had made his money supplying Cantonese labor to the railroads in Utah and Montana, paid little attention to the black people living in the mud-chinked log cabins down by the river, in the way a person would not pay attention to the indigenous animals that came with a property deed. Sometimes the blacks saw him smoking a cigar by the waterside at sunset, gazing at his cattle and freshly painted outbuildings and farm equipment and, most of all, his pillared house with its dormers and wraparound veranda and ventilated shutters on the windows.

Cod Bishop was not a man whose image you easily forgot. He wore yellow coach gloves for no apparent reason, and he had a way of turning his head so people speaking with him had to address his profile. Coupled with this, his abnormally long back had an inverted bow in it, reminiscent of a coachman's whip.

One evening he noticed a gopher mound and kicked at it with his shoe. He picked up a stick and jabbed it into a hole, then into another hole and another.

"How long has this been going on?" he said to a small black boy who was watching him.

"Suh?"

"These piles of dirt and rock, all this dead grass, the tunnels under the ground. How long have you people sat and watched this?"

"I don't know nothing about it, suh."

"Go get your mother."

The boy left but didn't come back. Cod Bishop threw his cigar into the river and walked up the slope to his house.

In the morning, he returned with two of his helpers, men with rolled sleeves and a determined look. Each was carrying a grub hoe in one hand and a bucket of coal oil in the other. One had a gunpowder horn hung from his neck. "Get started on this first one, and I'll flag the ones in the pasture," Bishop said. "Turn each mound into silt and ash. Kill every gopher that's down there. You leave one, you leave a hundred."

The workmen stuffed wads of paper down the holes and jabbed them deep into the burrows with sticks, then soaked the paper with oil and sprinkled gunpowder on it and dropped a lucifer match down the largest hole. The effect was instantaneous. Strings of smoke rose from the tunnels under the scarified ground and far out into the grassy perimeters. The air was filled with the smell of burning hair.

"Oh, what y'all doing?" a voice said.

Aint Ginny had come out of her cabin and was standing as small and frail as a stick figure behind the workmen, one hand gripped on a cane, her eyes the color of fish scale.

"Go back inside," one of them said.

"Y'all burning out their caves? You cain't do that, suh."

"Watch."

"They God's creatures. I feed them. I give them all names, too. They make their li'l squeaking noise when they hear me coming."

"You do *what*?" Cod Bishop said, approaching her, half of a smile on his face. He wore a tight-waisted coat and polished knee-high riding boots, his pants tucked inside them.

"The gophers ain't hurt nothing, suh. My grandson say there ain't none in the pasture. They got their li'l town down under the ground here."

"Go back into your cabin," Bishop said. "Don't try to intervene in the operation of my farm. You should know better than that."

"They suffering down there, suh."

"I've tried to be patient, Aunty. You're forcing my hand."

"Where Reverend Jasper at?"

"I suspect he's still in his grave. He's been there eighteen months."

"I seen him three days ago," she said.

Cod Bishop put on a world-weary face, then balled his fists and placed them on his hips, his coat stretching across his back, like a man lost in the most profound of thoughts. He studied the ducks pecking at their feathers among the flooded reeds, his cows grazing among the buttercups, the lovely green knoll that backdropped a collection of hovels. He turned to his workmen. "Get everybody out and soak it," he said.

"The other mounds?" one of them asked.

"All this," Bishop said, waving his finger at the cabins. "The privies, too. Rake the embers into the river. I don't want them blowing onto my rooftop."

"You're telling them to burn our cabins?" Aint Ginny said.

"I'm going to give each of you two silver dollars. I'll tell the colored preacher in town about your situation. There's a workhouse for colored in San Antonio. You'll be a lot better off there."

"I got the croup in my lungs, suh. They ain't gone take me. Where Reverend Prudhomme at?"

"The Prudhommes are not here anymore. That's one more reason you should seek help among your own people. But try to remember this, Aunty. You mustn't sass a white person again. I let it pass because of your age. Others may not be so kind."

She began to cry, tears running straight down her face onto her dress. He put his gloved hand on her arm and led her to the pasture fence. "Hold on to the rail till we bring the wagon down," Bishop said. "I don't want you getting hurt."

In minutes her cabin and the cabins of her neighbors were blazing, the flames flattening and whipping across her vegetable garden, curling and dissolving everything that grew there.

HACKBERRY SAW THE fire from his porch. He went into the house and came back out with his brass field binoculars. "What is it?" Ruby said from the doorway.

"Cod Bishop is burning out his darkies," he replied.

"Why would he do that?"

"Because he's a son of a bitch." The binoculars made a plopping sound when he dropped them back in their leather case.

"Where are the colored people?" she asked.

"Watching the fire."

"That's terrible."

"I'll be back in a little while."

"Where are you going?"

He seemed to consider the question. "I thought I'd throw a line in the river. It's not too late in the morning to catch a catfish or two. Tell Sid to clean up my fishing shack and put up the trail tent."

"What are you doing, Hack?"

"You got me. I've never been good at specificity."

"At *what*?"

"It means why worry about what hasn't happened yet," he replied.

He put a lead on a horse in the lot and led it to the shed where he kept his buggy. After he harnessed the horse, he got up on the buggy seat and picked up the reins.

"I'm going, too," she said.

HACKBERRY DROVE THE buggy up the county road and under the arch that gave on to Cod Bishop's property. By the time he reached the cabins, the logs had collapsed into mounds of flickering charcoal and soft ash. Except for Aint Ginny, the black people were climbing onto a flat wagon that would take them to town. Hackberry got down from his buggy. He was coatless and wearing a tall-crown Stetson that had sweat stains above the band, and a shirt with no collar. Bishop stared at him, his eyes dropping briefly to Hackberry's waist.

"This is not an official visit," Hackberry said.

"Then state your purpose."

"Aint Ginny has nursed half the white children in this county, including a few woods colts whose fathers wouldn't recognize them."

"I'm not a particular admirer of you, Mr. Holland," Bishop said. His eyes drifted to Ruby Dansen. "Nor do I approve of the way you conduct your personal life."

"Miss Ruby is my bookkeeper," Hackberry said. "She also takes care of my house. I'd like to call her my companion, but she's not. If you allude to her in a disrespectful way again, I'll bury you up to your neck in an ant pile."

"I'm sure you would, Mr. Holland. At least if you were drunk enough."

Hackberry scratched at his eye and gazed at the river. It was coppery green in the early sunlight, a long riffle undulating through gray boulders in the deepest part of the current. "Did you know Aint Ginny prepared breakfast for Davy Crockett and his Tennesseans on their way to the Alamo?"

"No, I didn't. And I don't care. She sassed me. Do you allow your servants to sass you?"

"I don't have servants. I'll take these people with me, though."

"Then your niggers await you, sir."

"We're not quite finished here."

"Stand back from me," Bishop said.

"I heard popping sounds on the road. I bet those were her preserve jars blowing up."

"I'm armed, Mr. Holland. I won't hesitate to defend myself."

Hackberry slapped him across the face. Bishop stumbled backward in shock, one hand rising to protect himself. Hackberry struck him again, harder, using his knuckles. "Apologize."

"I'm a white man, sir. I do not apologize to niggers."

"Don't address me as 'sir.'"

"What?"

"'Sir' from a man of your ilk implies we belong to the same culture. We do not."

"You cannot behave like this. You're an officer of the law."

This time Hackberry broke his nose.

"These men are witnesses," Bishop said. He had to cup his hand under his nose before he continued. "I've done nothing to provoke this."

Hackberry pushed him backward into the smoke from the cabins. He tore open Bishop's coat and pulled a five-shot nickel-plated revolver from his belt and threw it in the river. "Take off your clothes."

"What?" Bishop's face was trembling, his upper lip slick with blood.

"Strip naked and crawl into the ash."

"Somebody do something about this."

Hackberry knocked him to the ground and kicked him between the buttocks. When Bishop screamed, he kicked him again. Then a persona that invaded his dreams and shimmered in daylight on the edge of his vision stepped inside his skin and took control of his thoughts and feet and hands and the words that seemed released from a place other than his voice box. When these episodes occurred in his life, and always without expectation, he became a spectator rather than a participant in his own deeds. He saw his boot descend on Bishop's face and the side of his head and his neck and mouth; he saw Bishop's men trying to dissuade him, waving their hands impotently in the air, their mouths moving without sound, while Cod Bishop crawled for safety through hot ash like a caterpillar trying to crawl through flame. Someone was screaming again? Was it Aint Ginny or a child or Bishop? He didn't know. Then he felt a hand seize his upper arm. He turned his head slowly, blinking, the world coming back into focus, as though someone had removed an ether mask from his face.

"Hack?" Ruby said. "Hack, it's me. Enough."

"Enough what?"

"He's done."

Hackberry looked down at Bishop. "Get up and stop groveling around like that. Tell your darkies you'll make things right."

"Come home with me, Hack," Ruby said.

"What are you talking about, woman?"

"Let me drive the buggy. I've always wanted to drive one."

"That would be fine," he replied, widening his eyes. "Come along with us, Aint Ginny. The rest of y'all can come, too. Look at the rain and sunlight on the hills. I declare, if this world isn't a frolic."

Ruby held his arm tightly as they walked to the buggy, in a way she had not done previously.

A THUNDERSTORM STRUCK THAT night and lit the clouds with fireworks and filled the air with the smell of sulfur and mown hay and the fecund odor of spawning fish. It also pelted the fishing shack and the tent where Hackberry had quartered Aint Ginny and the other black people to whom he had given sanctuary. He went out on the porch and gazed down the slope at the tent swelling and flapping in the wind, an oil lamp burning inside. He went back in the house and began spooning soup from a kettle on the stove into a cylindrical lunch pail. Ruby watched him from the doorway. "I'll do it," she said.

"Do what?"

"Feed the old woman."

"I think it's tuberculosis, not croup."

"Better I do it than you."

"Why's that?"

"You're of an age when people catch germs more easily," she said.

"The reason I've reached my present age is I know how to avoid getting sick or shot or having someone stick a knife in me," he said. "Why are you looking at me like that?"

"I've just never understood why unteachable people waste their money on books," she said.

He draped a slicker over his head and carried the pail of soup and a wooden spoon through the rain into the tent. Aint Ginny was lying on one of the beds Felix had brought from the bunkhouse. Hackberry pulled up a chair to her bedside and filled the spoon and touched it to her mouth. "I'm going to have Felix carpenter a cabin with everything you need," he said. "You can stay here long as you want."

"That man gonna get you, Marse Hack. He's the kind come up on you with a dirk when you ain't looking."

"Cod Bishop? I hope he tries."

She opened her mouth as a tiny bird in a nest might, waiting for him to place the spoon on her lip.

"I was a little boy when we heard about the Surrender, but you saw it all, didn't you?" he said.

"I seen the Yankees burn the big house and chop up a piano in the yard. I saw them dig up our smoked hams. They dug them out with their hands, they was so hungry."

He stroked her forehead. "You go to sleep now."

He saw a shadow fall across his arm. He turned and looked into Ruby's face.

"The sheriff was at the door. He said Cod Bishop is filing assault charges against you."

"Remind me to shoot the sheriff."

"He said Cod Bishop is a sorry sack of shit and not to worry about it."

"I've always said the sheriff had redeeming qualities."

"Your supper is ready."

"I'm going into town for a little while."

"If you want to get drunk, do it here."

"I never drink in my home."

"That doesn't make sense."

"Getting drunk doesn't, either. That's why people get drunk. They cain't make sense of anything, least of all themselves."

"Thanks for explaining that. I'll throw your supper in the yard."

THAT NIGHT HE didn't go into town; nor did he drink. Instead he wrote in his journal, at his desk, in the light of a brass oil lamp that had a green glass shade as thick as a tortoise shell. His journal entries often dealt with historical events or, rather, the consequences he believed would ensue from them: the populist movement, the stranglehold on the dollar by industrial interests, the theft of public lands by the railroads, anarchists throwing bombs, and company ginks shooting down strikers on picket lines. These observations and notations, however, were secondary in importance to his entries about the depression and murderous instincts that were bedfellows in the Holland family, passing from one generation to the next, perhaps unto the seventh generation.

He had read and reread many times Thomas Jefferson's letter about the suicide of Meriwether Lewis and the fits of melancholia that Meriwether could avoid only by keeping his mind occupied. Jefferson, a child of the Enlightment who believed the unexamined life was not worth living, looked upon melancholia and self-destructive thoughts as the inevitable products of a brilliant and curious mind when it became idle. While a dolt remained as happy as a cloth doll with a smile painted on its face—even when the dolt was about to fall off a precipice—an intelligent person suffered the pains of the damned simply because he paused long enough to hear his own thoughts.

"What are you writing?" Ruby said over his shoulder.

"I try to sort my head out by writing about the things that fret me. Most of the time it doesn't work too well."

"What things?"

"I lose time. I step into a windstorm that's either outside or inside myself. Later I cain't remember exactly what I did there. Then it comes back to me in a dream. Sometimes it scares the bejesus out of me. My father is the same way. His name is Sam Morgan Holland. A lot of men died in front of his guns, from here all the way to Wichita and Abilene."

"He's a gunslinger?"

"A Baptist preacher."

"I'd like to meet him."

"I wouldn't wish my father on my worst enemy. If he gets sent to hell, I think the devil will quit his job."

She placed her palm on the back of his neck. "You're hot as a stove."

"What you saw me do to Cod Bishop, that's not me. It's a sickness that lives in me, but it's not who I am, at least not all the time. Maybe the Hollands got their bloodlust from the Indians. Or maybe we gave it to them. Whatever it is, we sure got it."

She took her hand away and gazed at the wallpaper. It was printed with small roses. "Who was the woman who lived here?"

"She called herself my wife. I'd call her otherwise."

"She hurt you?"

"I made my own bed. The fault is mine. I need to tell you something, Ruby. I made a mistake."

"About what?"

"With you. I made a mistake."

He saw the vulnerability, the flicker of injury, in her face before he had stopped speaking, and he hated himself for it. He set his pen down on the blotter and replaced the cap on the inkwell. "What I mean is I'm too set in my habits, too worn around the edges."

"You hear me complaining?" she said.

"When a woman loves a man, she knows it, and the man does, too. It's not a reasonable state of mind. It's kind of like having influenza."

"You think too much," she said.

"No, I don't. That's my problem. I don't think about anything. I just do it. Just like my father."

"Where are you going?"

"To bed. I love the rain and the lightning in the clouds. I chased cows all over Oklahoma Territory in storms like this. All that's ending. No one can know what that means unless he was there for it. It was a special time."

"What about Aint Ginny?"

"What about her?"

"Is she going to be all right in the tent?"

"I already moved her into the back room. You thought I'd leave her outside? Jesus Christ, Ruby, what do you think I am?"

He turned down the wick in the lamp until the flame died and a tiny ribbon of black smoke drifted through the glass chimney. He rose from his desk and went up the stairs and undressed and pulled back the covers on his bed and lay down and stared out the window at the flashes of electricity rippling through the heavens, not unlike ancient horsemen in pursuit of a golden bowl that somehow, millennium after millennium, eluded their grasp.

The storm had passed, and the thunder had rolled away and died in a diminishing echo among the hills, and the only sound in the house was the rain drumming on the roof when she undressed by his bedside and pulled back the covers and got in beside him. She laid her head on the pillow, her face pointed at his, her hair still up. "Do you want me to go?" she said.

"No," he said.

"I don't mean go from your room. From your house."

"No, I don't."

Her arm lay across his bare chest. "You're not interested in me?"

"How could I not be?"

"Then why do you stare at the ceiling?"

"I'm too old for you. I took advantage of your situation when you lost your job. You're poor and I'm prosperous."

"You get those notions out of your head."

"That I'm older than you? That I didn't make overtures to you when you were in a desperate situation?"

"That I'm a charity case."

"I said no such thing."

"There's a revolver sticking out from under your pillow."

"That's where I keep it when I sleep."

"What for?"

"My conscience bothers me. The men I've slain visit my bedside. Most of them are still in a bad mood."

"Don't make up stories that hurt you," she said.

"A man with a hole in his forehead standing by your bed is hardly a story. You haven't lived long enough. The dead don't let go of the world. That's why we put big stones on their graves. To hold them down."

"I think I should get back to my room."

He turned on his side and held his eyes on hers. "A girl like you is a gift. A rowdy man such as me is not. A few years with me and your youth would be gone. Not in a good way, either."

"Worry about yourself," she replied. She got up on her knees. "Look the other way a minute."

"What for?"

"Because I told you to."

When she took down her hair, it sifted across her face and shoulders. Her nipples were pink, the color and shade of the roses on the wallpaper.

"I told you not to look."

"I'm only human," he said. "Okay, whatever you say."

He turned his head and gazed out the window at the rain blowing across the yard. She spread her knees on his thighs and leaned down and kissed him on the mouth. She lifted his hand and placed it on her breast. "Feel that?"

"It's your heart."

"No, it's the way I feel about you."

"Let me up," he said.

"What's wrong?"

He sat on the side of the bed, in a male state, his hands propped on his knees. "I won't allow this of myself. You're a good girl. If we're going to be together, it'll be as man and wife. I'll go before the court and straighten out my marital status. I'll do the proper thing."

He was speaking with his back to her. She came around the side of the bed and stood in front of him. "You don't have to make promises or protect me."

"I certainly do, missy."

"I told you not to talk to me like that," she said.

"I never slept with a woman and went my own way in the morning. At least not when sober."

She placed her hand on his forehead and tilted his face up toward hers.

"I'm not a cow with a brand on it. You think I'd give myself to any man?"

"No."

"Then shut up."

She mounted him and placed him inside her, her eyes closing, her mouth opening in a large "O." The shadow of the rain on the window glass resembled ink running down her skin.

"Oh, Hack," she said. "Hack, Hack, Hack."

Even though the countryside looked as cold as pewter in the dark, he could smell the sun's warmth in her skin and hear her labored breathing on the top of his head and the blood whirring in her breasts.

Chapter 8

Nine months and eight days later, Ishmael Morgan Holland was delivered by a midwife on a cold winter morning that combined a flawless blue sky and sunshine blazing on the fields with a blanket of fog so thick on the river, Hackberry couldn't see the water or the giant boulders in the center of the stream. The midwife was a half-black and half-Mexican conjurer who blew the fire out of burns and cured snakebites in cattle by tying a piece of red string above the bone joint on the stricken limb. She had only one eye and was probably the ugliest woman Hackberry had ever seen. She told him she had seen Ishmael in the womb a week before the delivery, and a voice had told her he would be a king one day, unless he was betrayed by a man he dearly loved.

"Who's this betrayer you're talking about?" Hackberry said.

Her good eye bore into his face, vitriolic, glimmering in its socket. Her breath was as dense and fetid as a cave full of bats. "*Eres un* Judas *hacia tus hijos.*"

"Ride your broom out of here," he said.

After she left, he thought better of his words and tried to catch her and apologize, but she was gone.

"Why did you talk to her like that?" Ruby said.

"She said I was a Judas unto my children."

"Why would she say a thing like that?"

79

"How would I know? She's a crazy woman."

"Somebody is in a bad mood," Ruby said.

Four years later, he sued his estranged wife, Maggie Bassett, for divorce on grounds of infidelity. Not her infidelity. His. The inside of the courtroom smelled of cigars and unemptied cuspidors. The judge wore a gray-streaked black chin beard and had a large, deeply pitted, veined nose on which his spectacles perched like magnifying glasses on an owl. Hackberry could not stop staring at the strange optical effect created by the magnification. The judge's eyes reminded Hackberry of giant bugs trying to swim underwater.

"In the state of Texas, you cannot petition the court for the dissolution of your marriage because you, the plaintiff, have committed adultery," the judge said.

"I was trying to be gentlemanly," Hackberry said. "Discussion about marital congress is not something I normally engage in."

"Would you address the court in formal fashion, please?"

"Yes, sir."

"The point is you cannot sue yourself. Is that too difficult to understand?"

Hackberry gazed out the window as though perplexed, unsure of the right answer.

"You've submitted a list of your infidelities," the judge said, his finger pinched on a sheet of paper in his hand. "I cain't believe you've gotten this mess on the docket. What the hell is the matter with you?"

"Can I change the nature of my suit?"

"Can you *what*?"

Hackberry looked across the room at Maggie Bassett and her male companion, who had a shock of white hair like John Brown's in a windstorm, and a profile that matched, snipped out of tin, his eyes lead-colored. He wore button shoes and a bloodred silk vest and a tall collar and a black rain slicker he hadn't bothered to remove, glazed with sleet melting on the floor.

"By change my suit, I mean I would like to request a divorce from Maggie Bassett, also known as Maggie Holland, on the basis of the adultery she committed by sleeping with me," Hackberry said.

"Are you still a Texas Ranger, Mr. Holland?"

"When I'm not on leave and marshaling at the county seat."

"Then why don't you act like one? And stop addressing the court as though you're in a saloon."

"There is evidence that I was married to another woman, if not two, when I met Maggie Bassett, Your Honor. She was knowledgeable about both. That means she made a conscious decision to commit adultery as well as participate in bigamy. By anybody's measure, that's moral turpitude."

"The simple fact is she doesn't want to grant you a divorce," the judge said. "Nor does the court see any reason to grant you one. That said, I cannot for the life of me understand why a sane woman would want to keep a man like you around."

"It could be she wants my ranch and anything else of mine she can get her hands on."

"Mr. Holland, I'm not going to warn you again about your obvious disrespect for the court and this proceeding."

"I think it very likely that Maggie Bassett wants my assets, Your Honor. Her greedy nature and her addiction to laudanum seem to go hand in hand, although I'm not an expert in these matters."

"You're telling me your wife is addicted to opiates?"

"I'm just saying her marital habits are a bit unusual. I'm sorry, I meant to add 'Your Honor.' I'll start over. Your Honor—"

"You're about to find yourself in a jail cell, Mr. Holland."

"Judge, my poor skills with language are not allowing me to adequately convey my history with Maggie Bassett. Allow me to illustrate, Your Honor. I realized Maggie had eccentric tendencies when I found her in our bed with the Chinaman who was her opium supplier. When I expressed my puzzlement, she introduced me to the Chinaman and asked me to fix them a sandwich, since she was not disposed to go into the kitchen and do it her own self."

The judge touched his forehead like a man teetering on an aneurysm. "Mrs. Holland, would you care to address some of the statements your husband has made?"

She rose demurely from her chair. She was wearing a dark green velvet dress with a bustle and a fur collar, and boots that laced up to the knee. She had pale skin and soft brown hair she wore in swirls piled under a wide-brimmed straw hat. Her fingers were clamped on a small black cloth purse she held in front of her. Who would have believed her background? Not even Hackberry did.

"For a short time, I used a medication to control a nervous condition," she said. "The gentleman with me is Dr. Romulus Atwood, a specialist in these matters. He will testify that I consume no sedative stronger than warm milk."

"Romulus Atwood implants people with animal glands, Judge," Hackberry said. "He's sewn goat testicles on impotent men. The ones who have survived his procedures don't know whether to bleat or yodel."

"Be quiet, Mr. Holland," the judge said. He studied Atwood. "Were you ever a resident of El Paso?"

"Briefly."

"Rise when you address the court."

"Yes, sir, Your Honor."

"Were you ever known as 'the Undertaker'?"

"On occasion."

"For the four or five men you killed?"

"Those shootings were in self-defense and adjudicated as such, Judge."

"You were an associate of John Wesley Hardin?"

"I played cards with him. I wouldn't call him an associate."

"You wouldn't? What *would* you call him?"

"I'd call him dead."

"You think that's witty?"

"No, I would not try to be witty, Your Honor. I think Mr. Holland has sullied this lady's name. I think she's a good Christian woman, not an addict, and certainly not a miscegenationist."

"I don't like you," the judge said.

"Sir?"

"A killer carries his stink everywhere he goes. I want you out of my courtroom," the judge said. "As for you, Mr. Holland, I find against you. I think you're a dangerous, incorrigible man who has outlived his time and has no business carrying a badge and will probably come to a bad end. That said, I've heard you're a good father to your son. For that reason and that reason only, I'm not locking you in jail. I recommend that you care for your son and raise him right and forget all this silliness."

"I don't quite know how to take all that in, Judge."

"You can take it any goddamn way you want."

"Can I buy you a drink?"

"Not at gunpoint," the judge replied.

Hackberry went outside and stood a long time under a dripping mulberry tree. Across the dirt street, Maggie and the gunfighter who called himself a doctor entered a brightly lit café that glowed with warmth. The light had gone from the sky, and the sleet running down Hackberry's skin and bare head was cold and viscous and left a dirty purple smear on his face when he tried to wipe it off. Where was his hat? Had he left it in the courtroom? No, it was in his buggy. With his 1860 Army Colt revolver that had been converted for modern ammunition. How could he be so forgetful?

Those were the thoughts he was thinking when he retrieved his hat and wiped his face and hair with a clean rag and put on his hat and strapped the Army Colt on his hip and dropped his coat flap over the revolver's frame and the tiny notches filed in the wood grips. Then he crossed the street, never glancing down at the puddles he stepped in, the sleet hitting his face, his right hand opening and closing against his thigh.

He SAT AT a table covered with a checkered cloth and ordered a pot of coffee and a plate of hash browns and two fried eggs on top of a pork chop. While he cut his meat and speared it with pieces of egg into his mouth, his gaze stayed locked on Maggie and her companion, both of whom were sitting at a wooden booth no more than fifteen feet away, both trying to ignore him. Romulus Atwood had hung up his slicker, exposing his white dress shirt with balloon sleeves and a neckerchief a dandy might wear and a vest as bright as a freshly sliced pomegranate. Atwood glanced sideways just briefly, no longer than it takes to blink, and pulled the cuff of his right shirtsleeve down to the knuckle on his thumb.

When Hackberry finished eating, he wiped his mouth with his napkin and let the napkin drop to his plate. He got up from his chair and walked to Maggie and Atwood's booth, his Stetson hanging by the brim from his left hand. "You're looking mighty squirrel, Maggie," he said.

She set down her teacup. The color of her eyes changed from dark green to brown with the light and seemed to have no white areas. "Thank you," she said. "Are you doing all right, Hack? I worry about you sometimes."

"You know me. I try to stay out of the rain and not step on the cat's tail."

"Have you been introduced formally to Dr. Atwood?"

"Oh, yes, the Undertaker. That's quite a nickname. I heard you used to carry a cut-down under your duster."

Atwood grinned. "Not so, but pleased to know you just the same. Wes Hardin made mention of you on a number of occasions."

"What did you think of Wesley, Dr. Atwood?"

"People said he could read people's thoughts. That's why I never let my thoughts wander too far when I was around him."

"Did you know he headed up a lynch mob in Florida that burned a colored man alive?"

"Yes, I believe he referred to some hijinks in his youth. You and he had a go at it yourselves, didn't you?"

"I didn't quite get that."

"I think he said you spooked his horse while he was drunk. Then you put the boots to him before he could get off the ground."

"It went a little bit beyond that. I stomped his face in and broke his ribs and chained him in a wagon and nailed the chains to the floor. I busted him across the face with a rifle butt and took great pleasure in doing it. I guess you could say I flat tore him up before I came to my senses. I've always regretted that."

"We all get religion at some point in our lives," Atwood said.

"I wish I'd shot him. I wish I had shot a few of his friends, too. The world would be a better place for it."

Maggie Bassett's apprehension was obviously growing. She tried to signal the waiter for the check. Atwood began eating a slice of apple pie with a wood-handled fork, filling his jaw as a chipmunk would, a gleam in his eyes, as though injurious words had no effect on him.

Across the street, steam was rising from the back doors of a Chinese laundry. "You know why Chinamen get ahead of most white men?" Hackberry asked.

"Hack—" Maggie began.

"No, why is it that Chinamen are superior to the white race, Marshal Holland?" Atwood said.

"Because they work from cain't see to cain't see and take in stride all the abuse that white trash heap on them."

"I'm not following you."

"They're not human tapeworms. They don't sell ignorant people fraudulent medicines. They don't graft goat parts on a poor fool who cain't get his pole up."

"Hack, don't do this," Maggie said.

"Let him talk," Atwood said. "He's the law. And it looks like I might be his huckleberry."

"You know there's an ordinance against carrying a firearm inside the city limits?" Hackberry said.

"You're the only person I see carrying a gun, Marshal."

"Put your weapon on the table and stand up."

"I don't have one."

"Maybe it's my eyesight. Or I imagine things. Can I have a taste of that pie? I've always loved apple pie."

"Hack, please," Maggie said.

"He's all right," Atwood said. He set down the fork and pushed the plate to the edge of the table. "Here, let me wipe off the fork for you."

"You ever shoot a man in a poker game?" Hackberry said. "When he was raking in his winnings and about to head for the cribs upstairs? If you want to park one in a man's brisket, that's the time to do it. But you've got to have the right rig to pull it off."

"I don't do things like that."

"I bet you love your mother, too," Hackberry said. He pulled the fork from Atwood's hand and drove the tines through the man's knuckles into the tablecloth and wood. Then he ripped Atwood's sleeve to the elbow and removed the single-barrel .32 hideaway strapped under his forearm. Atwood's face was white, blood trickling through his fingers, his mouth quivering with shock, his hand impaled like a monkey's paw.

SOMETIMES IT WAS hard to turn it off. Hackberry pushed Atwood ahead of him into the street. The sky was laden with clouds that resembled smoke from an ironworks, swirling, unpredictable. "Walk to the jail," he said. "Don't look at me, either."

He pushed Atwood again. When Atwood stumbled, Hackberry hit him across the head with the revolver and sent him sprawling in the mud.

"He's no match for you, Hack. Please, this isn't necessary," he heard Maggie say. He felt her hands dig into his upper arm.

"I always thought you had pretty good taste in men. When did you take up with yellow-bellied back-shooters?" Atwood started to get up, but Hackberry kicked him again. "You stay where you're at."

"Hack," Maggie said, shaking him. "Hack! Did you hear me? Get out of it. Look at me. I'm Maggie. I know you. I know every thought you have. You're jealous and possessive. Now, stop what you're doing."

"Why are you with him?"

"Because I didn't have any place to live. Because I don't want to work in a whorehouse or teach children of ignorant cedar-cutters for thirty-five dollars a month in a mud-chink log house."

"Sounds like the girl I used to know," he said.

People had come out of the café and the saloon and the laundry, which always stayed open late, and were watching from the elevated concrete sidewalks inset with tethering rings. Hackberry picked up Atwood from a puddle and walked him off balance and stumbling to the jail. Out of the corner of his eye, he saw Cod Bishop, dressed in a crisp suit and bowler hat and a vest that looked like a cluster of wet dimes. "I saw all this, Holland," Bishop said. "One day you'll get your comeuppance. Your niggers will be of no help to you, either."

"Hold that thought. I'll be out in a minute," Hackberry said.

He locked Atwood in a cell in the rear of the jail. When he came back out on the street, Cod Bishop was gone. Maggie was not.

"Legally, I'm still your wife," she said. "That won't change."

"So call yourself my wife. In the meantime, I'll call myself the king of Prussia."

"Under Texas law, I own half of everything in your name."

"Then you should hire yourself a lawyer, one with better thinking skills than Romulus Atwood."

"I'll make you a proposal. I'll come back and be a good wife. You know everything there is to know about me. If we resume our marriage, there would be no surprises."

"Really? I heard only recently you worked in Fannie Porter's cathouse in San Antonio. Didn't you want to tell me that on our wedding night?"

"You never visited there or a place like it?"

"Working in a hot-pillow joint is not all you did, Maggie. You sewed me to a mattress when I was drunk and damn near killed me with a horse quirt. I don't think I'm up for a repeat on that."

"That's my point. You've seen the worst in me. I also remember a couple of things you seemed to like."

"Your wealth of experience in the erotic arts is undeniable."

"I didn't hear you complain."

"You're a handful." He paused. "So is a boa constrictor."

"Does Ruby's eye ever wander?"

"Don't be talking about Ruby. She's got nothing to do with this."

"She's young. A serving girl wants a strong and prosperous man to take care of her. It's nature's way. Later on she starts to have doubts."

He shook his head. "We're doing just fine," he said.

But Maggie had gotten to him. He remembered the times he had seen Ruby steal a look at the grocer's son, a tall blond boy reading for the law in Austin, and the day he caught her watching the Mennonite boy from down the road, washing himself under the windmill.

"We could make quite a pair," Maggie said. "I'm a good businesswoman. You know how to put the fear of God in the worst of men. We could write our names on the clouds."

"Ruby and I have a little boy."

"Out of wedlock, you do. I'm still your wife." She put her arm through his.

"You shouldn't have talked about Ruby that way," he said, stepping away from her.

"I'll be a good wife and a lover and a friend. We're two of a kind. We can take on the whole world, Hack." She looked into his face, biting down on her lip, her eyes brimming with certainty and promise. There was no question that she was one of the most beautiful women he had ever known. An empty hearse passed in the street, the rims of the wheels thick with mud and dung. Hackberry wiped his mouth with his wrist and widened his eyes and took a breath, staring into space.

"Atwood will go in front of the judge in the morning," he said. "Maybe you can pay his fine and take him home with you."

"Give me some credit."

"I do, Maggie. That's why you scare me."

"I want you, Hack. Look into my eyes and tell me I'm lying."

When she stepped closer to him, he felt a sense of arousal he thought he had gotten rid of long ago.

TWO DAYS LATER, he could not get Maggie's words about Ruby out of his head. It was Sunday. The windows were open, the river green and smoking in the sunrise. Ishmael was playing by the fireplace with a toy wagon Hackberry had carved for him, the wheels grinding on the wood floor. Hackberry could not remember a little boy who laughed and smiled as much. Ruby came out of the bedroom, dressed for church. "I heard Cod Bishop talking at the grocery store last night," she said. "He was telling people you whipped an unarmed man with a pistol."

"Did Bishop mention that the unarmed man was a lowlife bucket of goat piss by the name of Romulus Atwood who was fixing to drop me with a hideaway?"

"Cod Bishop also said you were escorting Maggie Bassett across the street."

"Cod Bishop says these things because he's a liar. Liars tell lies. That's why they're called liars."

"You were walking arm in arm?"

"No, I was not."

"Ishmael, will you stop that grinding?" she said.

"I don't want to criticize Maggie," he said. "I didn't do right by her. She's what she is. But I was not walking arm in arm with her, or escorting her anywhere, or having any kind of conversation that protocol didn't require."

"Ishmael, I said to put your wagon away. You can play outside with it."

"Don't take it out on the boy."

"Take out what?"

"You leave a teakettle on the stove, it boils over," he said. "Don't take your unhappiness out on others."

"Your wife was a prostitute. You were seen coming out of a café with her. But I'm not supposed to bring up the subject."

"Maggie was a schoolteacher when she was nineteen. She was a shootist in a Wild West show, too. She had some misadventures that put her in a bad way. I don't think it's fair for me to criticize her."

"I wish I could have done those things instead of waiting on tables and cleaning fish and washing clothes for deckhands fresh off a shrimp boat." She sniffed at her hand. "Maybe I should go scrub. Do I smell bad?"

"We don't have to do this," he said.

Ishmael scoured the wagon across the plank floor. "I told you to stop making that noise," she said. She jerked the wagon out of his hands and slammed it down on the mantel, breaking off one of the wheels. She picked up the wheel and looked at it helplessly. "I'll fix it. Stop crying," she said to the boy.

"Give it to me," Hackberry said.

"Don't touch me," she said.

"We're fighting over nothing, Ruby."

"Nothing, is it? You're with *her*, but it's nothing? Ishmael, be quiet." She bent over to pick him up. Her shoulders were firm and wide, her dress tight across her rump, her hair falling loose on her neck. Even under these circumstances, he couldn't ignore the level of desire he felt for her.

"Let me have him," Hackberry said.

"Don't you dare touch either one of us."

"Ruby, it pains me something awful to hear you talk like that. I'm just no damn good at this."

"Really? Will you be going to church with us this morning?" she said. "No? I guess I'll just take myself. What a fine day it's turning out to be, thanks to your former wife, schoolteacher and *shootist*."

"Who said you have to die to go to hell?" he said to himself.

"I heard that," she said. "Say it again and see what happens."

Chapter 9

HE EXPECTED HER to return from church by one P.M. He fixed lunch and set out plates and silverware and a pitcher of lemonade on the table, and put three encyclopedias on the chair where Ishmael sat when he ate with his parents. Hackberry shaved and brushed his hair and put on the suit he usually wore to church and town council meetings, then waited on the porch rocker. One o'clock came and went. At two-thirty he saddled his horse and rode north along the river, across the bottom of Cod Bishop's property, past the scorched remains of the cabins. Then he caught the road that led to the New Hebron Baptist Church, built on a rise just above the river bend. His heart was tripping as he hoped against hope he would see a picnic in progress, tablecloths and blankets spread on the grassy banks, or any other kind of normal event that would explain Ruby's failure to return home with their son.

But there were no horses or buggies tethered in front of the whitewashed building with the small stained-glass windows and the tiny bell tower tacked like an afterthought on the roof. He rode along the river's edge, past the frame house the minister called his "parsonage." The river was dark and swollen with rain in the shade and running swiftly beneath the bluffs and rocks on the opposite shore, creating a sound like a sewing machine, the riffle in the center flecked with tendrils of light and foam. Only three days ago hail had bounced all over the countryside. Now the trees were in full leaf, stiff against the blue sky, the pebbled bottom of the Guadalupe spangled with all the colors of the rainbow. This was the country that Sam Houston once called a fairyland, so verdant and cool and sprinkled with wildflowers in the spring that it seemed fashioned by a divine hand. It was a grand place, even though it was soaked in blood and haunted by the spirits of murdered Indians, many of them killed by Texas Rangers. Somehow the earth always cleansed itself of man's inhumanity, and if that was the case, he told himself, wasn't there an opportunity for the human family to do the same?

He rode slowly toward the arbor where the minister and Ruby and Ishmael were sitting at a plank table, the three of them reminiscent of a mythic family at peace with one another, the minister reading from a book that had a gold cross embossed on its black leather cover. Hackberry pushed his palms down on the pommel of his saddle, tightening his shoulders, straightening a crick out of his back. No one at the table bothered to look in his direction.

The minister, whose name was Levi Hawthorne, had been widowed the previous year at age twenty-five. His cheeks were rosy in spite of the ascetic nature of his face, his hair jet black and curled in locks on the back of his neck, like a painting of a British poet Hackberry had seen in a New York City museum. The members of his congregation said he had been inconsolable after his wife was struck by lightning while pulling wash off the clothesline behind the parsonage.

"There's Big Bud," Ishmael said, pointing.

"You call him Father. 'Big Bud' is a nickname," Ruby said. She stroked his head and pushed a strand of hair out of his eye. "You do not call your father a nickname." She turned her glare on Hackberry.

"I'm not supposed to worry about you or Ishmael?" he said.

Levi Hawthorne rose from the plank bench. He wore a dark suit that had been brushed to thinness and a white shirt with too much starch in it and cuffs too big for his wrists. "I'm glad you could join us, sir," he said.

"I don't join in where I'm not invited, Reverend."

"We were studying some passages from St. Paul's epistles to the Colossians," Levi said. His eyes went away from Hackberry's, then returned.

"Doesn't Colossians advocate restraint on sensual indulgence?"

"Why, yes, it does."

"That yonder is the woman I call my wife."

"Yes, she certainly is," Levi said.

"Even though some people would say otherwise," Hackberry said.

"It's not our province to judge others," Levi said.

"That yonder is my little boy."

"He's a mighty good one, too," Levi said.

"That's why I experienced a deep level of anxiety when he and his mother didn't come home for the lunch I set on the table."

"If there is anyone to blame, it's me, Mr. Holland."

Hackberry's eyes were dead, fixed on the minister's. "Did I say anyone was to blame?"

"No, sir, you didn't."

"Hack, we're going home now," Ruby said. "Get in the buggy, Ishmael."

Hackberry dismounted and lifted Ishmael in the air and set him on the saddle, then swung up behind him. He picked up the reins and stared at Ruby. "Think this is a peaceful stretch of country? Bill Dalton and his gang rode down that arroyo across the river not more than one year ago. They robbed the bank at Longview. How'd you like a bunch like that to get their hands on you?"

The blood had drained from around her mouth, to the point that she could hardly open her lips to speak. "Liar," she said. "Bully and cheap fraud. Murderer with a badge."

"I'm sorry for this, Mr. Holland," Levi said.

"You don't have anything to do with this, Reverend. I told you that," Hackberry said. "Go back to your biblical studies."

The minister sat back down at the picnic table, hanging his head, the back of his neck as red as sunburn. Hackberry felt Ishmael twist in the saddle. "Why's Mommy running away, Big Bud?" he asked. "Why's everybody mad?"

HACKBERRY'S BELLIGERENCE AND harsh words to the young minister were like an anchor chain he dragged with him through the rest of the day. He had another problem on top of it, one he hated to concede. Of the seven deadly sins, why was it he had to fall prey to the only one that had no trade-off? Unlike other sins, such as lust and gluttony and even sloth, jealousy brought no pleasure and instead, night and day, fed the fires of self-loathing and need and resentment of others. He could not get the minister's youthful face out of his mind, nor forget the reverential glaze in Ruby's eyes while the minister read aloud from his Bible.

The next night he rode into town under a sky veined with lightning that made no sound. The saloon was almost empty, its stamped tin ceiling pinging when the wind blew, the polished bar and the creosote-stained floor pooling with light that was the color of lead when trees of electricity exploded against the sky. A man was sleeping on his hands at a poker table in back. The bartender was eating a bowl of pinto beans with a spoon and reading a copy of the *Police Gazette*. A black man was cleaning the cuspidors with a rag. Dr. Romulus Atwood was standing at the bar, a shot glass of whiskey and a glass of beer in front of him, one pointy-tipped boot propped on the rail. His hand was wrapped with a fresh bandage.

Atwood touched his hat brim with one finger. His coat was pulled back over the pearl handle of a holstered revolver. "Just the man I wanted to see," he said.

"Get away from me," Hackberry said.

"I want to talk a business proposition. A smart man don't let his anger get in the way of his betterment."

"Who said I'm smart? Stay downwind from me, Atwood."

Atwood raised his beer glass and stared over the top of it as he drank, his eyes smiling.

Hackberry stood at the end of the bar, by the bat-wing doors, and ordered four fingers of whiskey in a beer mug. The wind filled the room with the smells of rain and ozone. He tilted the mug to his mouth and swallowed until it was empty, his eyes closed, the warmth of the whiskey spreading from his stomach into his viscera and genitals and arms and hands, driving the shadows from his mind, lighting places in his soul that, for good or bad, he seldom visited.

He called the bartender back three times. Maybe he drank half a quart. He wasn't sure. What did it matter? Was there any greater misery than living in the same home, in constant eye contact, with someone who had come to despise him? How had it happened? The answer wasn't complex. A young woman might be in need of a father on occasion, but that was not whom she dreamed about. Ruby had found a kindred spirit in the young minister, his fingernails as clean and pink as seashells on the cover of his Bible, his hair tousling in the breeze, his clean-shaven cheeks bladed with color, while at home she had to contend with a man who slept with a gun and believed specters stood by his bedside.

"Looks like you got an edge on, Marshal," Atwood said, pushing his glass along the bar as he approached Hackberry.

"You still here?" Hackberry said.

Atwood looked over his shoulder. The bartender had gone to the outhouse. The man sleeping at the table had been taken home by two of his friends. The black man was sweeping the sidewalk outside the bat-wing doors. "I'll keep it short," Atwood said.

"Say it and be done, because right now I'm of a mind to shoot you."

"Maggie's got snakes in her garden. You know what I mean by that, don't you?"

Hackberry glanced out the bat-wing doors at the rain blowing in the street. "You seem to be either a slow learner or you have a hearing impairment, Dr. Atwood."

"I was a special deputy in the Johnson County War up in Wyoming. Two train carloads of us from Texas went up there and got things straightened out. You heard about it?"

"As I recall, you terrorized the countryside and put the small ranchers out of business."

"What we did was hang cattle rustlers. One of them was named Cattle Kate. That's where I got over my inhibition."

"Which 'inhibition' is that?"

"About bringing justice to a woman who asked for it—who begged for it."

Hackberry let his gaze rove over Atwood's face. It looked as hard and carved as knotty pine, the eyes shiny, floating in their own liquid, as though diseased.

"I'll put it this way," Atwood said. "I lost my virginity a second time. I got over the notion that a troublesome woman deserved special consideration because of her gender."

"You lynched a woman?"

"It was a collective endeavor."

Hackberry drank from his mug and looked in the mirror. "Tell me what's on your mind or get out of my sight."

"Five hundred dollars and you won't see Maggie Bassett again. I'll buy her a train ticket. The two of us will just go away. Probably out to San Francisco or up to Alaska. The gold fields are booming. She won't be back. That's guaranteed."

"On the train? Maggie will just go away?"

"That's it."

Hackberry nodded. "She throw you out?"

"What do you care?"

"I was just speculating. Maggie was always good about taking in strays. She usually kept them around. You must have done something pretty rank."

"You could say I wasn't in accordance with her conjugal ways, if you get my drift."

"I'm going to use the jakes," Hackberry said. "Don't be here when I come back."

"It's not me who has a woman problem, Marshal," Atwood replied, rolling a cigarette. "I went looking for you at your ranch earlier today. That old nigress there said Miss Ruby and the boy went down the road to the Baptist church. She thought you might be joining them. When I got to the church, there wasn't anybody around, not unless you count your son, who was playing by himself in the backyard of the parsonage."

"Ishmael was by himself?" Hackberry said, not looking up from his drink.

"That's what I said. I asked him where his mama was at. He said, 'Inside making lemonade with the reverend.' I took a look through the back bedroom window. Ruby and the preacher were going at it like two beavers chewing on a log."

Atwood crimped the ends of a cigarette and stuck it into his mouth and lit it with a match he scraped along the underside of the bar.

"You tell quite a story," Hackberry said.

"I'm just passing on information, one pilgrim to another."

"That's thoughtful of you, Dr. Atwood. Excuse me a minute."

Hackberry walked through the saloon, past the billiard table, and out the back door into the wind and drizzle, his ears filled with sounds like an avalanche sliding down a mountainside. He went into the outhouse and closed the door and set the wood peg in the hasp and urinated through the worn, smooth-edged, beveled hole on which hundreds of men had squatted since the 1870s, depositing the only contribution to the earth they would ever make. That's why they scratched their names on walls and carved them on trees and rocks, why they hung their bodies with weaponry and scalps and rode their horses along the edges of precipices in electrical storms. They wanted to deny the reality of their short duration from their mothers' birth pains to the day someone placed pennies on their eyes, the insignificance of their daily preoccupations, the fact that the imprint of a leaf in an ancient riverbed had more permanence than they.

These were things he had learned not to speak about, in the way a blind man does not try to tell the sighted that vision has little to do with light. But who was he to think himself superior to others? Whatever wisdom he possessed always seemed to come from a bitter cup. The only real lesson he had learned in life was that a man's greatest gift was his family. Now he was about to lose it.

Was Atwood lying? A man could conceal love, but a woman could not, no more than a tropical flower could refuse to bloom. Only a fool would deny the obvious effect the minister had on her. Hackberry had become a spectator in the hijacking of his wife's affections. The image of the minister's beardless face floated before his eyes.

He buttoned his fly and washed his hands in water he dripped from a wood bucket and dried them on a towel hanging on a nail by the back door. Then he sat down on the stoop and listened to the rain tinkling on the tin roof, his mind too tired to think. "Marshal Holland," he heard a voice say.

The black man who had been sweeping the sidewalk was standing in the alley at the corner of the saloon, his hair beaded with raindrops, his trousers held up by rope.

"What is it, Markus?" Hackberry asked.

"The man in there with the bandage on his hand? He told Mr. Bill he'd work behind the bar so Mr. Bill could be with his sick wife."

"Good for him."

"He said something behind your back. He called you a bad name."

"Like what?"

"I don't like to speak them kind of words, suh."

"Thank you for telling me, Markus."

"Marshal Holland, you ain't listening. I seen him put his hand under the bar like he was checking something."

"Check what?"

"Suh, I don't want to borrow trouble."

"Go down to the sheriff's office and tell him what you told me."

"If it's all right with you, I'd like to go home."

"That would be fine, too. Is your family all right?"

"Yes, suh, they surely are."

"I'm glad to hear that."

Then the black man was gone and Hackberry was left alone with his thoughts and the sound of the rain on the roof, his holster creaking against his side when he straightened his leg to ease the discomfort from an old bullet wound, one that either the season or circumstance had a way of giving new life.

HACKBERRY REENTERED THE saloon and stood with one foot on the rail at the back end of the bar, his left hand resting on top of it. As Markus the saloon swamper had said, Atwood was acting as a substitute bartender, reading the newspaper, disengaged, glancing up occasionally at the rain blowing on the front windows.

"Give me a beer and an egg," Hackberry said.

Atwood filled a mug from the tap and broke a raw egg in it and set the mug on the bar. "You calling it a night?"

"Not quite. You got a clear look through the preacher's window?"

"A show like that? What do you think?"

"Ruby has a tattoo on her shoulder."

"Then she must have a twin sister, because the woman I saw had a body as pink and unmarked as a baby's butt."

"Thought I had you," Hackberry said. He drank the beer to the bottom, swallowing the egg yolk, his eyes lingering on Atwood's.

Atwood laughed to himself.

"Something funny?" Hackberry said.

"Maggie always said you were a smart man, the way you read Charles Darwin and encyclopedias and such."

"She overestimated me."

"You said it, I didn't."

"I'm slow on the uptake, Dr. Atwood. You have to he'p me here."

"You're right, the girl you live with—Miss Ruby, that is—has got a tattoo on her left shoulder. It's a rose, I believe. Bright red."

Hackberry rubbed his face with his palm. "I'm going over to my office and write up a report on your solicitation to commit murder. A warrant for your arrest will probably be issued by tomorrow afternoon."

"You take a mean revenge on a man who merely offered to buy a lady a train ticket, Mr. Holland. I guess that's the plight of a cuckold. If the woman strays, it's usually because she's not getting what she needs at home. Must be hard to live with."

"Could I have one of those peppermints in that jar on the shelf?"

"Bill saves those for ragamuffins."

"He doesn't mind if I have one or two when I come in."

Atwood picked up the jar and removed the glass cover. "He'p yourself."

"You take one, too."

"No, thanks. There's something demeaning about a man sucking on candy. I think it's got something to do with a desire for the mother's teat."

"Ride out. And not just out of town. Ride till you're in a place I'll never see you again."

"It's a free country."

"Not for you."

"Have another peppermint," Atwood said, tilting the jar toward Hackberry. "Get you a shitpile of them."

"Know why a diamondback rattles?"

"Because he's fixing to strike you?"

"That's what stupid people think. He rattles to let you know where he is so you won't step on him. If you don't step on him, then he's not required to bite you."

"A man learns something new every day," Atwood said.

Hackberry began walking toward the bat-wing doors, his boots echoing in the cavernous room. A gambler playing solitaire at a felt table looked up, then shifted his gaze to the playing card he had just turned over. The saloon windows were black, running with humidity, a rainy cool smell like sulfur and fish drifting through the doors. He waited to hear Atwood replacing the glass top on the peppermint jar, but instead he heard a duckboard creak behind the bar and then a scraping sound like a heavy object being dragged from a shelf.

Hackberry turned with a fluidity age had not taken from him, and drew the Army Colt, crouching slightly, driving back the hammer with the heel of his left hand, angling the barrel up so the round would clear the top of the bar, squeezing the trigger less than a half second later. The Colt bucked against his palm, a twist of yellow and red flame leaping from the barrel.

But just before the hammer struck the base of the .44 brass cartridge, Hackberry knew the origins of his rage had little to do with Romulus Atwood. Atwood was not a noun, not an adverb, not an adjective, not even a symbol; he was a surrogate, and a piss-poor one at that. The target of Hackberry's wrath was miles away, probably asleep in his parsonage, dreaming of Ruby and her countrywoman's breasts and the allure of her thighs and the way she moaned when he entered her. Or tossing with guilt over his new role as an adulterer and a hypocrite and the wrecker of another man's home.

The ball caught Atwood high up on the chest, just below the collarbone. He crashed against the bottles on the counter behind him but held on to the cut-down double-barrel ten-gauge he had pulled from under the bar. Hackberry fired twice more, splattering blood on the mirror, then shattering it, unsure where his rounds had hit Atwood. One barrel of the ten-gauge went off, pocking buckshot in the tin ceiling, raining down strings of termite-generated sawdust. Hackberry went around the end of the bar and saw Atwood on his back against an ice cooler, trying to lift the ten-gauge again. Hackberry cocked and fired his revolver until the hammer snapped on a spent cartridge. Atwood had lifted one foot in a futile attempt to protect himself; a round had torn through the sole of his boot and exited on the other side and blown away two of his fingers. But these were not the images Hackberry would remember when he thought about the systematic dismemberment of the Undertaker. Three feet in front of him, he swore he saw the minister's disembodied face painted on the smoke, the blush of innocence on his cheeks, his eyes serene and undisturbed by the gunfire and shattered whiskey bottles and blood speckling the coolers.

Hackberry lifted the shotgun from Atwood's grasp and broke it open with one hand and shook the fired shell and the unfired shell loose from the chambers, then tossed the shotgun over the bar.

The thumb of Atwood's bandaged hand was pressed to a hole in his throat, his lips pursed like those of a man who had stepped barefoot on a rusty nail and whose pain was so intolerable he dared not move. Atwood pulled at Hackberry's pants leg with his other hand.

"I cain't he'p you," Hackberry said.

Atwood's voice gurgled in the back of his mouth. Hackberry holstered his revolver and squatted down, his knees popping. "You want a preacher to read over you?"

"How?" Atwood whispered.

"How what?"

"How did you—"

"How did I know you were about to back-shoot me? I didn't hear you put the cover back on Mr. Bill's peppermint jar and set it on the shelf, like you were supposed to. So I knew you were headed for the scatter gun."

Atwood closed his eyes and then opened them again, as though losing consciousness or perhaps because he couldn't accept the fact that such an insignificant choice had cost him his life.

"If you believe in perdition, this is your last chance to avoid it, Doctor. Want to tell me the truth about Ruby and the minister?"

Hackberry said. His eyes were veiled as he waited and hoped that Atwood would not sense his desperation and terrible need to purge himself of the poison Atwood had planted in his soul.

A word seemed to form in Atwood's throat, then die in a grin on the edge of his mouth. His eyes remained open, staring at nothing, while a spider crawled across his cheek.

Hackberry got to his feet, off balance, the blood draining from his head, his hand still tingling from the recoil of the revolver. He pulled the cork from a whiskey bottle and drank, then pushed through the bat-wing doors, tilting the bottle skyward, while the few onlookers in the street backed away from him as they would from a half-formed creature born before the Creator made light.

Chapter 10

He DIDN'T COME home for two days. When he did, she was in the bedroom, packing her trunk. "Stop by to use our indoor plumbing?" she said without looking up.

"Where are you going?"

"California. Or somewhere out *there*." She lifted her face toward the window. "Don't come after us."

"*Us?*"

"You think I'm leaving without Ishmael?"

It was early morning, the flowers in the garden blue with shadow, the windows closed. He could smell his odor in the closeness of the room. "I have to know the truth."

"About what?"

"Before I killed him, Romulus Atwood said he looked through the parsonage window and saw you and the minister going at it. He described the rose tattooed on your shoulder."

She turned around. "Ishmael climbed through a fence and chased a white-tail. I went after him and caught my blouse on the wire and tore the buttons. Reverend Levi gave me a shirt to wear."

"He he'p you put it on?"

She folded one of her dresses and placed it in the trunk, her back stiff with anger. She said something to herself.

"I didn't catch that," he said.

"I said I feel sorry for you. Leave us alone, Hack. It didn't work out. End of our romantic tale on the Guadalupe."

"Don't leave me, Ruby. I won't drink no more. Or at least I'll try."

"You know what Reverend Levi said about you? You have the capacity to show love and mercy but not the will to sustain it. He said his father was the same kind of man. You grew up in a time when mercy was an extravagance. I thought that was well put."

He opened a window. The coolness of the morning had died; the sun's heat was already rising off the lawn. "Where's Ishmael?"

"He had croup all night."

"Respiratory illness runs in my family."

"So does insanity," she said.

"I cain't see anything straight, Ruby. I got something on my conscience, too. I don't do well with problems of conscience."

"I don't want to hear it."

"I blew Atwood apart a piece at a time. While I did it, I think I wanted to put the minister's face on his. In spirit, I was killing a man of the cloth. I cain't make that go out of my head."

She closed the trunk. There was neither anger nor sympathy in her expression. She was wearing an ankle-length dress with puffed white sleeves. "I'll write."

"Remember when we first met. I called you 'dutchie.' I thought you were going to give me a slap across the head. That's when I knew you were the girl for me."

"We weren't meant to be together," she replied.

He looked into the emptiness of her eyes and knew that no power on earth could change what was about to happen. Atwood may have been a liar; Ruby may have told the truth about the torn blouse; the minister may have been innocent of guile or design; but there was no denying the fact that her love for Hackberry had taken flight, in the way that ash rises from a dead fire and breaks apart in the wind and is never seen again.

"You meeting him out west?" he said.

"I haven't told him where I'm going."

"But you will."

"A boy needs a father."

He felt his face flinch. "Get out of my house," he said.

It wasn't over. Sick and hungover, he followed her outside as she and Ishmael got into her hired carriage. Unable to control his despair, repelled by the funk in his clothes and the stink of his breath, he waved his arms lunatically in the middle of the road. Inside the dust, he saw Ishmael looking back at him from the carriage seat, his mouth forming an "O" that made no sound.

Nor was Hackberry done two hours later when he saddled his horse and rode to the train depot and saw the locomotive and string of boxcars and two Pullman sleepers and a caboose head out of the station into a wide bend by a river where cottonwoods shaded the tracks. Like the pitiful fool he was, he spurred his horse along the tracks, whipping it with the reins, ignoring the wheeze in the animal's lungs, the labored effort over rocks as sharp as knives. He didn't give it up until he had blown out his horse, one he loved, and was left standing by the tracks, his horse heaving on its side, its tongue out, the train disappearing between hills in the middle of which a rainbow arched out of the sky, as though heaven and earth were mocking him in his defeat.

He pulled loose the marshal's badge from his shirt and flung it into the deepest part of the river, then sat down on a rock and wept.

His insomnia and depression and lassitude and devotion to whiskey went on for a year. Ruby sent him a postcard from New York City. On the postcard was an artist's sketch of a Ferris wheel and the pier at Coney Island. The card read, "It's not your fault, Hack. A leopard cannot change its spots. I hope you are well—Ruby." At Christmas she mailed him a photograph of her and Ishmael, who was sitting on her knee in a sailor suit. There was no inscription on the photo and no note in the envelope. Nor was there a return address. The minister had left town three weeks after Ruby did, destination unknown. A parishioner said, "I never saw a man go

downhill so fast. You'd think Old Nick was riding on his shoulder."
Hackberry contracted a private investigation agency in Brooklyn.
The investigative report read:

A woman named Ruby Dansen worked briefly as a cook in a
foundling home located in the Five Points area. Her companion,
name unknown, was apparently a consumptive who sold bread
rolls door-to-door. He claimed to be a minister but was asked not
to visit the foundling home, lest he infect the children with his
illness. Ruby Dansen often had a child with her. Supposedly Irish
hooligans in her building tried to extort her wages and she beat
one of them nearly to death with a piece of iron pipe.

Three months ago she did not show up for work. Neither she
nor her companion nor her child has been seen since.

Please let us know if we can be of any further service.

Hackberry got put in jail twice on drunk and disorderly charges
and sank into all the solipsistic pleasures of dipsomania, a state of
moral insanity that allowed him to become a spectator rather than
a participant in the deconstruction of his life. Also, if he wished, he
could visit the path up Golgotha without ever leaving his home.
Who needed nails and wooden crosses and the Roman flagella
and the spittle of the crowd when an uncorked bottle of mescal or
busthead whiskey was close by? The normalcy of the elements, a
restful night's sleep, rising to meet a new day, the journey of the sun
from east to west, all of these were replaced by delirium tremens,
flashes of light behind the eyes, blackouts, obscene memories, and a
thirst in the morning as big as Texas.

Abnormality became his norm. The man he once knew as Hackberry
Holland mounted his horse, bade the world a fond farewell, and went
somewhere else. The wretch he left behind was hardly recognizable.
The aforesaid were the words he used to describe his own descent into
the abyss, as though he took solace in being the architect of his own
destruction.

That was when Maggie Bassett came back into his life. She threw
out his whiskey and cleaned and scrubbed his house and washed his

clothes and put his employees on a regular schedule and balanced his books and wrote letters of goodwill to friends he thought he had lost. She cooked for a bunkhouse full of men, broke hardpan prairie with a single-tree plow, bucked bales and gelded and branded his livestock, and in calving season shoved her hand up to the armpit in a cow's uterus with the best of them. She took credit for little and did not demean or judge, and when his mind finally cleared, he admitted she had probably saved him from the asylum or drowning facedown in a mud puddle behind a saloon.

There was only one problem about living with Maggie Bassett: In his wildest imaginings, he could not guess what went on in her head. He suspected it would take two or three centuries to decipher who she was—in large part because she didn't know, either.

Seven months after Maggie moved into the house, Hackberry received a letter from Ruby Dansen. He read it, put it back in the envelope, and set it on a table in the living room. He said nothing of the letter to Maggie. That evening, at dinner, Maggie said, "I have a confession to make."

"What's that?"

"I helped rob a bank."

"You were bored and the Dalton gang needed an extra hand?"

"You know who Harry Longabaugh is?"

"A tall, self-important pissant with a lopsided head who never had a job other than slopping hogs? Calls himself the Sundance Kid?"

"Harry is handsome and a gentleman. I had the good fortune to know him several years ago. 'Know' in the biblical sense," she said. "How do you like that?"

His pale blue eyes were flat, his mouth dry. "At Fannie Porter's cathouse in San Antonio?"

"No, Harry and I went to the opera together, then to a very elegant restaurant, Mr. Smarty-Pants. He asked if I'd ever stopped a train or a held up a bank. He said you really hadn't lived till you'd stuck a gun in a bank president's face or blown open a safe full of John D. Rockefeller's money."

"You did not rob a bank, Maggie. Do not mention robbing banks to me again. Do you understand me?"

"I was trying to be honest with you. I saw Harry on the street yesterday. I don't think he saw me. I just wanted you to know."

He set down his knife and fork. "You saw him *here*?"

"His back was to me. Harvey Logan was with him. Believe me, it was Harvey. Nobody ever forgets Harvey Logan."

He picked up his knife and fork again, his forearms resting on the edge of the table. "I don't believe you."

"I don't care if you do or not."

"You think I'm jealous of a man like Longabaugh? I wouldn't cross the street to watch a rabid dog rip out his throat."

"Did you know your knuckles are turning white?"

"Because I'm wondering if I'm married to a crazy woman. Have you heard what cowpokes say about the women at Fannie Porter's brothel? 'Their homeliness is never held against them.' You take pride in knowing the clientele of a place like that?"

"You have the cruelest mouth of any man I've ever met."

"I saw you looking through the mail this morning. I think you read Ruby's letter. I think that's what this Longabaugh thing is all about."

"You left it open on the table. How could I not see it? She's using the child to extort you."

"I guess you didn't read the whole letter. The preacher was hit by a tram. He's dead. She's a good young woman who doesn't deserve the hardships of widowhood."

"You concede I saved you from destitution, yet you sit at our table, eating the food I prepared for you, and praise the merits of a girl who deserted you when you needed her most. Does that strike you as a bit unusual?"

"Maybe it explains my problems with women. I've always been a poor judge of character."

She threw her glass of sun tea in his face.

He slept little that night and woke at dawn and reread Ruby's letter. She was in Trinidad, Colorado, with Ishmael, working for an organization he had never heard of. He shaved, put on a suit, strapped on a money belt, and wrote Maggie a note:

I hope to be back home in ten days. I have to ensure my son is provided for. I'm sorry about last night. The next time I act in a willful or vain manner, you have my permission to put poison in my food, if you are not already planning to do so. Were you actually involved in a bank robbery? I think one of us is crazy. It's probably me. Take care.
    Your loving husband,
        Hack

He tilted his note into the light and reread it, wondering what his words actually meant. How could he communicate with a person who changed personalities the way other people changed their underwear? Sometimes during their most intimate moments, when he was convinced she was not acting, he would look into her eyes and take away only one conclusion: She could hold two contrary thoughts simultaneously with complete comfort. How many men could say that about their wives?

THE TRAIN RIDE to Trinidad took three days and required two transfers. It was a strange journey. At dawn, the train entered the Great American Desert, a pre-alluvial world of mesas and dry streambeds that antedated the dinosaurs and remained untainted by the Industrial Age. Far up the track, after sunset, he could see the glow of the firebox when the train arched around a bend, smoke and sparks blowing back from the locomotive, and men the conductor called "hoe boys," for the grub hoes they carried, running along the tracks, trying to grab a boxcar on the fly. Where did they come from? Why weren't they working and taking care of their families instead of racing on foot, grabbing on to a steel rung that could tear an arm from the socket?

Hackberry had seen mountains before, in Mexico and Southwest Texas, but they were little more than piles of crushed rock compared to the South Colorado Plateau. The peaks of the mountains disappeared into the clouds, their slopes so immense that the forests in the ravines resembled clusters of emerald-green lichen on gray stone. In the early morning, when he stepped down on the platform in Trinidad, the air was as cold and fresh as a block of ice, white strings of steam rising off the locomotive, baggage wagons rattling past him, the streets lit by gas lamps, and behind the city, a mountain as flat-sided and blue as a razor blade soaring straight up into the sky, touching the stars. He felt he had arrived at a place he might never want to leave.

He had telegraphed his arrival time to Ruby but had not asked that she meet him at the station. Regardless, there she was, in a frilly white dress that went to her ankles, a thin pink sash around the waist, a flat-topped, narrow-brimmed straw hat with a black band set squarely on her head. Ishmael was perched on a bench, wearing a suit and a matching cap and shiny black shoes with silver buckles. "There's Big Bud!" he shouted.

"How you doin' there, little pal?" Hackberry said. He scooped up Ishmael and bounced him up and down and whirled the two of them in a circle. "My heavens, what a powerful little fellow you are. I declare, you're a grand little chap. Isn't he, Ruby?"

She beamed at the two of them, as though a family picture that had broken on the floor had been picked up and glued together and replaced on the nail.

He set ishmael down and hefted up his suitcase, the stars still glimmering in a sky that was the color of gunmetal, while down below, at the bottom of Ratón Pass, the dawn was spreading in a yellow blaze across the plateau. "I understand the hotel here has a fine restaurant," he said.

"We've heard," she said.

Did she mean anything by that? No, he mustn't have those kinds of thoughts, he told himself. He gazed at the brick-paved streets by the depot, the vapor rising from the storm drains, the wet sheen on the slate roofs, the aggregate effect of a city built out of rock quarried from the mountains in whose shadows it stood, a smell in the air that bespoke of factories and a new era, one that wasn't all bad. *If you want to restart your life, could you find a better place than this one?* a voice whispered inside his head.

"I'm happy you told me where y'all were," he said. "I hired a detective to find you. You're a pretty good hider."

"It wasn't intentional."

"I think about you often."

"You do?"

"Well, of course. Why wouldn't I?"

"The night Levi was hit by the car—" she began.

"Don't give misfortune a second life, Ruby."

"He was using morphine. He said it was for his consumption. That wasn't true. He was in despair. He called himself an adulterer."

"He was a widower, and you were a single woman who left the company of an older man, one who never acquired any wisdom about anything. Neither one of you was an adulterer."

Nothing he said seemed to register in her eyes.

"Are you all right?" he asked.

"I don't know what I feel right now. I resolved in New York I would never cause harm to anyone again. I feel selfish. I don't trust my instincts or my thoughts."

"Water runs downhill whether you think about it or not."

"Where did you get that?"

"Probably from somebody who cain't tell bean dip from pig flop."

He and Ruby crossed the street, each holding one of Ishmael's hands, a trolley grinding past them. They sat by a window in the hotel restaurant where they could see the train pulling out of the station on its way to Walsenburg and the snowcapped roll of the Rocky Mountains.

"What can I order, Big Bud?" Ishmael asked.

"You can order whatever you want, little pal," Hackberry said.

"A waffle?" he said.

"I think you need a stack of them. That's a mighty nice suit you're wearing."

"It's from the dry goods store where Momma works. We have to take it back later. She has to take her dress back, too."

Ruby's face turned red.

"I thought you worked for a miners' organization," Hackberry said.

"During the day I'm a secretary at the Western Federation of Miners. Sometimes I work at night or on the weekends at a milliner's."

"Who takes care of the boy?"

"We have a children's room at the union hall."

"You're working two jobs? Why didn't you tell me?"

"I felt guilty for leaving you. I wasn't fair to you. Are you happy with Mrs. Holland?"

"What?" he said, unable to follow the change in subject.

"With Maggie."

"I'm in her debt, as I am to you. In my earlier life, whiskey made most of my choices. Now I have to live with them."

He signaled the waiter so he would not have to continue talking about Maggie. After they ordered, he went to the men's room and washed his hands and cupped water on his face. Then he looked in the mirror. Who was he? The sum total of his deeds? He would have liked to scrub most of them out of his life. When he went to bed at night or took a nap in a shady hammock, the same images waited behind his eyelids: flashes of gunfire in a darkened alleyway lined with the cribs of working girls, a cowboy buckling over from a shotgun blast inside a pen filled with squealing hogs, a runaway horse stirrup-dragging a dead man past a bank he had just tried to rob.

Unfortunately, part of the problem was that those images were not altogether unpleasant, particularly when he had to deal with the restraints of what was already being called "the modern era."

As Hackberry reentered the dining area, he looked at the tables and at the men in narrow-cut tailored suits and the ladies in hats holding their silverware the way easterners did, taking small bites of their food, chewing slowly before they swallowed. In their world he would never be more than a sojourner, a man for whom an incremental redemption could not take place.

He sat back down at the table and placed his hand on the back of Ishmael's neck. The coolness of the boy's skin and the flutter of his pulse made something inside Hackberry melt. "You're a mighty fine little fellow, did you know that?" he said.

"I can already read. Without ever going to school. Momma taught me."

"That's because she's a good mother. And she's a good mother because she's got a good son."

"Are you gonna come live with us?"

"I'm probably just visiting right now."

"Why can't you live with us?"

"How about you come down to Texas and stay with me?"

"Without Momma?"

"We'll work all that out."

Hackberry could see the confusion growing in the boy's face. He looked at Ruby.

"There's the waiter with your waffle, Ishmael," she said. "Let's eat and talk later."

"You said Big Bud might be staying."

Her cheeks flushed again.

"I plan to stay as long as I can," Hackberry said, patting the boy's back. "Maybe we'll take a train ride up to Denver and visit Elitch Gardens and see a moving picture show. Have you ever seen a moving picture?"

"No, sir."

"I haven't, either. We can do it together," Hackberry said. "That's the way you do things, see? Together. That makes everything more fun, doesn't it?"

"You're not going off, are you?" Ishmael said.

"No, not at all," he said. "My schedule is just a little uncertain right now. I declare, this is a nice town."

His head was pounding. He couldn't eat his steak and eggs. He stood up from the table and removed his hat from the back of the chair. He put a ten-dollar gold piece by his plate. "I slept in a bad position last night. I'll walk up and down a bit and meet y'all in the lobby," he said.

"We need to get back home," Ruby said. "I have to be at work by ten."

"Tell them you're sick and you're not coming in. The unions are supposed to be sympathetic with women's problems, aren't they? You want me to talk to them?"

She gave him a look that was just short of a slap. He went out into the cold and walked around the block, then sat down in the lobby next to a potted palm. His hands were shaking, but not from the cold. When she entered the lobby with Ishmael in tow, he stood up, his Stetson hanging from his fingers against his trouser leg, his heart beating. "I say everything wrong," he said. "I brought you a rose."

"I need to go home before I go to work. Can you get us a carriage?"

"Sure. I'll take care of Ishmael."

"You don't need to."

"Where do you live?"

"That's not important. Walk outside with me."

They went out on the sidewalk. She put Ishmael inside a carriage and turned back to Hackberry, her face a few inches from his. She had buttoned the stem of the rose inside her shirt. The wind was feathering her hair around the edges of her hat. The curvature of her chest was like a dove's. He had never seen a woman whose mouth was so inviting. "Do you love her?" she asked.

"She took care of me when I couldn't get a saucer of coffee to my lips."

"My question was an honest one. Will you answer it?"

"There's different kinds of love."

"Which kind did you have for me and Ishmael?"

"A kind that's more than I can explain," he said. "A kind that's not in the past tense, either."

Her eyes seemed to go inside his head. "I'll be finished at the union hall at five o'clock if you want to see us."

"Of course I want to see you. Why won't you tell me where you live?"

"It's not the best part of Trinidad. We'll come to the hotel."

"You don't have to hide your circumstances from me."

"Don't ever tell me about the debt you think you owe someone else, Hack. You understand?"

"I do."

Then she was gone and he was left standing alone on the elevated sidewalk, the stars fading into the harshness of the day as though they had never been in the sky.

Chapter
11

SHE SAID SHE and Ishmael would meet him in front of the hotel at seven P.M., but he thought it unseemly that she and his son should have to hide the whereabouts of their home and circumstances. He found out where they lived from a miner in the saloon next to the union hall, then went back to the hotel and dressed in a light blue coat and Confederate-gray trousers and a beige shirt and a black string tie. He brushed his Stetson and had his cordovan boots shined in the lobby, all the time wondering about the fleeting nature of life and the way one or two seemingly insignificant choices could open the door to a kingdom or sweep a man's destiny into a dustbin.

He bought a whirligig for Ishmael and a bouquet and a box of candy for Ruby, and hired a carriage to take him up a canyon that seldom saw direct sunlight and probably had been worked by individual prospectors for float gold and abandoned when the mother lode was never found. The road wound along a stream lined with rocker boxes and desiccated sluices and houses that were hardly more than shacks; the stream was a trickle at the base of the canyon, its exposed rocks greasy with an unnatural shine.

Hackberry leaned forward in the seat and spoke through the viewing slit to the driver. "What kind of place is this?" he asked.

"One to stay out of," the driver replied. His back was massive and humped like a turtle's shell, his coat splitting at the shoulders, his neck thick and ridged with hair beneath his top hat. The accent was Cockney. "They drink out of the same creek they build their privies on. They live like animals. There's an invalids' home here, too. Not a pretty sight."

Hackberry looked out the carriage's side windows. The canyon was precipitous and rocky and unsuitable for habitation. The only flat ground where a shelter could be built was close to the stream. He leaned forward again just as the carriage jolted across a deep hole. "Tell me something," he said.

"What might that be, sir?"

"Why would anyone want to live here?"

"That's a good question."

"It's not a question."

"I don't get your meaning," the driver said, raising his voice above the noise of the wheels on the road.

"Nobody *wants* to live in a place like this. They live here because they're poor and they have no work. Nobody wants to be poor and without work."

The driver turned around. He looked into Hackberry's face as though seeing it for the first time. "Your destination is right ahead, sir," he said. "Should I wait, or will you be having a jolly night with a lady friend in this splendid little spot?"

AFTER THE CARRIAGE driver rumbled back down the road, his whip and his crushed top hat lying in a puddle of dirty water, Hackberry knocked on the door of a paint-stripped, rotting frame house with a tiny porch and bare yard and a privy and wash line in back. What he could not get over was the absence of any distinguishable color in the canyon, as though the sky and earth had conspired to rob its inhabitants of hope or joy.

Ruby was obviously surprised when she opened the door. "I said we would meet you at your hotel. How did you know where we lived?" She looked around the disarray of her small living room, pushing her hair up, her face flustered. "How did you get here?"

"In a carriage."

"Where is it?"

"I sent the driver on his way."

"A top hat is floating in a mud hole."

"I think he needed to check on his family, an emergency of some kind. Do you have a neighbor I could pay to drive us to town?"

"I never know what's in your head. Or when you're lying. No one does."

"You don't need to hide your situation from me, Ruby. I want to be your friend."

"Come in."

Their level of privation filled him with shame. Through the side windows he could see the backyards of the neighbors, house after house, the children in rags, grimed with dirt, some with rickets and others with runny noses.

"The driver told me there was a house for invalids here'bouts."

"Up the road. Most of them have lost arms or legs or eyes to dynamite. Some have the consumption. They're called 'lungers.'"

"I think you should leave here."

"And go where?"

"Wherever you want. I'm still a fairly well-to-do man."

"And your wife will have no objection?"

"I control my own finances."

"That's not Maggie Bassett's reputation."

"Why do you badmouth me, Ruby?"

"Why did you ask about the invalids' home?"

"It doesn't seem right these men should be hidden away," he said.

"Do you want to visit them?"

"Probably not."

"No one else does, either."

"Maybe they chose their lot," he said before he could stop himself.

"They chose to blow up themselves for the Colorado Fuel and Iron Company?"

She was wearing a long pleated green dress with a white blouse she had probably washed in a tub behind the house for the express purpose of eating dinner with him and his son. And now they were arguing. Over what? The misfortune of men for whom they were not accountable.

"I don't know about these things," he said.

"Maybe it's time you learned."

She had not taken the candy or the bouquet or the whirligig or even acknowledged them.

"I brought y'all these," he said.

"That's nice of you."

"I'm not good at expressing my feelings," he said. "That's probably why I've committed so many violent deeds in my life. But I flat-out adored you, Ruby."

"Do you love me now?"

"What do you think? Ishmael was my darling little pal, and you were my darling companion."

"You want us to move back to Texas?"

"If you like. But I'm legally bound to Maggie. I cain't change that."

"I see," she said. She glanced over her shoulder at Ishmael, who had just come out of his room.

His face lit when he saw Hackberry. "Hi, Big Bud," he said.

"How you doin', you little woodchuck?" Hackberry said.

"I'm not a woodchuck."

"I know that," Hackberry said.

"I'll fix something for us to eat here. We don't need to go to town," Ruby said.

"That's not the plan. I have us a reservation at the best restaurant in Trinidad. The kind of place Yankee swells eat in."

"Then what *is* the plan? Tell me, would you please? Yes, I would love to know the plan."

Hackberry couldn't find words to answer her question. In the room's silence he could hear the wash flapping on the line, the door to the privy slamming on its hinges, a ball of tumbleweed slapping against the window. The light had gone out of Ishmael's face. "Is something wrong?" he said.

Two hours later, when Hackberry returned to the hotel, a telegram was waiting for him in his key box. Without reading it, he folded and placed it in his coat pocket and rode upstairs in the birdcage elevator, determined that the content, whatever it was, would not control him. But before the operator could open the collapsible door, Hackberry split the envelope and unfolded the square of yellow paper the telegrapher had handwritten the message on. It read, "Harry and Harvey at house. Afraid. Come home. Maggie."

He went to the telegrapher's office, but it was closed and would not be open until eight A.M. He bought a Pullman ticket for a train headed south at 4:17 A.M., then walked back to his hotel room and lay on the bed and stared at the ceiling until it was time to leave. *Woe be unto the wicked,* he thought. He couldn't remember if the admonition was from the Bible or if he had made it up. Why did it matter? Regardless of what he did, the end result was the same: broken trust, flaming buildings, spilled blood, and the object of his affection eluding his grasp. "Dear Lord," he said to the ceiling. "I get nothing right. If you want me to wear sackcloth and ashes, I'll gladly do it. I've got nary an answer to my troubles."

If there was a response, he did not hear it.

MAGGIE WAS WAITING for him in the buggy when the train pulled into the station at dawn three days later, the air brown with dust, the eastern sky as red as a forge. She had fixed coffee and hot milk for him in a covered pail. He drank it with both hands as she drove the buggy out of town, her shoulders erect, her face tight. She glanced sideways at him. "You miss me?"

"In your telegram you said you were afraid."

"I was. Answer the question."

He studied the side of her face. "Of course I missed you. You're my wife. Where are they?"

"Where are who?"

"Longabaugh and Harvey Logan. Who else would I be talking about?"

"I don't know where they are. They came to the ranch."

"What for?"

"Old times' sake. They don't need a reason. Maybe they plan to rob a bank."

"You let them in?"

Her cheeks were blotched with color.

"They were in our home?" he said.

"Harvey was drunk. Harry went to buy more liquor. I was alone with Harvey."

He waited for her to continue, but she didn't.

"Stop the buggy," he said.

She reined in the horse and glared into his face. "What?"

"What did Logan do?"

The rims of her nostrils were white, her cheeks bladed.

"I've been on a train three days, two of them in a chair car," he said. "Now, tell me what happened or get out and walk."

"Sometimes I hate you," she replied. She pulled the top of her blouse loose from her skin, her chin up.

"Logan did that?" he said.

"With his cigar. I hid in the canebrake. I could hear him looking for me, beating the cane with a stick."

His eyes searched her face. "Why did you let them in?"

"I didn't have a choice."

"You said you were out of the life forever."

"No one says no to Harvey Logan when he's drunk. Not even Sundance."

"Where are they?"

"Probably at Miz Porter's."

"They're living in a brothel?"

"She holds parties for them." She rested her hand on his. "Let them go. You're home now."

"They told you they're going to rob a bank?"

"No, they didn't. You're not a lawman now, anyway. I cleaned the house. I put flowers in every room. I baked a white cake with strawberries. Come home, Hack."

"Did Longabaugh put his hand on you?"

"No."

"Did he eat off our plates? Did he use our dinnerware? Or sit on our furniture?"

Her eyes started to tear.

When they reached the ranch, he went into the house and came back out with his Army Colt and saddlebags and entered the barn and saddled his horse. She followed him inside, silhouetted in the doorway against the red sky. He hung his pistol belt on the pommel and swung into the saddle. "You're pretty as the sunrise. But the contradictions in your eyes confound me and turn uncertainty into a way of life."

"Stay."

"Then tell me the truth."

"You just heard it," she said.

He stooped as he rode under the door frame. He heard a drop of rain tick on the brim of his hat. He turned in the saddle and looked down at her. "Did you think I'd be unfaithful to you in Trinidad?"

"Not if you were sober."

"That's not much of a recommendation."

"It's as good as you'll get."

From atop the horse, he could see the curled flesh above her breast where she had been burned. "You put me in mind of a line from William Blake. The one about the canker in the rose."

She took a pin out of her hair and reset it, her eyes empty. "Sundance is faster," she said. "But Harvey is the one most apt to put you in a box."

HE PAID A brakeman to let him and his horse ride most of the way to San Antonio inside a slat car loaded with baled cotton and barrels of pickles that leaked brine on the floor. It was dusk when he rode into the section of San Antonio that had been the concession of the city to Old Nick since the 1870s. Most of the cowboys had departed since the coming of the railroads and the outbreaks of tick fever and the closing of the Chisholm and Goodnight-Loving trails, but others had taken their place: gandy dancers and cardsharps and drummers and pimps and derby-hatted salesmen and slaughterhouse meat-cutters who washed off in a horse tank and left the water dark red before entering the saloon.

Busthead was fifteen cents a glass, mug beer a dime. There was always a free lunch on a counter. The dirt streets were lined with wood buildings that had never been painted. Seagulls spun in circles above a garbage dump next to a dilapidated loading chute where the train tracks used to be. Hackberry rode past a dance hall and a gambling house and a café that never closed. A calliope was playing in the middle of the street. On the corner of South San Saba and Durango was a two-story brick building with a wide balcony and wood pillars. The light had turned to purple horsetails in the sky, and he could smell rain and feel the barometer dropping, and for a moment thought he heard thunder, like cellophane crackling. He unlaced his saddlebags and pulled them from his horse's rump and draped them on one shoulder, then stepped up on the porch of Fannie Porter's infamous bordello.

The woman who met him at the door had a British accent and did not vaguely resemble an ordinary madam. "You look like a weary traveler," she said. "Are you in need of a boardinghouse? I'm afraid this one is only for ladies."

He removed his hat. "Do you know a Mr. Longabaugh or his associate, Mr. Logan?"

Her face was rosy, her eyes thoughtful. "I don't think I recall those names offhand. What did you say your name was?"

"Hackberry Holland."

"Were you an officer of the law at one time?"

"I was. I'm not now. Mr. Longabaugh and his associate paid a call at my home. I'm sorry I was not there to greet them. Perhaps I could leave them a message."

"These may be cattle buyers you're referring to. Most of the cattlemen gather at the saloon. You're welcome to come in, if you like. You seem to be a man of manners and education."

"Not really. San Antonio is the only place in Texas that will allow me inside the city limits."

She winked. "Let sleeping dogs lie, Mr. Holland."

"Always," he said.

Chapter 12

THEY WERE SITTING at a felt-covered card table, next to a faro wheel, playing dominoes. Two years earlier he had seen their ink-drawn likenesses on a circular handed out at the Texas Ranger headquarters in Austin. The taller man was more than six feet and had been called "distinguished-looking" in the circular. Hackberry thought otherwise. The taller man, Harry Longabaugh, alias the Sundance Kid, had a head that seemed dented on one side, or a bit warped, as though the bone had gone soft. Harvey Logan, alias Kid Curry, was cut out of different stuff. On first glance he seemed to have the features of an ordinary workingman, until one realized that the large nose and luxurious mustache were a distraction from the defining attribute in his face: namely, the moral vacuity in his eyes.

Longabaugh was bareheaded, his hair neatly combed, his beard less than two or three days old; his friend wore a derby and a gold stick pin and a gold watch and chain and rings on his fingers, although his nails were rimmed with dirt. The business suits of both men had lost their creases; their shoes were scuffed and powdered with dust and manure. They had the appearance of men who had never decided who they were or in which century they wished to live. Longabaugh seemed to have a habit of breathing through his mouth and staring at a thought six inches in front of his face. The opacity in Logan's eyes and the thickness of his mustache made it impossible to read his expression, provided he ever had one. Neither man appeared to be armed.

Hackberry set down his saddlebags on the bar and watched the two men in the mirror. Several prostitutes in dance-girl costumes were gazing down from the balcony rail and smoking hand-rolled cigarettes.

"Send a shot and a beer to those fellows at the table, will you?" Hackberry said.

"They buy their own drinks," the bartender replied.

"I owe them a round."

"Not here, you don't."

Hackberry set his Stetson crown-down on the bar. "This is a tough place. Could I have a beer? With an egg in it?"

"Coming up."

Only one, he thought. What was the harm? It wasn't busthead or tequila. He watched the bartender draw the beer and rake off the foam with a wood spatula. "Now a bottle of Jack Daniel's for my friends. I'll carry it to the table. That's all right, isn't it?"

The bartender took a square uncorked bottle of whiskey from the back shelf and set it on the bar. He set three shot glasses next to it, his grimed fingers inserted inside each glass. "Anything else?"

Hackberry flipped his saddlebags over his shoulder and walked to the felt table by the faro wheel with the whiskey and the glasses. "You boys mind if I sit down?" he asked.

"Suit yourself," Longabaugh said.

Hackberry set his saddlebags on the floor next to his chair. "Thank you. I've been riding trains for four days. I still hear the wheels clicking on the tracks."

"We know you?" Logan said.

"Probably not. Two or three years back I saw y'all's faces on a circular regarding a bank robbery in New Mexico. You were cleared of the charges, though."

Longabaugh put a peppermint in his mouth and sucked on it. He smiled with his eyes. "Can we help you with something?"

"You boys know a lady by the name of Maggie Bassett?"

"That's twice you've called us boys," Logan said.

"Figure of speech. Maggie says y'all came to our house."

"You're her husband?" Longabaugh said.

"Yes, sir. You were just in the neighborhood, knocking on doors and such?"

"Mr. Logan and I are buying cattle hereabouts. I knew Miss Maggie from a few years ago. We stopped by. She gave us a glass of lemonade. Out on the porch."

"You smoke cigars, Mr. Logan?"

Logan opened his coat, exposing an inside pocket with a silver case stuffed in it. He looked down at it as though he had never seen it. "Yes, I do. Would you like one?"

"I don't smoke."

"You're a lawman," Longabaugh said.

"A Texas Ranger and a city marshal at various times. These days I'm neither." Hackberry squeaked the cork out of the whiskey bottle and poured into their shot glasses. The smell of the whiskey rose into his face with the allure of a dangerous girlfriend's embrace.

Longabaugh took a sip from his shot glass. "Maggie told you something about our previous relationship?"

"I was wondering how men treat women where you boys come from. You speak like you're from up north, Mr. Longabaugh. Are women treated respectfully where you grew up?"

"I'm from Pennsylvania. It's little different from Virginia. Does that answer your question?"

"How about you, Mr. Logan? People treat women fine where you come from?"

Logan cleaned his nails. "If you got a burr in your britches, you ought to take it somewhere else."

"Me?" Hackberry said.

"I suspect it's got to do with Maggie Bassett. I married a jenny-barner myself. The secret is to keep an empty space in your head about what they've touched, particularly with their mouths."

"I'm not sure I heard you right. Married a what?"

"A jenny-barner. A whore. The challenge is to find one that don't have clap or the rale. The homeliest ones are the best. They're certainly the most grateful."

"I never thought about it in those terms. Would you call my wife homely, Mr. Logan?"

"I wouldn't call her anything. It was Sundance who wanted to visit your place," Logan said. He lifted his empty beer mug to the bartender and held up two fingers.

"One for me, too," Hackberry said, raising a finger. "Somebody burned my wife's chest with a cigar."

Longabaugh began stacking dominoes, steadying them with one finger when he thought they were about to fall. "Sometimes people who use opiates see unicorns eating the tulips in their gardens."

"My wife is no longer a user of narcotics. But if she were, she wouldn't know she had been burned with a cigar?"

"Maybe she has ringworm," Longabaugh said.

Hackberry's right hand rested under the table. "Maggie says you're fast."

"At what?"

"Putting pennies on a man's eyes."

Longabaugh knocked over a stack of dominoes. "I never shot anybody. Don't plan to, either. Somebody has been selling you fairy tales."

"Why did y'all hurt her?"

Longabaugh was hunched forward, his eyes unfocused, his coat pinched against his narrow shoulders. He wore an unbuttoned checkered vest under his coat, with a watch and fob and chain pinned to it. He rubbed one hand on top of the other, his calluses whispering across his knuckles. "Neither me or Harvey has ever hurt a woman. Don't be saying we did."

The bartender set down three mugs of beer on the felt and went away.

"Let's stop this serious talk," Longabaugh said, his eyes brightening. "It's about as pleasant as a sermon in a church house that doesn't have windows."

He tipped the bottle to the rims of the three mugs. Hackberry's gaze never left Longabaugh's face. The whiskey bloomed in an amber cloud inside the beer and ran with the foam over the side of Hackberry's mug, dripping onto his knuckles.

"Life is short. Isn't that right, Harvey?" Longabaugh said, clinking Logan's mug.

"Who did she claim did it?" Logan asked.

"Who burned her?"

"That's what I said."

"That would be you, Mr. Logan."

Logan's gaze wandered up the wall, his eyelids fluttering.

"She said you were drunk."

"Drunk or not, I didn't do it. If I did, I'd tell you. Then one or both of us would probably commit a rash act. But I don't get in gunfights over a damn lie."

"Believe what he says, Mr. Holland. Harvey keeps the lines simple. With Harvey, what you see and hear is what you get."

Hackberry searched the faces of both men, the clicking of the faro wheel growing louder inside his head. Neither man blinked.

"If you're holding something under the table, it had better be your dick," Logan said.

"I'm afraid you're a little late, partner. There's a .44 Army Colt pointed at your scrotum. I cut an 'X' in the nose of each round in the chambers. It makes an exit hole the size of a plug in a watermelon."

For just a moment Logan and Longabaugh seemed frozen inside a sepia-tinted photograph, their affectation of modernity a poor anodyne for the shabbiness of their lives. Hackberry waited for a tic in one of their faces, the movement of a finger on top of the felt, the flex of a jawbone, a quiver around one eye. The faro wheel stopped; the moment passed.

Hackberry raised his hands above the table and pointed his index fingers at the two men and cocked his thumbs. "Had you going."

"You think that's cute?" Logan said.

"You wet your pants?"

"Fuck you I did," Logan said.

"Your language is unseemly, Mr. Logan."

"Look up on the balcony," Logan said. "See the woman on the end? That's my wife. One signal from me and she'd stuff a porcupine up your ass. Or put a cupful of bird shot in the back of your head, whichever you prefer."

The woman upstairs pulled up her dress, exposing her bloomers and a cut-down single-barrel .410 shotgun strapped to her thigh. She smiled.

"Harvey doesn't mean anything," Longabaugh said, resting his hand on Logan's forearm. "We're not armed. Tell Maggie I hold her in the highest regard. She was always a charmer."

"Tell her I said she's a snake and a lying whore and full-time bitch on top of it," Logan said. "There's nothing wrong with her a bullet in the mouth wouldn't cure."

"See you down the road," Hackberry said.

"You'd better pray you don't," Logan said.

Hackberry heard someone laugh behind him. He got up from the table and slung his saddlebags on his shoulder and drank his beer mug empty, then set it on the bar and walked out of the saloon into the street, trying to pretend he had not made a fool of himself and been bested by a homicidal moron.

The woman he lived and slept with was a manipulator. The only joy he could take from his situation was that he was no longer in her debt. Whether the court granted him a divorce or not, his moral obligation was over. He went to the telegrapher's window at the train station and sent the following message to Ruby Dansen:

> *We can be a family again full-time. Say yes and I will be*
> *there. Love to you and that little fellow,*
> *Big Bud*

The only problem he had now was a level of thirst normal people would never understand. A brush fire raged and withered into ash. A thirst for whiskey did not. The rain was spinning like glass out of the sky. He went into the middle of the street and began turning in a circle, his arms stuck out by his sides, his face lifted to the clouds, his mouth wide. The calliope was still playing, although its operator was nowhere in sight. Hackberry knew an ocean of beer and Jack Daniel's would never quench the flame inside him. But a man could try.

HE WOKE UNDER a freight wagon. The rain had stopped and was dripping off the eaves of the shacks that lined the alleyway where he had passed out. His gold watch was still in his pocket, his saddlebags in a puddle of water, his .44 in his hand. He rotated the cylinder and counted the rounds in the chambers. None of them had been fired. He opened the cover on his watch and looked at the time. Only five hours had elapsed since he'd confronted Longabaugh and Logan. The calliope was still playing, the lights burning in several buildings along the street. A man wearing rubber pants and suspenders and a long-sleeved striped shirt, his hair parted down the middle, came out of a saloon's back door, his arm around a Mexican girl. "You gonna make it, sailor?" he said.

"What was that?" Hackberry said.

"You're listing, bud."

"What day is it?"

"Same day it was when you pissed out the window of the gambling hall," the man in rubber pants said.

"*Pobrecito*," the girl said.

"Who you talking about, girl?" Hackberry said. "Who are you people?"

The man and the girl dropped their eyes and didn't answer. Hackberry walked unsteadily down the alley into the street, knocking against a trash can and a rain barrel, the ground tilting as dramatically as a seesaw. A wagon splashed through a deep hole and splattered him with mud. The horses and wagons and buggies and water troughs and buildings on the street were whirling around him as though he were standing in the midst of a funnel. He stepped up on a wooden walkway in front of a barbershop and sat down on a chair someone had left outside. He folded his hands between his knees and hung his head as though in mourning, hoping he wouldn't get sick. Would his alcoholic misery never end? Dawn was a few hours away, and his entire day was already a bed of nails. In spite of his condition, he now had a chance at a new life, with a family and the simple pleasures whiskey had stolen from him.

He looked up and down the walkway. He could smell coffee boiling and meat and hash browns and eggs cooking on a griddle. Then Harry Longabaugh and Harvey Logan came out of a café, backlit by the electric lights. They were admiring a palomino gelding with a gold and silver tail tethered to a hitching rail. Neither man looked in his direction. Logan was puffing on a cigar that looked like a stick protruding from his thick mustache. Longabaugh stretched and gazed at the eastern sky, as though in anticipation of another fine day.

What a joke, Hackberry thought. Men for whom he had nothing but contempt had extricated him from a problem he had thought unsolvable. *Here's to you, boys,* he thought. *May you find a shady place when you get to the big blaze below.*

Then he watched Harvey Logan some more and realized he had been slickered by a man who had the psychological complexity of a centipede. Logan had taken the cigar from his mouth and was blowing on the tip, heating it into a red coal. A winged cockroach, as thick as a man's thumb, was crawling up one of the wood posts that supported the colonnade. Logan blew softly on the cigar's tip one more time and touched it to the roach's head and watched the roach sizzle and fall to the walkway. He ground the roach into paste under his boot, then rocked on his heels and resumed smoking the cigar.

"She was telling the truth, wasn't she?" Hackberry said behind him.

Logan sniffed at the air and didn't turn around. "You smell puke?" he said.

"He can't hardly stand up, Harvey. Let it go," Longabaugh said.

Logan yawned. "Yes, time to hit the mattress." He fished in his pocket and flipped a silver dollar over his shoulder onto the walkway. "There's a bathhouse run by a Chinaman down the street. He sells powders for crab lice, too."

Logan and Longabaugh walked toward the livery, chatting about a baseball game that was to be played that morning. Hackberry hooked one arm around the wood post, barely able to keep from falling into the street, his thirst so great he would have swallowed a quart of kerosene if it were handy.

Chapter 13

MAGGIE COULD FEEL the days starting to dwindle down. The nights were cool and damp, the autumnal change stealing across the land, bleeding the sky of its summer light and drying up the water in the creeks and burning the bloom on the flowers. For Maggie, it was a bit like watching the world come to an end. Since she was seven years old, she had experienced moments like these, and rather than achieve understanding of them, she'd discovered they grew worse as the years passed. They always occurred when she was alone and the house played tricks on her mind and whispered words to her that were unintelligible. Her breath would suddenly come short, as though someone had pressed his thumb against her throat, and a sensation as gray as winter would foul her blood and invade her glands and turn her skin to sandpaper.

She looked at the scorched chunks of limestone in the fireplace and the ashes and twists of burned paper that had been there since spring. She wondered if she should build a fire. Her body longed for the comfort of a warm hearth and the cheery petals of flame on a big log. But she knew the house would be overheated in minutes, and if her husband walked in, he would have one more tool to use against her, to take power from her, to reassert himself as head of the household.

You have a hard edge, Maggie, her father had said when she was fourteen, just before he put her on the train for New Mexico. *You don't give quarter. You need to learn mercy, girl. I guarantee you'll like the boarding school. You'll find kind and genteel folk there, people who'll set a better example than I have. God be with you.*

Benedict Arnold, she had thought. *Weakling and scapegoater of your daughter.*

When she was seven, he had given her a puppy named Napoleon. He told her not to leave Napoleon alone in the yard or coyotes would get him. Then, after infecting her with the cruel image of her puppy being torn apart, he went to town and told her to help her mother, who was eight months pregnant.

Maggie was playing jacks in the barn when she heard her mother call from the bedroom window. She started out the door, then stopped. Napoleon had climbed up on a stack of hay bales and was chasing his tail in a circle. "Come down here, you bad dog. I have to see what Mommy wants," she said.

Napoleon tumbled backward, wedging himself between two bales.

"See what you've gone and done, you silly puppy," she said.

She heard her mother call again, louder this time, a thread of pain in her voice. Maggie climbed up on a bale, trying to reach down and catch her pup by the neck. Finally, she was able to get her hand under his stomach and lift him over the bale and skid down on the barn floor with Napoleon held against her chest. She brushed the straw off his face and set him on a folded tarpaulin and looked for a piece of twine to tie through his collar. "I'll be there in a minute, Mommy," she called through the barn door.

There was no reply. Napoleon took off running deeper into the barn. "Napoleon, you're going to get a spanking with a newspaper," she said.

But she didn't spank him. Nor did she go in the house. She listened to the silence a moment, then sat down and resumed her game, bouncing the rubber ball off the plank floor and scooping up as many jacks as she could while the ball was in the air.

Her father returned from town a half hour later. She heard him cry out from inside the house, then he was at the barn door, his face like a collapsed balloon, both of his hands shiny with blood.

"Where have you been?" he said.

"Here, in the barn."

"Doing what?"

"Guarding Napoleon, like you told me."

"I told you to watch your mother."

"No, you said not to leave Napoleon alone. You said the coyotes would eat him."

"Your mother didn't call you?"

"Napoleon fell between the hay bales."

"You helped the dog but not your mother?"

"She didn't call me anymore. What's wrong, Daddy?"

"Your mother is dead." He squeezed his temples with his thumb and the tips of his fingers, his face riven with either sorrow or wrath. "Oh, Maggie."

She realized he was weeping, his back shaking. He put his hand down to hers. She stared at her jacks and rubber ball on the floor, and at Napoleon chasing a butterfly in the sunlight. She wanted her father to pick her up and hold her against him. She wanted to smell the warm odor of his skin, the cologne he put on his jaw and neck.

"Come inside," he said. "The baby is stillborn. We need to wrap him in a sheet. Your mother needs to be washed, too. No one must see her like this."

"Like what?"

"What do you think, girl?"

"She called me twice and—"

"*Twice?*"

She tried to think what she should say next. "It got quiet. Napoleon was whimpering. I thought Mommy was all right."

He released her hand. "You *thought*?" He looked at her as though he didn't know who she was. "Go on with you, now. Get the sponges and a pan of water from the kitchen. Get two sheets out of the closet."

She began to sob, hiccupping, her shoulders jerking.

"It's not your fault," he said.

She lifted her face to his. She felt a breeze on her skin, a coolness around her eyes.

Then he said, "I should have known better. You were born selfish, just like your grandmother."

He never spoke again of her failure, but sometimes he would look at her as though gazing at an instrument of the Creator's punishment rather than a daughter. Never again did he set her on his knees, or play games with her, or take her with him to his land office in town. There was an unrelieved weariness in his face, like that of a man with a stone bruise forever inside his shoe.

He didn't visit her on Christmas or Thanksgiving at the boarding school, and he didn't attend her graduation when she was sixteen. His excuse was his lack of funds and the probability that his investment in cattle futures was about to send him into bankruptcy. When she was called to his deathbed, she refused to hold his hand or kiss his brow or acknowledge his attempt at an apology. The minister and physician in attendance were appalled. Maggie Bassett, age seventeen, could not have cared less about their condemnation.

THAT MORNING THE mail carrier had delivered an envelope postmarked in Denver and addressed to Hackberry. The bright blue calligraphy obviously belonged to that poseur Ruby Dansen. Maggie steamed open the envelope and removed a single piece of folded paper. A lock of blond hair fell out. The note read, "Ishmael just had his first real haircut. He thought Big Bud might like this."

The note was unsigned. Maggie picked up the lock of hair from the floor and replaced it inside the sheet of paper and stuck the paper back inside the envelope and resealed the envelope with paste. Then she propped it against a flower vase on the dining room table, wondering what she should do next. Unfortunately, when it came to future events, she had a trait that sometimes frightened even her. She did not make decisions based on the results of a conscious process. Instead, her decisions seemed made for her by someone else, perhaps a little girl who lived in a dark place inside her, a place where Maggie the adult would never go by herself.

Where was Hackberry? He had been gone over two days. Did he

get into it with Harvey Logan? She touched the burn on her chest. Had she made herself a widow? Maybe that prospect wasn't entirely bad. She saw herself standing by an ornate coffin in the Holland family cemetery, bereaved, the mourners passing in review, squeezing her hand or patting her cheek. No, she must rid herself of thoughts like these. It was not her intention to have them or see these images. No, no, no, that was not she. The images were just a trick of the mind.

So much for that.

In the morning a boy on a mule delivered a telegram from the telegrapher's office at the depot. The name "Holland" and the rural route number were written in pencil on the envelope. "Where might this come from?" Maggie asked, smiling at the boy.

"I wouldn't know, ma'am."

"You don't think it's bad news, do you? People always say wire messages contain notices of accidents and deaths and such."

"The telegrapher listened to the tapping on the key and wrote out the message. He didn't seem to give it much mind, if that he'ps you at all."

"It certainly does. You're a very nice boy. You're a good-looking boy, too. You like lemonade?"

"Yes, ma'am. Everybody does."

"Why don't you come to see me sometime? We'll have some."

"If I'm out this way, yes, ma'am. Thank you."

She gave him a dime and watched him climb up on the mule, waiting to see if he would look back. But he didn't. *Innocent boy,* she thought. *Better to learn about the nature of the world from a gentle hand rather than a coarse one. I wish I had been so lucky.*

Where was the telegram from? It could be from the Ranger Frontier Battalion in Austin. Her husband had talked of getting back his badge. Or it could be from Denver. She steamed open the envelope. The message read, "Yes, Yes, Yes."

It was not signed. It didn't have to be. It was from Denver, and it contained an affirmation to a question obviously asked by the addressee, Hackberry Holland. She folded the telegram and replaced it in the envelope and resealed the flap and set the envelope by the letter propped against the flower vase.

She sat on the porch most of the afternoon and into the evening, without eating supper, and watched the leaves toppling out of the trees onto the surface of the river, gathering into channels between the rocks, then eddying and sinking beneath the current as though they had never been part of a wooded hillside. The sky turned the color of torn plums. Just before the stars came out, she saw a mounted man approaching the front lane; he sat tall and erect in the saddle, the stirrups extended two feet below the horse's belly.

She rose from the chair, her hands knotting and unknotting at her sides. *Destroy the letter and the wire,* a voice inside her said.

No, I'm not afraid of the dutchie, or whatever she is.

She stiffened her back and set her jaw and fixed her gaze on the horseman, determined not to be undone by self-doubt. The horseman rode by and disappeared into the dusk.

She woke at sunrise and began fixing breakfast. She heard the foreman and the hired hands driving the Angus across the river to a pasture that hadn't been grazed during the summer. She heard the cook washing a bucket full of tin pans and forks and knives and spoons from the bunkhouse under the spigot on the windmill. Then someone hollered out, "By God, there he comes!"

To the waddies and farmhands and drifters who worked for him full-time or came and went with the season, he was a composite of Captain Bly and Saint Francis of Assisi and somehow always one of their own. Down at Eagle Pass, he had beaten two of King Fisher's old gang almost to death with a branding iron. He had turned loose a caged cougar in a Kansas saloon that refused to serve Texans. On the Staked Plains, he froze to the saddle returning a kidnapped three-year-old Comanche girl to her parents. If he hadn't been a drunk, he could have been a congressman or the owner of an internationally famous Wild West show. Why did she stay with him? The answer was not one she liked. He was wealthy, at least by the standards of the times, and second, when it came to adversarial and life-threatening situations, he never winced. When she was with him, no one short of Genghis Khan would bother her.

She stepped out on the porch and saw him at the bottom of the lane, his hat tilted back, the sunset on his face, a bouquet of flowers propped across the pommel. He was wearing a dark suit and a blue silk vest, clothes he must have bought in San Antonio. She went back into the house and ripped pages from a Sears, Roebuck catalog and stuffed them among a pile of kindling. Her hand was trembling when she lit the paper. She stood back as the fire caught the draft and twisted into a yellow handkerchief through the chimney. She dropped the telegram and letter from Denver and the lock of Ishmael's hair into the flames and watched them blacken and curl and dissolve into carbon and then into ash, her face glowing from the heat.

HE REMOVED HIS hat when he entered the house, and tossed his saddlebags onto the divan. The boards under the carpet creaked with his weight. "I almost forgot how beautiful you always are, regardless of the hour," he said.

"Did you make a side trip somewhere?" she said. "Maybe to Canada?"

"If that's what you call falling into a bathtub full of whiskey."

"I thought we were done with that."

"*You* were. *I* wasn't. Now I am. I think."

"You found Sundance and Harvey?"

"I wouldn't call either of them the thinking man's criminal. I just had to knock on one door in the brothel district. Fannie Porter's place."

Her gaze left his. "You came home to shame me?"

"I never held your past against you. I'm just telling you where I went. I didn't accomplish much by it, either."

"Much of what?"

"Logan and Longabaugh said they didn't hurt you. Later I saw Logan burn a roach to death with his cigar. So I knew he'd burned you, too."

"You didn't call him out?"

"No."

"That doesn't sound like you."

"I was drunk. I looked for Logan after I slept it off. He and Longabaugh had both left town. I feel like somebody spit in my face."

"You tried. That's all that counts."

"You told me the truth, didn't you, Maggie? Please say you told me the truth."

"I won't discuss this anymore. You use the whip and rub salt in the cut."

"That's not my intention."

"I kept the white cake in the icebox. I'm glad you weren't hurt. Do you want coffee?"

He looked at the dining room table and flower vase on it, the place where each put mail addressed to the other. "I didn't get no mail?" he said.

"We got an invitation to a garden party at the mayor's house. I think we should go, don't you?"

"I thought I might hear from the Ranger Frontier Battalion in Austin."

"Were you expecting something from Ruby?"

"Not necessarily," he said. "I need to lie down. It's been a long trip."

"You don't want any cake?"

"Maybe not right now."

"Undress and I'll bring it to you in bed."

"I'm plumb wore out, Maggie."

"You're glad to see me, aren't you? That's what you said. Let me take care of you."

He went upstairs and sat down on the side of their bed and gazed out the window at a cloud in the west, one that was bottom-lit a bright gold by the late sun and swollen with rain and trailing horsetails across the sky. For just a moment he wanted to drift away with the cloud and break apart in a shower over a wine-dark sea filled with cresting waves that never reached land. *Yes, to simply slide down the shingles of the world,* he thought, *and be forever free, swimming with porpoises and mermaids. What's wrong with that?*

He heard Maggie coming up the stairs, saucers and cups and silverware clinking on a tin tray. He lay down and turned his head toward the window and placed the pillow over his head, pretending to be fast asleep.

EVERY DAY FOR a week he went to the post office, but there was no letter from Ruby. He also went to the telegraph office at the depot. The regular telegrapher was down with influenza. His replacement told Hackberry that no wire had come for him since he had taken over the key.

"The other man didn't receive one?"

"I'll look through his carbon book," the replacement said. "No, sir, I don't see it. 'Course, he's been ailing awhile. I can telegraph your party and check it out."

"Let's give it a try."

Hackberry wrote out a message similar to his first telegram, asking Ruby if she wanted for him and Ishmael and Ruby to be a family again.

A week passed with no response from Ruby. When Hackberry returned to the telegraph office, the same telegrapher was still on the key.

"Nothing came in for me?" Hackberry said.

"No, sir. We would have delivered it."

Hackberry sat down in a wicker chair by the telegrapher's desk. The window was open, the breeze warm and drowsy and faintly tannic with the smell of fall. A passenger train was stopped on the tracks, the people inside it stationary, like cutouts. "The season is deceptive, isn't it? It sneaks up on you. You turn around and it's winter."

"I'd be happy to send off another message," the telegraph operator said.

"It wouldn't do any good. She's a union woman. She moves around a lot. I'll try again directly."

The telegrapher nodded to show he understood. "It's a mighty nice day, isn't it?"

Hackberry didn't go home. Instead, he rode into the country, out where the train tracks followed the river through limestone bluffs and cottonwoods whose leaves trembled with the thinness of rice paper. He tethered his horse and lay down in the shade of the trees, in the coolness of the wind off the water, in the moldy smell of leaves and night damp that never dried out during the day. It was a fine spot for a rest, to close one's eyes and let go of the world and abide by the rules of mortality; in effect, to let the pull of the earth have its way, if only for a short while.

He fell asleep and awoke in the gloaming of the day, the air dense, like the smell of heavy stone prized from a riverbed or the smell of a cave crusted with lichen and guano and strung with pools of water. At first he didn't remember where he was; then he saw the train wobbling around the bend, its passenger cars fully lighted, not unlike an ancient lamplit boat crossing a dark lake. He could see the figures inside the passenger car clearly: a conductor in a stiff cap and buttoned-down uniform similar to that of a ship's captain; a teenage girl who seemed to smile from the window; a nun wearing a wimple and gauzy black veils that accentuated the pallor of her skin; a man in a plug hat with buckteeth and greasy hair that was the color and texture of rope, all of them moving irrevocably down the track into hills whose lines were dissolving into nightfall.

What was the destination of all those people? Why did he have the feeling their journey was a statement about his own life? He got to his feet unsteadily and mounted his horse as though drunk. The evening star was rising, like a beacon to mankind, but it brought him little comfort. Was there any doubt why men killed one another? Not in his opinion. It was easier to die in hot blood than to watch your death take place incrementally, a day or a section of railroad track at a time.

When he arrived at his house, Maggie was waiting for him in the doorway. "I was worried," she said.

"You thought I was in the saloon?"

"You could have been hurt, or worse. How was I to know? I care about you, whether you're aware of that or not."

He walked past her into the living room. Wet leaves were pasting themselves against the windows. He had not slept with Maggie since returning from Colorado. She seemed to read his thoughts.

"Am I your legally wedded or not?"

"You are indeed that," he said.

"Then treat me in an appropriate fashion."

"You once said we're two of a kind. That's not true."

"You want to explain that?"

"I'm not deserving of you. You're a far better person than I am, Maggie. You tolerate the intolerable. You're a remarkable woman."

"I think that's the finest compliment I've ever had."

He put his hat on the rack and rubbed one eye with the back of his wrist, the floor shifting under his feet. "We got anything to eat?"

"I fixed you a steak sandwich and potato salad. Go upstairs. I'll bring it to you. This time you'd better not go to sleep on me."

"I won't," he said.

"We were meant to be together, Hack. It's the two of us against the world. We'll have a grand time of it. I promise."

On the Marne,
1918

Chapter 14

WHEN ISHMAEL WOKE, the walls of his trench were seeping water and the dawn was colder than it should have been, the sky an unnatural and ubiquitous pale color that had less to do with the rising of the sun than the passing of the night. The terrain was cratered and devoid of greenery or vegetation, glistening with dew and in some places excrement, the root systems of grass and brush and trees long since ground up and pulped and churned by the treads of tanks and wheeled cannons and the boots of men and the hooves of draft animals and marching barrages that exploded holes so deep into the earth, the tons of dirt blown into the air were dry and eclipsed the sun at high noon and robbed men not only of their identities but their shadows as well.

Except for their uniforms, the men of color Ishmael commanded could have been mistaken for the French Zouaves and other colonials on their flank. Most of them were asleep, wrapped in their blankets or greatcoats, some with their rifles and packs on the fire steps that ascended to the top of the trench. Their Adrian helmets were strapped under their chins, their putties stiff with mud, their faces soft inside dreams, their arms crossed peacefully on their chests. They made him think of sleeping buffaloes, humped up against one another, each trying to avoid the telephone lines and pools of dirty water strung through the bottom of the trench and the constant ooze from the basketlike weave of sticks holding the trench wall in place. In the soup of animal and human feces and the offal of war, they made him think of children, in the best possible way. In moments such as these, he tried to suppress his affection for them, lest he become too attached.

Most of them were former National Guardsmen from New York and in peacetime had been porters and draymen and scullions and hod carriers and janitors. They loved their uniforms and marching on parade and seldom complained about the food or verbal abuse from white soldiers. They loved the army in spite of the fact that the army and the country sometimes did not love them. Their courage under fire left Ishmael in dismay and unable to explain how men could continue to give so much when they had been given so little.

The third time he was about to go over the top, he said a prayer that became his mantra whenever his mind drifted into thoughts about mortality and the folly and madness and grandeur of war: *Dear Lord, if this is to be my eternal resting place, let me be guarded by these black angels, because there are none more brave and loving in your kingdom.*

He gazed through a periscope that gave on to an immense stretch of moonscape chained with flooded shell holes and barbed wire that was half submerged in mud six inches deep that never dried out. In the distance he could hear the dull knocking of a Maxim, similar to the sound of an obnoxious drunk who taps a bony knuckle on a locked door after he has been expelled from a party. The fog from the river was white on the ground, puffing like cotton on the floor of a gin, shiny on the tangles of wire, sometimes breaking apart in the breeze and exposing a booted foot or a skeletal hand or a face with skin as dry and tight as a lampshade protruding from the soggy imprint of a tank tread.

"We going this morning, Captain?" a voice behind him said.

Ishmael lowered the periscope. It was Corporal Amidee Labiche, a transplant from Louisiana who had moved his family to the Five Points area in New York.

"Hard to tell," Ishmael said. "Have you eaten yet?"

"No, suh."

"It'd be a good idea."

Labiche's greatcoat was buttoned at the throat. He had a small head and big eyes and gold skin dotted with moles that resembled bugs or drops of mud. "Why's it cold, Captain? It's summer. It ain't supposed to be cold, no."

"We're not far from the river. The clouds are low, and the heat from the sun doesn't get through."

"It ain't natural, suh. Nothing about this place is natural. We're going, ain't we?"

High overhead, Ishmael saw three British planes headed toward the east, straining against the wind, their engines barely audible. "Most likely," he said.

"I wrote a letter to my wife and daughter. I'd like you to keep it for me."

"You're going to come through fine. You'll mail it later yourself."

"I'd feel better if you kept my letter, Captain."

Ishmael placed his hand on Labiche's shoulder and smiled. "Listen to me," he said. "You've been over the top six times. You're going to make it. The Germans are through and they know it."

"I feel like somebody struck a match on the inside of my stomach. I never felt this way."

"Fix us some coffee, Corporal."

Labiche breathed through his mouth as though catching his breath. "What time we going, suh?"

"Who knows? Maybe after the planes come back. Maybe the Huns will throw it in."

"I don't know why I cain't get warm, suh."

Ishmael tapped him on the chest with a fist. "See the light in the east? It's going to be a grand day."

"Yes, suh."

"Now, let's be about it. Let's show them what the Harlem Hellfighters can do."

"It ain't supposed to be cold. That's what I cain't figure. That's all I was saying."

"Start getting them up."

"The letter is in my back pocket, suh."

Ishmael went to his dugout, one whose walls were held in place by sandbags and planks from a barn, whose only light came from a candle that burned inside a tin can. He opened the leather case in which he kept his notebook, his stationery, a calendar on which he marked off the days, a copy of *The Rubaiyat of Omar Khayyam*, and letters from his mother. In the same leather case, he had placed a letter that he had just received and for which he had no adequate response or means of dealing with, as if he'd discovered the return of a lump a surgeon had removed from his body. It was dated June 3, 1918, and began with the words "Dear son." Those two words had not only drained his heart but filled him with a sick sensation for which he didn't have a name. It wasn't revulsion or anger; nor was it the loss and abandonment that had characterized much of his childhood as he and his mother moved from one mining town or logging camp to the next. The sickness he felt was like a cloud of mosquitoes feeding on his heart. The only word for it was fear, but it was not of an ordinary kind. It had no face. He feared not only that the words written on the paper were full of deceit but that he would fall prey to them and be forced back into the past and become once again the little boy who believed his father would keep his word and return home to his family.

Ishmael flattened the letter on the table and continued to read his father's words, like a man determined to overcome a seduction or undo the devices of an enemy.

I wrote several times but learned only recently that you were commanding a different unit than the one you led in Mexico. I went down there to find you and got myself captured and treated pretty roughly by a few of Pancho Villa's boys, although I can't blame them considering the damage we did to the poor dumb bastards we always seem to pick on. The irony is I wandered into a straddle house where some of your men were hanged and others ambushed. I made it back to Texas carrying a religious artifact I think someone would like returned to him, but that's another story. The point is, I didn't find my little chap.

I let you down. I had telegraphed your mom about getting

back together, but I never heard from her again and assumed
she had said good riddance, for which I don't blame her. My
letters to her were returned marked addressee unknown. I
have never stopped thinking about either of you. My wife
Maggie divorced me and took half my property and lives as a
respectable and prosperous woman in San Antonio, although
I suspect she has her hand in the whorehouses there. You and
your mother have every right to bear enmity toward me, but I
would love to have the chance to see you both again.

   Tell me where you are and I'll be there, whether you are in
France or Belgium or Germany or the United States. In my
own mind, I'm still your Big Bud and you're my little chap and
your mother is my darling companion. I realize that's a mighty
big presumption on my part.

   Your father,
   Big Bud

Ishmael rolled the piece of stationery into a cone, touching the
tip of it to the candle flame, and watched it burn. Then he blew
out the candle and rose from the table and put on his steel helmet
and attached the lanyard to the ring on the butt of his .45-caliber
double-action revolver and stepped out the doorway into the trench,
just as he heard the three observation planes fly back over Allied
lines toward the rear, the flak from German anti-aircraft hanging
harmlessly behind them against a porcelain-blue sky.

BUT THE ORDER to go did not come. Not that morning nor that
afternoon or evening. At nightfall, the batteries of French 75s began
slamming doors, each cannon firing a minimum of fifteen gas and
explosive shells a minute, blowing up the enemy's wire, knocking
the trenches to pieces, the explosions flickering miles behind German
lines, where an occasional shell struck a fuel depot or a field hospital
or ambulances parked in a woods or by luck landed in the midst of
a reserve unit, blinding and maiming and dismembering, diluting its
spirit before it ever moved into the line.

At 0500 the next morning the guns went silent. The stillness was so pervasive and numbing, Ishmael felt he had gone deaf; he thought about Quasimodo swinging on the giant cast-iron bells in the tower, delighted to hear the only sounds available to him, the same ones that had destroyed his eardrums.

A flare popped in the sky, briefly illuminating the greasy shine on the surface of the flooded shell holes, the greenish uniforms and bloated bodies of German sappers who had been caught in their own wire and cut to pieces by Lewis guns, a disemboweled horse whose eyes were as bright as glass. Then the flare died, and the shadows of the blasted trees and corkscrew pickets and timber posts anchoring the coils of wire dissolved into the darkness.

Up and down the line, Ishmael's men waited at the foot of the fire steps and ladders that led to the top of the trench, their long, slender bayonets like the tips of lances on their rifles. He pressed his eyes against the viewing slit of the periscope. A cold ribbon of light, the color of blue ice, had just broken on the eastern horizon. Behind him, he heard the sound of bagpipes rising and fading and then trilling inside a gust of wind.

He glanced at his watch. 0507. "Slam the doors one more time," he heard himself say under his breath, his chest rising and falling, his stomach churning. *Keep Fritz down in his trench just three more minutes. Make him crawl and defecate in his underwear. Make his glands bleed with fear. Make him become as we are.*

But the 75s were done for the day. His men were cloaked in shadow against the trench wall, some of them shaking visibly, their chin straps pulled tight so their teeth didn't rattle. At exactly 0510 the entire line erupted with the blowing of whistles, the grinding of telephone boxes, the clatter of equipment, the labored sounds of men lifting themselves over the top as though loads of brick were strapped to their backs, the first ones over already dropping as the Maxims came to life beyond the German wire.

Ishmael held his breath and went up the steps behind Amidee Labiche. His face was slick with sweat, the wind like ice water inside his shirt. He could see the muzzles of the Maxims flashing in the gloom, the rounds thropping into the bodies of men on either side. How could so many of the enemy have survived the eight-hour barrage of the French 75s? They had even established a salient, jutting out of their lines like the point of a ship equipped with automatic weapons, mortars, flamethrowers, and gas pumped through funnels from compressors in the rear. He had never felt this cold or naked. No, "naked" was the wrong word. He felt a sensation that could be compared only to having his skin stripped away with pliers.

The salient contained sharpshooters with scoped rifles and machine gunners who had positioned the barrels of their Maxims across sandbags so the rounds would spray the field chest-high. There would be a sound like a wet slap, and the man next to him would grunt as though he had stepped on a sharp stone, then he would go straight down on his knees, his ability to breathe gone.

Ishmael wondered how he could have been so cavalier about the corporal's preoccupation with the coldness of the countryside. Amidee Labiche's perception was not imaginary. The unseasonal temperature was only a precursor of what lay on the other side of the Great Shade, a landscape where the rain did not fall and the sun did not shine, and where love and human warmth and charity and the bonds of one's family held no sway, where regret was a constant and sorrow for one's foolish mistakes abided forever. In seconds an illiterate farm worker, probably with the face of a goat, wearing a cloth-covered piked helmet, would squeeze a trigger a quarter of an inch and stitch Ishmael's chest and leave him gasping on the ground.

The corporal was running beside him, his bayonet-fixed rifle pointed in front of him. Either pistol or trip flares were descending above them, burning as brightly as a welder's torch inside the smoke and dust. Somebody on the right, perhaps a British noncommissioned officer, was yelling, "Form it up, boys! Form it up! We'll break their fucking line! Follow me! Follow me!"

What madness, Ishmael thought. *At the behest of strangers, we charge with pistols and bolt-action rifles into machine guns. Where are the kings, the generals, the lords of the parliament, the senators and congressmen? Where are those who would not allow us into their clubs? Would they like to gaze upon their work? Would they be willing to change places with those they have sent to transform Eden into hell?*

Then he realized that his anticipation of death at the hands of a Saxon pig farmer was unfounded. He did not know where the artillery barrage came from. They were sixty yards from the German salient now, too close for the gifts of the Krupp family to lob shells without killing their own. But that was exactly what happened, although the barrage came at a forty-five-degree angle, perhaps from enormous cannons mounted on railway cars. The shells were not spread out; they detonated one after another in a straight line, blowing holes so deep that the earth geysering into the air was as dry as baked sand.

Ishmael felt that his legs were locked in concrete. Three men trying to run to the rear were vaporized into a bloody mist. He saw Amidee Labiche turn and stare into his face, as though an unfair trick had been played on them, waiting for Ishmael to tell him what to do.

Then the earth seemed to explode under his feet and lift him inside a windstorm that blinded his eyes and deafened his ears and stopped his mouth with dirt. He struck the ground with such force that his brain seemed to disconnect from its fastenings, his eyes bulging from his head. A smell like rotten eggs rose from the hole he was lying in while dirt clouds rained down on his face. He was sure that Amidee Labiche was sitting next to him, on the incline of the slope, his face powdered with dust, his Adrian helmet still on his head, his lips arterial red when he tried to speak.

What is it? Ishmael said.

Mail my letter.

My legs are gone. You have to mail it yourself.

I'm dead.

Sorry, Amidee. I didn't know that. Is it bad being dead?

Amidee held out the letter to him. His fingerprints were stenciled in blood on the flap. *Take it, suh. Please.*

Chapter
15

ISHMAEL AWOKE ON a cot in a tent billowing with wind, the sky beyond the tent flap marbled with maroon and black clouds that could have come from a fire or just the setting of the sun. Someone had removed his shirt and placed a catheter on his penis and draped a blood-speckled cloth on his hip and rib cage. His skin looked white and rubbery and seemed to glow with an iridescence not unlike that of the bodies in a charnel house. He reached down to touch his legs.

"I wouldn't move around too much. There's still shrapnel in your side," said a French colonel sitting next to his cot, one leg crossed on his knee. He wore a mustache and the red cap of a grenadier and a dirty khaki jacket without insignia or epaulettes and rumpled trousers tucked inside riding boots. He also wore one of the new mechanical hands, with flexible metal fingers that were oiled and bright and tapered and shiny, and a metal sheath that fitted over the forearm, like a knight's armor.

"I can't feel my legs," Ishmael said.

"You've had a spinal injection."

"My legs weren't amputated?"

"We thought you might want to keep them. There's shrapnel in your side, though, perhaps close to an organ or two. You must not take any more morphine. There's an 'M' painted on your forehead. Do you understand what I'm saying to you?"

"I had a dream."

"You'll probably have many, most of them bad." The colonel picked up a metal bedpan and rattled it. "This is what they've taken out of you so far."

"Where is Labiche?"

The colonel shook his head.

"The corporal. He was next to me when the shells started coming in."

"You were by yourself when the litter-bearers dug you out."

"No, he was sitting a few feet from me. Inside the shell hole."

The colonel patted him tenderly on the arm. "When your men broke the German salient, the first thing they did was look for you."

"What's that odor?"

"That's the fellow on the next cot. He was loading a phosphorus shell when it blew up."

"I saw Labiche. Before the explosion and after. He talked to me."

"You were buried alive. Only your hand was sticking out."

"He told me he was dead."

The colonel stood up and gazed into Ishmael's face. "Are you cold? I can put a blanket over you."

"He wanted to give me a letter. It was for his family in New York."

"This happens when you are gravely wounded. You feel there are things you must take care of. Sometimes you feel a terrible obligation to people you haven't thought about in years." The colonel picked up a box from under the bed and sorted through it with his mechanical fingers. "Here are the things from your dugout and your pockets. I suspect this is the letter you're talking about. See, it was here all the time. The address on it is in New York City." The envelope was creased and smudged with dirt, stenciled with blood.

"There was another letter. One I was supposed to take care of. I can't think clearly."

"Rest. You'll be going back to America soon. There is nothing to worry about. Listen. The guns are quiet. Look at the sunset. It's a grand finish to a grand day. We broke the spine of the Boche and hammered them into the dirt. They'll never invade France again."

Ishmael felt himself slipping loose from the conversation, his vision blurring, the smells of urine and medicinal salve and trench foot and gangrenous flesh growing more and more distant. *I will never forgive my father, never answer his letters, never be undone by his guile,* he thought. *He left his family to founder by the wayside. Would that I could drain his blood from my veins.*

Later, Ishmael could not be sure if he spoke these words aloud or to himself, or if they would have made any sense to his friend the colonel. When he awoke in the middle of the night, the sky was totally black except for a flickering of either cannon fire or electricity on the horizon. The man who had been burned by a phosphorus shell was carried away on a litter like a lump of bandaged charcoal, replaced with a man who had neither arms nor legs.

Top of the bloody evening to you, Ishmael thought. *Would you call this a grand end to a grand day? How about a game of checkers?*

IT WAS A dry September, the kind that brought no relief from summer's heat and left the rocks in the streambeds white and dusty and printed with the scales of insects that normally lived below the water's surface. Hackberry was determined to bring in a prize crop of pumpkins from the three acres down by the river where he grew vegetables that were for his personal use. Each morning he hoed out the weeds in the rows, and each evening he hauled water in barrels from the river and walked down the long lines of pumpkins, stringing water from perforated syrup cans that hung from a yoke stretched across his shoulders.

The sun had just dipped behind the bluffs on the far side of the river, splintering like a red diamond inside the cottonwoods, the river riffling slate-green through the shadows, when Hackberry heard a motorcar—actually, a touring vehicle that resembled a tank—coming up the dirt road, its heavy chassis and spoked wheels churning up huge amounts of dust, most of it drifting across his field and into his face.

The driver wore goggles and a duster and a cap. Not so the passenger in back. The latter stepped down on the ground like royalty from a carriage, dressed in a sky-blue silk shirt, a gray flop hat with an oxblood fur band, laced boots, and skintight striped trousers hitched high up on his hips so they accentuated his heart-shaped butt. The man removed his hat and pushed back his silvery blond hair, then unbuttoned his fly and cupped his phallus in his right palm and urinated in the middle of the road.

Two years previous Hackberry had seen the same man through a spyglass, in the early dawn at the base of a sunlit mesa, and in that moment had known he was looking at a man who had no category. Hackberry set down his water buckets and walked toward the touring car as the visitor stuffed his phallus back in his fly and buttoned up.

"I have indoor plumbing if you'd like to use it," Hackberry said.

"Don't need it," the man said. He extended his hand. "I'm Arnold Beckman. You may have heard of me."

Hackberry kept his eyes on Beckman's and did not raise his hand. "You have business with me?"

Beckman took a handkerchief from his pocket and blew his nose in it. "I understand you're looking for your son. I think I've found him."

The accent was European, with a tinge of Cockney, as though Beckman had gone to the wrong source to learn English; the aquiline profile was marred by a chain of pitted scars that went down the cheek and onto the neck and into the shirt collar. His skin looked untouched by the sun, a pallid hue in it that was more green than white.

"How would you know anything about my boy?"

"I heard of your situation through your neighbor."

"You're a friend of Cod Bishop?"

"I made an inquiry with a United States senator. Your son is in the Fitzsimmons army hospital near Denver. Is it true you were a Texas Ranger?"

"At various times."

"I've been looking for one Ranger in particular. He killed several Mexican soldiers in a bordello, including a general. Splattered them all over the rocks. He also burned a hearse loaded with some merchandise of mine."

"I hope you find him. This man sounds like a dangerous character. Probably of low morals, too. This happened in a bordello?"

"Are you familiar with the bordello I'm talking about?"

"I try to stay out of them. I already know my son's whereabouts,

Mr. Beckman. I have recently written to him and hope to hear back soon. Thank you for the information regardless."

"The man who burned my merchandise also stole a religious relic from me."

"Bones and such?"

"No, a sacramental cup. The woman who ran the bordello claimed to have no knowledge about it. Her name was Beatrice DeMolay."

Beckman's eyes seemed to be six inches from Hackberry's, although the two men were standing three feet apart.

"You said 'was'?"

"Yes, I did. Does that upset you?"

"I've known men like you. You're cut out of different cloth."

"Could you back up on that? I missed the allusion," Beckman said.

Hackberry leaned to the side and spat. "I've seen your handiwork. Flies are usually buzzing over it. Like a trademark."

"I'm opening up an arms company in San Antonio and Houston and New Orleans. I'm currently buying up captured and surplus infantry weapons from all over Europe, maybe the Orient, too. I could use a man like you. Do you think you could get my relic back?"

"No."

"Why not?"

"Because I don't have any idea what you're talking about. What did you do to the woman at the bordello in Mexico?"

"What does any man do with an attractive whore? I fucked her until her brains were running out her ears."

"I got to tend to my pumpkins."

Beckman stuck a piece of paper in Hackberry's pocket. "I'm staying in Austin. You have two days."

IN THE EARLY-MORNING hours he woke to rumbling sounds he associated with dry thunder or a herd spooking on an unfenced stretch of hardpan. He looked at his bedside clock. It was 4:16. He went to the living room and stepped barefoot out on the porch. In the distance he could see a light burning in his neighbor's house. The sky was black. A solitary bolt of lightning quivered whitely on the horizon, then disappeared. Inside the wind he could hear cattle lowing and the sweep of the trees by the river. He went back to sleep.

When he got up to fix breakfast, he glanced through the kitchen window at his pumpkin field. He stared at it for a long time, and at the slat fence on his hog pen and the barbed wire on the south end of his pasture. He poured a cup of black coffee and sat down at the kitchen table and drank it without sugar, then washed the cup under the hand pump in the sink and set it in the dry rack. Without bothering to shave, he put on his Stetson and saddled his horse and rode to the home of Cod Bishop.

He tapped on the door and waited. He could see the partially grassed-over area down by the river where, years ago, Bishop had burned the cabins of the black people living on his property, the scorched bricks and boards and sunken piles of ash still visible, as though the soil under the fire was incapable of restoring itself.

Bishop was wearing a Japanese robe when he opened the door, a monogrammed handkerchief in the breast pocket. "Why are you on my porch, Holland?"

"Arnold Beckman says you're a friend of his."

"He's a business associate."

"I never could understand the word 'associate.' It seems to cover everything."

"If you're drinking again, seek help from a physician or the temperance people. But leave."

"Somebody cut my wire and let out my Brahmas and busted down my hog pen last night. Most of my pumpkins are ruined. I'm going to spend most of the day rounding up my stock."

"Why are you telling me about it?"

"You hear or see anything unusual early this morning?"

"No, I did not."

"Your light was on at about four-twenty. It was a warm night. You must have had your windows open."

"I was in my office. I heard thunder. I don't know anything about your pumpkins. Now go home."

"Arnold Beckman has been making inquiries about my son. Did you tell him about my boy?"

"The one you drove from your home? How dare you speak to me like this?"

"You once said I was going to get my comeuppance."

"If I said something like that, I was probably justified. But I don't remember doing so. Regardless, I'm not the issue. You're a violent and primitive man, pitied by your neighbors and, by all accounts, an embarrassment to the Texas Rangers. There's a foul odor about you that you're not even aware of. Be gone, sir. You gave up your claim to membership in decent society many years ago."

"Cod, I'm convinced God sent you here to show us the fallacy of white superiority. Don't hide your light under a basket. Many are called, but few are chosen."

Bishop slammed the door in his face.

DURING THE MORNING and early afternoon, Hackberry and three of his Mexican workers salvaged a wagonload of his pumpkins and mended the hog pen and the barbed wire in the pasture and rounded up most of his stock. While he drove his cattle back into the pasture, he never took his eyes completely off the bluffs along the river or the dirt road that led to his house, or the deep green arbor of oak trees on the far end of his property. At three o'clock he left his horse saddled in the lot and went into the house and shaved and bathed and put on fresh clothes. Then he put a jar of lemonade and a jar of mustard and a loaf of bread and a chunk of uncooked roast and a whole onion and a fresh tomato in a canvas bag, along with a box that contained his stationery and fountain pen and postage stamps. He also picked up his holstered .44 Army Colt, the loops on the belt stuffed with cartridges, and hung it on the pommel of his horse, along with the canvas bag. He went into the barn and picked up an iron rod that had a wood handle on one end and on the other a hooked tip, blackened by fire.

The river was so low he could ride his horse across it on a sandbar. He came up on a stretch of beach shadowed by cypress whose lacy branches were turning gold with the season. Above him were gray limestone bluffs carpeted on top by lichen and moss and hollowed with depressions Tonkawa Indians had ground corn in. He rode up a sandy path lined on either side with fallen stone, and dismounted in front of a cave and tethered his horse to the limb of a willow tree. Down below, under the riffle flowing between two giant bounders, a shaft of sunlight had pierced the trees and lit the pebbled bottom as brightly as a rainbow.

A folding canvas chair was propped against the cave wall. He built a fire and cut strips from the uncooked roast with the bowie knife he had taken off the Mexican soldier he had killed two years earlier, and hung them on the iron rod and propped the rod across the rocks that ringed his fire. The smoke flattened against the roof, then corkscrewed through a crevice that formed a natural chimney into the top of the bluff. He sat down in the canvas chair and began a letter on top of his stationery box.

Dear Ishmael, it read.

> *I hope you received my earlier correspondence. Whether you have the opportunity to answer my letter is not important at the moment. I am writing to warn you about a man named Arnold Beckman. He has taken an interest in me for reasons I won't go into now. He has also used his contacts, all of which I suspect are nefarious in nature, to find out the name of the hospital where you are recuperating from your wounds.*
>
> *Have nothing to do with this man or his minions. He's an arms dealer, and like most arms dealers, he sells to both sides. I also believe him to be a sadist. In a word, he's evil.*
>
> *I love you, son. I let you and your mother down. One day I hope to make it up to you.*
>
> *Write when you have time.*
> *Your father,*
> *Big Bud*

A shadow fell across his handwriting. He began to write a postscript, not looking up. "You're standing in my light," he said.

"Saw your smoke. We were hunting down below," a voice replied. The speaker was rail-thin, over six feet, his shirt unbuttoned on a bony chest, his hair streaked with gray and soggy with sweat, tied up on his head. He propped his long rifle butt-down in front of him and leaned on it. It was a Mauser, one with a straight bolt. He grinned. "Sir? Are you there?"

"All the property from here on down to the river is mine. I don't allow hunters on it."

The second man was smaller, hatchet-faced, his sleeves cut off at the armpits, both of his arms tattooed with blue ink that had started to fade. He had black hair that grew like snakes, and a lazy eye that drifted back and forth in the socket the way a marble would. He carried a double-barrel shotgun crooked over his arm, the breech open, both chambers loaded. His body odor seemed to hang like an invisible curtain over the cave's entrance. "What's the good of a big ranch if you cain't hunt on it?"

"I don't believe in hurting animals unnecessarily."

"A rancher who sends his cattle to the packer but don't hurt them? That's a challenge to my thinking powers."

Hackberry capped his fountain pen and put it and his letter inside his stationery box and replaced the top on the box. "I'd figured y'all would be along."

"What's that you say?"

"If you dog somebody, don't silhouette on the crest of a hill. Don't aim your binoculars into the sun, either."

"Why would we be dogging *you*?"

"You got me. Why not make a clean breast of it? Dip your soul in the Jordan, know what I mean? I think it was y'all cut my wire and busted up my hog pen and trampled my pumpkins."

"My opinion is you've got your head up your ass."

"Cod Bishop and Arnold Beckman will leave you twisting in the wind. You take the risk, they take the profits. Sound like a good deal to you?"

"We'll be going. We didn't mean to bother you," said the man with the rifle. He grinned again, as though he could hardly contain his goodwill.

"I got a question," said the man with the lazy eye. "Is that a cap and ball?"

Hackberry's revolver lay on a flat rock on the other side of the fire, its belt coiled around the holster. "I had it converted for cartridges many years ago. I hardly shoot it these days. Want to shoot it?"

"You can leave it where it's at."

Hackberry propped his hands on his thighs and stared into the fire.

"Got yourself in a bind?" said the man with the lazy eye.

"That's what age does. Your judgment goes. You want to believe in your fellow man, but you end up in sackcloth and ashes, wondering how you could be such a fool. Doesn't seem fair, does it? You boys hungry? I got plenty."

The man with the rifle smelled himself. "Thank you. Maybe later. We got a job to do."

"You don't get it, do you, son?"

"Get what?"

"You shouldn't try to outsmart your betters."

"Our betters?" said the man with the rifle.

"That's right. Somebody hired you to follow me around, then report back to them. Instead, you got ambitious and decided to find out what was in this cave. Unfortunately, there's nothing here except cougar bones and bat shit. So now you've made enemies with a man who in his youth put a number of people on the wrong side of the grass, and in the meantime you got yourself crossways with Arnold Beckman."

It was silent in the cave. Hackberry leaned over and removed the onion and tomato and jar of lemonade and loaf of bread from the bag and set them on a flat rock. He sliced open the bread longways with the bowie and bladed mustard on it, then began halving the onion.

"Say all that again," said the man with the rifle.

"I was trying to say I feel sorry for you."

"Sorry for *us*?"

"You were probably unwanted at birth and had parents that were either poor-white trash or one step this side of feral. There's no fix for it. The seed goes from generation to generation like congenital clap. I've heard Bedouins are warned not to shake hands with Southern poor whites. You sniff your armpits and blow your nose on your napkin and spit on the floor and wonder why nobody likes you. On top of it, pert' near every one of you was beat on with an ugly stick. That's what I mean about life not being fair."

"I think you got rabies from these bats," said the man with the lazy eye.

"Son, have you looked in the mirror lately?"

Hackberry squatted by the fire and began picking the strips of cooked roast off the iron rod with the tip of his bowie, laying them out on the bread.

"I've had all of you as I can take," said the man with the lazy eye. He shut the breech of his shotgun. "Lay the knife down." The man with the rifle reached over and picked up Hackberry's revolver and tossed it behind a rock.

"I wish you hadn't done that," Hackberry said.

"That old revolver is the least of your problems," said the man with the lazy eye.

"You trespass on my property, you lie to my face, you disturb my meal, and now you treat my possessions with contempt. You boys really piss me off. I hate stupid people. It's a character defect I have never overcome. I work on it and work on it, and then a pair like you comes along and all my efforts go down the drain." Hackberry's face pained as he got to his feet, his joints creaking.

"You better close your mouth," said the man with the lazy eye.

"That's what I mean. Stupid to the core," Hackberry said. "Your mother must have been impregnated by a yeast infection."

He fitted his hand around the wood handle on the iron rod and rammed the heated tip into the scrotum of the man with the lazy eye, then swung it across the face of his partner. The man with the lazy eye dropped his shotgun and grabbed his genitalia, his mouth wide open, as though his jawbone were broken. Hackberry hit the other man again, splitting open his forehead, knocking him into the cave wall. He picked up the weapons of both men and flung them end over end into the river.

"Who paid you?" he said.

"Nobody," said the man with the lazy eye.

"This running iron I'm holding is of historical importance," Hackberry said. He held the tip of the iron over the fire. "I took it off the man who figured out how to change the XIT brand into a star with a cross inside it. The owners of the XIT let him off for showing them how he did it. I can show you how to do it, too. On your back or on your chest."

"Then do it, you nasty old crock," said the man with the lazy eye.

"I'm glad to hear you say that."

The man with the lazy eye blanched, his jaw tightening.

"That's not what I mean," Hackberry said. "I'm glad to see you're not totally worthless. Here's the reality of our situation. If you torture a man, he'll tell you whatever you want to hear. It's a waste of everybody's time, including the victim's. Besides, it's not something I do. So that's it. *Adiós*."

"What?" said the man with the split forehead.

"Git. Don't come back. Next time out, I'll hurt you."

The man with the split head had pressed his hand to his wound and was staring at the bloody star on his palm. "What the hell you call this?"

"Practice," Hackberry said.

He gathered up his revolver and holster and belt and sat back down in his chair, blowing out his breath, trying to catch a glimpse of the sky beyond the cave's entrance. Then he set his stationery box on his lap and began to address an envelope to Ishmael. In seconds he was deep in thought about Ishmael. When he glanced up again, his visitors were gone.

Chapter
16

THE HOSPITAL OUTSIDE Denver had been converted from a nineteenth-century army fort whose two-story buildings had the wide porches and stucco walls and red Spanish-tile roofs of army forts all over the burgeoning New American Empire. Ishmael had been placed in a ward with eight other officers, then moved to a private room, one that had a radiator and a private bathroom and a lovely view of the shade trees on the grounds and, in the distance, mountains whose peaks gusted with snow in the sunset.

"Why the special treatment?" Ishmael asked the orderly.

"You probably have friends in high places."

"Must be a mistake," Ishmael said.

"You need anything, Captain?"

"I didn't sleep much last night. Could you give me a touch of something, nothing too strong?"

"Better talk to the doc."

"I don't want to bother him. Don't worry about it."

"I'll see what I can do, Captain."

"Thank you."

He hadn't lied. He seldom slept through the night without dreaming, and as the French colonel had warned him, his dreams were not good ones. Neither were they nightmares, at least not in the ordinary sense. They were not filled with gargoyles and improbable events; they were simply a replay of events he had witnessed or images he had seen. Maybe that was what made the dreams so disturbing: They weren't creations of the mind; they were an accurate replication of the world. The bigger problem was he couldn't shut them down, as he did during his waking hours. Also the images told a story that few wanted to hear and that he did not wish to impose upon others.

Some German infantry units were issued a bayonet that had sawteeth along the crest of the blade. When it was extracted from the victim, particularly when the entry wound was in the upper torso, the sawteeth ripped loose bone, cartilage, lungs, kidneys, liver, and entrails like viscera in a slaughterhouse. One way or another, the French sent a message to the Germans: Any soldier captured with a sawtooth bayonet not filed flat on the spine would suffer a fate that no civilized person would ever want to hear about. To Ishmael, the stories had seemed apocryphal, not unlike the accounts of women chained to machine guns or bottles of German schnapps laced with cyanide left in trenches for French soldiers to find. Anyway, why was dying on a sawtooth bayonet more inhumane than death by a flamethrower or mustard gas that boiled the eyes in their sockets and coated the inside of the lungs with blisters and pustules?

Ishmael and his men had gone over the top through six hundred yards of machine-gun fire and artillery rounds loaded with gas, the air so thick with smoke and dust that the sun had turned to an orange wafer, metal flying through the air with a dry spitting sound like someone blowing abruptly through a peashooter. Men were crumpling all around him; some were caught in the wire and trying to free themselves with their bare hands; some were atomized. In the background was the constant knocking of the Maxims, as dull and unrelenting as a woodpecker tapping on a telephone pole. Suddenly, Ishmael and ten others, all of them gray with dust, as featureless as aborigines, were standing on the lip of the enemy trench, firing point-blank into the Germans trapped below, then jumping into their midst, clubbing heads with rifle butts or pistols and double-edged trench knives with brass knuckles on the hand guard, impaling or beating to a bloody pulp every enemy soldier who didn't surrender and sometimes those who did.

Both French soldiers and members of his regiment were leaping over the trench, driving deeper into the German line. Others were rounding up the Germans who had thrown down their weapons and raised their hands. Ishmael shucked the spent shells from his revolver and reloaded each chamber, his fingers shaking uncontrollably. On his left, he saw the French Legionnaires piling into the trench, some picking up German stick grenades and stuffing them in their belts. Something else was going on, too. A crowd had formed at a bend in the trench, each soldier trying to look over the shoulder of another. Someone was shouting in German.

Ishmael tore the wrapper off a candy bar and began eating, trying to close his mind to what may be happening farther down the trench. Then a man screamed. Ishmael could not tell if the voice belonged to the man who had been shouting in German. The scream contained no hope, only terror and pain.

He walked through the clutter of haversacks, ammunition boxes, gas masks, knee mortars, stretchers, pistol flares, telephone wires, shell casings, wire cutters, blood-caked bandages, first-aid kits, ration tins, rotted food, newspaper that someone had cleaned himself with, ammunition belts and boxes of potato mashers and rifle grenades fitted into their compartments like eggs in a carton, then pushed his way through the Legionnaires, who were bunched tightly together. He saw what they had done and tried to look away in the same way you would if you opened a bedroom door at the wrong moment.

A German soldier in a dirty gray uniform was sitting with his back against the trench, his legs splayed, his bucket helmet lying beside him. He had a long face, like a horse's, and bad teeth and flaxen hair and defensive wounds in his hands and a large wet area around his thighs where he had soiled himself. A sawtooth bayonet had been driven through his left eye socket, all the way to the hilt, pinning his head to the wall.

They were Legionnaires, many of them criminals, Ishmael told himself later. *If they hadn't joined the Legion, they would have been on Devil's Island. They were victims themselves, sent into the lines as cannon fodder. What they did is not their fault.*

But rationalizing the scene in the trench was not an easy job. These men had descended from the same tree and were made of the same flesh and blood as their victim. Their crime was not committed in hot blood, and their choice of a victim was arbitrary. Ishmael had seen three other German prisoners captured with rifles that had sawtooth bayonets. One had gotten a punch in the face; nothing was done to the other two. Later, the executioner of the German solider, a peasant from Brittany, made coffee and smoked cigarettes and chatted with his comrades a few feet from the body, as blithe as a bridegroom on his wedding day.

Psychiatrists might assure their patients that dreams were only dreams and they disappeared into the daylight. But psychiatrists had no cure for the truth about man's capacity for cruelty. The ancient Greeks understood that, and so did the growers of the opium poppy. The gift of Morpheus brought not only sleep but oblivion. You just had to be careful, a little touch now and then. You did not think of it in a self-serving or profligate way. You chewed the tablet gently, your eyes closed in a demonstration of gratitude and reverence. You let the granules slide down your throat with your saliva, and you swallowed with the words "thank you" on your lips. How could any gift from the natural world be bad? Morphine healed all wounds and lifted all burdens. The tranquillity it purchased was ethereal, if not holy.

The orderly kept his word and placed a vial of pills under Ishmael's pillow. That afternoon, when Ishmael woke from his slumber, he felt the wind blowing through the window like a cool burn on his skin. The snow on the peaks of the mountain was feathering against the sky. Then a figure stepped in front of the window, blocking out the sun. It took a moment for Ishmael's eyes to adjust. He studied her face and the redness of her mouth and the trimness of her body and her elegant clothes and the thickness of her hair. Though she was an older woman, she was one of the loveliest women he had ever seen.

"I'm Maggie Bassett. I used to be your father's wife or animal trainer, take your choice," she said. "My, you've grown into a big boy."

SHE WAS WEARING a purple dress with a silver and ivory brooch at her throat and high-heeled boots and a tall domed black hat with a floppy brim. She sat down in a chair by the widow and removed her hat and brushed her hair out on her shoulders. It was dark brown and looked freshly washed and dried, reflective of light, soft on her skin. "You don't remember me?" she said.

"I remember the name," he said.

"Probably not in the best way. Hack and I weren't a good match. Was it bad over there?"

"In the trenches? Not always. I wouldn't believe all the stories you hear."

"Is your mother alive?"

"Why wouldn't she be?"

"I heard she was involved with anarchists or something. In a mass killing."

"She was at the Ludlow Massacre, right down the road. The miners were on strike. They weren't anarchists."

"You have unusual attitudes for a professional soldier."

"I'm a soldier, not a company gink. The Colorado militia was doing Rockefeller's dirty work."

"You're certainly your mother's son. I always admired her. I think she and I have a lot in common."

"Nobody is like my mother."

"We both got involved with a man who has ten inches of penis and three of brain."

"You talk pretty rough."

"You don't know the half of it, sweetie."

"Why are you here?"

"I believe I helped deny you the home and family you should have had. I have a conscience, believe it or not."

"You came here to tell me that?"

"No, to offer you a job with an export-import company."

"Oh yeah?"

"It's a consortium. We have an office in San Antonio. Our warehouses are in Houston and New Orleans." Her gaze went away from his, out the window. "See how the trees flutter in the wind? This is such a fine time of year. You lived here when you were a child?"

"We lived in a sump outside of Trinidad. My mother worked two or three jobs to feed us."

"Where is she now?"

"Wherever the union sends her. She went to see Joe Hill before he was executed by firing squad in Utah."

"Who?"

"The songwriter. He was framed by the mine owners."

"I see," she said. "But she's not an anarchist or a Communist?"

"I never asked her."

Maggie approached the bed. Her eyes moved over his face. "I rode two days on the train to be here."

"That's very nice of you."

"I was a prostitute and helped rob a bank. But I never hurt a child. Except you."

"You don't owe me anything."

She placed her hand on his forehead. "You're hot."

"It's the radiator. It's got its own way. It turns itself on and off at the wrong times." He tried to smile.

"The radiator is cold. You have a fever."

"That's why sick people go to hospitals. They have fevers and such."

"You talk like your father."

"I talk like the people in the mining and log camps where I grew up."

She unbuttoned the top of his pajamas and placed her hand on his breast. "Your heart is like a drum."

"You could fool me."

"I came here as a friend, not to embarrass you."

"I heard you were a schoolteacher. I don't understand why an educated woman would marry my father."

"He's far more intelligent than he pretends. That's what his enemies never understand about him. Until it's too late."

"I don't like to talk about him," Ishmael said.

"Do you want anything? I brought you some fruit. I don't know if you're supposed to have it."

"That's kind of you. Thank you."

"You'd better get used to me. We're going to be seeing lots of each other."

She removed the sheet from his legs. His pajama bottoms were cut off at the tops of his thighs. His wounds were wrapped with medicated bandages all the way to the ankles. In places he had bled through. She put her hand on his lower abdomen and then on his thigh. "I can feel the heat through your skin. How many places were you hit?"

"There are men in the ward you don't want to look at. Their families cry when they see them."

"I want to do something for you," she said.

"No, you shouldn't have those kinds of feelings. I had a good life as a child."

She leaned down and kissed him on the mouth. One of her tresses fell on his cheek. He thought he smelled lilacs in her hair.

"Did you enjoy that?"

"What am I supposed to say?"

She kissed him on the mouth again, then gazed into his face. "Let me."

"Let you what?"

"Let me do what I can for you."

He shook his head on the pillow. "You don't need to worry about me."

She stroked his hair. "You're big and you're handsome, yet you're like a little boy."

"I wish you wouldn't say things like that."

"Am I too old?"

"No, ma'am, I don't think that at all."

"Then you mustn't refuse me. I'll be deeply hurt."

"What are you doing?"

"Closing the door."

"It's almost lunchtime," he said. "Look, I'm being processed out of the army. At my request. When I'm well and released from the hospital, we'll get to know each other."

"I told the orderly I'd brought you something. He won't be back until much later." She moved the chair in front of the door and pulled the curtain on the window, dropping the room into shadow.

"Miss Bassett, I prefer you not do this."

She sat in the chair and removed her high-heeled boots, then

stood up and undressed with her back to him. She lay down on the
bed and pulled the sheet up to her shoulders; she kissed him on the
cheek. She slid her hand down his stomach. "Look me in the face
and tell me you don't want me here." When he didn't speak, she
teased his lips with her finger and touched his teeth. "You resemble
both your parents."

"Miss Bassett—"

"Do this for me, not for you. That will make it all right. You're
a gentleman. That has special meaning for a woman of my
background." She got up on her knees and placed him inside her, her
eyes closing, her mouth parting. "Tell me I'm not a bad girl. Tell me
I've done something good for you, something no one else could do
as well. But tell me that only if it's true."

It is, he thought. Then he shut his eyes and felt himself nodding
off, floating out of the room to a place where the snow was blowing
like cotton candy, where the cigarette trees and lemonade springs
beckoned, where childhood and adult love and all the gifts of this
world seemed to crest and fold inside him and then burst achingly in
a fountain of colored light.

Vaguely, he remembered her placing either her breast or a soft pear
in his mouth. Was that what happened? Could you confuse those
two images? He drifted into a sleep that was as deep and warm and
secure as the sleep of an unborn child suspended inside its mother's
fluids. He wondered if someone had injected him with morphine. As
if she read his thoughts, she stroked his forehead to reassure him that
no harm would come to him. She was so quiet when she closed the
door behind her that he hardly knew she was gone.

When he woke, a half-eaten pear lay on his nightstand.

HACKBERRY TRIED TO put his mind inside Beckman's but knew it was
a waste of time. Beckman traveled across international boundaries
at will, hiring and using and discarding people as convenience
demanded. If he sent more men onto Hackberry's property, they
wouldn't be white trash hired out of a saloon. If he used guile, it
would be of an intricate kind, the sort that no one saw coming and

left people bereft of their dignity and resenting themselves the rest of their lives.

Hackberry had not shown anyone the chalice, if that was what it was. The inlay in the top of the cup, and the metal framework securing it, were obviously gold. The jewels were anybody's guess. How valuable could it be? Beckman was a businessman about to embark on a new venture, one that involved the sale of arms all over the world. Would he bog himself down in Southwest Texas over a religious artifact, one he was not sure Hackberry had in his possession? It didn't fit.

And what had happened to the woman at the bordello where the black soldiers had been lynched? She might have been a brothel operator, but Beatrice DeMolay had character, the kind you didn't acquire by simply sitting in a church house.

Hackberry rolled back the rug in his office and opened the trapdoor that gave access to the underside of the house. The house had been built in 1854, when mounted bands of comancheros showed up unexpectedly in front yards, wearing army coats with no shirts, their silence more piercing than a scream, their deeds of the next few minutes involving flame and prickly-pear cactus and leather thongs and levels of pain an unsuspecting pioneer family previously considered unimaginable. Hackberry reached down and lifted the rosewood box he had wrapped in a piece of canvas, and laid it on top of his desk. He opened the box and stared at the chalice, pressed tightly inside the green satin padding that lined the bottom of the box.

The stars were bright over the hills, the river shining in the darkness. He touched the tips of his fingers to the onyx goblet that held the golden cup. The lines in his fingers seemed to glow on its surface. For some reason he could not explain, he knew that Arnold Beckman represented something much larger than himself, and that Beckman's mission had somehow intersected with Hackberry's life for a reason, and that neither of them would ever be the same again.

He closed the box and tilted it upward so he could see the small cross and "Leon" carved in the wood. What was the provenance of the artifact? Mexico was in chaos. Both sides hung trees with corpses; almost every village in the north and the south had an adobe wall scarred with a jagged line of rifle fire. Bolsheviks and American mercenaries down there were as happy as pigs in slop. He knew no one in Nuevo Leon who might know the story behind the rosewood box and its contents.

They were coming, though. He knew this in the same way he had known John Wesley Hardin was coming, that wildfire and dust storms would follow prolonged drought. No matter which way you ran at philosophy or religion, there was no denying that certain individuals would find each other. No matter what they did, there was a magnet that would draw them together, and in an instant they would recognize each other and realize they were more alike than different. They would also recognize that that knowledge would save neither from his fate.

All the lights were off in his house, the windows open, the curtains straightening in the breeze. He wrapped the box in the piece of canvas and took it upstairs and placed it under his bed. He stared through the window at the myrtle bushes in the yard and the heat lightning above the hills and was sure that someone on the hillside, on the far side of the river, was looking at him with binoculars. He took an empty hatbox from a closet and wrapped it in a blanket, then went out to the barn and placed the hatbox and blanket inside a big bucket, along with two bricks, and tied a long piece of clothesline to the bail and walked to the old water well his father had dug by hand in 1859. He lowered the bucket down the brick sides of the well until it swung just above the water's surface, then cinched the clothesline to the winch.

When he walked back to the kitchen door, he didn't look to the right or the left, as though confident that no one had been watching.

The next night, when he arrived in Austin, the drought had broken and rain was tumbling on the city like broken crystal from a black sky, the lamps burning brightly atop the bridge over the Colorado River. He wondered if this moment marked a new beginning in his life.

ARNOLD BECKMAN WAS staying at the Driskill, a grand hotel on the corner of Sixth Street and Congress. A fete of some kind was in progress, one that attracted hundreds of guests and onlookers who were bunched up at the entrance. Not far away were a magnificent railroad station and City Hospital, the latter remarkable in its own right for its twin spires and ceiling-high windows and ventilated shutters and first-and-second-story wraparound verandas, a Caribbean echo of a more genteel era. The stone-paved street at its back door shone with the dull coppery glow of a rain-streaked alleyway in an Edgar Allan Poe story, although there was little romantic about the two types of vehicles parked on it, namely, motorized ambulances that brought in new cases of Spanish influenza, and the mortuary carriages that transported them to the graveyards where convicts in shackles, with rags tied over their mouths and noses, were forced to bury them.

Not a time to brood, Hackberry told himself. The Grim Reaper drew his scythe across all; why give him even a minute he had not earned? Time to join the revelers, to clatter the dice out of the cup, to have a talk in public with a man who funded slaughter and gloried in forcing submission on others. There was more than one way to bust a cap.

Hackberry went through the back door into the kitchen and on through a pair of swinging doors into a dining room hung with chandeliers and paneled with hand-carved mahogany. The tables were set with gold plates and silver bowls of water that had flowers floating in them. The men wore tuxedos; the women were dressed in gowns that probably came from New York or Paris. There were barrels of iced-down oysters lined against the wall; the serving tables were loaded with glazed hams, roast beef, smoked duck, pheasant, redfish and speckled trout, and every kind of side dish and dessert. White-jacketed black men worked feverishly at the bar to keep up with the orders. At the head table, up on a dais, sat the guest of honor, Arnold Beckman, dipping his cup into a bowl of champagne punch.

Hackberry sat down in an empty chair at a table in back. A waiter asked him for his order.

"Bourbon and water," he said.

"Yes, suh. Be right back wit' it."

"Tell you what, a rainy evening warrants a cup of tea and a bit of lemon. Can you do that for me?"

"Yes, suh."

The change of order surprised even him. Why had he done it? When it came to alcohol, he could not be accused of a halfway commitment.

Secretly, he knew. Every drunkard has many moments of shame that live like carpet tacks in his memory, but the one Hackberry could not deal with was his impotence when Harvey Logan had mocked him in front of the café in San Antonio's brothel district, clattering a dollar on the plank sidewalk, telling him to take a bath. No, it was worse than that, so shameful he couldn't think about all the details.

The master of ceremonies was introducing Beckman, who was wearing a white suit and a silk shirt as black and lustrous as oil, with tiny purple flowers stitched on the collar, which gave the impression of a man who had no label, no design, no need to be other than what he was. He had fled his own country rather than serve the imperialistic schemes of Kaiser Bill. He had fought the Turks alongside the Anzacs at Gallipoli and helped arm the Bedouins in the desert with T. E. Lawrence. He had been in Russia with the American Expeditionary Forces—with the marines, in fact—and had seen the bloody hand of the Bolsheviks at work, the same group that now threatened to infect the American workforce with their false doctrines.

Beckman listened with one arm placed stiffly on the table, his face lifted, his smile frozen, as though praise made him uncomfortable. Then the master of ceremonies gave him the podium. The bones in his face were like a bird's, perhaps a hawk's, but they seemed too small, too delicate, for the martial precision in his speech. A tooth would show when he paused, his expression softening, as though he were suppressing a memory from the war out of courtesy. The blueness in his eyes deepened as he looked into their faces, bonding with them, drawing his energy from the goodness they all shared. His silvery-blond hair hung in strands on his cheeks, as it would on a careless schoolgirl's. His listeners were enthralled. He was an imp, a hawk sailing on the breeze, an androgynous mix that was unthreatening and reassuring, like a mythic creature rising from an illustration in a book of fairy tales.

The Great War was not over, he said. It was just beginning. When he used the word "war," his chin had a way of lifting, exposing the chain of scars that dripped down inside his collar. The time to act was now. Do not listen to Wilson about a League of Nations. The Reds were spreading from Mexico into the American West. The federal prison at Yuma was already full of them.

The waiter put a teacup and saucer in front of Hackberry. Beckman finished, and the audience stood and applauded for almost a minute, the floor shaking. Hackberry looked around. Were these people out of their minds?

A few moments later he walked to the dais. Beckman was eating a steak, his elbows out, his wrists bent like hooks when he sliced his meat. He was talking to a woman on either side of him, his gaze never registering Hackberry's presence.

"How'd you get your scars?" Hackberry asked.

Beckman looked at him. "What scars?"

"The ones you kept reminding us you have."

"Mustard gas."

"You manufacture it?"

"Did you bring me something or not, Mr. Holland?"

"I was cooking up a meal in this cave I use as a fresh-air office when two of your fellows tried to give me a bad time. Have they checked in yet? Maybe they found what you're looking for. By the way, I had to take their guns from them and throw them in the river."

Beckman wiped his mouth with his napkin. "Did you, now? Your escapades seem to have no end. Would you like to join us?"

"I think not." Hackberry was wearing a powder-blue sport coat and dark slacks and a plum-colored tie and shined needle-nose boots. "Forgive me, ladies, for disturbing your dinner. Mr. Beckman thinks I have something that belongs to him. He's not only an arms dealer; he sells to both sides. He also steals from both sides. You know the Spanish expression *sin Dios, sin verguenza*? It means 'without God or shame.' Can y'all tell me why a man like him would lay claim to a religious artifact, what he calls a sacramental cup?"

The two women gazed around the room, their faces like dough pans. Beckman dipped his cup in the dredges of the punch bowl and filled it with pink champagne and melting sherbet. He snapped his fingers for one of the black servers to refill the bowl. "Do you want to be escorted out, Mr. Holland?"

"Thanks for the offer. I'll try to hobble out on my own."

"You're a public fool, sir. An object of pity."

"I cain't deny it. My boy got blown up on the Marne."

"Yes?"

"I was told the surgeons took a shovel load of shrapnel out of his legs and side."

"If you're telling us the world is a charnel house, you've arrived a bit late with the news."

"What'd you do to the woman at the brothel?"

"I know everything about you, sir. You destroyed your family and ruined your career as a lawman. Take your tattered mantle somewhere else."

"If I find out you hurt her—"

"Good night, Mr. Holland."

Beckman resumed talking to the two women as though Hackberry were not there.

HACKBERRY WALKED BACK through the kitchen and into the street and stood in an alcove where a horse-drawn carriage was parked. The paving stones were as brown and shiny and humped in the rain as loaves of bread. Along the wall was a row of paint and thinner cans. Over his shoulder he could see the empty bowl the waiter had taken from Beckman's table. One of the horses stretched forward, spreading his legs, and urinated on the stones. Hackberry grabbed a half-empty can of paint thinner and filled it up.

He went to the kitchen door. The waiter was chopping strawberries for the punch. Hackberry came up behind him and placed a dollar bill in his hand. "There's a lady with two children who needs he'p crossing the street. Would you take an umbrella to her, please?"

"Yes, suh."

"I'll watch the bowl."

"Where's she at?"

He hadn't lied. "Right on the corner."

He couldn't go through with it. He went back outside and poured the can in the gutter, then began walking toward a saloon, fog rising in sour flumes from the sewers.

No, he wasn't done with Arnold Beckman, just as he had never been done with Harvey Logan. He turned around and walked back through the hotel kitchen and into the dining room. In Hackberry's absence, the waiter had refilled the punch bowl and set it by Beckman's elbow.

"What's the expression about a bad penny?" Beckman said.

"You like the punch?"

"You did something to it?"

"Don't make enemies with people who have access to your food."

"Really?" Beckman drank from his cup, licking a piece of strawberry off his lip. "Have breakfast with me in the morning. Great fortunes are made only twice in a nation's history. During its rise and during its fall."

"I had an experience with Harvey Logan that I've drug around like a corpse on a chain. It happened when I was so drunk I couldn't stand up. Ole Harvey treated me like spit on the sidewalk. Harry Longabaugh had to intercede on my behalf. That was a special kind of humiliation. Logan topped it off when he threw me a dollar and told me to take a bath and buy myself a can of crab lice powder."

Beckman worked a piece of food from his teeth with his thumbnail, then sucked the spot clean. He laughed without making any sound.

"I deserved his scorn," Hackberry said. "That's what makes it so bad. I tried to catch up with him and even the score, but he killed himself after he got shot in a train robbery."

"Why are you telling me this?"

"Because I never thought I'd meet a bucket of shit that would equal Logan's standards. Then you came along."

"I see. So now you can have a second run at it?"

"No, I've pretty well shot my wad, and I don't consider myself a threat to nobody. But if I find out you hurt Miz DeMolay, I'll probably forget my Christian upbringing."

Beckman hooked his arm over the back of the chair. " 'Before me, every knee shall bend.' "

"You're Jesus?"

"I was just borrowing some of his rhetoric," Beckman said.

"Enjoy your punch. Cross my heart, I didn't put paint thinner and horse urine in it. You can ask the waiter over there, the one I sent outside while I guarded the bowl."

Chapter 17

THE SHERIFF'S NAME was Willard Posey. Some thought him ill suited for the job, with his sunken cheeks and firehouse suspenders and peaked forester's hat and clothes hanging straight down on his emaciated frame. People would have laughed at him except for a spark in one eye that seemed to say, *Do you really want to do that?*

Early in the morning, four days after his return from San Antonio, Hackberry heard a knock on his front door. He looked through the small window in the top of the door but could see no one. He unlocked and opened the door. "Mind telling me why you're squatting down on my porch?"

Willard squinted at him from under his hat brim. "I was trying to see that cave up on the bluff where you go for your meditation or afternoon nap or whatever unusual activity you're up to."

"Why are you interested in my cave?"

"Because your friend and neighbor Cod Bishop says that's where he saw you throw a couple of rifles into the river."

"Cod Bishop is a pea brain."

"You didn't throw two rifles in the river?"

"It was a rifle and a shotgun."

"Any particular reason you'd be throwing firearms in the river?"

"A couple of vagabonds threatened me."

"Know their names?"

"I didn't ask."

Willard stood up, straightening his back. He wore a shoulder holster without a coat, his badge on his belt. The shoulder holster was black and contained a nickel-plated revolver with white handles. "How you like my new motorcar?"

"It's an eye-catcher."

"I got it for a song."

"What happened to the top?"

"The previous owner cut it off with a hacksaw. Come on, let's take a ride."

"What's going on, Willard?"

"I hope you already ate."

TWO MAILBAGS, THE drawstrings pulled tight at the bottom of each sack and tied to a rock, had bobbed down the river, finally swinging into a pebble-bottomed green pool by the bank, oscillating on their tethers. A black child who was the first to see the sacks walked to the pool and smelled an odor that made him gag, then he ran to find his father. One hour later, a deputy used a boat hook to pull the sacks onto a grassy stretch by the water's edge. He and another deputy loosed the drawstrings and worked the canvas off the two bodies inside, both of which were blue and naked, the wrists bound in back with baling wire. One of the deputies vomited.

Willard parked his car in the shade. When he opened the door, it screeched like a tin roof being prized up with a crowbar. "Coming?"

"I can see from here."

"Will you get out of the motorcar, please?"

Hackberry walked within a few feet of the bodies. He cleared his throat. "That's the pair."

"It looks like they went out pretty hard. Ever seen that done to somebody?"

"Close to it. In Mexico."

"Why would anyone do that?"

"For purposes of information, obviously. Is this why you brought me out here? To ask unintelligent questions?"

"They didn't tell you what they were after? Why they followed you to the cave?"

"No, they didn't. The split in that fellow's head? I put it there with a running iron. I poked the other one in the jewels. The iron was right warm when I did it. That's the only mark I put on them."

"That sure clears it all up. Out of nowhere, you bust one man in the head and burn the genitalia on another? Seems like ordinary, reasonable, everyday kind of behavior."

"The one with the split head threw my pistol across the cave. I believed they were about to put the boots to me. I took it to them first."

"What did they want?"

"Food, money, whatever they didn't have to work for."

"Did anyone ever tell you it's rude not to look at people when you talk to them?"

"I had an indirect run-in with Arnold Beckman down in Mexico a couple of years back. I think he sicced these two on me."

"Who is Arnold Beckman?"

"An arms dealer. He's fixing to bring a lot of business to the state."

"What does that have to do with you?"

"Nothing. There was a woman down in Mexico. She ran a brothel. She saved my life. Maybe he did her in."

"Put your handkerchief over your nose. I want to show you something."

"I'm going back home."

"You're not going anywhere." Willard squatted on his haunches, the back of his neck tan and leathery in the sunlight, wadding a bandana in his fist and pressing it to the lower half of his face. He pointed with a pencil. "Look at their wrists. The wire is almost to the bone. They were probably alive when they went into the water. They drowned an inch at a time. Whoever did this wasn't satisfied with tormenting them from head to foot."

"Spend a little time with Beckman. You'll have a better sense of things."

Willard stood up and stuffed the bandana in his back pocket. He turned to the wind, his face clearing. "You're withholding information in a criminal investigation, Hack."

"About *what*?"

"If Beckman is after revenge, why didn't he have you killed? Why would he torture these two?"

Hackberry gazed at the horizon. "Looks like another storm is blowing up. See the dust climbing in the air? This time of year it turns purple against the sun. I love Texas."

"You have something that belongs to him, don't you?"

"The only thing any of us owns is six feet of dirt. You know who said that? Leo Tolstoy."

"Where's this Beckman live at?"

"I don't know. The last time I saw him, he was staying at the Driskill in Austin. For some reason he had the impression I contaminated the punch bowl he and his lady friends were drinking from."

Willard chewed on the corner of his lip and looked sideways at the clouds of rain on the horizon. "You're a vexatious man."

"Vexatious?"

"Yes, there are times when I'd like to shoot you."

"I feel the same way. Toward my own self, I mean."

"Get in the motorcar. I'll drive you home."

"No, sir," Hackberry said.

He began walking on the deer trail that paralleled the river, his shadow moving upstream against the current, the gaseous autumnal smell of the woods enticing him into its embrace, the coldness of the shade not so much a prelude to winter as a respite from the evil that men did unto one another.

HIS PROBLEMS WITH the sheriff weren't over. After he arrived back home, the rain strong enough to sting his face, he saw the bucket he had lowered into the well with a hatbox and bricks inside. It was lying on the grass, its contents spilled out. Just then Willard drove up and parked by the rose bed in the side yard. His car door screeched like a shard of glass shoved into Hackberry's eardrum.

"I thought we were done," Hackberry said.

"Not hardly. A Mexican woman on the river found a pair of

bloody britches buried in her cornfield. In the pocket was a drawing of what looks like your property and the cave up on the bluff. There was also a drawing of your house with a question mark over it. Somebody wrote down the word 'gold' with another question mark. Want to explain all that?"

"Maybe the fellow read too many books."

"What's in the cave?"

"Bones and bat shit."

"What are the bucket and bricks and cardboard box about?"

"I've been picking up trash and such."

"With a bucket tied to the winch on your well?"

"I was fixing to untie it."

"You figured if Beckman's people came on your property, they'd look in the well first. Even if they didn't try to get in the house, you'd know they were here."

"Anything on this property is mine. They got no right to it. That's the issue, at least as I see it."

"The issue is a double homicide."

"Their kind always end the same way. If not here, somewhere else. They dealt the hand."

"No, they didn't. You engineered this."

Hackberry took off his hat and blotted his face on his sleeve. "That's a goddamn lie."

"You're not going to talk to me like that, Hack."

"Well, you'll just have to live with it."

"You're going to end up in my jail, partner."

Hackberry put his hat back on. "It won't be the first time."

"That's the first truthful thing you've said today."

Hackberry watched Willard drive away. He remained in the yard and stared at the sky and the way the lightning bloomed silently in the clouds. How could so much force and power exist in the natural world without leaving a trace of its presence? It began as a flicker and then spread through thousands of miles of firmament in seconds and died inside an ocean of purple smoke. The magnificence of the moment could have been borrowed from Genesis. But what, if anything, did it portend? Was he simply another fool who wanted to believe he saw meaning in the skies when others did not? Was a terrible or grand event in the offing? The Great War had cost more than twenty million lives. Maybe peace would finally come to the world and the lion would lie down with the lamb. Maybe that was what the magnificence in the heavens indicated, like Yahweh hanging the archer's bow above a flooded world.

In a pig's eye.

Hackberry picked up the bucket and bricks and hatbox from the ground and threw them inside the barn, then went in the house and fell into a deep sleep on his couch while the rain danced on the roof.

WHEN HE WOKE, he felt so rested he thought he was still dreaming. The storm had passed, and the house was cool and dark and filled with kaleidoscopic fragments of light generated by the clouds in a blue-black sky, the dripping of the rain as musical as chimes outside a window he had failed to close. Had he slept through the day into the night or into the next morning? It didn't seem possible.

He saw headlights on the road. The lights turned up his lane and shone directly into his living room and then went black, filling his eyes with rings of color. He opened his front door, unable to believe what he was seeing, the coolness of the late evening ballooning inside the doorway.

The car was big and heavy and bright blue, a REO with four doors and a collapsible top and whitewall wood-spoked tires; the hood ticked with heat. A uniformed chauffeur got out and opened the back door, and a woman stepped out on the gravel and opened a parasol over her head. Hackberry clicked on the porch light.

"Are you shocked?" the woman said.

"I thought you were dead," he said.

"Why would you think that?"

"I heard the Communists had found their puritan selves and were shooting people right and left down there."

"Do I look dead?"

"You look wonderful, Miss Beatrice. Would you come in?"

Her chauffeur stood behind her. His uniform was gray and stiff, as if it had just been ironed, his skin so black it had a purple sheen, his cobalt-blue eyes incongruous in their intensity and color.

"My driver hasn't eaten. Would you mind?" she said.

"Whatever is in the icebox."

The chauffeur followed her through the door, removing his cap and placing it under his arm.

"Sit down, Miss B.," Hackberry said. He turned to the chauffeur. "I didn't get your name."

"Andre."

"Andre, your supper ware is in the far left-hand cupboard. Reckon you can find it?"

The chauffeur blinked to show he understood and went into the kitchen. He had not bothered to say "yes" or "yes, sir" or "thank you."

"Does he have a speech defect?" Hackberry said.

"He's aware of what you just indicated to him."

"Pardon?"

"You instructed him to use the tableware reserved for the servants. The tin plates and jelly glasses, the ceramics that are cracked or chipped. You reminded him he's a man of color."

"I'll feel bad about that the rest of the night," Hackberry said, then thought, *Why did I just say that?*

"I came here for two reasons. I won't take up much of your time."

"Take all you want. You didn't come here to fight with me, did you?" He tried to smile.

She was sitting on the couch, her folded parasol propped against her thigh. She wore a dark dress and a short blue velvet coat and a brooch that resembled a white rose at the top of her blouse. Her face was unlined and seemed to have no makeup on it. The lamp was bright behind her hair, which she wore in a curl at the back of her neck. "I spoke to you harshly in Mexico."

"I don't remember it that way. It looks like you're doing mighty well. You're visiting here?"

"I bought a vaudeville and motion picture house and an apartment building in San Antonio. I'm also buying a restaurant and amusement pier in Galveston."

He sat down in a deerskin chair by the fireplace. "You didn't hit oil somewhere, did you?"

"On land I bought at Goose Creek."

"You're making that up?"

She smiled.

"Good heavens," he said. He was uncertain what he should say next, even more uncomfortable about broaching the question that had been with him since Arnold Beckman's visit. The fireplace smelled of soot and the coldness in the stone. "I was going to ask you something rather personal."

"Go ahead."

"It's of a delicate nature."

"Mr. Holland, would you please stop acting like this?"

"Let me get a fire started."

"I'm going to leave."

"Arnold Beckman came by in his motorcar and introduced himself. He said something about you and him that was a little more than I could study on, if you follow me."

"No, I don't follow you at all."

"He said y'all were intimate."

His face burned in the silence.

"Why would that bother you?"

"Because I respect you. Because you saved my life. You were a friend to my son. The thought of that man with you makes my stomach turn."

"It didn't happen."

"I knew it didn't. I knew you wouldn't allow that. Knew it all along," he said, patting his knees. "Yes, ma'am, I surely did."

"My second purpose in coming here has to do with your welfare," she said. "Before you burned the hearse, did you take something out of it?"

"A few coins and currency, as I recall. Some candlesticks that turned out to be brass."

"Anything else?"

"Maybe a papist artifact came into my possession. That's the least of my troubles."

"What other troubles do you have?" she asked.

"The blood of innocent people on my hands. Sometimes I feel as if I'm living in a dream. I never drew down on a man who didn't draw on me first. Then I went down to Mexico and killed women and children and old people on a train loaded with Villa's soldiers. I'd give anything in the world if I could draw a big 'X' through that terrible day in my life."

He didn't want to look at her eyes. But he did. They were moist, the pity in them unmistakable.

"Miss Beatrice, I'd appreciate it if you didn't look at me like that."

"Has Beckman sent people to your house?" she said.

"A couple of them. They got greedy. He put them in mail sacks and dumped them in the river, still alive, with their hands bound behind them. He did some other things to them that are better not talked about."

"Where's the cup?"

He shook his head. "I didn't say I had a cup. I said I had an artifact. It was probably stolen from a chapel in a ranch the revolutionists occupied."

"Beckman won't rest until he gets it back."

"Is it the gold or the jewels? Why does Beckman want it so bad? He's probably one of the richest men in the state."

"You haven't guessed?"

"I'm not that smart."

"Andre, come in here," she said.

The chauffeur appeared in the doorway, holding a tin plate with a ham-and-onion sandwich on it. His eyes looked like they had been transplanted from a zombie. "*Oui, mademoiselle?*"

"Andre is from Haiti," she said. "He used to be a voodoo priest. He was defrocked for killing a man. I think he actually killed several men. Now he works for me. Why does Arnold Beckman want the cup, Andre?"

"Because he drank from it."

"Who is 'he,' Andre?"

"Our Lord, *mademoiselle*."

"See? Simple," she said.

LATER THAT NIGHT he wrote in his journal, *I have the feeling a burden has come out of nowhere and been set squarely upon my shoulders. I am not sure what the burden is. I know I do not want it.*

As he reread his words, he felt a level of fear in his stomach that made sweat break on his forehead. He slowly tore the page from the binding and continued tearing it into tiny pieces until it no longer existed.

Chapter
18

MAGGIE BASSETT WAS a believer in extreme measures. In every situation there was a winner and a loser. Those who pretended otherwise not only invited their fate but deserved it. Ask the animals whose heads ended up stuffed and stupid-looking on a den wall, while down below their killers shook the ice in their drinks and adjusted their scrotums and talked about the gas wells they were drilling in a pristine lake. Ask the Mexican girls who delivered on their knees behind a saloon for pocket change. The peons who had their land stolen for five cents an acre. The poor Negro wiping out a cuspidor with his bare hand, grateful for his job.

At Fannie Porter's place, she got to meet all the pilgrims in *The Canterbury Tales,* stringing in one door and out the other, each more hungry and base and self-deluded than the next. The setting of the sun didn't hide iniquity; it revealed it, as with kicking over a rotted log. City councilmen brought their mistresses to the cock- and dogfights down the street. People with syphilis of the brain had arguments with the moon to the delight of the spectators on the sidewalks. She serviced prison administrators who worked convicts to death and fed them weevil-infested food while they did it.

The sexual menu was wide open. Politicians showed up with gift certificates that had a six and a nine printed on them. There were private arrangements for clergy and men who wore hundred-dollar suits and freshly laundered white shirts as soft and smooth as ice cream, gold tie pins the size of an elk's tooth. No girl was too young, no man too old. When the men smiled, their faces turned into Halloween masks.

This was the milk of human kindness she read about?

In the American South, you fucked down and married up. Her bed smelled like a seagull's nest.

Twenty million dead in the war, and in the final weeks they were still killing so they could go back home and resume cleaning chimneys and breathing coal dust and textile lint and licking the boots of the swells. Maggie wondered what the girls leaping like balls of flame from the roof of the Triangle Shirtwaist Factory would have to say.

There was no way to reach Ishmael's room without traversing the entire length of the open ward. She tried not to look into the eyes buried inside the swaths of bandages or see the tubes running from the catheters into drip jars, the stumps crisscrossed with stitches like trussed hams, a man with a cotton pad and a strip of tape across his face where his nose used to be, the sputum buckets by the bedsides of those who had been gassed. The astringency of the mops and pails used to scrub the ward barely hid the stench of the unemptied bedpans and the yellow-streaked bed linen piled in the corners.

She collided with a skeletal man on crutches whose pajama bottoms exposed his pubic hair. When he apologized, his face inches from hers, his mouth a ragged hole, she drowned in his breath.

She went into Ishmael's room and shut the door. *Safe,* she thought, then wondered why she'd chosen to think that particular word.

He was propped up on the pillows, his smile as big as a slice of watermelon.

"Are you ready?" she asked.

"For what?"

"For our train trip."

"I'm a little fuzzy on that."

"We're going to San Antonio. I've reserved a compartment on the Pullman car. You're being discharged from the hospital. Like we talked about."

He frowned. "I'm confused."

"Everything is taken care of. What a nice day for a train ride."

"I thought my mother was coming here this week. Or maybe next. I know she was here."

He looked at Maggie uncertainly, as though she held answers to questions he couldn't formulate. He took a pill from a vial and broke it between his teeth and drank from a glass on the nightstand. "Sometimes I feel like a balloon bumping along the ceiling."

"Your mother was here last week. She left to go back to her job in New Mexico."

"I remember. That's true. Tell me again why we're going to San Antonio."

"You have an executive position waiting for you. Whenever you're able to start work. It's stuffy in here." She tugged open a window, hitting the frame with the heel of her hand, her jaw flexing. "There. Someone is burning leaves. Smell the chrysanthemums and the snow up in the hills. Don't you want to be outside again?"

"Did you talk to my mother?"

"I think she bears me a grudge. I don't blame her."

He sat up and hung his legs off the side of the bed. He picked up two walking canes that were hooked on the nightstand. "I can walk by myself to the bathroom now. I've tried to ease off the pink lady, too."

"What's the pink lady?"

He rattled the vial of pills. "The orderly is named Mike. He's a good fellow. The physicians can be hard-nosed. Did you bring another fruit basket?"

"No. Do you feel tension or nausea at all?" she said.

"Not now. I wake up at night. It passes, though."

"What passes?"

"The dreams. I read awhile and maybe crush a half pill in water, and then I'm all right. There's a man in the ward who has to wear a plastic face. He drinks absinthe. I've heard it's made from wormwood and destroys the brain."

"Don't talk about these things. You'll be throwing away all your medications soon."

"Watch this." He got to his feet and walked slowly toward the bathroom, his upper arms ridging. His back was tapered like an inverted triangle, his waist narrow, his buttocks small. She felt her nipples harden, a flush prickle her throat.

"Hurry up. We have things to do," she said.

"I'll have to be in the bathroom a while. Then we'll talk about my mother. You're going a little fast for me."

"Your mother is going to be fine. If you want, I'll get in touch with her. Everything is taken care of."

She heard him clatter his walking canes against the bathtub, then sit heavily on the toilet.

"Close the door for me. Don't look, either," he said.

"I'm going to take good care of you," she said, pulling the door shut, averting her eyes.

For a moment she actually meant it. No, it went deeper than that. She *did* want to take care of him. There was no doubt about the way she felt when she widened her knees and placed him inside her, like a wand that electrified her and made her go weak all over. His body was a massive sculpture carved from rose-colored alabaster, his chest flat, his nipples small, his breath sweet. When she came, she had to fight to suppress the sound that rose from her throat.

Why was he taking so long? She looked around the room. *The fruit,* she thought. *Get rid of the fruit.*

She dumped the basket into the trash can by the bed, then glanced outside and saw a skinned-up motorcar canted on its frame, driving through the parking area, the back bumper wired in place, a side window that looked like it had two bullet holes in it. The driver wore a slug cap and had the tight face of a boxer or someone who had been worked over with a slapjack or a sock full of sand. The woman in the passenger seat wore a lavender and yellow dress and a bandana over her hair. She seemed to look straight at Maggie, although the sun was obviously in her eyes. Maggie stepped back from the window. She could not believe her bad luck. It didn't matter if she had been recognized or not. Within minutes, Ruby Dansen would be inside the hospital.

Maggie's head was spinning, her heart rising into her throat. *Do not be at the mercy of fate. Passivity and mediocrity ensure failure and belong on the same daisy chain. When challenged, there is no such thing as excess. Turn their viscera into a tangle of oily snakes.*

The Gospel according to Maggie Bassett.

As though her thoughts could redirect her destiny, she caught a break. Ruby's driver had driven through the parking area twice, drawing the attention of a uniformed policeman, a fat Irish dolt with a florid face and a mustache like rope who had cloves and whiskey on his breath by ten A.M. He had stopped Ruby's driver and apparently told him to get out of the motorcar and explain the pocked holes in the side window, tapping it with his nightstick, his mustache flattening in the wind, his lips moving rapidly, the driver probably sassing him, fists balled.

Little miracles have a way of happening, don't they, you German cunt or whatever you are.

Maggie found the orderly in the hall. "Come with me," she said.

"And do what?" he replied, half smiling.

"You're Mike, aren't you? Captain Holland's friend?"

"I don't call him 'nigger lover.'"

"Pardon?"

"They say that's why he's getting out of the army. The army didn't treat his outfit right. He says the French gave them the credit they deserve. It's not what people like to hear."

Mike had a high forehead and mousy hair and thin shoulders and a nicotine odor that made her hold her breath. She pulled him into a windowless alcove that contained two chairs used by visitors; unresisting, his arm was boneless and flaccid in her grasp. She pushed him down in one chair and sat in the other, taking his hand in hers.

"What's going on?" he said.

"There's a woman outside named Ruby Dansen. She claims to be Captain Holland's mother. She's not. She's an aunt by marriage who treated him brutally when he was a child. She's also a Communist and has been committed twice to an asylum."

The smile left his face. "What's she doing here?"

"Causing trouble." Maggie leaned forward, her gaze fixed on his, rotating her thumb inside his palm. "You have to help me. We need to move Captain Holland now."

"What for?"

"She'll cause a scene. She'll convince somebody at admissions that she's his mother. He's being discharged today. He doesn't need a crazy woman screaming at him. He also doesn't need to revisit his miserable childhood."

"I don't know, ma'am. I don't like the sound of this."

She tightened her hand on his and leaned forward, her other hand settling on his thigh, the thumb working into the muscle. "Please."

His gaze broke. "Tell me what you want me to do."

"Put Captain Holland in a wheelchair and take him to the side door. My car and driver will be waiting. Hurry up."

"You think we might meet up later? You and me?"

"It's a possibility. But there's something else you have to help me with."

"*Have to?*"

She ignored the challenge. "You're already aware Captain Holland has needs for certain medications the hospital doesn't always provide."

"No, I'm a blank on that."

She opened her purse so he could see inside it. "I have to give him this. It's perfectly safe. It will quiet his nerves."

"Hypodermic needles are way above my skills, ma'am."

She laid a twenty-dollar bill across his palm. "No, they're not."

"And we're gonna see each other a little later, maybe tonight?"

"Yes, I would like that."

"Even though you've got a driver and a motorcar and you're probably going away somewhere?" His eyes crinkled at the corners.

"We're staying close by," she said, breathing audibly through her nose.

"I bet you forgot your fruit basket. You wouldn't want to leave that behind, would you? The captain was sure fond of it. A couple of bites and I would have sworn he'd been on an opium pipe."

"Well, you're certainly an observant and enterprising little fellow, aren't you?" she said. She took another twenty-dollar bill from her purse. "If this doesn't work out, you'll be visited by people who will do things to you that you thought happened only in nightmares."

HACKBERRY WAS FIXING dinner on his wood cookstove when he heard the screech of Willard Posey's car door out in the yard. He waited for the knock on the door; it didn't happen. He flipped the two boned pork chops in the skillet with a fork and watched them sizzle. He cut two huge slices of bread from a loaf and browned them in butter and stuffed the pork chops between them with a layer of ketchup and skillet gravy and onions and tomatoes and mayonnaise on top; then he filled a glass with buttermilk and sprinkled hot sauce in it. He looked out the front door. The car, absent the roof that had been hacksawed off, was parked on the edge of the lawn. No Willard.

He put his sandwich on a plate and pushed the back door open with his foot and filled his mouth with meat and bread and saw Willard down at the river, lobbing pebbles in the current, his back turned. Hackberry walked down the slope, his boots crunching on the gravel. Willard's cotton shirt was bunched where the strap of his shoulder holster angled between his shoulder blades; his back was stiff, like that of an angry man on a parade ground. The river was low, a dull green, insects hovering in clouds above the riffle in the fading light.

"Does strange behavior intrigue you, or do you just enjoy prowling around behind people's houses at dinnertime?" Hackberry said.

Willard sidearmed a rock across the river and watched it bounce off the opposite slope and roll down to the water. He turned around, his badge and holstered white-handled revolver at odds with his sun-darkened skin and the shadow and gloom that seemed to surround his person.

"What the hell is wrong with you?" Hackberry said.

"Not a goddamn thing."

"When did you start swearing?"

"Just now."

"Your wife throw you out?"

"I'm not married."

"In my case, that would mean there's at least one less unhappy woman in the world. I don't know about you."

Willard dusted off his hands. "You don't square with me, Hack. But you keep leaving your problems on my doorstep. What do you think I should do about that?"

"I wish I knew what we're talking about."

"The sheriff in Bexar called me about this woman DeMolie or whatever—"

"It's DeMolay. You're an intelligent man. Stop talking like an ignorant peckerwood."

"The sheriff doesn't believe she's just an ordinary businesswoman who got rich in the oil patch. He says she ran a place called the House of the Rising Sun in New Orleans. When it got shut down, she went to Mexico. Now she's here."

Hackberry sat on a stump and set his plate by his foot, making sure he didn't kick dirt in it. "Tell me what you're so hot about, and don't tell me it's because of Miz DeMolay."

"I'm mad because I have to protect an old, willful, blockheaded, womanizing crazy man from himself."

"I'm not old."

"You came out of the womb old. You walk around like every page in the Bible is glued on your clothes. One match and you'd go up in flames."

"I've never heard it put like that."

"That's because sane people fear provoking someone who left his mush in the oven too long. What's that red stuff floating in your milk?"

"Hot sauce."

Hackberry went back to eating, pausing only to drink from his buttermilk. Willard's face looked like smoked pig hide under the brim of his hat.

"I'm going to tell you what the sheriff told me," Willard said. "If you act on this information, I'm going upside your head with a two-by-four."

Hackberry stood up with his plate and glass in hand, then leaned down without bending his knees and set them on the riverbank. "Don't speak to me in that fashion again, son."

"You test people's charity," Willard replied.

"Maybe so. But I'm done on this."

"The sheriff said a man tried to throw acid in the DeMolay woman's face."

Hackberry's gaze drifted down the river to a canebrake where a calf was caught in the mud and bawling for its mother. His eyes were unfocused, seemingly disconnected from emotion. "Who was the man?"

"The sheriff doesn't know. He doesn't want Miz DeMolay in his county. He says good riddance."

"I appreciate you coming by."

"Look at me, Hack. Don't think the thoughts you're thinking. It's 1918. We're in modern times now."

"Two years ago, when I was blowing the feathers off Mexican peons, I got a different impression. It must be me."

His name was Mealy Lonetree. Some thought his first name was the short version of "mealymouth." Not so. Mealy was a fixer, a man whose face made you think of a fire hydrant wearing a derby hat. He was the man you saw if you wanted to buy or sell stolen property; hire an arsonist to torch your business for insurance purposes; extort, kidnap, blackmail an enemy; or make your cheating wife or husband disappear. All jobs were subcontracted, so there was never a trail back to the client. His felonious assault price list, one his father had used in the Irish Channel of New Orleans, offered blackened eyes, a lead pipe across the nose, broken fingers, stab wounds, a gunshot in the leg, an ear chewed off, or "the big job." There was a surcharge for photos.

Mealy ran a laundry and Turkish bathhouse in San Antonio's old brothel district, which was now licensed and zoned and had its own directory, called the Blue Book, containing the names and addresses of more than one hundred bordellos and gambling houses. The entrance to Mealy's office was on an unpaved alleyway, the windows blacked out, a bell on the door. Up and down the alleyway, prostitutes were smoking marijuana openly on produce crates in front of their cribs, some talking to soldiers in campaign hats and puttees, the late sun molten and dust-veiled, as it had been when Hackberry stumbled into Beatrice DeMolay's brothel in Mexico two years earlier. He stepped across a ribbon of green sewage filled with items he would rather not think about and entered Mealy's office without knocking.

Mealy was behind his desk, pear-shaped, dandruff on his black coat, a red paper carnation in his lapel, his eyes disappearing into slits when he smiled. A book of accounting figures was open on his blotter. "Mr. Holland, I'm so happy to see you. Please have a seat."

"How's life, Mealy?"

"What can I say? The world doesn't change. So I don't, either."

"Know a lady named Beatrice DeMolay?"

"I know who she is."

"Somebody tried to throw acid in her face."

Mealy put down his pen. He flattened his hands on the blotter, deep in thought, his fingers splayed. He drummed his fingers in a long roll. "You're not going to hurt my feelings, are you? You don't think I'd be associated with hurting a woman?"

"No, you wouldn't, Mealy," Hackberry lied. "That's why I came to you and not somebody else. I need the man's name."

"Ask the lady."

"She wasn't at her apartment. I don't know how much she'd tell me, anyway."

"Nobody in San Antonio is gonna throw acid at somebody without permission. And the person who asked for permission would probably be run out of town. If you want those kinds of lowlifes, go to New Orleans. She ran a house there. It was in Storyville. The House of the Rising Sun."

"You're from New Orleans."

"That's why I can speak with authority on the subject."

"How about Arnold Beckman? You ever run into him?"

Mealy was shaking his finger in the air before Hackberry had finished his sentence, his chin raised defensively. "I have nothing to do with the man you just mentioned. I didn't say anything about him, either."

"He's a pretty bad *hombre*?"

Mealy stood up from behind his desk. He seemed shorter and fatter, his hips wider, than when he was sitting down. "What if I buy you some supper? I know how you like Mexican food."

"I already ate. Beckman is behind this?"

"You think a man with that kind of wealth confides in a man like me?"

"Why did you mention New Orleans?"

"Because that's where the lady is from. Before Storyville got shut down, it was filled with the worst pimps in the country. Cut a girl's face with a razor, put lye in her food. You name it, they'd do it."

"All right, if the man Beckman hired to blind and disfigure Miz DeMolay is from New Orleans, what would his name be?"

"Mr. Holland, I always liked you."

Hackberry nodded but didn't reply.

"Don't be dragging me into trouble with this man from Austria," Mealy said. "This Hun. That's what he is, a Hun, right? We just fought a war with those guys. What are they doing over here?"

"Give me a name."

"Jimmy Belloc. Some people call him Jimmy No Lines. Get the picture?"

"He's in New Orleans?"

Mealy's face had turned gray, his yellow tie crooked on his coat, like a snake with a broken back. "Maybe. Or maybe he's still in town."

"You're a little emotional this evening. How do you know this?"

"I saw him two days ago. On the street, right by Alamo Plaza. He recognized me. I kept going."

"What's he look like?"

"He was in a fire. Maybe when he was a little kid. He's been stuck with the same face all his life. Mr. Holland, I don't like being caught between people. Don't tell anybody what I told you, suh. We got us a deal on that?"

"I would appreciate you not mentioning I was here, Mealy."

"You were here, Mr. Holland. And maybe I got to pay for it."

"I'm sorry you feel that way."

"It ain't the way I feel. It's the troot'." Mealy looked seasick.

Hackberry took a jitney across town to Beatrice DeMolay's apartment building. This time she was home.

Her apartment could be entered only through a brick-paved courtyard. The beds were weedless and sprinkled with wood chips and planted with hibiscus and hydrangeas and banana stalks that grew in thick clumps, and windmill palms and caladiums and orange trumpet vine and blood-red bougainvillea that reached to the Spanish grillwork on the balcony. Her face showed no surprise when she opened the door. Inside the confines of the courtyard, the air felt suddenly cold and dank. A light rain had started to fall, and raindrops were ticking on the elephant ears and philodendron, the sun buried like a mean red eye inside a bank of dark clouds. "Heard you had some trouble," Hackberry said.

"Really?" she replied.

"Thought I'd drop by."

She smiled. "I thought you might be around."

"Pardon?"

"Come in."

God save me from lightning, earthquakes, flash floods, and women who can make you feel like a snail on a hot sidewalk, he thought, trying to keep his face empty, removing his hat as he stepped inside. "Why did you think I'd be around?"

"Because you're a thoughtful man, even though you pretend you're not."

The windows of her apartment were ceiling-high, the rugs probably woven in Persia, the hand-carved antique furniture wiped and polished, darkly reflective.

"Tell me what happened," he said.

"There was no moon. Someone knocked. I turned on the outside light and opened the door. The lightbulb had been unscrewed. I saw a jar in his hand. I slammed the door just as he threw it."

"You saw his face?"

"I'm not sure. Maybe he was wearing a mask."

"What kind?"

"One that people might wear on Halloween or during Mardi Gras. Sit down, Mr. Holland. It's good of you to look in on me. But you shouldn't be disturbed by this."

"I'm not disturbed. The man who did it is going to be disturbed."

"Sooner or later, Andre and I will find him."

"Andre is the zombie?"

"You shouldn't talk about him like that."

"What's his formal title? Voodoo priest who kills people?"

"Would you like a glass of wine?"

"No, have supper with me."

When he told Mealy he had already eaten, he had told the truth. He had not gone to the woman's apartment intending to ask her out. The words came out of his mouth before he could think. How could he discuss in a public place what they needed to discuss? What was actually on his mind? He didn't want to answer the question.

"Did the mask look made of rubber? Rubber with a reddish tint?"

"Come to think of it."

"I don't believe you were looking at a mask, Miss Beatrice. Do you recognize the name Jimmy Belloc?"

"No."

"How about Jimmy No Lines?"

Her eyes were moving back and forth. The rain had turned to sleet and was hitting as hard as rock salt, sliding in serpentine lines down the fronds outside the windows. "Jimmy No Lines lived in the French Quarter. I think he did errands for Mealy Lonetree." She paused. "Did I say something wrong?"

"I was just wondering if there was such a thing as an honest man in the city of New Orleans."

"Many people ask that."

"Arnold Beckman is behind this, isn't he?"

"Of course."

She clicked on a lamp. The shade was hung with gold tassels and painted with multicolored flowers that glowed like moths. She sat down on the divan and pulled the crystal stopper from a decanter of sherry. She filled one glass, then started to fill another.

"No, thank you, ma'am, I'm not good at taking one drink." He sat on the other end of the divan, his hat on his knee, his legs too long to put in a comfortable place. "I don't want to take up a lot of your time, Miss Beatrice. I'd like to be done with my own troubles, but I don't know as I ever will. This stuff about a cup Jesus might have drank from is a little more than I can handle. The cup doesn't have anything to do with my life, but I'll be damned if I'll let the likes of Beckman get his hands on it."

"He believes the only artifact that has more power is the Spear of Longinus. According to the legend, it was the one used by the Roman soldier to lance the side of Jesus."

"That sounds like a story out of the Middle Ages. I don't know as it'll quite get through the wash."

"I had the impression you were a believer."

"The question is, a believer in what?"

"Give the cup to a church. Beckman will leave you alone."

"A Mexican padre in sandals and sackcloth is going to protect it?"

"Send it to Rome."

"I didn't see the Vatican's name on it."

"You're living in the wrong century, Mr. Holland. When you thought General Lupa was going to put you to death, you told him you had locked John Wesley Hardin in jail. You said you wanted that information on your grave marker. You showed a level of acceptance that probably unnerved him. The American West is gone. Beckman won't meet you in the street with pistols."

"He doesn't have anything I want. If he kills me, he still won't get the cup. I should have been embalmed a long time ago, anyway. About dinner, Miss B.—I didn't mean to impose myself."

"I have two parasols. There's a Mexican café on the corner."

THE WIND WAS cold, the rain blowing in ropes off the rooftops when they reached the café. It was smoky and warm inside, most of the food prepared on an open stone pit, the walls hung with banderillas and goatskin wine bags and sombreros and piñatas wrapped with crepe paper. Rather than wine, she ordered a cup of coffee with her dinner. "Did you find your son?" she said.

"He's in an army hospital outside of Denver."

"Is he all right?"

"He probably hasn't had a chance to answer my letters."

She waited for him to continue.

"I called the hospital. An administrator said Ishmael was inching along." His eyes went away from hers.

"How bad was he wounded?"

"He was at the Second Battle of the Marne. It was the last chance for the Germans. I hear they fought like it. I wish I'd been there."

"What would you have done?"

"Got him back home. Nursed him. Made up for not being there when he was little."

"You mustn't talk about yourself like that."

"I cain't figure you."

"Because of the type of businesses I've run?"

"That's not an inconsequential consideration."

"I've never been interested in people's condemnation of me. Do you care what people think about you?"

"In my case, most of what they think is true."

"I respect the women who work for me. Few people realize how much courage it takes to be a prostitute."

He found himself glancing sideways at the other tables.

"Do you know what a girl in the life has to endure?" she said. "The outrage men commit on their bodies. The punches in the face. Do you know how many of them are murdered each year?"

"I think I'm going to have an ice-cold Coca-Cola. You want one?"

"No, thank you."

"Miss Beatrice, I went to a sporting house years ago, down on the border. I've always been ashamed about it. Not because I slept with a woman for hire. I was ashamed because I took advantage of her poverty and her race. I'm going to have a beer now."

"Sure you want to do that?"

"No, but I'm going to do it anyway."

"Why?"

"I don't know. I never have. Here's our food. Boy howdy, doesn't that look good?" He kept his eyes lowered until the cold, sweating bottle of Mexican beer was in his hand and its brassy taste in his mouth, like an old friend moving back into the house, ready to set up shop.

"What are you planning to do, Mr. Holland?"

"Eat this food and walk you home."

"Then what?"

"Take care of business," he replied.

A half hour later, he stood with her at the entrance to her apartment house. The moon was up, and the banana plants and elephant ears and philodendron were beaded with water, like big drops of mercury.

"Would you like to come in?" she said.

"I'd like to, but I cain't."

"Are you going to drink?"

"I'm not sure," he said.

"Please come inside."

"That would make me awful happy. I want to get my boy back. But I want to get his mother back, too. Her name is Ruby Dansen. She was a good girl and deserved a lot better than me."

"That's a pretty name. Good night, Mr. Holland."

"Goodnight, Miss B."

He watched her go inside the apartment, then began walking toward his hotel, trying not to think too hard on the deception Mealy Lonetree had perpetrated on him, at least not until he could do something about it. He stopped at a package store and bought a pint of whiskey and drank it as he walked, a thick layer of white fog swirling around his knees, the whiskey flooding his throat with a golden airiness that could not be measured.

Chapter 19

ISHMAEL FELT THE train tilt and begin its abrupt descent down Ratón Pass, its wheels locked, screeching down the grade with such intensity that the inside of the Pullman room trembled and the closet doors swung open and shook on their hinges. He lay on his side in the bed, in his underwear, watching the pinyon trees and ponderosa and outcroppings of rock and the steep slope of the mountain slide past the window, the woman's body molded against his, her breath on his neck, her hand resting on his hip.

It was funny how he sometimes thought of her as "the woman" rather than as Maggie Bassett. Maybe that was what she intended. She made herself into all things woman. She was lover, caretaker, mother, and confidante. "Provider" might be another word. The injection she had given him before they left the hospital was more than a temporary flight from pain and worry that the Greek god Morpheus usually offered. The hit had traveled up his arm and spread through his body like the Red Sea, turning his eyelids to lead, filling him with a sense of pleasure and warmth that bordered on orgasm, taking him to a sunlit place where the earth jutted into infinity and the stars plummeted past him into a heavenly abyss.

"Are you awake, sleepyhead?" she said.

"I was watching the rocks and the trees. The grade is dropping so fast, I dreamed we'd fallen in a hole."

"We'll be in New Mexico in a few minutes. In another hour we'll be in Texas."

He tried to turn his head to see her face, but she was pressed too close. "I don't remember getting on the train. How did I get to the station?"

"You were sedated."

He closed his eyes and opened them again, the canyon dropping into shadow on a curve, the couplings jarring. "My mother was coming to see me. She didn't show up?"

"It's the medicine. You have things turned around. I left a message and a phone number. If you like, we can call her when we reach San Antonio."

"How do you know where she is?"

"The people we work for can find anyone, Ishmael. Did you know you might be in motion pictures?"

"What are you talking about?"

"With your looks and physique? The man I work for, the man you'll be working for, owns part of a film company in Pacific Palisades."

"I don't know where that is. I feel strange. Like bees are buzzing under my skin."

"We'll go out to the Palisades. I've been there. It's right on the ocean. They say it's the place where no one ever dies. The man I work for says that's why people love motion pictures. They believe the actors in the film become immortal. If they can associate themselves with the actors, they become immortal, too."

"Maybe they should visit the Marne. It might cure them of their thoughts on immortality."

She spread her fingers on his stomach, then moved them down into his shorts and touched him. "We can pull the shade. The door is locked, and the porter won't bother us. I told him not to come by unless we call him."

"I don't feel too well right now."

"Would you like something to eat?"

"Just some water. Or something with sugar in it. Anything sweet. I don't know why I have this feeling inside me, this humming in my blood. What did the doctor say when I checked out?"

"He said good-bye. Stop talking about the hospital. That's all behind us now."

He turned on his back, forcing her to look into his face. "Maggie," he said, not as a question.

"Yes?" she replied.

"You're Maggie. That's all. My head wasn't working right for a while."

"It's good to be silly sometimes," she said. "When I was a little girl, I was punished for being silly. My father didn't like little girls being little girls. His daughter was supposed to be serious and dutiful. If not, he'd find ways to hurt her without ever laying his hands on her."

"What kind of work was your father in?"

"I don't talk about him much. Or even think about him. Bad ole me. He's been feeding the worms a long time now. I think he found the right role in life."

He raised himself on his elbow and looked into her eyes. He had no idea what thoughts she was thinking or if she had any idea how her words could frighten. "A French colonel warned me in a field hospital."

Maggie's face darkened, as though the shadows on the canyons' walls had moved across it. "Warned you about what?"

"Morphine."

"That's all bugaboo. It comes from a plant. It's a gift of the earth."

"So is poison ivy."

"Don't be clever. Cleverness is for people who have nothing to say."

"I feel like I have a fever. I can see flashes of light inside my head when I close my eyes."

"You have to forget the war. My grandfather was at Shiloh. He could never stop talking about it."

"Maybe we can go up to the dining car in a little while. Is it far?"

"Just one car up. I'll get the porter to help us. We'll have a delightful meal, then we'll be in Texas and you can leave all your bad memories behind."

"I don't think it works like that. It'll just take a little time. Then I'll be fine."

"See? I told you. You're a dear man. You make me twenty years younger."

"I remember my mother saying you were an outlaw woman."

"Do I look like an outlaw?"

"Outlaw women are not beautiful?"

She pressed his head against her breast and kissed his hair. "I just want one promise from you. It's not a lot."

"I don't think making promises to people is a good practice."

"Don't ever turn your back on me. You're young and you'll make mistakes, and I'm talking about mistakes with other women, but it will only be temporary. Then you'll come back home, and everything will be all right, and I'll forgive you because you're young. But you must never renounce me, or call me old, or say I'm not a part of your life anymore."

"Why would I do that?"

"Because you're young and you think you'll stay that way. We're out of the Pass now. We're about to see a dead volcano and miles of prairie with antelope and deer on it. You should see the sunrise here in the fall. The hillsides are still green and look soaked in blood just as the sun breaks over the hills. Isn't the natural world a grand place, Ishmael? Clear and pure and free of mankind's evil. Hold me."

"Do you know you're shaking?"

"What a silly thing to say," she said. She buried her face in his neck, her teeth biting tenderly into his throat.

HACKBERRY RETURNED TO his hotel room and sat on the side of his bed and finished the pint of whiskey. Then he unsnapped his suitcase and removed a canvas U.S. cavalry water bucket, the soft, collapsible kind that could be dipped by hand in a stream or tied by a rope to the handle and cast out into the current, where the water was deeper and cleaner. He had bought it in a secondhand store after he heard Ishmael had joined the army and become an officer in the cavalry. He had never used it to draw water from a steam or well or pond; he had always kept it dry and brushed free of dust and on a peg in his tack room. Every time he looked at it, he thought of his son and pretended that in some fashion he was at his side.

Its only utilitarian purpose was to carry the items associated with his trade: a set of brass knuckles he had never used; a pair of manacles whose spring mechanism and locking steel tongs he kept oiled and cleaned; two boxes of ammunition; his bowie knife in the beaded scabbard; his 1860 converted army revolver; a blackjack with two lead balls sewn in tandem inside a hand-stitched leather sock mounted on a spring and wood handle; and a Peacemaker .45 single-action revolver presented to him in a ceremony by an officer of the Colt Company at the Brown Palace Hotel in Denver.

Mealy Lonetree lived in an apartment above his office on the alleyway in the brothel district. He was packing a suitcase on his bed when Hackberry pushed open the door. Hackberry was wearing his slicker buttoned over his gun belt. The door had not been locked, and he wondered at the casualness of Mealy's omission. Mealy looked over his shoulder at Hackberry, then folded a pair of trousers and pressed them inside the suitcase and smoothed them flat with his palms. He didn't look up again.

"I'm just one of the little people, Mr. Holland. I don't got a choice about what I do a lot of the time," he said.

"Why didn't you tell me Jimmy Belloc or No Lines or Whatever worked for you in New Orleans?"

"He made collections, that's all. It was numbers money. It was innocent. The Italians love lotteries. Don't ask me why."

"Where is he?"

"A rooming house one block down from Fannie Porter's old place. He likes to be close to the colored cribs. Because of the way he looks. He can feel superior instead of being a freak."

"I wouldn't have forced you to give me his name. Why did you give me his name and hold back on me at the same time?"

"I got no answer."

"You'd better think of one."

"I'm nobody. All that stuff about sending out people to beat up other people with lead pipes and chew off their ears is crap. My clientele are pimps and working girls and thieves, all of them trying to screw each other. Look at where I live. How I look. How would you like to be me?"

"You wouldn't send me into a trap, would you?"

Mealy faced him, his eyes askance, shiny with fear, his doughy hands curling and uncurling. In the poor light, the dandruff on the shoulders of his blue serge suit glowed like tiny snowflakes. "Jimmy No Lines is a throwaway guy. Why go after a throwaway guy? Somebody wants to hurt Miss Beatrice. Maybe somebody wants to hurt you. Why help them do that, Mr. Holland? Go back home."

"Arnold Beckman again?"

"We have newspapers here. Those men who were pulled out of the Guadalupe inside mail sacks? They used to come to the cribs on this alley. They worked for Beckman down in Mexico, when he was supplying arms to Villa or Huerta or some of those other greasers they got there. The newspaper didn't say this, but I'll make you a bet: They went out hard."

"Give me the address of the rooming house," Hackberry said.

"Forget the rooming house. This time of night, check out Betty's Vineyard. He uses the back stairs, even there. Don't do this, Mr. Holland. Get out of town and give Mr. Beckman whatever he wants."

"What *does* he want?"

"I got no idea," Mealy replied, his expression miserable.

The madam's name was not Betty, even though the house had been known for years as Betty's Vineyard. Where the name came from, no one knew and no one cared. The house had been in existence since the days of the Chisholm Trail, which wended its way from Yoakum up through San Antonio and across the Red River into Oklahoma Territory to the railheads at Wichita and Abilene in Kansas. Betty's Vineyard was like a tattered replica of Fannie Porter's sporting house one block away. It was a termite-eaten Victorian, the paint curled into chicken feathers, slats broken from the veranda, the ventilated shutters cockeyed, the hinges bleeding rust, the carriage lanterns on the porch lit with blue bulbs.

A girl who looked like a maid opened the front door. "Come in, suh," she said.

Hackberry removed his hat but remained where he was. "I'm looking for Jimmy Belloc."

"Suh?"

He could see three men sitting on a couch in the living room. They looked white, but he wasn't sure because they were wearing hats and their faces were covered with shadow and they made a point of bending forward as they talked among themselves, the smoke of their cigarettes rising from between their fingers. "Go get the lady you work for."

"You the law, suh?"

"No."

"Miss Dora ain't here."

"Yes, she is." He stepped inside, his buttoned slicker suddenly too warm, the sleeves and shoulders too tight. He glanced up the stairway. A white man was walking up the stairs with a colored girl; their backs were to him. There was a light on in the kitchen. "Is that where she's at?"

"Yes, suh."

"Fetch her."

A moment later, a black woman emerged from the kitchen. She was big and wore a long-sleeved dark dress printed with flowers and buttoned at the throat, with a tasseled black silk sash and rough boots like a man's and strings of beads around her neck and glass rings on her fingers. "What do you want?" she said.

"A man named Jimmy Belloc. He's white."

"There ain't nobody here that goes by that name."

"Do you know where he is?"

"I never heard of him. Who are you?"

"A rancher from outside Kerrville. I'm a friend of Beatrice DeMolay."

"What's that got to do with me?"

"Nothing. I want Belloc."

"You didn't hear me the first time?"

"He's a burn case. He was in a fire when he was a child."

Her eyes stayed on his, not blinking. "Don't be giving me your truck."

"Can I have a drink?"

"Drink of what?"

"Whiskey. With a Mexican beer, if you have it."

"This ain't no saloon."

"You didn't blink."

"What?"

"A liar blinks at the end of a lie. Or he doesn't blink at all. A person telling the truth blinks in the middle of what he's saying. Did you know that?"

"We don't have no trouble here. This is a good house. I pay the right people so it stay that way. We don't allow no rounders or hoodlums."

"I used to be a Texas Ranger. I'm not now. But if I walk these three men on the couch outside, I'll treat them as though I'm still a Ranger. They'll never be back. Then I'll go upstairs and talk to some of your other customers. I don't care who you pay. They're not friends of mine."

In the background a phonograph record was playing, the mountain instruments and adenoidal voices flat and mournful:

> *Don't forget me, Little Bessie,*
> *When I'm near or far away,*
> *Just remember, Little Bessie,*
> *None will love you as I do.*

"What you want him for?" the woman said.

"To clear up a situation he's involved with. One you want to stay out of."

She rested one hand on the banister. There was a tension under her left eye that had nothing to do with fear. It suggested a level of anger he didn't want to think about.

"Get out," she said.

He put his hat back on and unbuttoned his slicker. He looked up the stairs. "Which room?"

"There ain't no guns allowed here."

"Go in the kitchen. Take the maid with you. If there's a phone back there, I'll hear you."

"I cain't go into y'all's houses, but you can come into mine. You can fuck my girls, but a black man gets lynched if he fucks yours. Who you think you are?"

He tried not to hear what she was saying, tried to ignore her presence and the distraction she represented. Something was wrong, but he couldn't put his hand on it. He placed one boot on the stairs, the heel of his right hand resting on the ivory grip of the Peacemaker. He looked into the woman's face. The hatred she felt for him was the kind that no one could confront in a rational manner; for her and her family, the injury probably began with birth in a dirt-floor shack and progressed to a lifetime of picking cotton until their fingers bled, watching a white overseer take any girl he wanted into the woods, being cheated of their wages, living with the daily awareness that a rope or a whip or a prison farm could be their fate.

The woman's upper lip was damp with moisture. She was breathing through her nose, her nostrils swelling. What was her name? Dora?

"I didn't do it to you, Dora."

"Do what?"

"Everything."

The record continued to play, the needle scratching on the surface.

> *When your hair has turned to silver,*
> *When your eyes have faded, too,*
> *Just remember, Little Bessie,*
> *None will love you like I do.*

"I want the man who tried to blind Beatrice DeMolay," he said. "I won't leave till I get him."

"Ain't nobody here thrown no acid in nobody's face."

"I didn't say anything about acid."

She curled one hand into a fist. "You didn't have to. Everybody on this side of town know about it."

The three men on the couch were motionless, their cigarettes burning in the ashtray, their eyes fixed on the rug. Hackberry stepped back from the staircase. "You three," he said.

They lifted their faces.

"Out," he said.

They didn't argue. He pushed the door shut behind them and locked the bolt. "Go in the kitchen now," he said to the woman. "If there's somebody up there with a gun, you'll be in trouble you won't get out of. If not from me, from others."

"Why you doing this to me?"

"I'm not your enemy. You'd like to believe I am, but I'm not. Now get in the kitchen. If you hear a gunshot, call the police."

He walked up the stairs slowly, each step creaking under his weight, his elbow holding back the flap of his slicker, his hand gripped tightly on the holstered Peacemaker. He could smell a sour odor rising from his armpits.

> *When the shots and shells are screaming,*
> *When the bitter duty calls,*
> *Just remember, Little Bessie,*
> *None will love you like I do.*

Where had he heard the song? It was a soldier's lament, one that went back to the Civil War, one his father used to sing. He thought of Ishmael in the trenches of France. He thought of his poor wounded boy and the fact that he might never learn his father loved him.

He reached the top of the stairs. The hallway was long, with a series of doors on either side, a single low-wattage unshaded bulb at the end. He slid the Peacemaker from his holster and lifted it free of his coat, his arm cocked at a right angle, the barrel pointed up. He opened the first door and pushed it back on its hinges. The room was empty, the bed made. He opened a second door. A light-skinned, flat-chested girl in a shift was sitting by herself on the side of a mattress, her bare feet hardly touching the floor. Her eyes looked as small as seeds. "The blackberry got the sweet juice," she said.

"Where's the burned man, missy?"

"Trick, trade, or travel, Daddy. What you doin' wit' that big gun? Bring it over here. I'll take care of it for you."

He smelled an odor like brown sugar spilled on a woodstove. "You been smoking opium, girl?"

"I ain't no girl. Ain't been one since I was twelve. That's how old I was when I got turned out. Come on, I'll show you."

"Where is he?"

"The burned-up man? Wit' Corrine. He used to like me. Now he say I'm too young. That show how much he know."

"Where's Corrine's room?"

"Last one on the hall. You missing out on a good t'ing."

He stepped back into the hallway and closed the door to the girl's room. The carpet on the floor was so thin, it felt like straw under his boots. A white man in a strap undershirt, his suspenders hanging at his sides, stepped out of a doorway, stared starkly at Hackberry and the gun in his hand, and retreated into the room, closing the door softly. Hackberry unscrewed the bulb by the window at the end of the hall, then stood next to the last door, his back pressed against the wall. He turned the knob and let the door swing back on its hinges.

There was no sound from the room. He stepped inside, his arm still cocked at a right angle, the barrel of the Peacemaker still pointed upward. A fat black woman was pouring a pan of dirty water into a bucket, her breasts hanging like watermelons out of her robe, a razor scar down one cheek that puckered her eye. "What you want?" she said.

But his attention was not focused on her. The man in the bed was sitting upright without a shirt, a coverlet pulled to his waist, his chest and shoulders wrinkled like pink rubber curdled by flame, his face a bowl of porridge with eyes, nostrils, and a mouth that had no lips.

"Step out of the bed and get your britches on," Hackberry said. "Keep your hands on top of the covers."

The man took a long time to speak. An object like a woman's brooch hung from a leather cord around his neck. "I really don't feel like it."

"I'm interested in the man you work for. Not you. We can talk in the alley. What's that around your neck?"

"My Purple Heart. I stubbed my toe on a dead Flip."

"You shouldn't have taken out your problems on Beatrice DeMolay."

"Who?"

"Get your pants on."

"I lost them," the man in the bed said. He looked at the woman. "You ever see this guy?"

"Maybe. Do what he say," the woman said. "Miss Dora gonna take care of this."

"Tell me what you want, chief," the man said. "I'm late for work. I'm the greeter at Delmonico's. Kids love me. I'm a real howl."

"Feel sorry for yourself on your own time," Hackberry said. He approached the bed and slowly pulled the coverlet off the mattress, letting it drop to the floor. The burned man was wearing undershorts and socks. The lower half of his body was white and completely unscarred.

"Get up," Hackberry said.

"No."

"Why make it hard on yourself? Why make it hard on the colored lady?"

"I ain't no lady," the woman said. "Get yo' ass out of my bedroom. I'm fixing to throw this bucket on you."

"You will not do that. Don't even pretend you plan to do that. I don't want to shoot a woman."

"You think I care about yo' gun? I seen you before. Where's your badge at? They take it away from you?"

"He's a lawman?" the burned man said.

"Off the bed," Hackberry said.

"I done warned you," the woman said. She flung the contents of the bucket on him, in his face and eyes and hair, sloshing his skin and hat and coat and shirt with a ubiquitous stench that was like effluent from a sewage line or shrimp that had soured in a bait well. He gagged and tried to wipe it out of his eyes and mouth and ears, then saw the man reach under his pillow and get to his feet.

Hackberry pointed the Peacemaker straight out in front of him, cocking the hammer, believing that it was already too late, that a fat, half-dressed, enraged black woman against whom he had no grievance had just ripped the hands off his clock.

He pulled the trigger without aiming. The roar of the .45 inside the closed room was deafening. The bullet blew through the burned man's shoulder and embedded in the wall and patterned the wallpaper with blood. But neither the burned man nor the enraged woman was through. The woman swung the bucket at Hackberry's head just as the burned man aimed and pulled the trigger on a small semiautomatic. The firing pin snapped dryly on a bad cartridge; the man jerked the slide to clear the chamber and load a second round.

The bucket cut Hackberry above the eye. He fired again without aiming, the Peacemaker bucking in his palm, flame leaping from the muzzle. The burned man crashed backward as though trying to sit on the sill and unable to find purchase, taking the broken glass and the shade down with him, his mouth open like a starving bird's.

Hackberry lowered the gun and stared at the destroyed window, his right hand shaking uncontrollably. Down below someone had turned on a light and was yelling for help. Hackberry hardly felt the blows when the black woman attacked him, trying to claw his eyes.

He shoved her away and leaned out the window, staring down into the circle of light where the dead man lay. A Mexican woman had rolled him over on his back and was holding his head in her lap. She looked up at Hackberry, blinking against the rain. He could see the hole in the burned man's stomach and the blood welling out of it.

"You the man did this?" the woman said. "Why you hurt Eddy? Why you come down to do this? Help! Somebody help!"

Chapter 20

THE SHERIFF'S SUBSTATION was located inside an ancient one-story brick building that smelled like stagnant water. It once served as the county jail and now contained two cells, neither of which had plumbing; they were used only to lock up drunks overnight.

Hackberry sat in a chair by a chain-locked gun rack lined with shotguns and Winchester lever-action rifles. The door to one cell was open, the other empty. The sheriff stood inside the open cell, looking down at a man in a plain oblong wood box; the dead man's body had been sprinkled with chunks of blue ice that a deputy had carried in a bucket from the saloon next door. "His name was Eddy Diamond," the sheriff said. "He did two years in Yuma for syndicalism."

"'Syndicalism'? Meaning what?"

"Stirring up union trouble in Arizona Territory. You all right?"

"I heard inmates go crazy in the cells at Yuma."

"Most people do when you lock them in an iron box in hunnerd-and-twenty-degree heat."

"How'd he get burned?"

"Some shit in the Philippines. Or Nicaragua. I forget which." The sheriff came out of the cell and closed the door behind him, shaking it to make sure it had clicked shut.

"You're sure his name was Diamond?"

"It was the only one he used."

"Did he have an alias? Like Jimmy Belloc or Jimmy No Lines?"

"Not to my knowledge." The sheriff had a drooping mustache and a lined face and a purple bump on the ridge of his nose. He had gotten out of bed to take care of the shooting and kept looking at the clock on the desk. "Don't study on this, Hack. You didn't have no choice."

"I got his name from Mealy Lonetree. I think he was the one who threw acid at Beatrice DeMolay."

"That's one woman I wish would move to Mars."

"That man in yonder is the one who attacked her. It had to be him."

"Diamond was in jail for disturbing the peace the night she says somebody threw acid at her."

"She *says*?"

"You in the habit of believing ex-whores?"

"She's a friend of mine."

The sheriff pulled on his ear. "Mealy gave you the name of this Belloc fellow?"

"Yes, he did. He also acted like he was standing on the edge of his grave."

"When was this?"

"About seven hours ago."

"He was," the sheriff said.

"Was what?"

"Standing on the edge of his grave. He hanged himself in his closet."

Hackberry stared straight ahead, his hands propped on his knees, his ears ringing. Then he gazed at the floor and at the dirt grimed into the grain of the wood, the cigar burns, the chewing-tobacco stains, the wisps of dried manure and horse hair that had fallen from someone's boots or spurs. "That doesn't make sense. Mealy was fixing to leave town."

"The coroner is putting it down as a suicide. Let it go at that. Stay away from this woman. These people are gutter rats. That includes the man you shot. At the inside, he was a whoremonger."

"I don't believe Mealy killed himself. I think Arnold Beckman is behind all of this."

"Could be. But bad-mouthing others isn't going to he'p you."

Hackberry looked at the floor and the way the leather was worn around the points and sides of his boots from sticking them into stirrups. When he closed his eyes, he saw the verdant land along the Guadalupe and bluebonnets blooming in the spring, bending and riffling in the wind, electric blue as far as the eye could see.

"Did you hear me?" the sheriff said.

"I'm not feeling too good right now."

"What's that stink on you?"

"I don't know. I'd like to go now. Do you mind?"

"Hell, no, I don't mind. Take your weapon with you. Get out of the goddamn country. I'll take care of the paperwork."

"You don't have to get your quills up."

"I'm doing this only because I remember the old days."

"That's good, because I wouldn't want you to do anything on my account. Don't let that dead man out of his cell, either."

"Say again?"

Hackberry went out the door, his face tight and numb with hangover, his gun belt and holstered revolver looped over his shoulder. The dirt street was empty, the stores and bordellos and saloons and gambling houses closed. His right ear was still partially deaf from firing the Peacemaker in the closed room, and the ground seemed to shift from side to side, as though he were on board a pitching ship. The rain had stopped, and the air was cold and smelled of wood smoke and somebody baking bread. Was a bakery about to open its doors? If so, would he be allowed inside? He had just killed an innocent man, a labor organizer, a decorated soldier, not unlike his son. If an unkind voice had told Hackberry he was the worst of men, absolutely alone and friendless, he would not have argued.

When he returned home later in the day, dehydrated and sick, trembling with fatigue, the boxlike phone on his living room wall was ringing. He picked up the listening piece from the hook and put it to his ear. "Hello?"

"How does it feel?" a merry voice said.

"Beckman?"

"Did you have an enjoyable evening in San Antonio?"

"I'll never give you what you want."

"This is just for openers."

"Have at it."

"You know the man you killed was a recipient of the Purple Heart?"

"That's right, he was."

"He was also awarded the Medal of Honor. The newspapers will have the full story within a day or so."

Hackberry felt one eyelid stick shut, as if the eye had dried up and turned to sandpaper.

"No philosophic observations?"

"You cain't buy me, you cain't scare me."

"Then why are you telling me that? You're a delight."

Arnold Beckman began laughing and continued laughing even as he was hanging up, as though his merriment were so genuine, he didn't care if others were privy to it or not.

THAT NIGHT HACKBERRY put on his canvas coat and a flop hat and went down to the riverside with a wicker chair and a bait bucket and a cane pole strung with a fishing line and a wood bobber and a treble hook and a weight made from a minié ball, and set up shop on the edge of the water. He baited the treble hook with a piece of liver and cast it close to an eddy behind a downed cottonwood tree where yellow catfish as thick as his upper arm hung in schools. But the real purpose of his visit to the riverside was not to catch fish. A few feet away, under a tangle of cable left over from a logging operation, was the hiding spot he had chosen for the artifact he now thought of as the cup. He had wrapped it and its wood case inside a rubber slicker, and then a tarp, and tied it with rope, and at night had buried it up the slope in a dry spot that never collected water.

He was not sure why he was drawn to this particular spot by the river on this particular night, but he knew his purpose did not have to do with fish. The truth was, he could not deal with the image of the burned man lying in the alley, his head resting in the Mexican woman's lap, blood pumping from the hole in his stomach.

Hackberry shut his eyes and opened them again, trying to restart his thought processes before they led him into the dark places that were a trap, never a solution. He looked over his shoulder at the tangle of cable and the burial spot he had planted divots of grass on. *I don't know if you actually used that cup or not, but I need some he'p.*

He was surprised at his request. He had never been keen on prayer and in fact was not exactly sure what it consisted of. In his experience, religious moments tended to occur when people were about to fall off a cliff or get rope-dragged through a cactus patch.

I was set up, but I doubt if anybody will believe that. Were it not for the sheriff in Bexar County, I'd probably be charged with manslaughter. The sheriff in Bexar County is not the type of man I want to be indebted to. I'm open to any suggestions you have, sir.

There was no reply. The moon was full above the hills, its mountains and craters and ridges like an enormous bruise on its surface. Hackberry looked again at the burial spot. *Tell me what to do, sir. Tell that boy in the brothel I'm sorry. Maybe he was a friend of my son. The prewar army was a small group. Sir, what am I going to do? I feel absolutely lost.*

He felt his cane pole throb in his hand. His bobber had been pulled straight down in the eddy, the moisture squeezing from the tension in the line, the weight of the fish arching the pole to the point of breaking. He slipped his hands down the pole and grabbed the line and twisted it around his wrists and pulled the catfish clear of the eddy and the rotted cottonwood, through the reeds and onto the bank, its long, sleek, grayish-yellow sides and whiskers and spiked fins coating with sand.

He put his foot across the fish's stomach and worked the treble hook free of its mouth, then picked it up by the tail, avoiding its spikes, and swung its head against a rock, slinging blood on the grass. He put the catfish in the bait bucket and squatted by the water's edge and began washing the blood and fish slime from his hands. The water clouded and the blood disappeared inside it, but he could not get the smell of the fish and what it reminded him of off his hands.

He got on his knees and scrubbed his hands with sand, accidentally knocking over the bucket, spilling on his pants the blood from the piece of liver he had brought for bait. He walked up the incline and sat down next to the burial spot, his arms limp, his head on his chest.

Me again. Everything I touch comes to the same end. I got nowhere to go. I got nobody to cover my back. He'p my boy, please, wherever he is. And if you can, he'p me keep my aim true and my eye clear. This isn't much of a prayer, but it's all I got right now. Amen.

Later, he looked from his upstairs bedroom window at the spot where the rusted cable lay and thought he saw a white light, like moon glow, radiating from the ground rather than from the heavens. Then a cloud passed in front of the moon, and the light disappeared from the embankment, and he realized it had been an illusion.

HE WOKE EARLY to the smell of coffee boiling and bread baking. He put on his trousers and boots and hooked his suspenders over his undershirt and went downstairs into the unheated house and saw a man's head go past the kitchen window. He opened the back door and saw a cook fire blazing by the edge of his flower garden, a piece of corrugated tin stretched across two rocks, the wind flattening the smoke on the lawn. Willard Posey was pouring water from a tin can into the coffeepot.

"I hate to ask," Hackberry said.

"Ask what?"

"You cook biscuits in everybody's yard?"

"Just yours," Willard said. "I made the coffee a little too strong and added some more water. You have any butter?"

"What's the problem of the day, Willard?"

"I figured you needed a friend."

"About the trouble in San Antonio?"

"Get us some plates. You have such a fine place here. It's one of the most peaceful spots I've ever seen. The envy of any normal man."

"Is this going to take long?"

"I'll try to keep it short," Willard replied.

They sat in straight-back chairs and ate off tin plates on the back porch, the sunlight spreading across the hills, the willows on the riverbank the color of old brass.

"Why'd you do it?" Willard said.

"Shoot the man in the cathouse?"

"Go to San Antonio."

"I owed Miz DeMolay."

Willard nodded. "That's not really why I'm here. I got a call from your former common-law wife. She didn't ring you?"

Hackberry stopped eating. "You're talking about Ruby?"

"Yes, sir, that's the name she gave me. Miss Ruby Dansen."

"Where is she?"

"She didn't say. She wanted to know where her son has gone to."

"He's in the army hospital outside Denver."

"She says your ex-legal-wife took him out of there. She said your ex-legal-wife is given to unscrupulous and devious activities. She also said your ex was the paramour of the Sundance Kid, although she didn't use the word 'paramour.'"

"Maggie Bassett took Ishmael out of the hospital?"

"On a train headed south. According to her, Maggie Bassett put your boy in a wheelchair and abducted him."

"You didn't get a callback number? You just dropped by and made breakfast in my yard and dumped all this in my lap without bothering to get a number?"

"She didn't give it. I asked."

"He was in a wheelchair?"

"That's what she said."

"What kind of shape?"

"I don't know, Hack. I felt obliged to tell you this. I didn't come out here to be your pincushion."

Hackberry stepped into the yard and knocked the crumbs from his tin pan. "I didn't mean to get crossways with you."

"I worry about you."

"So do I."

"There's people trying to mess you up. What bothers me is you seem to he'p them every chance you get."

"Deputize me."

"Wouldn't that be a step downward for you?"

"Pay me a dollar a year. You'll always know where I'm at. I won't be able to sass you, either."

"You still haven't learned to drive a motorcar?"

"Haven't had time to get a manual. Or whatever the directions are called."

Willard stared into space. "I think one of us ought to run off with the circus."

FOR ISHMAEL, THE nights and days at Maggie Bassett's house in San Antonio were not separated by the rising and the setting of the sun but by changes in the chemistry of his body and brain. Fatigue gave way to sleep and a moment's rest, then a sudden awakening on the Marne, where he found himself running through artillery fire, his legs caught in wet cement, the air bursts illuminating flooded shell holes stained yellow on the rims with mustard gas, dead men floating in them, their bodies bloated, their uniforms splitting on their backs.

The sunrise brought with it a pressure band along the side of his head, as though he were wearing a hat, and a third eye in his vision where ordinary images became part of an alternate universe, one that could easily suck him into its confines if he were not careful. A wrong thought was not a minor concern. One slip and he could find himself inside his third eye, where all bets were off and reason held no sway. He wondered if his brain were no longer attached to his skull.

Maggie brought him breakfast on a tray and opened the curtains so he could look out on the rolling countryside and the gray ruins of a Spanish mission and its two bell towers and the birds that rose from them in the morning and descended in droves at sunset. She washed him and medicated his wounds and changed his bandages. She read to him when he couldn't sleep, and put an Edison Amberola next to his bed so he could listen to recorded music on a cylinder. She also fixed him ice cream with crushed pineapple on it and insisted on hand-feeding it to him. When his skin burned for no reason, she took a very small pill from a vial and placed it in his mouth and lay by his side and held his hand in hers.

It was the other thing she did for him that he knew he could not live without. To deny his need was foolish; to deny the pleasure he derived from satisfying that need was even more foolish, somewhat like a man on the edge of orgasm telling himself he could be sexually abstemious if he so desired.

He didn't know what the hypodermic needle contained. She swore it was not morphine, just a harmless powder, a mild antidote to relieve the pain in his legs and the night sweats that soaked his sheets and left him depressed and trembling with cold in the morning, like a child who had wet his bed. She prepared the hypodermic needle twice a day in the kitchen, beyond his line of vision, but he could hear her drag the match across the striker on the box, then he would smell the pleasant odor of burning candle wax and another odor, one that seemed out of context, like someone splashing fireside bourbon into a tumbler.

In preparation for the procedure, she washed her hands with soap and water and disinfectant and always cleaned his skin with rubbing alcohol and a cotton swab before she pricked the vein, the blood rising through the needle into the glass barrel. Then she pushed down the plunger, looking kindly into his face as his mouth opened and his viscera melted.

"Why do I smell whiskey when you load the syringe?" he asked on their third day in San Antonio. He was sitting by the window in a wheelchair woven from straw, thirty minutes after an injection, the sky hung with warm colors that dissolved into one another.

"You don't like it?"

"I'm just not sure what we're doing."

"You're not a drinker. So I give it to you this way. A little wine for the stomach."

"How do you know I'm not a drinker?"

"Because you're nothing like your father."

"I remember him being a good father when I was little. I never understood why he left us or why he didn't visit or get in touch."

"He left you because he's a selfish, mean, murderous man. That's not an insult. It's what he is. Maybe it's not even his fault."

"He must have hurt you pretty bad."

"Your father made me have an abortion. He's a shit. What else can I tell you about him?"

"My mother said he liked children."

"Believe what you want."

"Maybe he didn't like me," Ishmael said.

She went into the kitchen and came back with a folded newspaper. She dropped it into his lap. "See what he's been up to."

The article about the shooting in the brothel was on the front page. The headline read: WAR HERO KILLED BY EX–TEXAS RANGER. The lead paragraph identified the dead man as a union organizer and a recipient of the Purple Heart and the Medal of Honor who had been horribly burned and disfigured during the Filipino Insurrection. It made no mention of the victim's arrest record. The shooter was a retired Texas Ranger and former city marshal who had been fired from his job for public drunkenness. His name was Hackberry Morgan Holland. A pistol had been found near the body of the deceased. The investigation was continuing.

"The sheriff will protect your father, so don't waste your time feeling sorry for him," Maggie said.

"How do you know?"

"They're corrupt."

"Not all of them."

"When I was a working girl, we had to give free ones. Want some names?"

"No."

She took the newspaper from his hands and dropped it into a wastebasket. "Would you like to go down to your office today?"

"Which office?"

"The one where you're going to work and make a great deal of money. Arnold wants to meet you. Tomorrow he'll be off to Galveston and Juárez. When you're better, you and I can go to Mexico with him. You can buy handmade lace and jewelry for the change in your pocket."

"I need to talk to my mother, Maggie. I don't know why she didn't come back to the hospital. You left a message?"

"I told you that. I told the hospital administrators how to reach us, too. I called her union in Santa Fe."

"I thought it was in Albuquerque."

"Maybe she's working in both places. Ishmael, your mother is probably under great stress right now. The U.S. Attorney's Office is arresting radicals all over the country. You know, because of the Italians putting bombs in people's mailboxes. I think somebody should drop a bomb on Ellis Island."

He stood up from the chair, waiting for the momentary discomfort and pain to leave. "I want to walk today. I don't care where we go."

"You're not ready. You need to sit down."

"I'm tired of sitting. I'm tired of lying in bed. Tell me about Arnold Beckman again. I can't keep some of these things straight in my head."

"You're still recovering. You were almost blown apart."

"The ones who were blown apart are still in France. Why does Beckman want me? I don't have much work experience outside the military."

"People love a hero."

"I'm not heroic."

"I've seen your medals."

"Most of them are French. Nobody cares about French medals," he said.

"It doesn't matter. People want appearances. I was a schoolteacher. Think anybody is interested in the history of a schoolteacher? But a reformed whore who still has her looks? Tell me men aren't interested. Women, too, if they're honest."

Ishmael picked up both his canes and walked to his bed and sat down heavily. He rolled down his pajamas over his bandages and peeled them free of his ankles and pulled on his trousers. He walked to the dresser without the canes and took a fresh shirt from a drawer and put it on and tucked it in and tightened his belt. He straightened his back, smiling. "Not bad, huh?"

"We have to be back by four."

"I thought we might eat in a restaurant."

"No, we have to come home for your medication. We have to keep the regimen," she said. "You need the right kind of food. Have you ever worked in a restaurant? If you saw the people who wash the dishes and prepare the food, you'd never eat out again."

"I think I've got too many punctures in me. I just want to go outside. I want to be in the sunshine again."

"I haven't done bad by you, have I?"

"You were swell. In every way."

"You used the past tense. There is no past tense between us."

"That went by me."

"Don't worry about all these little things. Let little people worry about little things. That's their job." She kissed him on the cheek. "That's a preview for when we come back. I want to give you the life you didn't have."

"My life has been fine."

She rested her head on his shoulder and placed the flat of her hand on his heart. "I'll make it finer. I'll be your mother and your lover and your sister and all things to you."

"Some might call you an unusual lady, Maggie."

"You're my big boy. Big all over. My big, lovely, delectable boy." She unbuttoned the top of his shirt and kissed his chest. "Precious thing."

Chapter
21

ARNOLD BECKMAN'S OFFICE building and the apartment he kept in it were not far away, on a green plain north of the city, in sight of both the San Antonio River and the ruins of the Spanish mission. The building was white stucco, with blue trim and a gray slate roof and balconies from which orange trumpet vine hung in thick clusters. But there was something wrong with its architectural design and ambiance. The colors were too bright, the windows too small, the flower beds unplanted and humped with manure that hadn't been worked into the soil. A solitary live oak hung with Spanish moss stood in front, half of the branches withered by lightning or blight. The adjacent lot was stacked with construction debris powdering in the wind. When Ishmael approached the building with Maggie Bassett, its symmetry made him think of a man about to sneeze.

Beckman's office had the same sense of ambiguity. It was filled with potted plants that had wilted, the drain dishes curlicued with grit. Most of the furniture was made of antlers and curved and debarked and shellacked wood that resembled bones, with rawhide and animal pelts stretched across it. High on the wall, behind the massive desk, was an oil painting of Robert E. Lee and Stonewall Jackson at an encampment, the men staring in opposite directions, the brushwork flawed in a way that made both appear cross-eyed.

"Drink?" Beckman said.

"No, sir. Thank you," Ishmael said.

"Have a seat."

"You'll have to excuse me. If I sit down, I have trouble getting up."

"You're a polite young man, Mr. Holland. I could use a few more like you."

Beckman's chair was pushed back from his desk. He wore an open shirt and a silk bandana tied around his neck; his legs were extended in front of him, crossed at the ankles. His face seemed possessed by levels of energy that his skin could hardly constrain. His movements were not movements but jerks, muscular spasms, twitches; his hands kept opening and closing. His eyes were a brilliant blue, constantly roving over Ishmael's person. He squeezed his scrotum. "You were at the Battle of the Marne?"

"Yes, sir, one of the battles, the last one."

"What did you think of the French machine gun, the Chauchat? What do they call it? The 'sho-sho'?"

"My men thought it was junk."

"What about the Lewis?"

"There's none better."

"Why not the Maxim or the Vickers?"

"They're too heavy and take too many men to operate. The Lewis is light. One man can run thousands of rounds through it without a misfire."

"I have a firing range in back. I'd like for you to demonstrate a few weapons for me."

"Why do you need me to demonstrate them?"

"I don't. I need to see how you'll demonstrate them to our clients."

"Who are your clients?"

"Let's go outside. I'll explain a few things to you. Maggie, will you fix me a vodka and orange juice with a couple of cherries and a sprig of mint?"

She looked at Beckman blankly. He had not asked her to sit down; he had hardly acknowledged her presence. "Sorry, I was daydreaming. What did you want?" she said.

He repeated his request and said, "Have you ever seen a more beautiful woman? Look at her. Ageless, not a wrinkle in her skin. Tell us how you do it, Maggie."

She went to the foyer and called to the maid and told her to fix Beckman's drink and bring it out to the gun range.

"See that?" Beckman said. "She stays young by not letting men boss her around."

"Refer to me again as though I'm a ventriloquist's dummy, and you'll wish you hadn't," she said.

Beckman smiled with his eyes and led the way to the range, the dimple in his chin glistening with aftershave lotion. The targets were all the same: the black silhouette of a man printed on paper that was mounted on a board forty yards out. The shooting tables and canvas chairs were arranged uniformly under a striped awning. In the distance, to the left of the range, Ishmael could see the bell towers of the mission. A cloud moved across the sun, dropping the countryside into shadow, lowering the temperature precipitously. He thought he saw men, maybe stonemasons, working on the mission. On the shooting tables were rifles and pistols and field boxes of ammunition.

Beckman gestured at the closest table. "Recognize these?"

"The Lee-Enfield, the '03 Springfield, the Mauser, the Mannlicher-Carcano, the .30-40 Krag."

"Let's see what you can do with them."

"I don't fire at that kind of target anymore."

The maid brought Beckman his drink. He drank from it. His lips looked cold and red and glossy, as though they had been freshly lipsticked. "You don't shoot at a target that resembles a man?"

"That's correct."

"Inside you asked me whom I sell to. I could tell you the world. But that's not accurate. I sell weapons to collectors, and I sell them to people who need them to defend themselves. I also supply them to motion picture companies."

"But your big purchasers are nations?"

"Not any nation. The ones in danger. Do you know who those happen to be?"

"I haven't thought about it."

"As soon as the Bolsheviks get things tamped down in Moscow, they'll be after East Europe. The Japanese want China's resources. They also want Southeast Asia. North Africa is up for grabs. The Arabs thought they were going to win their independence from the Ottoman Empire. Instead, they got royally screwed. You look uncomfortable."

"I need to sit down."

"Are you in pain?"

"It passes," Ishmael said, easing himself into a chair.

"You don't look well, Mr. Holland. Let me get you a drink."

Ishmael shook his head. The countryside was going out of focus, the birds from the bell towers freckling the sky. "I apologize. My knees get weak if I stand too long."

"That's understandable. I took one through the kneecap at Gallipoli. A Turk got me from one mile out. I had to hand it to the nasty bugger. It was a magnificent shot."

"I remember hearing of an arms dealer in Mexico. I never saw him, but I was told he was German or Austrian," Ishmael said.

"There were many. I was one of them."

"This one was in business with General Lupa. The Wolf."

"Lupa's nickname was a compliment. He was a swine."

"He lynched four of my men at a bordello. He lured others into a trap."

Beckman raised his eyebrows as though being forced to speak on an unpleasant subject. "Lupa was a bastard. I heard he was killed, maybe by his own men. I didn't do business with him, so I'm not well informed as to his fate."

"Did you know Huerta or Villa?"

"No, I supplied Emiliano Zapata, a true man of the people. He was pure of heart and wanted nothing for himself. He'll probably be assassinated. No Mexican story has a happy ending."

"I thought that was the Irish."

"They both get a regular fucking. It's the nature of the beast. Why grieve on it?"

"What kind of salary goes with the job, Mr. Beckman?" Ishmael said.

"Eight thousand dollars a year. To start. At some point, your commissions will be greater than your salary, and eight thousand dollars will seem a pauper's salary. Which of these rifles do you favor?"

"The .30-40 Krag. For its smooth action and the way you can keep loading while you're firing and never be empty."

"Shoot it for me."

"The angle of your range isn't good. I think there're some trucks down by that old mission. I don't want to use your targets, either, sir."

"That mission has been deserted for years," Beckman said.

"They're restoring it, Arnold," Maggie said.

"It's Sunday. Why would anyone be working on it today? I'm a bit tired of that bunch, anyway. They used the power of the church to challenge the title to my land. I had to cede them fifty acres along the riverside to keep what was already mine. Tell me the clerics don't know how to make the eagle scream."

"Ishmael doesn't want to shoot. Leave him alone."

"You don't want to shoot?" Beckman said.

"Another time."

"That's the way it was in the trenches?" Beckman said. "Let's take a bloody vote on it? Wait until the weather is nicer? Fritz might be sleeping in?"

"Not quite," Ishmael said.

"I'll be fucked if I see trucks or workmen there. What is it, four hundred yards? You think this .45 automatic will travel that far?"

"Arnold, behave," Maggie said.

"I'm sure Mr. Holland has an opinion. Do you have an opinion, Mr. Holland?"

"Don't wave that around," she said.

"This is perhaps Mr. Browning's best creation. Think it might reach the mission, wake up a few Irish immigrants who are probably drunk or dozing on the job?"

"Arnold, I mean it. Stop the histrionics before you hurt someone," Maggie said, pushing Beckman's wrist down.

"I'd like to try the Krag, Mr. Beckman," Ishmael said, picking up the rifle, working the leather sling around his left forearm.

"You worry over nothing. Watch," Beckman said. He pointed

the .45 in the direction of the mission and pulled the trigger seven times, his wrist bucking, the ejected shells bouncing on the table. "See? No one even noticed. People are being killed all over the world at this very moment. It isn't being written about or filmed, so it doesn't exist. The British sent hundreds of thousands into Maxim guns. I saw their bodies stacked like frozen cordwood. The incompetent bastards who sent them to their death wouldn't take time to piss in their mouths. But they're treated as fucking national heroes."

"I think we'd better be going," Ishmael said.

"Don't be a prima donna, Mr. Holland. I know you're a brave man. We'll take a drive and check out the cabbage eaters you're worried about. Darling Maggie will come with us, won't you, you lovely mog?"

"Of course," she said.

"What did you call her?" Ishmael asked.

"A mog. That's British slang for a cat. Look at her, sleek and lovely and about to spring. She'll ruin other women for you. After Maggie, they'll all seem homely as a mud fence."

"Thank you, Arnold," Maggie said. "But please shut up. I've never known anyone who can absolutely pump it to death."

"She's the only one I let talk to me like that," Beckman said. "Venus Rising in Texas, right out of the Gulf of Mexico, the sun bursting from her hair. The egalitarian queen and cowboy's delight."

"I'm warning you, Arnold," she said.

His face split into a smile; he clapped his hands like a magician making all bothersome complexities disappear. "Let's go see if we put any holes in the mission's walls. I don't want to bring the papists down on my head again."

THE AIR WAS cold, the sunlight harsh, as they drove in Beckman's open-top car to the Spanish ruins. Beckman was riding hatless in front, his hair blowing. "Told you," he said. "Half of them look like boiled red potatoes. I've yet to know a Paddy that wasn't a nigger turned inside out."

Maggie leaned forward and pushed him in the shoulder. "Will you stop that?"

"Admit it, you love it," he replied.

"I commanded colored troops," Ishmael said.

"I'm aware you did. So don't be so bloody serious. We can't seem to have any fun these days. Everyone has his own smug cause."

The driver parked in front of the mission. Ishmael and Maggie stepped down, but Beckman remained in the seat. He lit a cheroot and dropped the match on the ground, tilting his head back as he blew a stream of smoke into the wind. Ishmael waited for him.

"Go ahead," Beckman said. "I'll be along."

Ishmael talked with a foreman about the reconstruction, then finally said what was on his mind. "We were shooting down below. A round didn't stray this far, did it?"

"Not that we noticed," the foreman said.

"I'm glad. I apologize for disturbing your work. How old is this place?"

The foreman had a build like a beer barrel about to burst, the sleeves of his flannel shirt rolled up on his thick forearms, his face wind burned. "Two centuries, I suspect. Want to walk around inside?"

The wooden roof had collapsed long ago, and the rock walls had been blackened by fire, the apse piled with debris. Ash from a trash fire in back floated like hundreds of moths out of the sunlight into the nave.

"It's cold in here," Maggie said. Her hands were stuffed in a fur muff.

"You didn't 'love' what Beckman said, did you?" Ishmael asked.

"What was that?"

"He said you loved his racist sense of humor."

"I'm used to it."

"Tell me."

"Tell you what?"

"That you didn't like that comment about Irishmen and Negroes."

"No, I didn't like it. I've heard worse. Who cares? Why is it so cold in here?"

"Early winter, maybe."

"I don't like the cold," she said. "It's like being alone. I could never live in the North. I never liked winter or gloomy places. Why did you want to come in here?"

"It makes me think of all the people who stacked the stones in the walls or prayed in here or died here. I think they're still around, just like at the Alamo."

"You're talking about ghosts?"

"Sometimes I believe that all time happens at once. Maybe the dead are still living out their lives right next to us."

She removed one hand from the fur muff and slipped her arm inside his. "You're a strange boy."

"I like the way you stood up to Beckman. I just wish you didn't push him the way you did. Like you were having fun with him."

"Fun? There is no such thing as fun with Arnold. Don't ever underestimate him. He's lighthearted until he decides to become serious. Then he's dangerous. I'll put it another way: He's a short man no one thinks of as short."

"Maybe we should stay away from him."

"Arnold is the twentieth century. Be glad I found you, Ishmael, even if I have my warts."

"I've yet to see them."

She started to smile, then her gaze broke. "We should go now. Why talk about things no one can understand? One day we'll all be dead and none of this will matter."

"That's a grim way to think," he said.

"We have now. We have each other. You like me, don't you?"

"Sure. Who wouldn't?"

"Then let's talk about now and not these other things. I don't like to be cold. I don't like to be alone."

"I thought Beckman was joining us."

"Forget about him. You shouldn't be on your feet too long. Let's go somewhere warm. You're going to get sick. Your face looks chapped."

"Are you upset about something?"

"Why should I be upset? I don't want to see you get sick, that's all. Do you think I'm abnormal because I worry about you?"

He paused, his arms stiffening on his canes. White ash was drifting down on Maggie's hair, as soft as Christmas-tree snow. "I have to ask you something. Beckman knows a lot about Mexico and a general named Lupa. But he said Lupa may have been killed by his own men. I was at the bordello where Lupa died. General Lupa was killed by an American. The prostitutes told me they fought up in the rocks behind the bordello."

"You were at a Mexican whorehouse?"

"I was looking for my men. Lupa hanged four of them. For no reason. Before he hanged them, he made them drop their trousers so they'd die in a shameful manner. Then he ambushed a patrol I sent to find my men."

"Don't talk anymore of these things, Ishmael. Let the dead go. I'm cold."

"A hearse full of ordnance had been parked in front. Somebody set fire to it and all the weapons and ammunition inside, including machine guns. Nobody in Mexico burns firearms, particularly Mauser rifles and Maxims."

"What does this have to do with Arnold? He wants to give you a job. That's all that matters."

"There were bodies all around the brothel. I knew the woman who owned the brothel. She was gone when I got there, but the girls said an Austrian arms dealer was hunting for something in the ashes of the hearse. The girls also said the man who killed Mexicans all over the canyon was a Texas Ranger. I think he may have been my father."

"I don't want to hear this. It has nothing to do with us," she said. "I don't like talking about brothels, either." Her face had hardened, as though she were examining an image a few inches in front of her face, one nobody else saw. "Look out for yourself, Ishmael. I tried to take care of my mother. Instead of getting any thanks, I got blamed for her death."

"I see," he said, realizing she had slipped into a place that only she knew about or understood.

"You *see* what?" she asked.

He shook his head neutrally.

"This place is unsanitary. I want to go and not come back," she said, lifting a piece of ash from her hair and dusting it off her fingers. "Be nice to Arnold. He has qualities many people don't know about. He's fascinated with history. He has degrees from Heidelberg and Vienna. You keep staring at me. Why do you stare at me like that?"

"Sometimes you seem to have two thoughts in your eyes at the same time. Sometimes I can't figure out who you are."

"The person who's going to make you rich. How's that for starters?"

Beckman was waiting for them by the car, smoking his cheroot, not removing it from his lips, his teeth showing when he took a puff. "What kept you?"

"We thought you were coming in," Ishmael said. "You might enjoy it. Some of the murals are still on the plaster. Somebody cut the date 1730 on a flagstone. Would you like to take a look?"

"If I wanted to, I would." Beckman dropped his cigar on the ground and mashed it out with the sole of his boot. Then he cleared his mouth and spat.

"We're not in a hurry," Ishmael said.

"Are you hard of hearing?"

"No, sir."

"Then don't act like it."

"Maggie said you're a student of history."

"Look at me."

"Sir?"

"I said look at me."

Ishmael shook his head again, his eyes focused on empty space.

"I don't like repeating or explaining myself," Beckman said. "For you, I'll do it once. Most Christian churches are built on pagan sites. That's why Attila the Hun didn't sack Roman churches. He feared Odin, not a Hebrew god. Are you listening? I have the distinct feeling I'm not communicating with you."

"You're correct. I don't understand what you're saying."

"I don't trouble the spirits, and they don't trouble me," Beckman said. "Clear enough?"

"Yes, sir."

"You learn your manners in the army? If so, they taught you well."

"I learned them at home. From my mother."

"That's a good answer. That's why I want you to represent my company." Beckman's face broke into a grin as he shifted his attention to Maggie. "Ah, you're a magnificent woman, probably the bane of us all. Payment for the screwing we've given women since the time of Eve. What do you think of that, Mr. Holland? Do you think we shit our nest in that pleasure park between the Tigris and Euphrates?"

"Did you ever hear anything about a burned hearse down in Mexico, Mr. Beckman?" Ishmael said. "One that was loaded with ordnance owned by General Lupa?"

The wind gusted in the silence, speckling the air with dust that was cold and shiny, like mica. Beckman untied the bandana from his neck and whipped it into a rope and retied it around his forehead, pinning his hair to the sides of his face. His eyes were elongated slits, a canine tooth showing behind the curl in his lips. "No, I know nothing of burned hearses," he said. "Do you know there's a tic in your face, Mr. Holland? Do you have a nervous condition? Maybe an addiction of some kind? You should do something about that."

THE DAYS WERE growing shorter, the sun unable to warm the interior of Maggie's house, the rugs full of electricity. It was only five o'clock, and Ishmael could feel his spirits sinking. He paced the floor and looked out the window at the shadows on the lawn and the strips of gunny cloth whipping on a farmer's barbed-wire fence, a plowed field spiked with brown weeds. Maggie was cooking dinner in the kitchen, banging pots and iron skillets, scraping metal on metal. She had not mentioned his "medication," a word they both used more and more often. She dropped a skillet heavily on the stove.

"What's in the syringe?" he said from the door.

"You already know," she replied.

"Morphine you mixed with whiskey?"

"It's heroin. It turns to morphine inside the bloodstream. Some people smoke it. There are worse things around."

She was frying potatoes in the pan without a cover, the grease popping on the stove.

"Why don't you use a lid?" he said.

"Why don't you stay out of the kitchen?"

"What did I say wrong?" he asked.

"It's what you didn't say. Arnold was talking to me like I was trash, and you didn't say anything."

"I didn't think it would help."

"You didn't mind bringing up hearses and guns in Mexico. Why is it that I don't count? Get a plate out of the cupboard."

"I'm not too hungry."

"Oh, lovely."

"It's not the food, it's my stomach."

"Physician, heal thyself," she said, stabbing at a piece of meat in the skillet.

"You're talking about the medication?"

"The syringe is in the top drawer of my dresser. Make sure you get the mixture right. Or throw it in the garbage."

"I sent another telegram to my mother's union. She took leave. Maybe she's coming to San Antonio."

"Stop the presses."

He wiped his nose and scratched his arms. "You have some brandy?"

"In the cabinet," she said.

"I feel sick, Maggie. I can't help it."

He stared at the back of her neck, waiting for her to reply, his heart rate increasing, his breath growing more ragged. The Brits called it the black monkey. But it didn't just climb on your back. It turned its fleas loose on your skin and crawled inside you and clawed at your connective tissue, spreading a pervasive itch over your entire body, inside and out, even on your tongue. He wanted to scrub himself with a wire brush.

He went back into the living room and sat on the couch, a hot coal eating its way through his stomach. "Maggie?" he called.

She came to the kitchen doorway, steak fork in hand. "Decide what you're going to do?"

"I don't have any memory of leaving the hospital. I feel like I have holes drilled in my memory."

"Count yourself lucky. You should have seen the basket cases in the open ward."

"I didn't have to see them. I soldiered with them."

She went back into the kitchen. He squeezed his wrists, first one, then the other, as though trying to shut down the malaria-like sickness flowing through his veins. A moment later, he heard her sigh and the tinkle of the steak fork striking the bottom of the sink. He felt her weight on the couch, smelled the odor of cooking in her clothes.

"There's a price for everything," she said.

"Price of what?"

"You became an army officer and enjoyed the pleasures of your rank. You paid the cost in France. I was nineteen and treated like the queen at Miss Porter's whorehouse. I enjoyed it, too. Now I dream about every degenerate I helped degrade my body. You and I let others use us because we had no power. Once you accept that, you make a choice. You use your intelligence and never let anyone hurt you again. You also get even."

"What's Beckman after?"

"Control of the world, probably. How would I know? People are driven by their vices, not their virtues, Ishmael. Why climb up on a cross about it?"

"I'm going to have a brandy."

"You can do it that way if you want."

"What other way is there?"

"I used opium and laudanum for years. Now I don't. When you don't need it anymore, you put it aside. You think you can't go without it now, but I think you can."

"Does Beckman's interest in me have something to do with an arms deal in Mexico? With the lynching of my men?"

"Arnold's only interest is making money. Forget about Mexico and whatever happened there. They were killing each other on stone altars before the Spaniards ever arrived."

"I'm coming apart, Maggie."

"Tell me what you want to do. You want to lie down with me? You want me to do anything for you? Think of me as your movable feast."

"I don't know what I want," he said, his voice strange, removed from the person he thought he was. "I don't know who I am. I want a drink of brandy. Just a little. To take the edge off."

"With soda or ice or straight up?" she said.

Chapter 22

Ruby DANSEN WOKE at dawn in the chair car and looked out the window and saw zebras and giraffes and white horses and at least four elephants in a field, down by a smoking river, men in rolled shirtsleeves flinging armloads of hay from a flatbed wagon. Was she dreaming? The train rounded a bend and passed a grove of bare cottonwoods. The animals slipped out of view, clouds of white fog thicker than ever on the fields and river.

A soldier wearing a peaked campaign hat was standing in the aisle, close by her chair. He bent down and pulled a blanket up to her chin. "I put this on you," he said. "It's right chilly. You can sleep some more, and I'll bring you some coffee."

"Ishmael?" she said.

"Ma'am?"

"I thought you were my son. I was dreaming. I took him to the circus when he was three."

"You weren't dreaming, ma'am. That was the circus out there. Every kind of wild animal you can think of."

She tried to see beyond the caboose of the train, her breath fogging the glass. When she looked back at the soldier, she realized one of his sleeves was pinned to the shoulder. "Were you over there?"

"Yes, ma'am, I sure as heck was."

"Did you know Captain Ishmael Holland? He commanded colored troops."

"No, ma'am, I didn't. But I heard they done right well."

"How far are we from San Antonio?"

"We're fixing to pull into the station any time now. Are you all right?"

"Why, yes, I am."

"You were having a bad dream. That's what the cold will do to you. You cain't be getting that Spanish influenza, either. It can flat put you in a box."

"You've been very kind," she said.

"The Harlem Hellfighters, that was their name. Did your son come home okay?"

"No, he was wounded badly in both legs."

"I'm sorry. I hope things work out for y'all."

"I hate to ask you such a personal question, but maybe you can help me. When you were recovering from your injury, did you have trouble with any of the drugs you had to take?"

His eyes went away from hers. "I didn't learn anything over there but one lesson, ma'am: You get shut of the war as soon as you're able."

He retook his seat at the head of the car with two other enlisted men. One was asleep; one was reading a newspaper. The man who was asleep had a pair of crutches propped next to him; the man with the newspaper wore a rubber mask painted with flesh tones and a neat mustache.

ISHMAEL COULD NOT remember with exactitude how he got to the carnival. Maybe in a jitney or maybe a driver in a Model T picked him up on the side of the road. He remembered the loud ticking sound the engine gave off, like a clock mechanism working against itself, gnashing its own cogs and teeth into filings. He remembered the driver placing him in the front seat, sticking his canes snugly by his side. He remembered unstoppering the bottle of brandy again and working on the second half of its contents, his voice too loud inside the confines of the car, his allusions to Mexico and France and pulling a mule uphill loaded with two wounded men lost on his benefactor.

He saw the carnival through a brightly lit haze of dust, the Ferris wheel printed in multicolored electric dots against black clouds. "There," he said.

"You sure?" the driver said. "I think maybe you better go to a hospital. You were a soldier?"

Ishmael studied the driver's profile. "I didn't get your name. Do I know you?"

The driver looked at him and seemed to smile, not wanting to injure or offend. "I'm the fellow who picked you up."

Ishmael nodded as though a profound truth had been told him. "By that patch of weeds. That'll be good."

"Don't let the police get you, buddy. They can give you a hard time. I'd throw the bottle away."

The Model T stopped and Ishmael got out on the road, supporting himself with his canes. He stared back through the window. "Were you at Carrizal?"

The driver shook his head, his eyes sad, and drove away.

Ishmael walked through a pine grove, the needles as soft as a sponge under his canes, the brandy swinging in his coat pocket. He entered a clearing and passed horse trailers and tents and trucks held together with wire, and people cooking on hot stones and sheets of tin, their faces firelit, as supple and impassive as warm tallow, shadows leaping behind them.

He stopped and rested, leaning against a tree, and drank from the bottle, closing his eyes as the brandy slid down his throat and seeped like an elixir through his system and touched all the nerve endings in his legs with magical fingers. He worked his way up a path and across a railroad spur to the fairgrounds, sure that he was smiling, because the skin of his face was as tight as the stitching on a shrunken head. He could also smell his odor, similar to a horse blanket that had soured in a tack room, or the pot liquor in a jar of spoiled fruit.

He moved as stiffly as a straw man down the midway, surrounded by the popping of .22 rounds in the shooting gallery, calliope music, a barker describing the freaks on display in his tent, aerial rockets bursting into pink foam, the hand-carved facial starkness of the carousel horses rotating round and round, the squealing of the children, the smells of hot dogs and candied apples and buttered corn, the ventriloquists and magicians and hypnotists on the stages, fire-eaters blowing flame and the stench of burning kerosene into the night, the rattling of the mesh on the geek cage.

Ishmael stepped between two tents and leaned against a pole and drank again from the bottle, then entered the midway afresh, metabolically sealed and protected from the crowds of people parting in front of him like waves against a ship's bow. A frightened mother pulled her child from his path. A man flipping meat patties with a spatula looked up from his grill and said in a Down Under accent, "You're about to run aground, mate. Better find a dry dock."

The Ferris wheel was at the end of the midway, the gondolas painted with polka dots, lines of people with cotton candy waiting to board. That's where he would go, he told himself. He had more than eight dollars in his pocket. He would seat himself in a gondola and be subsumed into the sky, the heat and pain in his legs evaporating, the canes resting across his thighs in a dignified fashion, the last few swallows in the bottle available whenever he wanted them. He would remain in the gondola until his money was gone, rising again and again into gold-veined black clouds of which he had no fear.

That was when he tripped on a rubber power cord and fell headlong into a puddle formed by the overflow of a dunking machine on which a Negro sat dressed in the striped jumper and cord-tied pants and sockless work boots of a convict, his hair bejeweled with drops of water, his grin as self-abasing as the slice of watermelon and the Little Black Sambo painted on a sign above his head.

Somebody helped Ishmael to his feet and even fitted his palms on the canes. Ishmael gazed at the black man and at the onlookers and at the concessionaires and family people bunching up to see what was happening in front of the machine that allowed people to throw a baseball at a metal disk welded to a lever, sending the Negro plummeting into a horse tank.

"Men like this fought for our country," Ishmael said.

The onlookers made no response. Their faces were ovals, the eyes and mouths and noses little more than hash marks, neither good nor bad. The young boys wore slug caps, vests, knickers, dress shirts, ties, and Buster Brown shoes. There was nothing mean about any of them. Why couldn't they understand what he was saying? "You've been taught to disrespect the colored man. Don't let others use you like this," he said.

"You don't like it, go back where you came from!" someone at the back of the crowd said.

"All of you are better than you think you are," Ishmael said. "This is a poor man. He should be your friend."

"Nigger lover!" another man shouted.

"A colored man can't fight back. You let others make cowards and bullies of you."

A dirt clod flew out of the darkness and hit Ishmael in the eye. He raised his forearm in front of him, squinting into the brilliance of a spotlight a carnie worker had turned on his face. Inside the glare, he saw the silhouettes of three hatted men heading for him. One held a club; all three had badges pinned to their shirts. They grabbed him by the arms and led him behind the tents. He heard someone spear a baseball into the metal disk on the dunking machine and, a second later, the sound of mechanical release, like the heavy wood-and-steel trapdoor on a scaffold dropping, followed by a loud splash and the laughter of the crowd.

Ishmael freed one arm and ripped his elbow into the nose of the man holding him, cleaning the glasses off his face. The injured man cupped his nose, blood leaking through his fingers, inadvertently crunching his glasses under his boot. He removed his hand, his lower face smeared as though a burst tomato had been rubbed on it. "Bad choice, shitbird."

Another man pushed him to the ground; or maybe he just fell. One man stripped off his coat and searched it. He shone a flashlight on Ishmael's arms. "He's a dope addict."

Ishmael tried to get up and fell down again.

"What's wrong with your legs?" another said.

"Shrapnel," Ishmael said.

"Where?"

"On both legs, up to my hip."

"Here?" the man with the bloody nose said. "Or here? Sorry. How about here?"

Ishmael felt a sensation like a series of knife thrusts work its way up his thighs into his groin and turn his rectum to jelly.

"Where y'all want to put him?" one of his warders said.

"Good question. I don't want to babysit him till the drunk wagon comes by."

"I saw the Missing Link passed out behind the jakes."

"Put him in the cage?"

"He's a stewbum. Let him sit in his own shit. Maybe he's selling dope or white-slaving for the Cantonese."

"Is that right, you're on the hip?" the man with the ruined nose said. "That's what they call opium smokers these days. Chinamen that smoke it do it on their hip."

For the first time in his life, Ishmael knew what a black man felt when he listened to the rhetoric of the men uncoiling a rope, knotting it neatly, enjoying the oily pull of it through their palms.

THAT SAME EVENING Ruby Dansen took a jitney from her hotel to the address of Maggie Bassett, just outside the city limits, not far from a Spanish mission whose glassless windows had become red eyes in the last remnants of the sun. Maggie Bassett's house was built of purple and brown brick and gray river stone, with dormers and walls thick enough to ensure the house was cool in the summer and warm in winter. There were chairs and a table on the porch, chimes on the eaves, a garage with a motorcar inside, a Dutch oven in the side yard, a two-seat bicycle under the porte-cochere, a vine-threaded gazebo inside a grove of pomegranate and orange trees. It was the kind of home that advertised its excess and told others that necessity and need were never factors in the lives of those who resided there.

Ruby twisted the handle on the doorbell. She fingered her cloth purse and gazed at the mission and the tall grass blowing on the slope below it and wondered how much blood had been mixed in the earth here, how many Indians and Spaniards and Mexicans and white colonists and missionaries were buried anonymously in these hills, voiceless, their stories untold, their deaths not worth an asterisk, their last thoughts known only to themselves.

She also wondered what she should say to Maggie Bassett. What did you say to someone you quietly and dispassionately despised? She knew there must be words that were appropriate, perhaps created especially for this type of situation, maybe vituperative, maybe rigidly formal. Unfortunately, she didn't know what they were. The working girls she had tried to help over the years came from mill towns and skid-road logging camps where the timber beasts slid the logs down a mud-slick gulley lined on either side by brothels and saloons. The girls who worked in the cribs had grown up poor and unwanted, and most of them had been molested or raped by age fifteen, usually by a relative or a friend of the family.

But how could anyone explain Maggie Bassett? Educated at a boarding school. A schoolteacher. Heartbreakingly beautiful in the eyes of any man or woman. Her family rich. Yet she rented her body to scum like Butch Cassidy's gang, a collection of throwbacks who convinced themselves they robbed trains and murdered people because they represented the oppressed. If that weren't enough, she had been the consort of Dr. Romulus Atwood, who thought he was a shootist of world importance until Hackberry blew him out of his socks.

Then Ruby realized she was thinking in a proud way about Hackberry, and she forced herself to remember his abandonment of her and their son when they needed him most.

Maggie Bassett opened the door, her eyes full of daggers. "What do you want?"

"I'm Ruby Dansen."

"I know who you are. I said, what do you want?"

"I'm looking for my son, Ishmael Holland. May I come in and speak with you?"

"Yes, you may speak to me. No, you may not come in."

"I'm sorry you feel that way."

"How did you know where I live?"

"I suspect I could answer your question in several ways. Perhaps I asked others if they knew a local woman who was the town pump for the Hole-in-the-Wall Gang. Instead, I looked in the city directory, which is what most people do when they want to find someone's address."

Maggie Bassett's face never changed expression. "I don't know where Ishmael is. He went for a walk. He's rather moody sometimes. I suspect it has to do with his upbringing."

"You kidnapped a disabled man from a hospital and took him a thousand miles away on a train, and now you have no idea where he might have gone? Does that sound convincing to you?"

"He left earlier this evening. I didn't want him to, but that was his choice."

"Left with whom?"

Maggie's eyes were as unreadable as a cat's. "With *whom*? Your grammar is so impressive. I imagine that's a great source of pride for you."

"Why did you go to Denver to see him?" Ruby said. "Why did you take him out of the hospital? The orderly you bribed was fired."

"I didn't bribe anyone. I tipped an orderly who helped us."

"Why did you bring him to San Antonio?"

"To offer him an executive position with an international company," Maggie said. "To make up for the childhood that was denied him."

"He had the best childhood I could give him. He's also a friend to the working people of the world, something I don't think you could teach him."

Even before Ruby had finished speaking, she knew how foolish and self-righteous she sounded. Maggie had led her into a rhetorical trap.

"I forgot. Your friend Bill Haywood blew up the governor of Idaho," Maggie said.

"Those were false charges."

"If Bill Haywood and your greasy cohorts aren't the ones planting bombs in mailboxes, then who is? John D. Rockefeller?

J. P. Morgan? The pope?" Maggie Bassett waited, her head cocked. "Cat got your tongue?"

"I'd like to slap you."

"I suspect you would. When people of low intelligence run out of words and can't think very fast, their first option is usually to hit someone. It must be a terrible way to live."

Ruby felt small and cold on the porch, shrunken by the long train ride and the fatigue of the day, the pitiful amount of money in her purse and the fact that she hadn't eaten supper, all of it like a great iron chain weighing on her shoulders. "I started going to a Dutch reformed church for a while."

"I'm so happy to know that."

"I listened to this minister talk about our need to forgive others. He said we don't get any rest until we forgive. So I said under my breath that I forgave you for whatever you may have done to us, even though I really didn't mean it."

"So you're not true to your own religion?"

"That's correct. This time I'm going to say it to you and mean it. I forgive you. But that also means you don't exist anymore."

"What did you say? Say that again. What did you—"

"Before I go, can I ask you a question? Does the name Hole-in-the-Wall Gang have sexual overtones? I've always been puzzled by the name. I thought someone with your background might know the answer."

Ruby began walking back down the dirt road toward a country store where she could use a phone to call a taxi. The sun was a flickering scarlet diamond that somehow had created a patch of blue on the horizon. When the wind changed, she thought she heard the music of a calliope but knew her imagination was playing tricks on her.

ONE OF ISHMAEL'S warders held him by the arms and another by the legs. They swung him back and forth to gain momentum, then flung him through the back door of a darkened cage that faced the midway. When he landed on his spine, on a floor made from railroad ties, his mouth shot open and a ball of light exploded inside his head and turned his eyelids to tissue paper. He rolled over, groaning, urine and excrement matting in his hair and painting the side of his face. His warders were looking at him through the doorway. They wore peaked hats probably purchased from an army surplus store and long-sleeved cotton shirts and scrap-metal badges, and he knew he was in the hands of men whose fear was in direct proportion to the level of cruelty they visited on others. One of them released the rolled-up canvas at the top of the bars and dropped it to the floor.

"You got yourself in the honeypot, boy," he said. "The drunk wagon might be along directly. That's as good as it's gonna get." It was the man whose nose was bulbous and mottled purple and still dripping blood. "Got nothing to say?"

Ishmael lifted his cheek from the floor. "I'm Captain Ishmael Holland, United States Army," he whispered.

"No, you're my property and a liar on top of it," the man replied, unbuttoning his fly. "Relax. This is nothing. Wait till the two of us are alone." He cupped his phallus in his palm and arched a gold stream of urine on Ishmael's head and mouth and eyes. "Here's your canes. My name is Fred. I'm gonna have a hot dog, then I'll be back." He pressed an ax handle into Ishmael's thigh and twisted it. "Want anything?"

Ishmael passed out and went to a place and a particular evening in his childhood he had always associated with disappointment, an evening he had thought he would never want to revisit.

Big Bud had come to their home up a dark valley outside Trinidad, Colorado, with flowers and chocolate for his mother and a whirligig for him. And a promise to take Ishmael on the train to Elitch Gardens in Denver. Not only would he have ridden the roller coaster and pedaled a boat across a lake churning with bronze-backed carp; he would have seen moving pictures filled with Indians trailing feathered bonnets and stagecoaches caroming through clouds of dust, the driver and shotgun guard hanging on for dear life, the passengers firing black-powder weapons out the windows at their pursuers.

He would have been in a theater crowded with children whose mothers and fathers sat next to them, just as he would have been sitting next to his mother and father, the way families did.

But Big Bud and his mother had argued, and Big Bud did not keep his promise and instead went back to Texas on the train and never saw his son again. Now, inside the cage, inside the reek of feces that someone had tried to scrub out of the wood floor with ammonia, he began to create and superimpose a fantasy on his young life.

The sounds and activity outside the cage became the visit to the magical place where the train should have taken him and his father and mother. He saw the three of them spinning in a big teacup mounted on a stanchion that rose and fell against the sky; he saw them eating frozen custard with tiny wooden spoons out of paper cups, and ice cream wrapped inside a waffle, and sausages that were split open and stuffed with cheese and chives and rolled inside a chunk of warm French bread. He saw the three of them walking down the midway, his mother holding one of his hands, his father the other, swinging him over the electric cables that powered the rides. He knew that as long as they held on to each other, nothing in the world would ever be able to harm him.

Where's that fine-looking little chap? he heard his father say.

Right here, Big Bud, he answered.

I cain't find you, son. Where are you hiding?

I've fallen into a dark place. Why did you leave me?

Just hold on. I'll be there. I promise.

You promised before and left us. Why would any father do that to his family?

There was no answer.

Tell me where you are, Big Bud. I know you're out there. Can't you hear me?

Ishmael saw a work boot close by the corner of his eye. "Told you I'd be back," said Fred. He squatted down, a hot dog balanced in one hand. He tilted his head so he could look directly into Ishmael's eyes, and pulled up a chair. "Doesn't look like the drunk wagon is gonna be back. I told the Missing Link he could relax for a while. Look what I got you. A half-pint of white lightning. Open wide. You might have a future here."

Chapter
23

Rᴜʙʏ ᴡᴇɴᴛ ᴛᴏ a café down the street from the hotel where she was staying, and ordered a cup of tea and a plate of black bread with butter and a dish of apricots, and wondered how long her money would last, even if she starved herself.

A day of reckoning was probably at hand, and not the kind the IWW had hoped for. Wilson's imprisonment of pacifists and draft resisters and critics of the war, along with the jailing of union organizers in the western states and the execution of Joe Hill, had fed the agenda of the anarchists and produced a level of violence and fear that was a gift from a divine hand to corporate America.

Ruby finished eating and left a ten-cent tip for the waiter and went outside. In the next two blocks, she could see bars on both sides of the street, a tattoo parlor, pawnshops, stairs on the side of a decrepit building leading to a taxi dance hall upstairs, the windows open, filled with yellow light, the dancers moving like shadows. Again she thought she heard a calliope. She saw a glow beyond a copse of trees on the edge of the city, and a spotlight shining on a hot-air balloon, someone throwing Chinese firecrackers from the gondola, the electric flashes and strings of smoke out of sync with the staccato popping that was like rain clicking on lily pads.

A policeman was standing on the corner. He wore a high-collared brass-buttoned blue jacket and a lacquered helmet, the kind a British bobby might wear.

"Pardon me, is that a circus over there?" she asked.

"No, ma'am, that's the sideshow and the carnival that travels with the circus."

"I see," she said. She watched the balloon rise higher in the sky, the spotlight hitting on its silvery skin like hundreds of mirrors.

The policeman wore a short club and handcuffs on his belt and had a brush mustache and a merry smile. "Would you like to go there?" he asked.

"I was looking for my son. He loved to go to fairs and the circus when he was a little boy. I took him as often as I could."

"Your son lives in San Antonio?"

"You could say he's visiting. He was wounded on the Marne. His name is Ishmael Holland. Is there a jitney or a carriage that could take me to the carnival?"

"Yes, on the next block. You said your son's name is Holland?"

"You know him?"

"Is he related to a former Texas Ranger?"

"Yes, his father is Hackberry Holland."

The policeman's eyes met hers, this time in a different way.

"You know Mr. Holland?" she said.

"Not personally."

"My son shouldn't be walking about. His wounds are probably bleeding."

"That's a peculiar situation you describe, ma'am. I'm having a bit of trouble understanding what's going on here."

"My son fought in a war to help make the crown princes of Europe and Britain richer. The oil reserves in the Arabian deserts weren't a minor issue, either. Now he's impaired."

"Words such as those aren't much welcomed around here."

"That's too bad." She looked again at his eyes. "Was there something you were going to say about Mr. Holland?"

"He shot and killed a man in a colored house of ill repute. The man he shot was a syndicalist. At least that's what they're called hereabouts. Are you feeling all right, ma'am?"

"Yes," she answered, an army of needles marching down her neck and spine.

"You're a socialist?" he said.

"Yes, I am. I'm also a friend of Elizabeth Flynn and Emma Goldman."

"I don't know who those people are. Do you still want to go to the carnival?"

"I don't know if I have enough money for a jitney. Is there public transportation?" she said, the sound of her words unfamiliar, uttered by someone else, like soap bubbles rising one at a time in her throat, her mind unable to shut down the image of Hack Holland killing a union organizer in a brothel.

The policeman reached out and placed his hand lightly on her upper arm. "Steady there."

"I'm quite all right. I spent a long time on the train. I'm a bit tired, that's all. Why did Mr. Holland shoot the union man?"

"I don't know the details. The victim had been in prison for syndicalism. The radicals are upset because he was a war hero and that sort of thing." He waited for her to speak, but she didn't. "My fellow police officer parked down the street owes me a favor," he said. "I'll ask him to drive you to the carnival. Ma'am, did you hear me? Would you like my friend to drive you?"

"Yes. Please. That's very gracious of you."

"This isn't a city to have trouble in." The policeman gazed across the street, where two other policemen were dragging a man in a slug cap and disheveled suit out of an alleyway, through the garbage cans, throwing him onto the sidewalk. "I keep my own counsel about various things. You might do the same."

FOR HACKBERRY, THE end of the day had become a harbinger of death, not simply a gathering of the light on the horizon but a shrinking of it, a compression whereby darkness prevailed over goodness and drew the vestiges of the sun over the earth's edge, obviating the prospect of another sunrise, another spring, one of bluebonnets and buttercups and Indian paintbrush, another chance at undoing the past and reassembling the broken elements of his life.

His father, Sam Morgan Holland, had been a drover and a Confederate soldier and a violent and drunken man with a homicidal temper who had watched his entire herd, two thousand head, spook in dry lightning and turn in to a brown river flowing over the Flint Hills outside Wichita, Kansas. He had cursed God for his bad fortune and stayed drunk all the way back to Texas, and joined those who sat on the mourners' bench at the New Hebron Baptist Church, in despair and beyond the pale.

The terminology depended on a person's education, but the characterization of hopelessness and irrevocable loss was always the same. Women who killed themselves in sod houses in the dead of winter had "cabin fever." Those who studied the mystics called it "the long night of the soul" or "a time in the Garden." Others were simply called self-pitying drunks who were "weak" and would trade their souls for a half cup of whiskey.

Supposedly, Sam Holland found peace when he hung his guns on a peg in a brick jail on the border, and locked the iron door behind him, and rode away to become a saddle preacher on the Chisholm Trail. Hackberry had his doubts about the story. Blood didn't rinse easily from a man's dreams. Nor did memories of irreparable injury done to others.

Hackberry had experienced "spells" since he was a child. A spell could last fifteen minutes or days. The experience was the equivalent of weevil worms eating a hole through his heart while he watched a sky as blue and flawless as silk turn into a giant sheet of carbon paper.

Voices in his head. Night sweats in the middle of the day. Inability to breathe, as though someone had sifted a tablespoon of sand in each of his lungs. A sensation above the left ear that was like a banjo string being tightened around the scalp. People wondered why a man sat down on a stump and upended his shotgun and propped his chin on both barrels?

When he'd found Beatrice DeMolay's bordello in the high desert of central Mexico, he had thought a deliverance was at hand. Instead, he was tortured by fire and in other ways he could not completely remember; he also littered the landscape with the bodies of his tormentors. Then the cup had come into his possession. Was it an accident? Or was there purpose in his discovering it ironically in a hearse filled with ordnance?

As the light died on the horizon and the air cooled and grew dense with a smell like old leaves in a rain barrel, he walked down to the river and sat once again by the tangle of rusted cables where he had buried the cup.

He had read in his encyclopedias about the Arthurian search for the Grail and the stories of Knights Templar who supposedly returned from the Crusades with the shroud and pieces of the cross. He set little store by any of it. The one reference that wouldn't go away, however, was the name of the Grand Master of the Knights Templar. It was Jacques de Molay, burned at the stake in front of Notre Dame Cathedral at the close of the thirteenth century. With a minor contraction of the spelling, the name was the same as Beatrice DeMolay's.

Maybe it was another coincidence. That wasn't a word Hackberry's murderous saddle preacher of a father had much tolerance for. He called coincidence "the Lord acting with anonymity."

Could the cup be real, the one Jesus not only drank from but probably dipped bread in and gave to his disciples? The thought frightened Hackberry, not because the cup had been held by Jesus but because it had been entrusted to *him*, Hackberry Holland, whose record of chaos and mayhem and womanizing and bloodshed was legendary in the worst sense.

According to what he had read, Jacques de Molay had returned from the Holy Land with the shroud that had covered Jesus' body and, some believed, the Holy Grail. He and his fellow knights were arrested en masse on Friday the thirteenth, tortured unmercifully for days and weeks, and sent to their death as idolaters.

Hackberry looked at the evening star winking just above the hill on the far side of the river. He pared his fingernails with a knife and tried to create a blank space in the center of his mind where he could hide and think about absolutely nothing.

Forget about all the great mysteries, he told himself. If anyone ever figured them out, he hadn't seen the instance. What were the real problems confronting him? He had been lured into shooting and killing a man who was probably mentally impaired, someone who had been burned so badly he resembled a mannequin. Second, the issue with the cup was not about the cup but the fact that Arnold Beckman wanted it. And if Arnold Beckman wanted something, it was to make the earth a much worse place than it already was.

Hackberry rested his hand by the rusty coils of cable. What an unsuitable place for the cup, covered by the industrial detritus of the twentieth century. Time to move it. But where?

How did a cottontail elude his pursuers? He ran in a circle, then went down a hole or crossed water and left his enemy chasing a scent that had no end. A Comanche Indian up on the Staked Plains did the same: In blazing heat, in the midst of summer drought, he would put a pebble under his tongue to cause his mouth to salivate, then wander in circles and figure eights until the canteens of his pursuers were empty, and attack them at the end of a burning day. Hackberry would hide the cup in a place where Arnold Beckman's people had already been. The cave. Strange. According to the legends recounted in his encyclopedias, the cup had been hidden in a cave in southern France or perhaps western England, the last redoubt of the Celts.

He went back to the barn for a shovel. He thought he heard the phone ringing inside the house but paid no attention to it. He pulled on his gloves and stripped the tangle of cable free from the ground and threw it down the slope into the shallows. The ground was as loamy and soft as coffee grinds when he pressed down on the shovel blade and eased it under the box he had wrapped with a tarp and a rain slicker.

Then a phenomenon took place that had to be the result of natural causes. He was almost certain of this. The full moon had just broken through the clouds, as bright as silver plate. As he dumped the dirt off the blade of his shovel, the ground and air sparkled as though he had dug into a pocket of pollen. *Pyrite,* he told himself. The same false indicator that had sent James Bowie chasing after legends and silver and gold in San Saba County. Hackberry picked up the box and refilled the hole, stamping it down, ridding himself of thoughts about ancient myths and Crusader knights on the road to Roncesvalles or wherever they could bloody a sword in the name of Christianity.

Once again, he heard the phone ringing.

RUBY GOT OUT of the policeman's car and walked up the midway of the carnival. The hot-air balloon was now directly overhead, anchored by a rope, a man in a straw boater and a candy-striped coat tossing buckets of confetti and paper-wrapped taffy to the children below. But something was wrong. The people in the midway had divided into two groups. The larger crowd had gathered directly under the balloon, the children's hands outreached toward the gondola. Others had formed a crowd in front of a cage. When a child wandered away from the larger group toward the cage, a parent would rush over to him and immediately drag him back, fighting.

Ruby tried to see over the shoulders of the crowd gathered in front of the cage, one with wire mesh and bars. "What's happening up there?" she said to the man in front of her.

His teeth were the size of an elk's, his eyes as small as dimes. "The geek show. He's supposed to be the Missing Link. More like a rummy making a few dollars and having some fun."

Through the heads and hats and bonnets and thick necks and broad backs, Ruby saw a man trying to get to his feet inside the cage, then slipping on his buttocks, his clothes and skin streaked with filth. She felt her heart knock against her ribs, her breath rush out of her throat.

She tried to push her way through the crowd. The people around her smelled of sweat that had dried inside wool, onions and greasy meat, malt, unwashed hair, decayed teeth, and deodorant compounds smeared under their armpits. A man hit her in the breast with his elbow; a woman screwed her face into a knot and said, "Be careful who you're pushing, Swede."

Ruby went back through the crowd into the midway and circled behind the game booths until she found the door of the cage. Three men were sitting at a wood table outside it, drinking Coca-Cola and smoking. They wore badges and suspenders without coats and hats that shadowed their faces. One was short and wore a piece of tape across his nose; there was blood on his collar and the front of his shirt. An ax handle lay by his foot.

"Who are you?" she asked.

"The law. What can we do for you?" the short man said.

"No, you're not. You're ginks. That's my son in that cage. Did you put him in there?"

The tallest of the three put out his cigarette on the sole of his boot and took a sip from his Coca-Cola, gazing at nothing. "He was drunk and started a fight. We put him in there for his own protection. The city police are going to pick him up."

"You're a liar."

"He shouldn't have got drunk. If you want to take him home, be our guest," the same man said.

"What are your names?"

"Eeny, Meany, Miny, Moe. As in catch a nigger by his toe," the short man said. "Moe ain't here." The other two men tilted down their hat brims to hide their grins.

"My son was at the Marne. Where were you?" she said. "I promise you'll be held accountable for this."

"My name is Fred," the short man said. "That man in yonder assaulted me. To make sure everything is on the table, I bought him a bottle of moonshine. I could've had him locked up for six months. If I was you, I'd tuck my lower lip back in my mouth."

"What's your last name?"

"Beemer. Fred J. Beemer." He opened a pouch of string chewing tobacco and filled his jaw. He chewed it slowly and spat a long stream in the grass. "Nothing like a little Red Man."

"My name is Ruby Dansen. I want you to remember it."

"I'll carve it on my heart," Fred Beemer replied.

She pulled open the back door of the cage and stepped inside. The spotlights on the midway were iridescent, eye-watering, rimmed with humidity. Someone had cut Ishmael's belt in half and his trousers and undershorts had slipped down on his buttocks. His palms were printed with peanut shells and wet cigarette butts. His skull seemed translucent and red against the brilliance of the light. The people watching him through the wire mesh had the faces an artist would paint on a medieval mob—lantern-jawed, beetle-browed, unshaved, hair growing from their ears and noses, teeth the color of urine. They were the kind of people who attended public executions and delighted in blood sports. Were these the people to whom she had devoted her life?

She got to her knees and pulled Ishmael partially erect. Then she worked herself onto a chair and got his weight across her thighs, so he lay spread across her lap, his arms hanging loose behind him, the bones in his chest as pronounced as barrel staves, his face puffed, his eyes half-lidded.

The crowd stared at her, leering, fascinated.

"What have you done to my son?" she asked. "What have you done to my darling son?"

Chapter 24

THE CLOCK ON the kitchen windowsill said 9:03 when Hackberry answered the telephone. Outside, the sky was black, grit blowing against the pane. "Will you accept a long-distance call from Ruby Dansen?" the operator asked.

"Yes," he said, a stone dropping inside him.

"Go ahead," the operator said to the caller, then went off the line.

"Ruby?" Hackberry said.

"Who else?"

"Where are you?" he said.

"San Antonio. Ishmael is hurt. In a cage at a carnival. It's too much to explain. Can you come?"

"Ishmael is in San Antonio?"

"He's been living with Maggie. He left her house on foot and ended up at a fairgrounds. Some ginks with badges got their hands on him. He has bruises all over him."

"Why would they want to hurt Ishmael?"

"Their kind don't need an excuse. They treated him like an animal. They put him on exhibit."

"They did *what*?"

"I have to go. Can you come or not?"

"I don't have a car, and I don't know how to drive. I'll have to call somebody. Where are you now?"

271

"At the café by the fairgrounds, waiting on an ambulance. I have little money."

She told him the name of the hotel where she was staying. He remembered it vaguely, a place for transients, single men at the end of the track.

"Don't worry about money. Where's Maggie?" he asked.

"How would I know? Why did she take Ishmael out of the army hospital? Why this sudden surge of charity?"

"I quit trying to figure her out many years ago. Who put Ishmael in the cage?"

"There were three of them. One said his name was Fred Beemer. Fred J. Beemer."

Hackberry wrote on a pad. "They're deputies?"

"No."

"How do you know they're not?"

"Do deputy sheriffs in San Antonio carry ax handles?"

"I'll do everything I can to get there as soon as possible," he said.

"Maggie said she was arranging an executive position of some kind for Ishmael. Who is she working for, Hack?"

"I'd like to say the devil. But it's probably worse. The name Arnold Beckman comes to mind."

"Who?"

"I want to see you, Ruby. I've been wanting to see you an awful long time."

"Hurry, please," she said.

He gave her the name of a hospital. "Make sure the ambulance takes him there. It's the best. They're all busting at the seams with influenza patients."

WILLARD POSEY SENT a deputy to pick up Hackberry. An hour and a half later, he was at the hospital in San Antonio where he was supposed to meet Ruby, except there was no sign of Ruby and no record of a patient named Ishmael Holland. "They were here," Hackberry said to the woman at the admissions desk.

"I'm afraid they were not," she replied. "But I'll tell you who is: all the influenza patients on the gurneys in the hallway."

He and the deputy drove to the fairgrounds. It was Saturday night, and except for the carousel, the rides and concessions were open late, the ragged popping of rifles and the smell of gunpowder drifting from the shooting gallery. The deputy was a tall redheaded boy named Darl Pickins who wore a knit sweater with his badge pinned to it. Up ahead, on the midway, Hackberry saw a dunking booth where a waterlogged man of color was wiping himself off with a towel, preparing to retake his place on the dunking stool. A little farther on was a cage with a sign over it that read THE MISSING LINK.

"Darl, why don't you go back to the café across the street and have a cup of coffee?" Hackberry said. "I'll be along directly."

"Sheriff Posey said I'm supposed to stick with you."

"I bet he did. But right now I've got everything covered. I need you at the café in case Miss Ruby shows up there. If you're not there, she won't know where we're at."

"Yes, sir, I see what you mean."

"Then why aren't you headed to the café?"

"Sheriff Posey says you tend to get into things."

"The sheriff exaggerates and is a big kidder on top of it. Trust me on this."

"Yes, sir."

"Good-bye, now."

"I'll be at the café."

"That's the place to be," Hackberry said.

He walked to the cage. A man in rubber boots was hosing off the floor, skidding a gray froth of straw and water through the bars. Hackberry opened his coat, exposing his badge. "I'm looking for Fred Beemer and a couple of his colleagues."

"Down by the barbecue tent," the man with the hose replied, not looking up. "Doin' nothing, I suspect. They're good at it."

Hackberry continued down the midway, past the Ferris wheel, into a poorly lighted area where a purple-and-white-striped canopy rippled in the wind and three men sat at a table in front of an empty stage, eating barbecued ribs with their fingers. No one else was in the tent. In their peaked hats and long-sleeved cotton shirts, with their flat stomachs and tightly belted trousers, they could have been mistaken for lawmen of years ago—except for their inability to hold their eyes steadily on his as he approached their table.

"I heard y'all had some trouble."

"No, sir, no trouble here," one said. "Indigestion, maybe."

Hackberry looked casually over his shoulder, back down the midway, then at the men again. "Something to do with the Missing Link act. It is an act, isn't it? That's not a real missing link in there?"

"Search me," said a man with a strip of tape across his nose. "Why are you interested?"

"No reason. Is that an ax handle?"

"Possums wander in at night and chew on the electric lines. Who are you?"

"I'm a deputy sheriff over in Kerr County. I was looking for Mr. Beemer."

"What for?" the man with the taped nose asked.

"He's the fellow I'm supposed to see about the man y'all had to lock up."

"Why's Kerr County interested in a drunk man and drug addict in San Antonio?" the tallest of the three men asked. His teeth were tiny, hardly bigger than a baby's, his whiskers grayish brown, soft-looking, like winter fur on a squirrel.

"The man you refer to as a drunk and drug addict is my son."

The tall man lifted his face, so the colored lights from the Ferris wheel fell across it. "A woman took him away. She said she was his mother. I'd say she was a pain in the ass."

"How'd she take him away?"

"We didn't pay it no mind," the same man said.

"My son got blown up in France. From my understanding, he had a pint of metal in his lower body. Why would y'all put my boy in a cage?"

"Because he fell down in a puddle of water that had a power cable running through it," Beemer said.

"You put me in mind of the Sundance Kid," Hackberry said. "The way you scrunch your shoulders and tilt up your chin. I knew him and Harvey Logan, both."

"*I* look like the Sundance Kid?"

"Hand on the Bible. Logan was a dyed-in-the-wool killer and a five-star lamebrain. Sundance was just a lamebrain. Not even one-star."

"We were just doing our job," Beemer said. "Did we mention your son was stirring up nigger trouble?"

Hackberry pulled back his coat flap and hung it behind the butt of his holstered Peacemaker. "Could I see your ax handle?"

"Let's hold on there a minute," the tall man said.

"It's a little late for that. Things get loose on you, and you look back and nobody can figure out how it went downhill so fast. It's a dad-burned mystery."

"We can talk this thing out," the tall man said, his face marbled with the glow from the Ferris wheel, the skin under one eye twitching.

What Hackberry did next he did without a plan, without even heat or passion, except to ensure that Beemer received just due and the others were treated as adverbs rather than nouns. In reality, he went about the destruction of the three men as though chopping wood or breaking up old furniture or packing cases for burning. He beat them until they cowered on their knees, then he beat them some more, stomping their faces and heads into the soft dampness of the grass, spilling their half-eaten food on top of them. Then he pulled their wallets from their trousers and took a piece of identification from each man and tossed their wallets in their faces.

All three men were carrying a business card with the name of Arnold Beckman's company on it.

"Try to make more trouble for us, and I'll be looking you up," Hackberry said.

He wiped his hands on a towel, propped the ax handle neatly against a chair, and walked back down the midway to rejoin Darl

Pickins at the café, the carousel coming to life for no reason, the wooden horses whirling without riders.

MAGGIE BASSETT FOUND herself biting her lip in her living room, unable to gather her thoughts and rebuild her mental fortifications, staring out the window at the ruins of the Spanish mission to distract herself. How do you deliver bad news to a man who does not tolerate bad news but demands to hear it as soon as it happens? Better said, how do you report bad news to a man who requires full candor but is enraged by it?

She had one of the new candlestick telephones, made of brass, with a dial on it. It always gave her pleasure to use it. Now it felt like a lump of ice as she dialed Arnold Beckman's number.

As always, he didn't speak when he answered the phone, deliberately making his caller feel off guard, invasive, vaguely guilty.

"Arnold?" she said.

"It's you, Maggie," he said brightly. "What can I do for my favorite lass?"

"I don't know where Ishmael is."

"He ran off from your charms?"

"I'm serious."

She waited in the silence, a creaking sound in her ears, as though she were slipping to the bottom of a lake, its weight about to crush her skull. "Arnold?"

"How. Can. A. Crippled. Man. Disappear?"

"We had an argument."

"You know I do not like to repeat myself."

"Maybe he took a jitney. He was walking with his canes. He couldn't have gone far."

"Then why are you not out looking for the people who drive jitneys in your neighborhood? Or searching the ditches? Why are we having this conversation?"

"I've done everything you've asked. Everything doesn't always work out like we plan."

"When it doesn't work out, you fix it. But instead of fixing it, you've

called me. Our little girl wants her daddy to clean up her mess. Not a good attitude. What are we going to do about that, little Maggie?"

She felt a flush in her cheeks, a fish bone in her throat, words forming that she dared not speak. "I felt my first obligation was to apprise you of the situation. I plan to drive around town to places where he might have gone. He was drinking when he left. He's probably drinking now."

Before she had finished speaking, she felt weak, sycophantic, submissive to a man she secretly abhorred. She was breathing into the receiver, hoping he did not sense her fear and self-loathing. His words injured her in the same way her father's had, like paper cuts that she hid and nursed and carried until he unleashed more damage on her. When would it end? Only when she was able to vanquish her father's memory by either undoing Arnold Beckman or proving herself his equal. And the fact that she gave Arnold Beckman that kind of power only made her hate herself more. How sick could a person be?

"Are you there?" she asked.

"Indeed, my love."

"What do you want me to do?"

"Just continue being the lovely piece you are. You are a lovely piece, you know. And I've had it on every continent, with every race and every age. You're every man's wet dream, Maggie."

She felt her breath coming harder in her chest, her left hand opening and closing spasmodically, the nails pressing into her palm. She tried to speak firmly, to pretend she had not heard what he'd just said. "I'll take care of it. I shouldn't have let this happen. It's my fault."

"Don't worry. I'll send some men out. Did he hurt you or get out of hand, that sort of thing?"

"No, he's not like that."

"You still have the motherly touch. That's good. That's why I like you, Maggie. Having you in my stable is like having half a dozen women in one. I never know who I'm talking to. You're an absolute delight. I'm glad you're not a man. I might be afraid of you."

She heard a whirring sound in her ears, the same sound she had heard when she pressed her head against her mother's breast as a child. Why did she have memories of this kind? Why couldn't she catalog and compartmentalize her thoughts and deal with them one by one so they didn't control her life? Why couldn't she understand the tangled web that comprised her mind?

"I never know what to say to you," she said.

"Look on the light side of it. Maybe you spent too much time on your back. A touch of the wrong lad, and it shows up in the brain years later. Let's face it, you knew some scruffy characters. Hello?"

She was unable to speak.

"I'm just kidding," he said. "Don't be such a bloody prude. We're cut out of the same cloth. We're interlopers. That's why the people who sit at my table and eat my food and drink my wine hate the pair of us."

She lowered the receiver, widening her eyes, stretching her face, letting out her breath. She put the receiver to her ear again. "I forgive you for being obnoxious and vulgar, Arnold. I guess you came out of the womb that way. But you'll never speak to me like that again."

"That's my girl. Hang their scrotums on the point of your knife. Now get out there and find your war hero. We have an empire to build, Maggie. I want you to be my queen. You're an Amazon. Your thighs could span the Strait of Gibraltar."

She didn't say good-bye but simply hung the receiver back on the hook and looked at it as though his voice lived inside it. She was wondering if there was such a thing as the human soul. If so, how did one explain the existence of a man like Beckman? And if so, wasn't her soul already forfeit? Wasn't it better to believe in nothing than to make oneself miserable trying to solve mysteries the human mind couldn't fathom? Was not all of mankind adrift on a dark sea, without hope, at the mercy of undercurrents and waves as high as mountains?

Outside, the light had gone out of the sky and a burst of rain-flecked wind blew open one of the French doors, scattering leaves and pine needles on the rug, filling her house with the tang of late autumn and the holiday season. She had never felt more alone in her life.

AFTER ISHMAEL HAD been refused admission at the hospital and the ambulance had left on another call, Ruby had asked a jitney driver to drive her to a different hospital.

"It's the same all over town. More sick people than beds," he said.

"What about the army posts?"

"Fort Sam Houston and Camp Travis are quarantined because of influenza. I wouldn't get near either one of them."

"There has to be someplace I can take him."

"I know a clinic," he said. "It's not much, but they have medicine."

He drove them across the river into a bowl-like area dotted with shacks and mud-walled hovels. A dirty haze from the stacks of a rendering plant hung like strips of gauze above the rooftops. The electricity was out on the street where the clinic was located, and the glass on the oil lamps burning in the foyers was black with smoke; flashlights moved behind the windows.

She gazed at the litter in the open ditches, the privies that were nothing more than a chunk of concrete pipe screwed into a hole, the animal carcasses along the road, a corrugated shed by a stream where clothing was spread on the rocks to dry. "This is the Mexican district?" she said.

"Most of them are wets and don't bother nobody," the driver said. "They don't want to get sent back across the river, if that's what you're asking."

Women in shawls and men's coats and work shoes, carrying children in their arms or holding them by the hand, were gathered in the foyers. None of them looked injured or sick, simply tired and afraid and confused, as though waiting to be told what to do.

"Why are all these people here?" she asked.

"One of those sleeping cars for gandy dancers got hit by a line of freight cars on the wrong spur. It was one of those three-deckers, about as solid as an orange crate. They're still bringing them in."

"Do you know anyone in there? I don't speak Spanish."

"Sorry, I got to get back to the depot. That's where I get most of my fares."

She rolled down the window. An odor struck her face like a fist.

"Better roll it back up, ma'am," the driver said. "In back, they burn waste and bandages and things I won't mention."

"Pull up in front. You have to help me carry him in."

"I'm sorry, I have to go."

"No, you don't. You brought me here, and you're not leaving until my son is safely inside. Come around this side and help me lift him up."

The driver fiddled with his cap.

"Did you hear me?" she said.

"Yes, ma'am," he replied. "If you can pay me first, please."

The two of them got Ishmael inside and laid him in a hallway on a wood pallet covered by a blanket and a stained mattress pad. Amid the shadows and the flashlight beams and the press of bodies and people tripping over the patients on the floor and the incessant sound of coughing, Ruby tried to get the attention of anyone who could help. She knelt by Ishmael and formed a tent over him by propping her arms on either side of his shoulders. She twisted her head and tried to speak to the driver. "I'll stay here. You go find a doctor and tell him—"

The driver was gone. Through the entranceway, she saw a pair of headlights drive up the rutted road and disappear.

She got to her feet and began pulling the pallet closer to the wall, away from the flow of traffic through the hallway, the splinters tearing her flesh. She got on her knees and pushed, working the pallet an inch at a time into the shadows, between two other patients, away from the faces of frightened children in the flashlight beams, a nurse trying to squeeze through with an overflowing bedpan.

"There," Ruby said to Ishmael, even though his eyes were closed. "That will do for the time being. I promise I'll get us out of this. There are patients on either side of us. No one can step on us now. Can you hear me, Ishmael? Open your eyes. Please. Say something."

He did neither. She shook the person on the pallet next to Ishmael's. "Who's in charge here? Give me a name. I don't speak Spanish. Can you understand me? What is the name of the man in charge? I'm sorry to bother you, but you must wake up. Does no one here speak English?"

Then she realized she was addressing herself to a Mexican woman whose facial wrinkles were dissolving into the bloodless and pale and featureless anonymity of the dead. For a moment she thought she would weep.

Someone shone a light on Ruby's head. "Who are you? How did

you get in here?" a man's voice said. He was bald and potbellied and wore a white smock stippled with blood. "Who gave you permission to put that man here?"

"No one did. He's my son. He needs help."

"What's wrong with him?"

"He has shrapnel wounds all over his legs. Maybe they're infected. Maybe something is broken. He was beaten at the carnival."

"Move out of the way," the physician said, shining the light on Ishmael's face. "You shouldn't have put him here. All these people are contagious. Hold this."

He stuck the flashlight in Ruby's hand and knelt down and felt Ishmael's throat and lifted one of his arms, rolling back the sleeve. Then he unbuttoned Ishmael's shirt and trousers and felt his ribs and pulled the trousers lower and probed his abdomen and examined the bandages on his thighs. He took the flashlight back. "He smells like a distillery."

"Don't you dare talk about him like that. Half of Texas smells like a distillery. The half made up of Baptist hypocrites."

"You brought him to the wrong place. Get him out of here."

"He was wounded fighting for his country."

"This entire neighborhood will probably be quarantined. Do you want to spend the next six months inside this clinic?"

"We're already here. You have to help him. We have no other place to go."

"If you don't get him out of here, I will."

"No, you won't. If you try to eject him, I'll gouge your eyes out, and you'll have to perform your next surgery by touch. I pulled murdered children out of the cellar at Ludlow. Don't tell me your troubles."

The physician stood up and clicked off the light. She stood up also, her face no more than a foot from his. A nurse jostled against him and kept going. The physician didn't take his eyes off Ruby's. He removed a pair of scissors from a pocket in his smock. "Start with the bandages. I'll bring you a pan and a washcloth and some alcohol and iodine. Who beat him?"

"Ginks with badges. They said he started a fight. That's not true. He's a gentle boy. One of the ginks had an ax handle."

"I'll be back shortly. Don't touch the woman lying next to you. She may have had typhoid. I believe you're a brave woman, madam. But every night is Ludlow here."

For the next half hour, Ruby peeled strips of adhesive and gauze, yellow and stiff and crusted with salve, from Ishmael's wounds. Surprisingly, they were free of blood. She washed him all over as best she could in the semidarkness, stroking his brow, rebuttoning his shirt, reassuring him even though he seemed unconscious. The smells of ether and carbolic and iodine and an odor like woolen clothes that hadn't been hung in the sun for months began to feel natural, the way fog was, the way the hospital tent at Ludlow had been, the way the huddled masses carried with them a level of suffering and courage that few understood.

She had been self-righteous and too hard on the doctor, and she knew that if it were not for his kindness, the world would be much worse off. Still, she could not free herself of the collective face of the crowd who had watched her son's degradation inside the cage at the carnival. Didn't they understand who the enemy was, the ones who gave them bread and circuses and kept their attention directed elsewhere while they despoiled the earth and cheated and robbed the treasury and kept working people poor and uneducated? Why did the human race band together to participate in its own victimization?

Sometimes she wanted to dash her fists on the faces of the people she served. Was she more of an elitist than she thought? There were moments when she believed her social causes were manufactured, that her anger had more to do with her abandonment by Hackberry Holland than the suffering of masses. What a joke that would be. Years of devotion to a self-manufactured illusion, all because of a man. What would Emma Goldman have to say about that?

But as always, when she fell into self-destructive introspection, she had to remember an old lesson she had taught herself. People were not what they said. They were not what they thought. They were not what they promised. People were what they did. When the final tally was done, nothing else mattered.

Three feet away, a small boy was crying and holding on to his mother, who lay on a pallet, her lips congealed with a dry, gelatinous film. The mother was moaning, her eyes bright with fever, straw clinging to her hair and clothes.

"What's wrong with your mother?" Ruby asked the boy.

"She don't have water," he said. "There ain't no water."

"That's silly. Of course there's water. I'll watch your mother. You go ask the nurse for water."

"There's a big line at the faucet in the back. I ain't got a can." In spite of his tears, his face was dry, like a baked apple. He wore shoes without socks and a man's cap and two long-sleeved shirts instead of a coat.

"You stay right here and watch your mother. I'll be right back," she said. "That's my son, Ishmael. You have to watch him for me. Can you do that?"

He looked at her, uncertain. He started to speak, then stopped, as though he couldn't remember what he should say. His face started to crumble. "Is she going to die?"

Ruby bent over, eye-level with him. "No, we're not going to let that happen. Don't be afraid. Never be afraid and never be sad. Not for any reason. That's how we win. We never give up and we're never sad."

"I heard the doctor tell the nurse she might die. He was talking about moving her body. Why would the doctor say that if she's going to be all right?"

Ruby hugged the boy's head against her stomach, then worked her way to the rear of the building and out the back door, where she discovered what had happened to the water supply. The water line to the neighborhood had been cut in the train accident, and because the clinic had a cistern, everyone in the neighborhood had come to draw water from it. The only light in the backyard came from a metal barrel filled with burning scrap wood. A long line of people with buckets and tin cans and glass jars was strung from the faucet through the dirt yard into the alley, the firelight and shadows dancing on their faces.

She wondered if this were what hell was about. Not a place of punishment but of disparity. Those who had done nothing to earn their fate lived like this, while three miles away, others rode the Ferris wheel and children raised their hands joyfully to a hot-air balloon that rained down candy on their heads.

She bought a syrup can for a dime from an old man and waited her turn at the spigot. Between the buildings, she saw the headlights of two black four-door motorcars going up the street and circling back. The cars were too big, the paint too shiny and new, for the neighborhood. One of the cars had a bell with a clapper attached to the driver's door, the kind of bell police vehicles carried.

Five minutes later, she filled the syrup can and went back into the building. She almost collided with the little boy who thought his mother might die. "The doctor gave her some medicine," he said. "They're moving her to a bed." He reached out to take the syrup can from her hands.

"How's my son?" she asked.

The boy's face went blank. "They took him away. They must have found him a bed."

"Who's 'they'?"

"Two men. They picked him up from the floor and carried him out."

"Out where?"

"I don't know. They said everything was all right. I told them I was supposed to watch him. They said I did a good job. They work here, don't they?"

He caught the syrup can before it could hit the ground.

IN ISHMAEL'S DREAM, he revisited a scene that had less to do with war than with the aberrations it produced, images that were literally unimaginable because they had no precedent and their probability was nil and a witness had no way of possessing the empirical information or scientific knowledge that would allow him to understand what his eyes told him.

Ishmael had heard of experiments with phosphorous artillery shells but had never seen one fired. A rumor spread that the Brits on their flank were throwing a new type of grenade into Fritz's wire, with devastating effect. But what could be worse than a flamethrower or mustard gas or a direct hit on a field hospital by Big Bertha, a mortar that could blow a barn-size hole in the earth?

He saw an event that proved to him once and for all man's limitless ingenuity in manufacturing weaponry that canceled the laws of physics and created situations for which no one, particularly the victim, could have prepared himself.

The Germans had attacked before dawn, dressed in their green-gray uniforms that blended with the fog and the ruined landscape, wearing their bucket helmets and goggled gas masks, like space aliens, the wands on their flamethrowers flaring alight in two-second bursts.

The Brits began heaving grenades in their midst, throwing them like baseballs. The explosions took on the shape of giant furry spiders, the legs white and puffy and broken, thick as a man's thigh in one moment, spindly in the next, arching up and trailing down, all in an incandescent second.

Ishmael expected the screams to follow, as they always did when they were trapped inside a burning tank or when flames roared from the gun slits in a concrete pillbox. That wasn't what happened. The Germans who survived the initial explosion dropped their rifles and kept moving toward the British wire, their uniforms rent with pockets of the most intense, purest white light Ishmael had ever seen. The Germans made no sound, as though the trauma were of such magnitude that the human voice could not do it justice. The phosphorous burned its way through their bodies, punching holes that seemed to open on to infinity. And still no sound came from their throats. Only after someone began spraying them with a Lewis did they crumple and disappear inside the ground fog.

Later, Ishmael always referred to them as "the light bearers," and not in an ironic or cynical fashion. He saw them in his dreams with regularity and had come to think of them as friends who had seen the reality of war and knew the limits of human endurance, with whom he would never have to argue about the insanity of the modern era.

As he lay on the floor of the clinic, he felt someone lifting him to his feet and placing a blanket over his shoulders. His eyes were leaden, his head on his chest, but he was sure he was once again in the hands of friends, and they would take him to a safe place where he would never have to worry about anything.

Chapter 25

HACKBERRY AND HIS fellow deputy, Darl Pickins, could not find Ruby or Ishmael anywhere in San Antonio. Maggie Bassett's house was dark and locked and the motorcar gone. The clerk at Ruby's hotel said she had put her key in the box earlier in the evening, and he had not seen her since. Hackberry left a note.

"There's one other place," Darl said. "Across the river. A shantytown. The clinic there is sort of a dumping ground."

"For what?"

"Whatever the county won't treat." Darl put a piece of gum in his mouth and chewed while he drove and gazed out the side window at a *cervecería* hung with lights, the girls leaning against the wall outside, smoking cigarillos. One of the front tires slammed down hard in a rocky hole.

"I'm not in a good mood, Darl."

"They handle just about anything except dogs with rabies. Most of the wets go there. The hookers go there because the county would report them to the state health department, and they wouldn't be able to work. Can I ask you a question, Mr. Holland?"

"My title is Deputy."

"It don't seem respectful."

"What is it you need to know, Darl?"

"Did something happen while I was at the café and you was over at the fairgrounds?"

"Nothing of world importance, I'd say."

"Because this guy went walking past the café real fast, saying a crazy person tore the hell out of the three guys with an ax handle. More or less jumped up and down on their faces, too."

"Probably a Bolshevik agitator of some kind. I mean the man spreading rumors. That's how the Reds work. Always stirring up people's imagination. Would you drive us across the river now?"

"Yes, sir. Deputy Holland, we're on the same side, ain't we?"

"That's a funny question to ask."

"No, sir, it ain't," Darl replied, looking straight ahead.

They rumbled across the river on a wooden bridge and parked in front of the clinic. It was two-fifteen A.M. The electricity in the neighborhood was off, the building dark, the oil lamps in the foyer extinguished. A Mexican woman working by a battery-powered lamp in the small admissions office said no one by the name of Holland had been formally admitted to the clinic the previous night or that morning.

"He's big, like me. His legs are bad," Hackberry said. "He may have been beaten."

The woman shook her head.

"The lady who would have brought him here is named Ruby Dansen. She's a handsome woman. She looks like a Swede. Talks like a Yankee."

"No, I don't remember anybody like that."

"I do," a nurse said from the doorway. "She and a jitney operator brought the man in. They didn't stop at the desk. They put him on a pallet. She went out back and got in line to fill a water can for an influenza patient."

"Where is she?" Hackberry said, his heart pressing against his side.

"She and her friends took the man away," the nurse replied. "No, wait a minute. Some men in a black car came inside and lifted him up. Maybe she helped them carry him out, I don't remember. I know she was close by. We were terribly busy. I remember a little boy thanking her for helping his mother."

"Where did they take my son?" Hackberry said. "Who were the men in the black car?"

"I don't know. I'm sorry," the nurse said.

Hackberry felt Darl's hand on his shoulder. "We cain't do no good here, Mr. Holland. Let's go. We'll find him. I promise."

But they didn't find him. And when Hackberry returned home at six that morning, the sun looked like a broken egg yolk on the horizon, the fog on the river as toxic as the haze on the Styx.

He slept on the living room couch so he could hear the telephone if it rang. When he woke, he fixed coffee and eggs and a slice of ham on his woodstove, then ate and washed his face and brushed his teeth and shaved and put on fresh clothes. Through the front window, he saw a raccoon walking along the porch railing, his fat ringed tail flicking back and forth like a spring. Hackberry filled a bowl with fish scraps from the icebox, and a second bowl with water, and took them out on the porch and set them down not far from the raccoon. "Here you go, Poindexter. Chomp it down."

Then he saw a sight he wouldn't have believed he would ever see. Cod Bishop was coming up his lane on a groomed long-legged red gelding, sitting on an English saddle, wearing immaculate white jodhpurs and black knee-high boots and a riding cap strapped tightly under his chin. In his right hand, he held a tissue-wrapped box with blue ribbon tied around it. His face had the solemnity of a prune.

"Good morning, Mr. Holland," he said. "Looks like you have a fat little friend there."

"That's Poindexter. What are you after, Cod?"

"A word. May I get down?"

"I'm running behind on my chores at the moment."

"Do me the courtesy, sir."

Hackberry pulled his gold watch from his pocket and opened the cover and looked at it. Then he looked at the river and the bluffs and the fields but not at Bishop. "Get down if you like."

"Thank you." Bishop stepped as gracefully from the stirrup as a man half his age, his lips pursed. It was not Bishop's patrician airs that bothered Hackberry, or the way his long back bowed inward like a buggy whip, or the imperious cut of his profile; it was the meanness of spirit he disguised under any number of banners. There was no war he did not like, no cheap idea he did not support, no uncharitable, self-righteous cause aimed at the defenseless that he did not make his own. In moments like these, Hackberry sometimes wondered why anyone should object to a three-day open season on people in order to clean up most of the world's problems.

"I brought you some bonbons," Bishop said.

"You brought me candy?"

"I know we haven't been the best of neighbors. I'd like to make that right."

"Not on my account."

"Would you accept this gift?"

"Would you tell me what this is about, please?"

Bishop set the tissue-wrapped box on the top step. "I've formally broken off my association with Mr. Beckman." His words had held together until the mention of Beckman's name. Then an inflection like a loose electric wire crept into his voice.

"Why would you be ending your friendship with Beckman at this particular time, Cod?"

"I made a mistake. I got into a situation I shouldn't have." Bishop cleared his throat. "Would you forgive me, Mr. Holland?"

Hackberry shook his head. "No, sir, I cain't do that."

"Your father was a saddle preacher. Would he not advise you to forgive when someone offers his apology?"

"I think you waded out too far in the creek and got scared. I also think this has to do with my son's disappearance."

"I know nothing about that."

Hackberry picked up the raccoon from the porch and flipped him up on a shoulder. "Where's my boy?"

"Sir, I'm at a loss. I've come here in good faith. I'm a businessman who used bad judgment, and I want to own up to it."

"I think you know what happened to my boy. I also think Beckman hired you to spy on me."

"That's not true."

"Just what is it you have that he wants?"

Bishop wet his lips and blinked.

"That shouldn't be a difficult question," Hackberry said.

"Representation. That's what I was going to give him. Representation."

"He's an arms dealer. He's friends with princes and kings and Mexican generals like Villa. Why does he need to come to a hole in a road like this for representation? Stop fooling yourself."

"I shouldn't have come here."

"I've seen Beckman's handiwork up close, Cod. You're in bed with a snake. He staked out a *campesino* down in Mexico and let his men have at it. Want to hear the details?"

"No," Bishop said, a red knot blooming on his neck.

"Cod, if I lose my son, I cain't tell you what I'll do." Hackberry set down the raccoon on the porch and watched him waddle back to his bowl. He looked at Bishop again. "The thought of it scares me."

"I'll go now, Mr. Holland. I'll take back the gift. It was presumptuous of me."

Hackberry stared across the river at the willow trees on the bank and the stretch of sandy beach and the smooth, hard-packed path that led to the cave among the bluffs. "What did you tell Beckman about me? What did you do behind my back that scares you so bad?"

"I don't remember particulars. He bears you a grudge about something that happened in Mexico. I told him—" Bishop wiped his mouth, his eyes misting.

"Go on," Hackberry said.

"He said not to worry about you. That eventually you would fall on your own sword. He said you're one of those men who actually seeks his own death."

"He's probably right," Hackberry replied. "But it won't happen today. And when the time comes, I might have a lot of company for the trip across."

Bishop mounted his horse, his left hand shaking on the reins. He turned his horse in a circle, his face white. "You won't tell him, will you?"

"Tell who what?"

"Beckman. About our conversation. I ask this one favor of you."

"You're on your own, Cod. I'd better not find out you've held on to information about my son."

"Sir, can you show me a little respect? Just a little. We're both gentlemen."

"Tell that to the darkies you burned out of their homes."

Hackberry went back into the house just as the phone rang. It was Ruby.

SHE TOLD HIM of everything that had happened at the clinic in the Mexican district. She also said she had gone to the police and the sheriff's department.

"You told them about the motorcar with the bell on it?" he asked.

"Yes, the police said they don't go beyond the city limits. A deputy at the sheriff's department said their motorcars don't have bells."

"You're sure the car had a bell? On the driver's side?"

"Yes."

"Then someone is lying," he said.

"You believe the police or the sheriff's department abducted Ishmael?"

"I think it was somebody who works for Arnold Beckman."

"That's the second time you mentioned that name."

"He buys and sells arms all over the world. He believes I stole his property down in Mexico in 1916."

"What were you doing in Mexico?"

"Looking for Ishmael."

"You stole something from this Beckman man and he's holding Ishmael until he gets it back?"

"I cain't say that for sure, but I suspect he'll be getting in touch."

"Hack, I'm really upset by what you're telling me. Our son's life is in the balance because of some stolen property you won't let go of?"

"It's a little more complicated than that."

"It doesn't sound complicated at all," she said. "It sounds like your stubbornness at work."

"You don't cut deals with a man like Arnold Beckman."

"Not even to save your son?"

"You never play on your enemy's terms, Ruby. The day you accept Beckman's word about anything is the day he'll rip out your throat."

"I can't believe this is happening. What is it he wants so badly?"

"I said Beckman *thinks* I have something of his. I'm coming back to San Antonio. I'll see you at your hotel this afternoon."

"What about the men who put Ishmael in the cage?"

"What about them?"

"I told the police and the sheriff's office what they did to Ishmael at the carnival. They said they couldn't do anything about it unless the victim filed a complaint."

"I found the men who hurt Ishmael."

"What did they say?"

"Not much. They're probably filing assault charges against me today. But recently I shot and killed an IWW organizer. He was also a Medal of Honor recipient. So in terms of my legal troubles, those fellows at the carnival aren't high up on the scale. I'll be there directly."

"A policeman told me about the shooting. It must have been an accident. I know you would not deliberately kill a union organizer."

"But I did. And I cain't undo it. And that's the way it is."

He hung up before she could reply.

ARNOLD BECKMAN HAD summoned Maggie to his office. And "summoned" was the word. The times he had physically intimidated her were few. She felt safe inside her beauty and intellectual superiority and the uncomfortable levels of desire she caused him that he did not easily hide. But she knew that many of his emotions were infantile, and when he didn't get what he wanted, he was capable of destroying everyone and everything around him, including the objects of his affection. She also knew he delighted in witnessing others' pain.

When she entered his office, he was sitting behind his desk with a shot glass of what she suspected was tea; he never drank alcohol while he attended to business. Five other men she had never seen were sitting on the chairs made of animal hides and antlers and shellacked driftwood. One of them was Asian. She had no doubt about the kind of men they were. They wore clean work clothes and sat with their hats on their knees as though posing for a photographer, but they were unshaved and had profiles cut out of sandstone; the iniquitous light in their eyes was only the outer edge of their cruel nature. They were the type of men who wore their body odor as a weapon. Their self-worth was measured by the degree to which they could inspire fear in others. The woman who fell into their hands was never the same again.

From his vest pocket, Beckman took a bejeweled pocket watch no larger than a twenty-five-cent piece and looked at it. "Naughty girl," he said.

"I didn't get much sleep last night, Arnold," she replied.

"Unfortunately, none of us did, due primarily to one individual's negligence," he said. "Meet Jim and Jack and Jessie and Jeff. I call them the J Boys."

The smiles of the four white men were lascivious, their eyes lingering on her face and throat and breasts, one of them licking his bottom lip, each enjoying his moment in the magic kingdom, which to them was Beckman's office.

"And this is Mr. Po," Beckman said.

The Asian man bowed his head deferentially, his tan pate shining in the lamplight. He had a small mouth like a guppy's, and tiny hands, and small shoulders that he didn't try to disguise inside his tight-fitting suit. He also wore button shoes, although they had been out of fashion for many years.

"How do you do, Mr. Po?" she said.

The Asian man rose partway from his chair, his eyes lowered, then sat down again. Perhaps he smiled, perhaps not. He didn't speak. No one had asked her to sit down.

"Where is Ishmael?" she said.

"Snug as a bug in a rug, thanks to some friends of ours in the city," Beckman said.

"May I see him?"

"Miss your laddy, do you?" Beckman said.

"I don't know why you called me here. Would you please tell me? I would appreciate that very much."

"A bit out of sorts?" he said.

"Maybe I should leave," she said, trying to ignore the amusement in the faces of the J Boys, who were staring at her as though she were on a burlesque runway.

"No, leaving is not a good idea," Beckman said. He looked at his fingernails. "We need to get ourselves more tightly organized so we don't have a problem like this again. We can't have our war hero turning into a walkabout, can we? He doesn't appear to want his medication. Maybe you can do something about that."

"I'm not going to talk on this level with you, or in this environment, either," she said. "Maybe you didn't offer me a chair because this collection of white trash has already sat on all the furniture and you didn't want me to touch any of it. At least that's what I would like to believe. Regardless, I'll leave you to your friends and be on my way."

Beckman leaned back in his chair, grinning, lifting his hand to the four white men. "I'll see you gentlemen at the café at noon," he said. "Stay away from the whiskey and the ladies. I have a job for you."

They filed out of the room, their eyes straight ahead, their boots heavy on the floor, their odor sliding across her skin. Each waited until he was outside the door before he put on his hat.

"You never cease to surprise me, Maggie," Beckman said. "I wouldn't want to get on the wrong side of that bunch."

"Why are they here?"

"If they didn't work for me, they would be working for my enemies. Now sit down and let's talk business."

"Where is Ishmael?"

"Receiving the medical care he needs. We found him in a clinic across the river that's full of dying influenza patients. We probably saved his life. Do you know who Mr. Po is? From what I know about your history, you should."

"No, I'm sorry, I know nothing about Mr. Po, other than the fact that he seems to be the only gentleman in the room."

Beckman rubbed his eyes. "You're an absolute curse, Maggie. You're going to punish me because I was a little flippant with you?

Why do you think I keep you around? Yes, you're beautiful, but I hired you for your brains and your willingness to do bloody near anything to accomplish your goals. We're alike more than we're different. We know how the world works, and we don't buy in to the rot that turns men into sheep."

"Mr. Beckman telling truth. You are beautiful lady," Mr. Po said, as though reading the words one by one off a card.

"Thank you," she said.

"I speak French but not English so well."

"You speak fine," she said.

"Mr. Po has been a longtime friend of the British and the French in South Asia," Beckman said. "Soon he will be a facilitator for us."

"You're arming Orientals?" she said.

"Not just yet," Beckman said. "But their day in the sun is coming. Right now the issue is currency. As you probably guessed, they have none." He leaned forward, lacing his fingers on his desktop.

She waited. "Yes? Go on."

"So they've created a 'currency' of their own. You know what it is, don't you?"

"No," she said.

"No idea?" Beckman said. "Comes from a lovely red flower? Oceans of red flowers bursting from green husks? The Brits transported the seeds from India to China. We're actually getting in on things a bit late."

"You're going into the opium trade?"

"No, I'm an arms trader. I'm simply opening up my parameters regarding payment. I don't expect a goatherd to pay me in British pounds or American gold eagles. You'll be my liaison with Mr. Po. You'll probably have to travel overseas."

"I don't know about this, Arnold. I don't like it."

"You're telling me you never smoked opium?"

"I tried it."

"And you're still here, aren't you? Not only here, but you seem to have found the Fountain of Youth. Maggie, the potential with Mr. Po is unlimited. America's cities are filled with wretched, unhappy people. A man who cannot find fifty cents to feed his family will find five dollars to buy alcohol. Think of the amounts he will find in order to buy heroin."

Maggie's head began to throb, a nest of veins gathering in her temple. She was sitting in a chair framed out of elk antlers, the horn pinching into her back. "I have no knowledge of these matters. You'll be breaking the law. You'll be undoing your own enterprises. You're a smarter businessman than that."

"*We* are not breaking any laws. Mr. Po's transactions take place overseas. The vendors in this country will receive from him. The product grown in the Orient will be sold by him. And he will pay us for the guns we ship to friendly countries or democratic insurgencies."

"I'm confused. I don't want to talk anymore about this."

"You are not confused about anything, Maggie. You understand the nature of power. There are two kinds of people; those who have it and those who do not. Think back on what it was like when men such as those who just left here were your clients. No, don't put that pout on your face. The world fucked you, just as it did me. Now it's our turn."

"I want to see Ishmael."

"Listen to me," Beckman said. He lifted his chin and used one finger to trace the chain of scars that ran down his cheek and neck into his collar. "I got this in one of the early mustard-gas experiments. It involved putting the gas in an exploding shell. I also lost my sense of smell. The scientists who did this to me could not have cared less."

"Mr. Beckman say profane words but is a visionary," Mr. Po said.

"Time to make a choice, Maggie. You're on board the *Pequod* or not. But we're going to kill the great white whale with or without you, girl," Beckman said. "Think back to when you were nineteen and scared to death and glad to be offered a bare mattress and a water pan in a straddle house for the kind of roach bait that just walked out of here. Did you like their hands on you, their breath on your skin, their fingers knotted in your hair?"

Her cheeks were flaming, her hands clenched in her lap, her mouth so dry and her face so tight that she couldn't swallow or even blink.

Chapter 26

AFTER COD BISHOP left his house, Hackberry called the sheriff and asked a favor.

"You want Darl Pickins to drive you back to San Antonio?" Willard asked.

"Somebody has got hold of my son. I need to get him back."

"I just got two calls from the authorities in Bexar, Hack. Guess what they were about."

"I wouldn't know."

"Three security workers at the carnival got tore up by some wild man."

"That's too bad."

"The wild man who attacked them said he was a deputy sheriff in Kerr County. About six and a half feet tall. Maybe a little more. An older man. He said his son had been wounded in France."

"These were full-grown men, I assume. Not children or paraplegics?"

"Most likely."

"I think I know who they might be. The same ones who put my boy on display in the geek cage. I cain't imagine somebody putting the boots to them. That's a heartbreaking story."

"I swore you in as a peace officer. You don't have permission to beat the hell out of whomever you feel like."

"They had it coming."

"Your badge goes in your dresser drawer today, Hack. I'll pick it up the next time I'm out."

"I think I did the right thing."

"It might have been the right thing twenty-five years ago. You know what got Wesley Hardin killed?"

"A bullet through the brain. It does that sometimes."

"It's what his kind look for. From the day their parents throw them out with the slop jar. You're always skirting the edge of it. That's what I don't understand."

"Darl cain't drive me to San Antonio?"

"They're going to put you away, Hack. In Huntsville or an asylum or some other shithole you'll never come out of. Why do you let them do it to you?"

"Who's 'they'?"

"I give up."

The line went dead.

THE PITY THAT flowed in the veins and the cup of mercy that could fill the heart in a second had always remained mysteries to Hackberry. Their power was so great and disarming that he often feared them.

Of all people to cause these emotions in him, it had to be Cod Bishop. As Hackberry was trying to find somebody to take him to San Antonio, he looked out the window and saw Bishop walking through the pasture along the riverbank, toward Hackberry's house, without a hat or coat, staring furtively at the bluffs and the sky as though they contained either an omen or a threat. Even his gait seemed out of sync with the world; he walked as though his feet were sinking in snow or ice.

Hackberry went out on the back porch, hoping Bishop had finally decided to tell the truth about his relationship with Arnold Beckman. More important, maybe he knew where Ishmael was being held. Maybe Cod Bishop was on the verge of starting a new life.

Vanity, vanity. If ever Hackberry had seen a man in the midst of a nervous breakdown, it was Cod.

"What's going on, partner?" Hackberry said.

"I was digging in the ash, cleaning and stacking the bricks," Bishop said. "I'm not bad with a trowel and cement. I've worked right alongside many a tradesman."

"I'm not quite following you."

"Where the darkies used to live. There was a fire years ago, and they moved away. I'm rebuilding their houses." Bishop's white shirt was streaked with charcoal, the armpits ringed with sweat, a manic shine in his eyes. "I aim to find them and bring them back. What with modern communications, you can always find people."

Hackberry nodded. "Why don't you come in?"

Bishop looked over his shoulder. "I should be getting back. I need to order lumber and nails and shingling. Where do you think the elderly woman went to? I can't remember her name."

"That was probably Aint Ginny."

"Know where she might be?"

"She'd be pretty old."

"Yes, I guess we're all getting along in our years. You must take care, Mr. Holland. There's evil abroad in the world. All of us must be on the lookout."

"I'll make some tea. Come inside and rest a bit."

"That's very kind of you. I was speaking to the minister at the church. I told him how neighborly you've been."

Hackberry opened the screen door and waited for Bishop to walk ahead of him. Instead, Bishop stared across the river at the bluffs, as though trying to remember something that lay just beyond the edges of his memory.

"Is something troubling you?" Hackberry said.

"Why, no, not at all. As Little Pippa says, 'God's in his heaven and all's right with the world.' See the bluffs? In its way, they're our tombstone. We go into their shade and then rise again. It's all part of a plan."

"I never thought of it that way." Hackberry slipped his hand under Bishop's arm and helped him up the steps and into the kitchen. "I'm going to fix us a sandwich and some warm milk instead of tea. Then I'll drive you home in my carriage. I think you might have caught a chill."

Bishop sat down at the breakfast table and continued to stare across the river. He pinched his temples, his brow furrowing, as though someone had tapped a nail between his eyes. "I think I've done something terribly wrong, Mr. Holland. But I don't know what it is."

"Does it have to do with me or my son?"

"No, I gave up a secret, I think. I'm trying to remember what it is. I feel very bad about it. I can't bring it to mind. You think it's about the darkies?"

"Maybe you shouldn't fret on it right now."

"I look around me and all I see is darkness."

Hackberry looked into Bishop's eyes. They were as mindless as water in an empty fish bowl. "We'll have our snack, and then we'll give Dr. Benbow a call."

"The secret is about that cave, isn't it?"

"It could be."

"Thank you, Mr. Holland. It'll be good to have Aint Ginny and the other colored people back. It's funny how they get to be family. Then one day they're gone."

RUBY DANSEN HAD not slept more than two hours since Ishmael had disappeared from the clinic. She bought bread and a wedge of cheese and an apple from a grocery by the hotel and ate them in her room, then drank as much water as she could to kill the hunger pains in her stomach. She had money for perhaps three more days in the hotel, but not if she ate in the café down the street or hired a jitney to Maggie Bassett's house. So she put on the best dress she had, one made of maroon velvet; a gray hat that had a tall black feather in the band; and walked four miles in the wind to Maggie's home, her energy gone, her vision speckled with tiny dots.

This time she didn't twist the doorbell, she banged on the door with her fist. She saw Maggie's face appear behind a curtain, then the door opened and Maggie was glaring at her, her nostrils white around the rims. "Why are you hammering on my house?" she said.

"Where are you hiding my son?"

"I'm not hiding him anywhere. What's the matter with you? Why don't you go back to Denver? Why do you look at me as the source of all your problems? Why would I hide Ishmael? I think you're a lunatic."

"You're a liar," Ruby said. "Your friends kidnapped him from the clinic. Don't tell me they didn't. I was there."

"I don't know where he is."

"But you know where he was taken. You know they kidnapped him. You're disingenuous at best."

"Oh, there it is with the vocabulary again."

"You never answer the question. Everything that comes out of your mouth is to protect yourself at someone else's expense," Ruby said.

Maggie leaned out the door. "Who's with you? How did you get here?"

"I walked. I'm by myself."

"You walked from town?"

"What did I just say?"

Maggie looked at nothing, then back at Ruby. "I think of Ishmael as my son. I wouldn't see him hurt for the world."

"You whore."

There was a wrinkle of triumph at the corner of Maggie's mouth. "Let me remind you of your own rhetoric, Ruby. You said you forgave me. Now you walk miles to my home and beat on my door to insult me. Does that seem like rational behavior to you?"

"You take orders from company swells, Maggie. I talked with the IWW. Arnold Beckman is a union buster. He kidnapped my boy, and I think you know why."

Ruby waited, hoping Maggie would conclude that she possessed information which in reality she did not. But the eyes of Maggie Bassett never gave up secrets, never showed defeat or guilt or acceptance of responsibility and, more important, never lingered on the injury of others.

"Who says Arnold told me anything?" Maggie asked. "I don't take orders from anyone. Do you know what your hat reminds me of?"

"My hat?"

"Don't misunderstand me. It's certainly cute. Do you go to the flickers? Actually, people call them 'the movies' now. Arnold took me to his studio in the Palisades. You must come out there sometime. I think people would be dying to meet you."

"Have they hurt him?"

"Who?"

"My son."

"I have to run some errands. Do you want a ride back to town? I love your hat. It puts me in mind of Robin Hood's followers, medieval trolls on bandy legs toddling around the set, pretending they're part of a grand cause."

"I guess my trip has been a waste. Would you forgive me for what I'm about to do?"

"No more shopgirl silliness, Ruby. Bye-bye, now."

"Please give Arnold Beckman this message: If he doesn't return my son, I'm going to kill him."

"Why don't you tell him yourself?"

"Thank you. I will. In the meantime, I really need to do something else, for your sake and mine."

Ruby punched Maggie Bassett squarely in the face, knocking her on her bottom in the middle of the hallway.

WHO ARE YOUR *friends?* Hackberry wondered. *The ones who will lend you money in times of need? Pull you from a raging creek or a burning house?* No, the real ones were the people who granted a favor simply because you asked it of them. There was no interrogation, no weighing of the scales, no equivocation. They backed your play. They were the kinds of friends you never let go of.

He called Beatrice DeMolay's house in San Antonio and waited while the operator got her on the phone. "Miss B.?" he said.

"Mr. Holland?" she replied.

"I need some he'p."

"What can I do for you?"

"I never learned how to drive, and I need to get to San Antonio. The sheriff, in spite of the good soul he is, has pulled my badge. My boy has been kidnapped, most likely by Arnold Beckman's employees. Can I hire your man, what's-his-name, the zombie, to drive me around?"

"His name is Andre, Mr. Holland."

"Whatever. He looks like he could scare a corpse out of a graveyard. Can he come get me?"

"Yes, he can. I'm sorry to hear about your son. What does the sheriff's office say?"

"Take a guess."

"They're not interested?"

"They may have had a hand in it. The motorcar that took him away may have had a bell on it. Anyway, I don't have any credibility in San Antonio. I shot and killed a Medal of Honor recipient, and last night I worked over three thugs who had Beckman's business card in their wallets."

"I didn't get that last part."

Through the window, he saw two motorcars come down the dirt road and turn under the archway onto Cod Bishop's lane. One was the departmental car usually driven by Darl Pickins, and the other was the motorcar of Dr. Benbow, the part-time county coroner.

"Hello?" she said.

"Yes, ma'am. I know what Beckman wants. I'm not going to give it to him. There are many reasons why not, but the chief one is he will kill Ishmael as soon as he gets what he wants. Am I wrong?"

"That's exactly what he'll do."

"Thank you," he said.

"Andre will be on his way in a few minutes."

HACKBERRY CUT THROUGH pasture to the back of Cod Bishop's property, walking through the scarred area where Bishop had been recovering scorched bricks from the soil and scraping them clean with a trowel and stacking them as though reconstructing the past and undoing the harm he had visited upon the black people who were his charges. As Hackberry neared the main house, he saw the two motorcars parked by the barn. The red gelding Bishop had ridden that morning was in the lot, favoring one foot, half of the loose iron shoe visible beneath the horn.

Both barn doors were open wide. The dirt floor was broom-sweep-clean, the stalls free of manure, the baled hay still green and stacked both in the loft and high against the back wall, enclosed by a chain-latched chest-high slatted partition. Cod Bishop had always run a tight ship.

Darl was standing in front of an unlatched stall. Dr. Benbow, the part-time county coroner, was squatting next to Bishop's body, touching the neck, the ribs, and the throat. He stood up and put a notebook in his shirt pocket and inserted a pencil next to it. He was a gangly man with iron-colored hair that grew over his collar, and he was dressed in a black suit. He had hung his coat on the side of the stall and rolled up his sleeves to his elbows. Even though the air was cool and a breeze was blowing through the shade, he had broken a sweat. He seemed to stare at Hackberry without seeing him. "What's your opinion?"

"What's *my* opinion?" Hackberry said.

"You knew him pretty well. Or at least you lived next door to him for a couple of decades. How he'd end up in this predicament?"

"The crack on his head would probably be enough to do him in," Hackberry replied. "If that's what you're asking."

"Any one of the blows would be enough. I think one of his ribs punctured his heart. His thorax is probably broken, too. Would you answer my question?"

"Cod wasn't a careless man around horses. Also, he left them out most of the time. Sometimes in winter he'd put up the mares. I don't know why he'd have the gelding in the stall."

"Know anything about his state of mind? Has he been acting strange, behaving irrationally?"

"He was at my house this morning. I was fixing to call you, but he didn't want me to."

"Call me for what purpose?"

"I think he was having a mental breakdown. I believe his conscience was weighing heavily upon him."

"Would he walk his horse into a stall to abuse him? Because his quirt is over there by the broom."

"No, his livestock was his property. Cod did nothing that would devalue his property."

"What do you think, Darl?" Dr. Benbow said.

"I think somebody flat put it to him," the deputy said.

Hackberry and Dr. Benbow looked at him. "What do you base that on?" Dr. Benbow said.

"It's not for me to say."

"Yes, it is," Hackberry said.

"He was a widower," the deputy said.

"People have it in for widowers?" the coroner said.

"Mr. Bishop had an eye for the ladies. All kinds. Some with a wedding band on their finger."

"So he was fooling around with the wrong man's wife and got himself beaten to death?" Dr. Benbow said.

"I ain't sure who stomped him. But that horse didn't," Darl said.

"Talking to you is like the Chinese water torture, son. Would you get to it?" Dr. Benbow said.

"The loose shoe on the gelding out yonder is on the back foot," Darl said. "It looks like Mr. Bishop was hit several times. A horse pawing in the air might be able to do that. But most times a horse only gets you once when he kicks with his back feet, unless you're boxed in the stall with him. That didn't happen."

"Tell your boss to give you a pay raise," Dr. Benbow said.

"What for?" Darl said.

"You see beyond appearances. It's a valuable asset," the doctor said. "Wouldn't you say so, Mr. Holland?"

Hackberry gazed across the river at the bushes that shielded the opening of the cave in the bluffs. He wondered how soon Beckman's men would be there.

ONE HOUR LATER, Andre pulled up in the bright blue REO owned by Beatrice DeMolay, and got out and knocked on Hackberry's front door. He removed his hat when Hackberry unlatched the screen.

"Come in," Hackberry said.

"Miss Beatrice said I'm to bring you directly to her apartment, if you have no objection."

"I want to talk to you first. Come in and sit down."

"Where?"

"On a chair, where do you think?"

"I prefer to stand."

"That's fine. The last time you were here, I told you to go in the kitchen and he'p yourself to the icebox. I also told you where your supper ware was at. You and Miss Beatrice thought I was telling you to use only the dishes and forks and knives and such reserved for the he'p, namely Mexicans and people of color. That was not the case. My mother died in childbirth when I was a little boy, and her china has remained unused in the cabinet ever since. I don't eat off it, and I don't let anybody else eat off it, either."

Andre's face was impassive, his cobalt-blue eyes never leaving Hackberry's, his skin so black it glowed with the clean radiance of freshly mined coal.

"Here's the other thing I wanted to say," Hackberry continued. "If you choose to he'p me, you'll be at risk. That means dangerous men might be a stone's throw from us right now. Are you troubled by any of this?"

"No, I am not."

"You don't address other men as 'sir'?"

"If they request that I do."

"You're a regular blabbermouth, all right. Okay, here's what has occurred. My neighbor, Cod Bishop, was in the employ of Arnold Beckman. I believe Mr. Bishop saw me up in the cave in those bluffs across the river and told Arnold Beckman I had probably hid something there. Mr. Bishop was found dead in his barn this morning. This was after he tried to quit Beckman."

"Miss Beatrice has said I should do whatever you tell me."

"What I'm telling you right now, Andre, is to listen. I don't want you hurt. This is Texas. While you're working with me, you do not lay your hand on a white man."

"Why do white people always think black people want to put their hands on them?"

"I didn't say 'put.' I said— Never mind. If we have trouble with somebody and he needs shooting, I'll do it. Clear?"

"Yes, sir."

"A breakthrough," Hackberry said.

"Arnold Beckman sent someone to throw acid in Miss Beatrice's face. If I meet him, it will not matter if he is white or black."

"I spoke too soon. So be it. Better a sober cannibal than a drunk Christian."

"What does that mean?"

"Don't worry about it. We need to cross the river and go to the cave."

"If Beckman's men are watching, they will see us."

"That's the point, partner."

Chapter 27

Hackberry and the Haitian chauffeur crossed the river and climbed the trail to the cave's opening. Down below, the long knifelike yellow leaves from the willow trees drifted in the riffle, steam rising off the boulders inside the shade. Hackberry was carrying a two-gallon fuel can, a hand-notched wood plug in the spout, the coal oil sloshing inside.

"I'd like for you to stay out here, Andre, and have a smoke," he said. "Pay no mind to what I do in the cave. We're going to take our friends on a snipe hunt."

"What is a snipe hunt?"

"It means you convince a fellow he can catch all the snipe he wants if he holds a flashlight in front of an open gunnysack by a barbed-wire fence between the hours of eleven and midnight."

"Who would be so stupid?"

"It's a metaphor. It means you confuse and mislead and mystify your enemy. Stonewall Jackson said that."

"The general who fought for the preservation of slavery?"

"Not everyone is perfect. Anyway, if you glance to the north, you'll see the sunlight reflecting off a glassy or metallic surface. I have a feeling that's Mr. Beckman's people."

"Do you believe in the unseen world?" Andre said.

"I never had a choice."

"I don't understand."

"If I didn't believe somebody was up there, I'd be forced to believe in myself. For me, that's a horrible thought."

"You have tiny filings in the handles of your pistol."

"This is an 1860 Army Colt, converted for modern cartridges. Changing the grips won't bring back the men I killed. Plus, every one of them had it coming, and the world is better off without them."

"Do they visit you in your sleep?"

"You know the answer to that one."

Andre gazed at the willow leaves floating between the boulders, dipping in the chuck, disappearing in the sunlight.

Hackberry set the coal oil can on the floor of the cave and worked his way deeper inside, where the walls narrowed and the crevice in the roof allowed a glimmer of sky when the trees were not in leaf. He felt along a shelf until he touched a rock he had wedged in a hole and then covered with a huge rat's nest. He pulled the box, still wrapped in a rain slicker, from inside the wall. He knelt on one knee and unwrapped and opened the rosewood top and touched the smooth onyx of the cup with his fingertips.

Lord, they got my boy. They want your cup, too, but they'll have to kill me first and pry it out of my hands. I have to move us. I hope I am doing the right thing. I would like to drill a hole between the eyes of every one of those sons of bitches, but anger only clouds my reason and empowers my enemies. Be my light, my sword, and my shield.

Sorry for swearing.

For just a moment, he was certain he had taken leave of his senses. A voice outside himself, one he had never heard and loud enough to echo inside the cave, said, *I think I'll survive it.*

He stood up, the rosewood box still open in his hands. "Say again, please?"

There was no response. He was sweating even in the dampness of the cave, his ears popping in the silence. He heard a noise behind him.

"Did you want me, Mr. Holland?" Andre said.

"No."

"I heard you talking."

"I'm getting old. I talk to myself sometimes."

The Haitian looked up at the ceiling of the cave and at the pale glow from the crevice that operated like a flume. "Who was the other person?"

"What?"

"I heard someone speak to you."

"That must have been an echo. I told you not to pay me no mind."

"Do you want me to wait outside?"

"Yes. I'll be along shortly," Hackberry said, his hands cold and strangely dry on the box, his throat clotted with phlegm. "Come back here."

"What is it you want?" Andre said, frozen against the circle of blue beyond the cave's entrance.

"What did the voice say?"

"I'm not sure," Andre replied.

"That's what I thought. It was probably a rock tumbling down the hillside."

"Something about surviving."

Hackberry shook his head in denial. "That was me," he said. "People my age are always studying on mortality. It makes you a little crazy. You talk to yourself and don't remember what you said."

"Yes, sir," Andre said. He turned to go.

"We're not on the plantation. You don't have to call me 'sir.' I cain't stand servility. We taught it to y'all, and now it's the bane of your race and the disgrace of ours."

"Let me know if you need anything, Mr. Holland."

Hackberry watched Andre exit the cave, stooping slightly, his suit coat tightening across his back, his hands as big as frying pans. Hackberry lifted the cup from the green velvet cushion, wrapped it in the slicker, and replaced it inside the wall, then refitted the rock in the hole.

Why do you fear me? a voice said.

I didn't mean to give that impression. Please he'p me get Ishmael back. I don't care what happens to me. That boy has been paying my tab all his life. It bothers me something awful. I don't get no rest.

But the voice no longer had anything to say.

Hackberry pulled the wood plug from the spout on the fuel can and poured a zigzag pattern of coal oil along the floor of the cave, sloshing it on his chair and writing table. He threw the empty can outside the cave and heard it clatter in the rocks. "Confuse, mislead, and mystify," he repeated to himself. He latched the rosewood box and carried it outside and set it on top of a boulder, then rolled a newspaper into a cone and popped a match alight with his thumbnail and lit the paper and tilted the cone down until the flame almost touched his fingers. Then he tossed the paper into the cave.

Black smoke corkscrewed along the ceiling through the crevice at the back of the cave, rising in curds through the natural chimney into the trees atop the bluffs. Hackberry's chair and writing table crawled with fire, and the rats' nests in the cave's corners glowed and winked inside the smoke, but the flames on the floor were of low intensity and short duration, and other than blackening the walls, they had little appreciable effect.

"Why have you done all this, Mr. Holland?" Andre said.

"The men watching us are primitive people. As such, they believe that all other people act and think in the way they do. They think we're done with the cave and whatever it contained."

"Mr. Beckman is not a primitive man."

"You're wrong there, partner. Beckman is one cut above a man with a bone in his nose and a spear in his hand."

Andre didn't reply. Hackberry picked up the rosewood box and tucked it under his arm. "Time to hit the trail."

"Where are your friends, Mr. Holland?" Andre said.

"Pardon?"

"Your son has been kidnapped by an evil man. I suspect these are the worst days in your life. Where are your friends? There should be many at your side. Have they all deserted you?"

"I've driven the best people in my life from my door. That's not an easy fact to live with."

"You are a man of great humility."

"I like you, Andre. But if you don't shut up, I'm going to shoot you."

"Do as you wish."

Hackberry stared at the hillside where he had seen the sunlight flash on a reflective surface. But the only living thing he saw there was a cow walking out of the shade, a bell clanging under her neck.

"Andre, I'm beset by a great fear," he said. "No matter how this plays out, I think Beckman plans to kill my boy. A man like that never leaves a debt unpaid. That evil son of a bitch is going to kill my Ishmael."

"There are other ways to deal with this problem, Mr. Holland. You are a man of restraint. I am not."

Hackberry looked into the Haitian's eyes. What he saw there made him blink.

MAGGIE BASSETT DID not know what to do with her anger, or where to place it, or how to stop it from ulcerating her stomach. Ruby Dansen had punched her in the face and knocked her on her rump in her own house. Her puffed lip and the swelling in one nostril made her face look like it had been scissored in half and glued together unevenly. No man had ever done something like this to her, much less a woman.

She sat in her kitchen and held a piece of ice wrapped in a towel to her face, and reveled in one revenge fantasy after another about Ruby Dansen. And in so doing, she transferred more and more power to Ruby, a busybody waitress who thought she knew more about economics than the owners of U.S. Steel.

The thought of it made Maggie move the piece of ice from her mouth to her forehead. Again and again she saw Ruby's fist coming unexpectedly out of nowhere, landing like a set of brass knuckles in the center of her face, jarring her eyes in their sockets, rendering her helpless as she fell backward on the floor, afraid that more blows were coming.

Afraid? Of Ruby Dansen? She couldn't believe she'd just had that thought. That was impossible. She must never have it again. It was absurd. She had dealt with the likes of Harvey Logan and spent a week in Denver's Brown Palace Hotel with Harry Longabaugh. She'd even had a fling with Butch Cassidy. She knew that Butch was still alive, that he hadn't died in the shoot-out down in Bolivia. She had been the consort of the most famous outlaws in America. How many people could say that? Afraid of Ruby Dansen? How silly.

When she realized how foolish and revealing her thoughts were, she wanted to cry. Except no one was there to commiserate with her. She could almost hear Arnold's mocking voice as she told him of Ruby's visit. He would cherry-pick his way through every detail of her pain, stirring the pot, his eyes gleeful while he analyzed her weaknesses. When he tired of the game, he would offer to have someone visit Ruby at her hotel in the late hours, or escort her off the sidewalk into an alley. And after Arnold had dispatched the mess she had made, he would remind Maggie repeatedly of her ineptitude and her dependence upon him.

No, that was not going to happen, she told herself. When Maggie Bassett got even, she got even. For Maggie, the word "restitution" was a misspelling of "retribution." She did not believe in an eye for an eye, either; Maggie paid back with interest. And the beauty of her revenge was that she never told anyone about it, like a badge of honor you carried but never showed anyone. Her refusal to comfort her father on his deathbed, to even touch him, was not an act of vengeance. It was simply how she felt. Why pretend? He was not a loving father and had blamed her for her mother's death. She was supposed to get all weepy because he was dying? How stupid could people be? He didn't need her when she needed him. What was wrong with letting him check out on his own?

The real expression of her feelings toward her father came two years later, when she journeyed by train to the graveyard where he was entombed next to his wife under a huge slab of Italian marble, safely beyond her reach. It was sunset on a Sunday, the dogwood in bloom. A few families were picnicking on the grounds, the children flying kites against a magenta-tinted sky. Maggie removed a bottle of wine from a straw basket on her arm and sipped from it until the bottle was empty. Then she set it down and gathered up her skirts and urinated on the slab while the picnickers stared at her, aghast.

But an exorcism of Ruby's attack would require more than the price of a train ticket. And Ruby was not the only source of Maggie's anger. Arnold was becoming more and more of a problem.

His insinuations about her had become more common in their daily dealings, his disrespect for her and women in general more pronounced when a male audience was available.

Plus the question she kept trying to shove to the edge of her mind: What had he done with Ishmael? Over the years she had piece by piece gotten rid of her conscience, the way a person got rid of a worrisome appendage. She believed the conscience was little more than a set of ideas installed by others; she felt it had little to do with right and wrong and instead served the interests of the installers.

It was wrong to gas a soldier in the trenches but all right to burn him to death with a flamethrower? The railroads should be given every other section of land along the railroad track and regular people should get nothing? All men were brothers and equal in the sight of God unless they were dumb peons you could pay ten cents an hour? Every patriotic man should vote, but the woman who demanded the same right was branded a lesbian? Fornication was beyond the pale unless you did it in a city-sanctioned cathouse? Sometimes she wondered why she didn't join forces with Ruby Dansen.

Nonetheless, even in her anger, she could not stop thinking about Ishmael. Maybe that was why she kept her mind on Ruby in the first place. She had injected Ishmael, seduced him, and brought him to San Antonio so Arnold could satisfy his obsession over a religious artifact and get even with Hackberry Holland. But something had happened on the train ride down the southern Colorado plateau and through Ratón Pass. Lying next to Ishmael in the bed inside their private room, she had felt like both a mother and a lover, as though entering into an innocent form of incest and perhaps thereby restoring her youth. These were moments that others would not understand. Why should they? They hadn't been abandoned by their fathers and forced to work in a bordello, or live on the bread crumbs paid to schoolteachers. She thought about the slow rocking of the train descending the Pass and Ishmael's body molded to hers as they watched the pinyon trees and the great outcroppings of gray and yellow rock slide by the window, and for a second she thought she smelled the trace of shaving soap on Ishmael's neck, and felt the heat of his skin on her lips.

Maybe she was corrupt. But what she thought and what she did and what she felt were not necessarily part of one another. No one chose to be a prostitute. And once you became one, you either kept company with gunfighters and outlaws who protected you, or you ended up on the street at the mercy of pimps and Murphy artists and jackrollers and eventually went blind or insane with venereal disease of the brain.

Arnold ridiculed the life she had led. He always began with a compliment but ended by degrading her. If she told him about her feelings for Ishmael, he would only show amusement, his eyes lighting mischievously, the tip of his tongue sliding along his bottom lip, his face smug with what he considered his secret insight into her soul. Because that was always the message. Maggie deceived herself, but her mentor and protector, Arnold Beckman, saw through it all and liked and admired her just the same.

He had trained her how to think about herself, using flattery one moment and the threat of rejection the next. He was a master at it. The only thing he had not done to her was try to seduce her, and she was never sure why. Many men who visited bordellos feared intimacy; maybe he was one of them. Women were brought to his apartment by a pimp late at night, and he had a mistress in Galveston and perhaps one in Mexico City, but otherwise he rarely touched people, even to shake hands. She had never thought about that. He was cruel and allowed his men to do unthinkable acts to his enemies, but she could not remember the instance when he laid his hand on another man.

What she did know was his talent for making people resent themselves, cajoling them into their own self-destruction. In spite of knowing these things about him, she had allowed herself to be his ongoing victim. She felt sick to her stomach.

SHE DROVE HER motorcar to Arnold's building. She not only drove it to the building, she parked partly on the walkway and partly in the flower bed. When she saw no one through the office window, she climbed the stairs in the breezeway and banged on the apartment door. When he didn't answer, she shook the knob. "I know you're in there, Arnold," she said.

"What the hell do you want?" he called out.

"I want you to open the door."

"Come back another time, love."

"Want me to break a window? This flower pot should do nicely."

She heard his feet padding on the straw mat on the other side of the door. He slipped the bolt and opened the door partway, wearing a white bathrobe, his hair dripping. "Lost your mind, have you?"

"I need to talk."

"About what?"

"Ishmael."

"We did that this morning. What happened to your face?"

"An accident."

"You should do something about it. You look like someone sawed a perpendicular line down your face."

"I didn't come here to talk about myself."

"Of course not. You're the soul of goodness. Was it an old boyfriend? Tell me who he is and I'll take care of it. You can watch if you want."

The bathroom door was half open. She could see steam rising from a giant gold-plated tub submerged in the oak floor. "Bathing with a lady friend?"

"Not unless you care to join me."

"There are times when I hate you, Arnold."

"I give up. Come in. I must have clap in my brain." He walked toward the bathroom, jiggling his fingers over his shoulder for her to follow. He dropped his robe and descended the steps into the tub, easing into the water, resting his neck on a soggy velvet support between the faucets. He closed his eyes and sighed, his phallus rising to the water's surface.

"Do you have any embarrassment or shame at all?" she said.

"We're friends. The water is fine, in case you want to relax a bit," he replied, his eyes still closed. "Do my scars bother you? I bet you didn't know I had so many."

"I have an appendix scar. Does that count?"

"You'd be surprised how many women like to touch them," he said. "I've never understood that. I think women are more drawn to pain and violence than they realize."

"I'll talk with Hack. We'll get back the cup or whatever that thing is. I can do it. He listens to me."

"Tell me what's really on your mind," he said. "And don't tell me it's not about you. There's nothing you do that's not about you, Maggie. That's why I love you. You're feline from head to toe, and I mean every supple and sensuous curve in your glorious body. Come in here with me. It would be the greatest honor of my life."

"Don't hurt him," she said, surprised at the weakness in her voice.

"The war hero?"

"Stop pretending you don't know what I'm talking about. I know you, Arnold. I've seen what you've done to others who have gotten in your way."

"I think you don't know me well enough," he said. He opened his eyes and winked. "I've always wondered what the objection was."

"I think you're afraid of women."

He smiled to himself. "Test me."

"What's that smell?" she said.

"What smell?"

"Something is burning," she said.

"It's my sandwich. I was reheating it in the skillet. Turn off the stove for me, will you? People don't know what it's like to lose one of your senses. I'd give anything to smell a gardenia again. Why do you feel so sorry for Captain Holland? His legs are fine. He's handsome and has his whole life ahead of him. Why do you think me such an ogre?"

"You mock people. Me in particular."

"I do not. You intrigue me. I love to watch you when you look in the mirror. The way you touch a line here or there. You make me think of a little girl." He looked past her and raised himself in the tub. "There's smoke coming out of the kitchen. Would you get in there, please?"

She went into the kitchen and turned off the stove. She returned to the bathroom and put down the cover on the toilet and sat on it.

Through the window, she could see a solitary woman walking in the shade of the poplars that lined the road leading to Arnold's building. "Say of me what you will. But let Ishmael go. You've seen the pain of war. Why not act with mercy to someone who's shared your experience? He's done you no harm."

"I'm not the one standing in the way."

"Are you talking about my former husband?"

"He stole my goods. No one steals my goods, love."

"By 'goods,' you mean the cup?"

"The Grail."

"I don't believe that."

"You're not a student of history. Beatrice DeMolay is the descendant of the Crusader knight who brought it back from the Holy Land, along with the Shroud of Turin."

"The what?"

"The winding sheet of Christ."

"Why do you want a cup? What will you do with it?"

"Encase it in concrete under one of my buildings and never tell anyone where it is."

She stared at him, blinking, unsure what she had heard.

"I'll know where it is. But no one else. Not ever," he added. "Unless I feel like telling them."

He picked up a washcloth and wiped his armpits. She continued to stare at the curious combination of features that constituted his physiognomy—the slanted cheekbones and pointed cleft chin, the hooked nose, the analytical gleam in his eyes that dissected a person's mouth and hair and the shape of his ears and delighted in discovering imperfection, the chain of scars that resembled hardened pustules dribbling down his neck, the shoulder-length silvery-blond hair indicating either his disdain for sexual normalcy or the presence of a cruel woman inside his skin.

"The world hasn't been good to either of us, Maggie. When we leave it, we'll make sure no one forgets we were here. It's not a bad way to be."

"I don't think I ever really knew you," she said.

"Take off your clothes. I'll draw fresh water for us."

"Do you ever think about what awaits us?"

"The other side of the grave? The Great Judgment, that sort of thing?"

"Thinking about it is not exactly a lark."

"You die. Then you stay dead for a long time," he said. "Why do men love war? We become the givers of death, not its recipients. If we survive it, we have killed Death."

"You're the most depressing person I've ever known."

"You're depressed by the truth, Maggie. You look at me and recognize yourself. What you've never understood is that I don't have to own people. They discover themselves inside me. They genuflect before me like small children. I don't take power from people. They give it to me."

"You need to own the cup, though. What does that tell you about yourself?"

"It tells me you should watch your mouth."

She looked through the window at the woman walking from the road to the building's entrance. "Looks like you have a visitor."

"Send them away," he said. He squeezed the washrag on his face. "I'm sorry for threatening you. You're one of the few people in the world I respect. And it's because of your superior intelligence, although sometimes you do a magnificent job of hiding it."

"Ah, she's headed into the breezeway. I'll get the door," Maggie said. "You might put on your robe. I don't think she'll be able to handle your scars and your frontal nudity at the same time."

Chapter
28

Hackberry threw his saddlebags and a rolled blanket and a rolled slicker in the backseat of the REO and got in front with Andre, then watched him start the engine and step on the pedals and move the gear lever back and forth on the floor console. "So you got intermediate speed and high speed and reverse, all on that one stick?"

"First you must release the brake and start the engine," Andre said. "Otherwise, it does no good to work the gears."

"I gathered that. One floor pedal is to stop or slow down, and the other one lets you move the gears? That's what they call the clutch?"

"Yes, but all this must be coordinated. It is a complicated mechanical system that cannot be taken lightly."

"I appreciate your skill in these matters, Andre. Can I give it a try?"

"Do you think that is wise?"

"Probably not. I'll observe for a while."

And that was what he did, although his mind was not on the REO and its plush leather seats and polished mahogany dashboard and brass-rimmed, glass-covered instruments, nor the comfortable surge of its engine and the way the hood seemed to devour the roadway in the blink of an eye. He knew these aspects of the new era were all fine things to contemplate, but they had little to do with the mysteries whose solution had eluded him for a lifetime. He could not explain why the good suffered and could not understand how Creation could have brought about its own inception. Nor could he reason his way through the nature of divinity, or whatever people wanted to call it. He was sure, however, that somewhere on the other side of the physical world, there was a spiritual reality not unlike stardust shaken from the heavens. It animated the natural world in a way that had nothing to do with the laws of physics, and the irony was that no one seemed to notice.

In the span of one week, while prospecting in Chile, he had heard a throaty, sweeping sound on a wooded hillside that was exactly like a streambed roaring with water and mud and uprooted trees, all of it about to burst loose and turn the countryside into a floodplain. He told himself the sound came from the wind blowing at gale strength through the trees, except there was no wind and the trees were as still as the brushstrokes on a painting.

He heard rocks creaking and murmuring under the riffle in the river, sometimes with an actual clacking sound, like seals barking at one another.

He saw pools of quicksilver on the floor of a forest whose canopy was so thick, the moon wasn't visible when he looked up at the sky. The radiance from the forest floor cast no shadows, only light.

On a cold evening, when the sun had turned the hills into purple velvet, he heard a boom like buried dynamite or dry thunder in a box canyon where there was no footprint other than his own. The sky was the dark blue of newly forged steel, streaked with meteors as fragile as hailstones; the air was sweet and cold in his mouth and lungs and tasted like hand-cranked ice cream. There were no clouds overhead; there was no electricity flickering on the horizon. The total absence of sound following the boom made him wonder if he had gone deaf. "Where are you?" he shouted into the vastness of the canyon. "Show me where you are!" There was no acknowledgment of his inquiry, nor even an echo.

The REO hit a bump, and he realized he had nodded off.

"We'll be in San Antonio soon, Mr. Holland," Andre said. "Go back to sleep."

"I'm fine. I'd sure like to have a try at this."

Andre pulled to the side of the road and left the motor running. "Miss Beatrice has told me to do whatever you say. But I am also charged with protecting her motorcar."

"I don't plan on driving it into the side of a cow. What could go wrong?"

"Miss Beatrice says you are willful and get in trouble at almost every opportunity."

"I'll have to remember that."

"I will guide you through the process. Do not press too hard on the accelerator. If in doubt, take your feet off the pedals and let the car slow to a stop. That way, nothing bad can happen. Remember to guide the car in a straight line."

"I'm at your disposal."

They exchanged places. Hackberry gripped the steering wheel on each side and twisted it back and forth. "This has a right nice feel to it."

"Now put your left foot on the left pedal—" Andre began.

"Hang on!" Hackberry said. He let the clutch snap loose from under his foot and pressed the accelerator to the floor, straightening his legs, pushing himself deeper into the leather seat, the tires on the REO's right side skidding dirt and gravel along the edge of the rain ditch. He flew through a crossroads past a general store, swerving to miss a wheelbarrow a man had dropped as he ran for his life.

"You must take your foot off the accelerator! You must do it now, Mr. Holland!" Andre said. "Please, sir! Lift up your foot!"

"I already did! The pedal broke off!"

"Sir, look at the road, not your feet! Sir, please do not look at me! Look through the windshield at the road! What are you doing?"

"Cutting through the field. Nothing can happen out here in the field. I got it under control, Andre. Settle down."

"Sir, please do not be offended, but you are a crazy person!"

"A little bump coming up. Prepare yourself. Oops!"

Andre twisted his head and looked through the rear window. "Sir, you have ruined a man's fence! He's chasing us! I think he has a gun!"

"I'll talk to him later. I'm trying to concentrate. Control your emotions."

"Sir, there's a wash line ahead! Sir, these people will kill us!"

Hackberry ripped through a succession of three clotheslines, then swerved the REO and aimed it at a cornfield, clothes and bedsheets streaming from the car's windshield and fenders. The dry cornstalks flattened under the bumper and tangled in the wheels and undercarriage, the frame bouncing with such violence over the hard-packed rows that pieces of the motorcar's interior were flying through the air.

"I cannot believe this is happening to us," Andre said.

"It's not a problem. Now be quiet!"

"Look out! There's a haystack!"

"That's what I've been looking for. Now get ahold of yourself and stop all this histrionic behavior."

"This what?"

"I'll explain later. Put your hands on the dashboard. Here she comes!"

The REO piled into the haystack and came to a stop, hay collapsing around the windows, steam and the smell of burned rubber rising through the floor.

"How do you turn off the ignition?" Hackberry said.

"You ask me this now? Look behind us. There are people coming on horseback."

"They probably want to he'p. People are pretty neighborly here'bouts. Andre, if you're going to be taking me around San Antonio, you have to stop carrying on over a hill of beans. I'm just glad it was us driving and not Miss Beatrice. Anyway, let's fix it and be on our way. You can drive if you want."

"You are allowing me to drive now?"

"Yep, I'm plumb wore out. You didn't happen to bring any sandwiches or coffee, did you?"

Andre stared at Hackberry in disbelief.

"You're a mighty nice fellow," Hackberry said. "But let's face it, you definitely have a strange side to you. You were a voodoo priest?"

"Why do you bring up the subject of voodoo at this particular time?"

"I have to read up on it. From time to time I develop an abnormal bent myself. We might make a good team."

RUBY DANSEN COULD not untangle her thoughts as she walked up the road in the shade of the poplar trees to the building owned by Arnold Beckman. She was too tired, too hungry, and too forlorn to think in a rational way. Besides, what good did it do? She had learned long ago that orderly procedure and the world of courts and legality and collective reasoning, if there was ever such a thing, had little meaning when it came to the application of justice. The courts were the sanctuary of the rich and the bane of the poor. The radicals sometimes won in the streets but never in the courts. Patience was an illusion, faith in the process the equivalent of a Chinese opium pipe.

She had been to the sheriff's office and the city police department. At best, they were no help. At worst, they were in the employ of Arnold Beckman. Her son had been abducted from a public clinic, in front of witnesses, and had disappeared into a black hole. No one knew where he was, and no one cared. She stepped out of the shade into the sunlight, her eyes red, her skin chafed by the wind and dry as paper, her chest constricted as though her breath had been vacuumed from her lungs. She was glad she didn't have a pistol in her purse, because there was a very good chance she would use it.

She entered the breezeway. The doors to all the offices were locked. At the head of the stairway was a heavy door with a brass knocker. She mounted the steps and lifted the knocker and beat it as hard as she could against the steel plate. Maggie Bassett opened the door, her mouth swollen, dried blood on one nostril. "Here to attack me again?" she said.

"Where is he?"

Maggie turned her head, her hand still on the door. "Arnold, I think Miss Dansen wants to speak with you."

Ruby brushed past her. Then something happened that Ruby wasn't expecting: Maggie's fingers fumbled at her wrist. "Be careful, girl," Maggie whispered.

"Say that again?"

"Nothing," Maggie said, her face pointed down.

Ruby walked into the living room, the rug deep under her shoes. Through a half-opened door, she saw a man rising from a floor-level bathtub, working a robe over his shoulders. His body was almost hairless and striped with scars that could have been inflicted with a lash or a knife or both; his thighs were thick and shaped like a satyr's. He closed his robe and tied a laminated golden cord snugly around his hips. "You're who?" he said.

"Ishmael Holland's mother. What have you done with him?"

"Nothing. I offered him a job."

"You're well known to us. You're a liar and a union buster and a tool of the warmongers."

"Really, now? Who is 'us'?"

"The Western Federation of Miners and the United Mine Workers of America and the Industrial Workers of the World."

"Are the Molly Maguires in there?"

"You'd better wipe that smirk off your face."

"You would rather Captain Holland not work for me because I'm a capitalistic warmonger? I fought against the forces of Kaiser Bill, just like your son, even though I'm Austrian by birth. How many profiteers went up the slopes at Gallipoli, madam? How many were with Lawrence in the Arabian Desert?"

"You tell me where my son is, or I'm going to do something extreme."

"No, what you will do is turn your twat around and take it out of here."

"I've checked you out, Buster Brown. You're a fraud. You got your scars in a Malaysian prison. You were a pimp."

Maggie looked at Beckman. "What's she saying?"

"I have no idea. Ask her," he replied.

"Where did you get your information, Ruby?" Maggie said. "Arnold has been in several wars."

"So have carrion birds," Ruby said.

"Arnold, you were at Flanders fields. Tell her."

"Get her out of here," Beckman said.

"Maybe you should leave, Ruby," Maggie said.

"Why do you let a man like this give you orders?" Ruby said.

"He's my employer."

"Did you sleep with my son? Is that how you got him down here?" Ruby said. Her cheeks pooled with color in the silence. A bird flew into the window glass. "You scheming bitch," she said.

"Let's be done with this. Call the police, Maggie," Beckman said.

"Be done with this?" Ruby said. "You kidnap my wounded son and say 'be done with this'?"

"Madam, you have invaded my apartment, and you refuse to leave. I think you may be impaired."

"Something is burning," Ruby said.

"No, nothing is burning. Nothing here needs your attention," he said. "There is only one duty you have to perform here, and that is to leave. Can you understand that? I look upon your son as a brother-in-arms. I can make him rich. Instead of thanking me, you come to my home and call me a pimp. Do normal people do that sort of thing? Would you please leave before you shame yourself and Captain Holland any worse than you have already?"

Ruby sniffed at the air again. "You could burn your building down. Is that the door to the kitchen?"

"What do you think you're doing?" Beckman said. "Did you hear me? Where are you going?"

"Checking out your digs. What a grand place," she said. "The building looks like a constipated circus elephant, but your apartment is elegant. You have all the new appliances and cookware? I was right, it's a bit smoky in here. Maggie should take better care of you. What a lovely stove."

"Get on the phone," Beckman said to Maggie.

Maggie didn't move.

Ruby dragged the heavy skillet off the stove. She dumped the sandwich on the floor and went back into the living room. "This is for the miners at Ludlow and Cripple Creek and the boys who didn't come back from the Marne."

She swung the skillet at Beckman's head just as he raised his forearm to protect himself. The blow caught him on the cusp of his forehead, cutting a red star in the skin, scraping a layer off his nose, knocking him into the wall. His face went white with shock. The next blow caught him on the elbow, the next squarely across the face, slamming him into the wall again.

He cupped his hand to his nose, strings of blood hanging from his fingers. She kicked his shins, forcing him to drop his hands and bend forward, then swung the skillet sideways against his ear, flattening it into his scalp. "Tell me where he is or your brains will be on the carpet," she said.

Beckman was half-collapsed against the wall, holding one hand to his nose, lifting the other for her to stop. He removed his hand from his nose so he could speak. "You could break a man on the wheel, woman, I'll grant you that. But you're stupid and ignorant. I am not the source of your problem. Your former common-law husband is."

Ruby raised the skillet again.

"Don't do it," Maggie said. "Please. This will not get your son back. You've seen Arnold's scars. He's not afraid of pain. Talk to Hackberry. He'll not listen to me, but he will to you."

Beckman picked up a candlestick phone from a table by the bathroom door and dialed the operator.

"Ruby, please," Maggie said. "We can work this out."

"With a man like this?"

"Hackberry's stubbornness brought all this about," Maggie said.

"I should have hit you with this skillet instead of him."

Beckman had the police on the line.

Ruby dropped the skillet on the rug and wiped her hands on her sides. She looked at Maggie. "You betrayed Ishmael and handed him over to this piece of scum," she said. "I think you're the most treacherous person I've ever known."

"Say what you want. What you're doing is stupid."

"Unless you give back my son, I'll follow you and this man to the grave."

The whites of Maggie's eyes were threaded with tiny broken blood vessels, as though she were on the verge of crying. Ruby walked out the door onto the landing. She thought it was over. Then she heard Maggie behind her.

"You don't know what you've done," Maggie said.

"Then tell me."

"He has Ishmael. With a snap of his fingers, he can turn your son's life into the death of a thousand cuts."

THE REO BROKE down twice on the way to San Antonio, and it was evening before Hackberry and Andre arrived at the city limits.

"Where do you want me to drive Miss Beatrice's destroyed motorcar now?" Andre asked.

Hackberry gave Andre the directions to Ruby's hotel. Hackberry went inside and was told that Miss Dansen was not in her room and had not left a message. He got back in the motorcar and tried to think clearly. "Do you know where Beckman lives?"

"Out by one of the old missions," Andre replied. "I don't think it is advisable to go there."

"Why shouldn't we?"

"Because you do not go into your enemy's lair. You catch him when he is outside it. Then you isolate him and do what you wish."

Hackberry studied Andre's profile against the sunset. "Sometimes you can give a fellow a chill."

"Members of the army came to our village and told me to close my church and the school I helped build. I told them I would not. So they stole my children. These men were whoremongers and did not have families and cared nothing about innocent children who did not understand the nature of evil and thought all men were good."

Hackberry looked through the windshield at the men in unironed clothes on the sidewalk and a fire burning in a trash barrel and the lights coming on in the cafés and bars along the street. A Salvation Army band was playing on the corner. "Go on," he said.

"They would not give my children back. One night I caught three of the kidnappers. I trussed them with rope and gagged them and hid them in a cart, under the feces of my pigs and cattle, and took them into the jungle. By sunrise, they had given up their former way of life. There was no good deed they would not grant me, no information they would not gladly share. I was no longer a priest then, except for the love and sorrow I carried in my heart for my children. No one can understand the nature of loss until he has lost a child. But the loss is far worse when others have stolen your children and done things that even they will never tell anyone."

"What did you do to them?"

"I showed them that it was possible for them to become children again. They reached a point where nothing of the adult remained. The adult had died during the night. They looked shrunken, even in size. They made mewing sounds rather than words."

"What happened to your children?"

"I don't know. The three kidnappers had given them to others. The villagers said they were eaten by the Tonton Macoute. This is not true. I am certain they are in heaven, and sometimes I think they speak to me. But I do not know the manner in which they died, and I am filled with a great sadness when I imagine what may have been their fate."

It took Hackberry a moment to speak. "Go by Beckman's place."

"I think this is a bad choice," Andre said.

"It's not up for a vote."

THEY DROVE UP a dirt road lined with poplars, then saw a building that was dark except for one light in an upstairs window. Andre pulled the REO into the deep shade of the poplars and cut the engine. "Once or twice a week he has visitors about this time of the evening."

"What kind of visitors?"

"A procurer delivers Mexican girls. The procurer is also a trafficker in opium. He works for a Cantonese man associated with the Tongs in San Francisco."

"Beckman has only Mexican girls brought to him?"

"They are the ones who are most available. The supplier of girls may be more than a procurer and vendor of opium."

"Would you please just spit it out?"

"He hangs up the girls on a hook in a doorway and puts on a pair of tight yellow gloves that he keeps in a special drawer. The bodies of Mexican girls have been found in the garbage dump, badly beaten."

"Who told you this?"

"Mexican families across the river. They know nothing about Mr. Beckman. They don't even know his name. They simply say there is a man with hair like a woman who lives by one of the old missions and that he will pay large amounts of money for a pretty girl who is a burden to her family."

"That's hard to believe."

"They do not go to the police because they are afraid they will be sent back to Mexico. Will you answer a puzzle for me? We all know that starving people will eat members of their own family. Knowing this, why should we be surprised at anything they do?"

"You're a grim fellow, Andre."

"You avoid the problem. Tell me now, do you want to knock on Mr. Beckman's door? Maybe we will save a young girl's life. Or maybe not. Maybe after we leave, he will pick up his telephone and have your son killed. Do you want me to park in front? I'm waiting."

A red spark still burned in the hills beneath a patch of blue sky. Hackberry picked up his saddlebags from the backseat and set them on his lap. "Head down to those Spanish ruins," he said, removing a spyglass from one of the bags. "We'll see what Mr. Beckman is up to. Maybe he'll take us to my son."

"He is not a stupid man."

"Like me?"

"Why would you say such a thing about yourself?"

"Because I made a mess of my life and hurt many people in the process. The one I hurt the most was my son, and I cain't forgive myself for it."

Andre looked straight ahead and said nothing until they arrived at the ruins, then it was only to ask if Hackberry wanted him to go to town for food.

"That's a good idea," Hackberry replied. "Maybe get something for the night air, too."

"You mean brandy?"

Hackberry thought about it, his hands dry and rough as he rubbed one on top of the other. "I could sure use one of those Cherry Mash candy bars. They're a treat, aren't they?"

Chapter
29

As ANDRE DROVE away, Hackberry spread his slicker on the ground by a crumbling stone wall and used his saddlebags as a cushion for his back, then draped his blanket over his shoulders and pulled the segments of his spyglass into a long tube. He could see shadows moving on the shades of the lighted second-story windows, but there was nothing out of the ordinary about them. He gazed through the spyglass until his eye became tired and watery, and the sky filled with bats and swallows.

He could not get Andre's story of the kidnapped children out of his mind, and he wondered how Andre had not gone mad. He also wondered if he was soon to join the ranks of those who carried images in their heads that were the equivalent of hot coals.

The moon resembled a wafer broken crookedly in half from top to bottom. Beneath it, the sun had refused to die, creating a bowl of light between the hills that dimmed and grew in intensity and then dimmed again, like the refraction of candles on the inside of a gold cup.

Not far away was the site where 188 men and boys were killed on the thirteenth day of a siege that had left Mexican soldiers piled to the top of the walls surrounding the mission known as the Alamo. On the last night of their lives, did the moon rise in the same fashion, signaling that an ancient event of enormous significance was about to repeat itself? The buglers behind the Mexican ramparts were blowing "El Degüello," black flags flapping on the regimental staffs, signaling no quarter. Did the men and boys defending the mission's walls hold hands and tremble as they assembled for a final prayer? Did their fear suck the moisture from their throats and mouths and leave them with a thirst that could never be slaked? Surely the dust blowing from the plains in clouds that looked like swarms of insects wouldn't conspire to clog their nostrils and mix with their sweat and turn their faces into death masks before their time? This could not happen to *them*, could it?

An even more troubling thought confronted him. Was the cruciform shape of the ruins where he sat a coincidence or a suggestion of the fate about to be imposed on his son?

Hackberry untied one of his saddle bags and removed his Peacemaker and the bowie knife that was honed with an edge like a barber's razor and sheathed in a double-layer deerskin scabbard. At what point could a man justifiably go to the dark side and take on the characteristics and deeds of his enemies? He knew stories from old Rangers about the raids on Indian encampments, and the denial of mercy to even the smallest or the oldest in the tribe. The rationalization was always the same: The Indians, particularly the Comanche, had committed atrocities against innocent farm families and missionaries or sometimes a lone trader whose wagon was loaded with pots and pans and machine-made clothes and whiskey. But Hackberry always had the sense that the thundering charges upon the wickiups and the storm of bullets and the burning of the Indians' food and blankets and buffalo robes were intended to be repeated until there was not one Indian left alive south of the Red River.

He felt very weary, in the way he had felt weary when he had committed himself to a dissolute life, and no sooner had he closed his eyes than his head nodded on his chest. He felt his pistol slip from his grip and his bowie knife slide off his thigh. In his dream he saw Ishmael as a little boy in a suit and tie and short pants and shoes with buckles, an Easter basket on his forearm, a pet rabbit inside it. Ishmael looked up into his face. *Why did you leave us, Big Bud?*

I didn't aim to.

That's what you did.

It just happened. I didn't have a lot of smarts back then. I walked off without knowing the awful mistake I'd made.

You could have come back.

I tried. I wrote and telegrammed your mother. I never got a reply, no matter where I sent my messages.

We were poor and needed your help. Why wouldn't she answer?

It was obvious. She wanted shut of me.

Help me, Big Bud.

He'p you how? What's wrong?

It's dark here. It smells like leaves and wet stone. The voices around me belong to bad men.

Son, this is driving me crazy. Tell me where you are.

Hackberry reached out to touch him, but Ishmael's image withered away like a sand effigy caught inside a windstorm.

THE MAN ASSIGNED to watch and take care of him was named Jessie. That much Ishmael knew. The rest was a puzzle, other than the fact that Jessie didn't like his assignment. Ishmael's eyes were sealed with cotton pads and adhesive tape, shutting out any glimmer of light from the match he heard Jessie strike on a stone surface to light his cigarette. He could hear water ticking from a pump into a bucket, and he could smell the coldness in the stone or bricks or concrete that surrounded him, and he could smell an odor like wet leaves in winter, but he guessed the bucket was made of wood, perhaps oak, and the odor of a cold woods on a January day was a self-manufactured deception because he did not know what his four captors, all of whom seemed to have names that began with the letter "J," were about to do to him.

"You really a war hero?" Jessie said.

"No," Ishmael said, turning his padded eyes in the direction of Jessie's voice. He could hear Jessie draw in on his cigarette, the paper crisping.

"My friends say you're a war hero. You calling them liars?"

"Most of the heroes I knew are still on the Marne."

"They say you commanded nigra infantry."

"That's correct."

"Teddy Roosevelt said he had to force them up San Juan Hill at gunpoint."

"Double-check your information. Colored troops saved the Rough Riders' bacon."

Ishmael heard the cigarette paper crisp again, then felt Jessie blow the smoke across his face.

"Not a good time to be a smart aleck," Jessie said.

"What do you get out of this?"

"How much do I get paid?"

"Yes."

"My reg'lar pay for doing my job. It's called company security. Not that much different from being a watchdog for Uncle Sam."

"You work for Arnold Beckman, don't you?"

"Me? I wish. We call ourselves private contractors."

"What is it that Beckman wants so bad?"

"You don't listen, do you, boy?"

Ishmael felt the heat from the cigarette close to his cheek. Then the heat went away. He heard Jessie sucking his teeth.

"My father will catch up with you," Ishmael said. "He has a way of leaving his mark."

Jessie was sitting close to him now, breathing through his nose, his breath crawling across Ishmael's face. "From what I hear, he's not the fathering kind. You're lucky he didn't strangle you with the umbilical cord."

Ishmael felt encased in a sarcophagus. He was strapped to a bunk bed, his ankles bound with rope, his wrists cuffed to a wide leather belt buckled around his waist. He kept his head still, his eyes pointed at the ceiling, as though he could see through the cotton pads. He said nothing.

"Did I call it right?" Jessie asked.

"How do you know anything about my father?"

"My uncle by marriage was Harvey Logan. In case you don't know who that is, he rode with the Sundance Kid and Butch Cassidy.

He said your father was a derelict he gave a dollar to so he could go to the bathhouse."

"I know who Harvey Logan was."

"He was a card. He had your father's number, all right. I remember him drinking a mug of beer on the porch with his feet on the railing, laughing about it."

"I need to use the bathroom."

"Did you hear what I said? My uncle was a member of the Hole-in-the-Wall Gang."

"I need to use the bathroom pretty bad."

"Then you're shit out of luck."

"You taped my eyes. That means I might have another reason to run. If that happens, where does that leave you?"

"I don't think you got that picture right. You got needle scabs on your arms for all the world to see. If you get turned loose, your brains will be mush. Nobody is going to care what you say. You'll be on a street corner, drooling in your lap."

"Walk me into the bathroom. I can't see. I can't go anywhere. My hands are manacled."

"That's right, they are. So I'm supposed to unbutton your britches?"

Ishmael squeezed his eyes shut behind the pads, his bladder about to burst. "If I develop uremic poisoning, I may die. How will you explain that to Beckman?"

"I didn't tell you I worked for Mr. Beckman. You got that? You're starting to piss me off, boy. I'm not somebody you want to piss off."

"Let me explain something to you, Jessie."

"How do you know my name?"

"Your friends used it in front of me. My father is coming. After you chloroformed me, I saw him in a dream. He's going to do something terrible to you and your friends. I don't want that to happen, mostly for his sake. Maybe you didn't choose the life you lead. Maybe there's a better way of life waiting for you."

"Shut your mouth."

"I need to use the bathroom."

"How about this instead?"

Jessie wrapped Ishmael's head as tightly as a mummy's with a towel, then slowly funneled a full bucket of water in his mouth and nostrils, pausing only to ensure that none of it was wasted.

HACKBERRY LIFTED HIS watch from his vest pocket and clicked open the case and looked at it. It was gold and as big as a biscuit. Where was Andre? The moon was higher, bluer, the clouds drifting across its broken edges. In the west, the sky was flickering with electricity, the hills green and undulating and as smooth as velvet, like topography beneath a darkening sea. He thought he could smell rain. He put on his slicker and slung his saddlebags over his shoulder and began walking back toward the city. He glanced once at the windows of Arnold Beckman's apartment, but all of them were dark, and he could see no signs of movement.

What had happened to Andre? Where was Beckman? No car had left the building. Did he go to bed this early? Hackberry walked the four miles to town and used a pay phone to call Beatrice DeMolay.

ANDRE WAS PUTTING his bag of groceries on the passenger seat of the REO when the police pulled in behind him on the side street and cut its lights. A bell was attached to the outside of the driver's door. The two policemen who got out wore dark blue uniforms with high collars and brass buttons. They both had mustaches, and each carried a revolver in a holster and a short, thick wooden club hung on his belt from a rubber ring. One officer looked at the broken headlight on the driver's side, and at the cornstalks matted in the bumper and the grille, and ran his hand along the scratches and dents on the finish. "Who's the owner?" he asked.

"Miss Beatrice DeMolay," Andre said.

"You work for her?"

"I'm her driver."

"Where'd you get the accent?"

"I'm originally from Haiti."

The officer stuck his head inside the driver's window, then withdrew it. "What were you doing inside that old mission?"

"I drove someone there for Miss DeMolay."

"And vandalized the car while you were at it?"

"The car was in a mishap. A friend of Miss DeMolay was learning how to drive."

"We got a complaint about a darky looking in people's windows. One driving an expensive car that might be stolen. Did you take a peek through somebody's window tonight?"

"I will not speak on this level with you. I am also requesting that your friend take his hand off my arm."

"What did you say?"

"Do not place your hand on my person. I will do whatever you ask. But you will not treat me as you normally treat people of color."

"Maybe you should rethink that statement."

"The issue is not me. Nor is it you. There is a struggle going on around us you do not understand. Your lack of education prevents you from seeing these things. If you are in the service of Arnold Beckman, he will take you to hell with him. Mr. Beckman may be in league with the Evil One."

"That about rips it for me," the officer said. He pulled his club from its rubber ring and pushed it into Andre's breastbone. "Get into the backseat of our car."

"You mustn't do this."

"I know the reputation of the DeMolay woman. She was a white slaver. I don't know what that makes you. But we're going to find out. Now you get your black ass in the car."

"I have groceries to deliver to Mr. Holland. I cannot go with you. Miss DeMolay has given me orders to stay with Mr. Holland and to do what he says and make sure he remains safe. I do not have a choice. He has sent me for food, and that is what I have done. Maybe you can follow me to the ruins of the mission. He will tell you these things are true."

"I think you'd make a great contribution to the workforce at Huntsville Pen," the officer said. He began jabbing the club into Andre's sternum.

Andre fitted his hand on the officer's throat and lifted him into the air as he would a piñata. The officer's eyes bulged, his mouth gurgled, his face turned from pink to purple while his feet churned in the air and his hands tore at Andre's wrist.

"I will release you now," Andre said. "I hope you will not bear me ill will."

Then a flash and a sound like a firecracker exploded inside his head, and the sidewalk slammed against his face as though he had fallen from a ten-story building.

HACKBERRY HAD USED a pay phone in a drugstore on a corner where the streetcar stopped to load and discharge passengers, the connector rod sparking on the cables overhead. The car was open on the sides, and he could see women and men in formal dress stepping off the car and walking toward a lighted café. He had forgotten it was Sunday, a day for families and people in love and those on meager budgets who went from their church meeting to a warm café that was considered a treat. How long had it been since he had done these simple things?

Beatrice DeMolay picked up the phone on the second ring.

"Has Andre contacted you?" he asked.

"He's not with you?" she said.

Hackberry closed the door to the phone booth. "We were watching Beckman's building from the Spanish ruins. I asked Andre to take your motorcar and find us some food. He didn't come back. I walked to town."

"Did you have mechanical trouble?"

"Not exactly. The car is going to need a little external repair. The fenders and grille and bumpers and such. Maybe some touching up inside."

"What happened?"

"I took over the wheel for a little while. The pedal got stuck. The one that controls the gas."

"You wrecked my car?"

"We ran through some wash lines and a cornfield and maybe a fence and bumped into a haystack. I cain't quite remember the sequence."

"I don't believe I'm hearing this. You let Andre drive off by himself with the car in that condition?"

"It probably sounds worse than it is."

There was a long silence on the line. "I'll call the police department. In the meantime, I want you to come to my apartment. You and I need to have a serious talk."

"I want to confront Beckman."

"All you think about is confronting people, Mr. Holland. What has it gotten you?"

"Ma'am?"

"Look at your situation. Why don't you try thinking about something before you do it?"

He felt a catch in his throat. "I'll try to find him, Miss Beatrice."

"No, you won't. I'll handle it. Do you have any idea how the San Antonio police will treat Andre?"

"I have no doubt at all," he said. "I'm sorry I tore up your car. I'll have it fixed."

She was talking when he replaced the receiver on the hook. He stared at the phone, his ears ringing, his brow cold, his hands stiff when he tried to close them. He wondered if he was coming down with influenza. He went to the soda counter and asked the clerk for five dollars in change.

Outside, fog was rolling in from the river, clean and white and damp-looking, gathering as thick as cotton in the streets. The sky was sprinkled with stars and streaked by meteorites that turned into flecks of ice, the thunderheads in the west pulsing with tiny forks of electricity. Why didn't witnessing the antithetical nature of creation and the radiance of the universe bring him peace? Why couldn't he be in alignment with himself the way the planets and stars were, all of them hung like snowy ornaments on a tree by Druid priests? He sat back down in the phone booth and called the sheriff in Kerr County at his home. "Is that you, Willard?" he said.

"Who'd you think it was?"

"I need your assistance."

"What did you get yourself into now?"

"You name it."

"Where are you?"

"San Antonio. In a drugstore downtown."

"I don't hold any sway there."

"That's not what I'm asking for."

"You're asking me to give your badge back. The answer is no."

"I need somebody to cover my back. I cain't go up against all these sons of bitches by myself."

"You want me to call the sheriff or the chief of police?"

"These are the ones I'm having trouble with. My son is kidnapped. I may never see him again. I need your damn he'p, Willard."

"No, what you want is the Earp brothers and Doc Holliday to walk down to the O.K. Corral with you. The old days are gone, Hack."

"Not for me."

"Your old friends work in sideshows. Frank James sold shoes in Fort Worth. What does that tell you?"

"It tells me you cut bait on a friend. Give me your deputy's phone number. That young fellow, Darl Pickins."

"What for?"

"The boy has sand, unlike some others I know."

"Come around him and I'll lock you up," Willard said, and hung up.

Hackberry watched the streetcar going through the intersection, the cables dripping sparks overhead, the passengers sitting on the open benches in muffs and scarfs and fur-trimmed coats, snug among one another, the fog puffing around them as if they were travelers on an ancient ship.

Chapter
30

Hackberry felt like a beggar at her door. As the taxi drove away and he mounted the steps to her apartment, he tried to repress his resentment for her condemnation of him. Before he could tap on the door, it opened. She was wearing a dark green dress with a white collar, almost like a Victorian affectation, her hair in a bun, her face pale, free of makeup. "Andre is in jail," she said. "My attorney is there now. He was struck in the head by a policeman."

"What for?"

"The police say he tried to strangle an officer."

"Did he?"

"Probably."

"They'll put him away."

"No, they will not. Do you want to come in?"

"Thank you. How will you stop them?"

She didn't reply, her eyes lingering on his.

"You have something on them?" he said.

"What do you think?"

"Sorry way to run a railroad," he said.

"I see, you subscribe to a higher morality?"

"No, I don't have any moral authority in anything," he replied.

He looked at the rows of books on her living room shelves, the ornate furniture, the thick drapes, a big brass clock on the mantel, a log burning in the fireplace. Her home was a study in stability, the kind that was personal and seemed to have no antecedent and was not cultural or inherited. He rubbed his hand on his mouth. He would have cut off his fingers with tin snips for a drink. "I hung up on you because you hurt my feelings. The truth is, I'm short on friends, and I fear that my ineptitude is going to get my boy killed."

"What do you plan to do, Mr. Holland?"

"Take it to them. Under a black flag."

"Try to listen to me. Arnold Beckman wants the cup. He won't rest until he gets his hands on it. You have to use your wits. Odysseus used his intelligence to defeat his enemies. You have to do the same."

"I should put a Trojan horse in Beckman's backyard?"

"Don't mock me."

"What if I told him I'd give him the cup? What if I told him he could have me with it?"

"He would take the cup and then kill you. I suspect he would not do it all at once, either."

"You're preaching to the choir."

"And you'd put yourself in his power anyway?"

"If it would get my boy back. Ishmael could be released to you. You're a good diplomat. You could work it out."

"You know better, Mr. Holland."

"That cup was supposedly used by Jesus Christ at the Last Supper. If that's the case, why aren't I getting any he'p from Upstairs? What am I supposed to do?"

"I'm going to meet my attorney at the jail, then take Andre to a hospital. Do you want to come?"

"No, I have to find Ishmael's mother."

"Let me ask you a personal question. When this is over, do you plan to be around?"

"Around where?"

"San Antonio. Kerrville. Wherever."

"I'm not keen on travel." He waited for her to reply, but she didn't. "What kind of question is that?" he said.

"I was just curious. You're an unusual man, Mr. Holland."

"Can you call me Hack?"

"Formality has its purpose," she said.

He tried to see into her eyes, but she tied on her hat and didn't look directly into his face again.

He took a cab to Ruby's hotel. At first he did not recognize the woman retrieving her room key at the desk. From the back, she looked like a countrywoman whose hat was on crooked and whose hair had come loose and fallen in long wisps on one cheek, as though she were too tired to push it back in place. Then she turned around and looked straight at him, even though there were other people in the lobby. "Hack?" she said.

"How you doin', Ruby?"

"I just got your message."

"Where've you been?"

"At Beckman's. Out at the army base, too. I talked to a colonel. I thought they might help us."

"What'd he say?"

"They have their own problems. Can we sit down?"

"You went to Beckman's on your own?"

"I'll tell you about it. I really need to sit down first."

He was disconcerted by her eyes. He had forgotten how beautiful and mysterious they were, deep-set like a Viking's, the color of violets.

"Did someone drive you? Did you take a taxi?" he said.

"No, I walked. It's all right, Hack."

"No, it isn't."

He looked for a place to sit. The lobby had retained a gloomy form of elegance with its floor-standing ashtrays and potted palms and musty sofas and newspapers scattered on an oak table lit by a lamp that had a big rose-colored glass bubble for a shade. He put his hand on her elbow and walked her to a tasseled sofa by the window. She seemed to take no notice of his touch.

"You were at Beckman's apartment?"

"I hit him with an iron skillet. Several times. I wanted to kill him. If Maggie Bassett hadn't intervened, I probably would have."

"Then you just walked away?"

"Beckman wasn't in any condition to stop me. I forgot to mention something. Earlier I hit Maggie in the face with my fist."

"We need to move you away from this hotel."

"Why?"

"Beckman sent a man to throw acid in Beatrice DeMolay's eyes. What do you think he'd do to you?"

"It's Ishmael I'm worried about. Maggie warned me. I acted stupidly."

"Maggie did? After you hit her?"

"She's a jack-in-the-box."

"You were always heck on wheels. Remember when you threw the cherry pie in the congressman's face?"

"I did that?"

"In the hotel restaurant in Galveston. That's how we met."

"I'm really tired, Hack. I think I'm going to pass out."

"I need to tell you something. Ishmael came to me in a dream just this evening. It was a strange moonrise. The moon looked like a broken wafer. The moonlight was in the dream, like it was part of what was happening to Ishmael. He was a little boy again, dressed in his Easter suit, with a rabbit in a basket. He was trying to tell me where he was. I think I'll see him again and he'll tell me where he is. Maybe in a dream tonight."

She gazed at him woodenly, her lips moving as though she'd misunderstood his words.

AFTER THE SECOND bucket of water had been poured incrementally on the towel, Ishmael felt his lungs turn to fire and his heart swell to the size of a cantaloupe; he saw a great pink balloon inflate inside his head and suddenly pop as though it had been touched with a hot cigarette.

When he woke, someone was blotting his face with a towel. "Who are you?" Ishmael said.

"My name is Jeff. You're a tough guy."

"What happened to Jessie?"

"I sent him to make a snack. He was a little rough on you?"

"I have to use the bathroom."

"I'm going to unhook one of your hands and walk you to the water closet across the room. You don't want to take the pads off your eyes. You know why, too. We're in agreement on that?"

"I understand."

"I'll be up the stairs. All the doors are locked. You cain't go nowhere. Don't get ideas."

Ishmael nodded to show he understood.

"This doesn't have to end in a bad way, buddy," Jeff said. "Just don't give the wrong guy trouble. Come on, get up. Easy does it. There you go."

Jeff fitted his hand under Ishmael's left arm and walked him across a floor that felt paved with bricks, then left him inside a wood cubicle that had a door with a latch on it. "The chain is on the left-hand side of the box. Pull it when you're through," he said. "There's a roll of paper on the floor. Sorry about all this."

Then why are you doing it to me?

"What was that?"

"Nothing," Ishmael said. "Thank you for your consideration."

He sat on the toilet and felt in front of him to ensure that the door was shut. He peeled one eye pad partially back with his thumb and realized he was sitting in darkness. Through a crack in the wall, he could see water seeping through the stones below a ground-level window, and he guessed his basement prison was located close to a river or a lake. A solitary palm tree was silhouetted against the moon, its fronds straightening in the wind. Low in the sky, perhaps on the western horizon, a lake of electricity seemed to be flaring inside a storm bank. From somewhere above, he could hear the voice of the man who had almost drowned him: "The guy doesn't know anything. If he did, I would have gotten it out of him."

"Who told you to question him?" Jeff's voice said.

"Mr. Beckman wants something from the guy's father. I was helping out."

"Listen, Jessie, we're paid to do what Mr. Beckman tells us. Right now that means we find the soldier's mother."

"What for?"

"She beat the living shit out of Mr. Beckman. With a frying pan."

"You're kidding."

"Tell him that."

"Where is she now?" Jessie asked.

"That's what we have to find out."

"Then what?"

"You get to enjoy yourself."

"Like you don't want to have a crack at her?"

"I hear she's a looker, all right."

"Why's our hero taking so long?" Jessie said.

Ishmael pulled the chain on the water box, sending a torrent through the pipe into the toilet bowl.

HACKBERRY RENTED SEPARATE rooms on the top floor of a ten-story hotel on Alamo Plaza. While the bellhop put Ruby's suitcase on the luggage stand, Hackberry opened the French doors to the balcony and gazed down on the gazebo and wooded park in the center of the plaza and at the streetcars and colonnades over the sidewalks and the headlights of the motorcars wending their way into neighborhoods that were covered with trees. "Come look, Ruby," he said. "Isn't it grand? Look at the carousel."

She stood next to him, motionless, staring down at the plaza, her shoulder barely touching his. "We took Ishmael there on his first birthday," she said.

"I sat on the wood horse with him. He pointed at you every time we went around. Then he kept looking backward at you."

"I want to sleep now, Hack. In the morning we'll start out fresh."

He couldn't take his mind off the memories the carousel brought back, and he said nothing in reply.

"No one in Kerrville would help you?" she said.

"The law isn't there for individuals. It's there for people as a whole, or at least for chosen groups. Most of the time it serves the general good, but often at the expense of individuals. It's the secret nobody talks about."

"I don't care about any of that. I want to kill Arnold Beckman. Or hire someone to do it."

"That's not like you."

"That's what you think."

"Better go to sleep, Ruby," he said, his reverie broken. "Thinking at night isn't good for anybody. I'm three doors down."

IN HIS ROOM, he sat on the side of the bed and called Beatrice DeMolay. "I didn't know if you'd be home," he said. "Are you all right?"

"Yes, I just returned from the jail with Andre," she said. "He wouldn't go to the hospital. I got a call from your friend Sheriff Posey. He seems worried about you."

"Willard called?"

"He thinks you're angry at him."

"I knew Willard would come around. What did you tell him?"

"Nothing. Where are you?"

He told her the name of his hotel and his room number.

"I'm going to see Arnold Beckman in the morning," she said.

"This is the man who tried to blind you, Miss Beatrice. Stay away from him. Ruby already tore him up with an iron skillet. I suspect he's not in a good mood."

"She attacked Beckman? You'd better get her out of town."

"When we get our son back."

"You have to trust me, Mr. Holland."

"Tell Andre I'm glad he's doing okay."

"He's not okay. They treated him worse than they would an animal."

"Miss Beatrice, you cain't negotiate with Beckman. His kind only understand force."

"You're wrong," she said. "His kind understand money. That's their weakness."

"When I first came by the cup, I got drunk in a cantina and passed out in a pole shed full of manure. You came to me in a dream. You stroked my forehead and kissed me on the mouth. You told me I was chosen. You called me '*mi amor.*' You put me in a state of arousal. But I was just flattering myself. You were telling me I'd been given an obligation of appreciable significance, one I probably wasn't going to like."

"That's more detail than we need to hear, Mr. Holland."

"It's what happened," he said.

"There's a historical fact I think you have a right to know. It's not meant to upset you or to indicate I necessarily believe it's anything more than coincidence. In a small museum in Paris, there is a painting of Jacques de Molay's death by fire in front of Notre Dame Cathedral. Standing in the crowd is a man who looks exactly like Arnold Beckman."

"Miz DeMolay, you're a nice lady, but the wingspan of a moth is the wingspan of a moth. I'm going to bed now. Take care of yourself and Andre. Check with you later."

He quietly hung up the receiver and lay down on top of the covers and went to sleep with his clothes on, his fingers folded on his chest, the light burning, hoping Ishmael would speak to him again.

BUT HE HEARD no voices during the night and saw no images in his dreams. When he woke in the morning, he was not sure where he was. He sat on the side of the bed, the covers slipping off his legs, and tried to reconcile the sun shining on the balcony and the ornate normalcy of the room with the prospects the world offered him on that particular day. He had no legal authority and was powerless against the forces that had taken his son. He felt as though fate had imposed upon him a role he had seen many hapless individuals play when one day they discovered that they were absolutely alone, that no one believed their story or understood the nature of their loss and the depth of their grief. They may have had only one eye in the kingdom of the blind, but they did have one eye. Unfortunately, no one could have cared less.

He looked at his watch. It was 6:14. He opened his saddlebags and laid out his possessions and went into the bathroom and brushed his teeth and shaved and took a hot bath and put on a clean shirt and socks and underwear. He called down to the desk and ordered a plate of steak and eggs and a pot of coffee, then called Willard Posey in Kerrville. "Miz DeMolay said you were looking for me."

"I was wondering if you'd gotten yourself shot or if you'd set fire to a church or a saloon or anything like that," Willard said.

"Will you give me back my badge?"

"I talked with the state attorney's office."

"Did you hear me?"

"No, you're not getting back your badge. Now will you shut up a minute? He says Beckman has broken no laws. Does the state attorney like him? No. Does he fear him? He wouldn't say."

"You asked him that?"

"Forget the state attorney. What is it Beckman wants from you? You keep asking for he'p, but you're not willing to trust me with your secrets. I'm pretty wore out with it."

"I have a cup Jesus may have used at the Last Supper."

"You picked it up at an attic sale? How you fixed for Gutenberg Bibles?"

"It's encased in gold and jewels. It probably goes back at least to the Middle Ages." Hackberry could hear a sound like someone drumming a pencil on a desk blotter. "Are you still there?"

"I don't know what to say. There are rumors you were hit in the head with lightning when you were a child. Some say it was an improvement."

"You think I want a problem like this?"

"If what you say is true, give it to somebody. The Catholic Church or the Dunkers or the Holy Rollers, whoever. I'm embarrassed to have this conversation."

"You have three children, Willard."

"Don't drag my kids into this."

"That's the point. You cain't bear to think of them in the hands of a man like Beckman. Why should it be different with me? Do you have any idea what he may have already done to my son? You want me to tell you where I've hidden the cup?"

"No."

"Why not?"

"I don't know why not. You quit fretting me like this. You've got a talent for dropping an awful burden on a man's back with no warning."

"How's it feel?" Hackberry said.

"THERE'S A WAY," Ruby said later in the morning, when he walked her to a café. His hand was cupped on her elbow as they crossed the streetcar tracks.

"To catch one of Beckman's men if they come after you?"

"I think that's what we should try."

"That's like starting a fire to put out a fire. Sometimes you end up with two fires."

"Desperate situations, desperate measures," she replied.

"Here's another one: A bad idea is a bad idea."

"You think women are weak? That we have to be protected?"

"A group that pours acid in mailboxes isn't in need of protection." He felt her eyes on the side of his face. He was afraid to look at her.

"Don't tell what I'm going to do and what I'm not," she said.

"I'm not about to. I learned my lesson," he said.

"Are you patronizing me?"

"No."

"Then why the remark about suffragettes?"

"I once got kicked in the head by a bull named Original Sin. That's a fact."

"So don't say anything."

They stood on the curb, waiting for the traffic light to change. He forced himself to look her in the face.

"Got you," she said.

They sat at an outdoor café under a colonnade and ordered coffee and pie.

"We have to do something. We can't let events control us," she said.

He watched a streetcar pass, the wheels clicking on the tracks. "It's a fine day. Most days are. If a person can keep that in mind, every option is his."

His statement struck him as banal, and he thought he had lost her attention. The waiter brought their order.

"There's a man watching us," Ruby said. "Across the street. By the gazebo."

"Why do you think he's looking at us?"

"He was on the corner by the hotel when we walked out. I know a rounder when I see one."

Hackberry picked up his coffee cup and looked out the side of his eye at the park. "I don't see him."

"He's gone. He was unshaved and had on a floppy hat and was wearing tight pants tucked inside his boots."

Hackberry removed his billfold from his breast pocket and took three hundred-dollar bills from it and passed them under the table to Ruby.

"What's this for?"

"You need it. I'm going to walk you back to the hotel now. I'd like for you to stay in your room until I return."

"What are you going to do?" she asked.

"See Beckman."

"What will that accomplish?"

"I don't know. I wish I did." He blew out his breath, his strength gone. "Ruby?"

"What?" she said, setting down her fork.

"I admire you. I always did. I admire everything about you. You and Ishmael are the best human beings I ever knew. You know what remorse is? It's losing your family and knowing you're to blame. It's why I've killed people all these years."

The people at other tables stopped talking, their silverware suspended over their plates, their mouths frozen in midsentence.

Chapter
31

LIFE CHEATED A man in many ways. The secrets of Creation remained the secrets of Creation. A man's worst experiences were not healed by time but waited for him like a dark cocoon breaking open when he closed his eyes at night. And the comforting virtues of patience and charity often held no sway over irascibility and fear of death. But the greatest cheat, the one a person never got over, was betrayal by a friend and the subsequent loss of faith in one's fellow man.

After Hackberry took Ruby back to the hotel, he hired a jitney to drive him to Arnold Beckman's office and told the driver to wait while he went inside. The secretary was a small Asian woman who wore big glasses and made Hackberry think of a smiling goldfish. "He's not here right now."

"Do you know where he is?" Hackberry asked.

"Are you Mr. Holland?"

"How do you know my name?"

"Mr. Beckman said you might be here this morning. He left this for you."

On the piece of notebook paper were an address near the brothel district and the words "See me." Hackberry folded the paper and put it in his shirt pocket. "How did Mr. Beckman know I was on my way?"

"He's a very intelligent man. He always tells me to anticipate the

357

needs of my friends. He says a good businessman is a good listener. He says the client or customer will always tell you what he needs if you will listen."

"You like working for Mr. Beckman?"

"Yes, he is an old friend of my grandfather, Mr. Po. Do you know Mr. Po?"

Where had he heard the name? Something to do with the West Coast. Maybe the Tongs. "Is your grandfather in the export-import business?"

"Yes, perfume and exotic fish and teakwood furniture. He is very famous in the Orient."

"It was nice meeting you. If Mr. Beckman calls, tell him I'll be there in a few minutes."

"I will call him right now."

"That would be fine," he replied.

Hackberry went out the door and replaced his Stetson on his head and got inside the jitney, handing the driver the slip of paper given him by the Asian woman. "Know the neighborhood?"

"Yeah, but I usually don't take people down there at this hour of the day. You're sure that's where you want to go?"

FIFTEEN MINUTES LATER, he arrived at a paintless two-story building with wood cornices left over from the 1870s, located on a brick street that was cracked and sunken through the center and pooled with rainwater. Dirty children with rickets played on the sidewalks; the garbage cans had been knocked in the gutters. The day was bright and sunny and cool, but the air smelled of excrement and garbage and damp alleyways. Two black women without coats stood against a wall on the corner, overly made up, wearing straw hats with cloth flowers sewn on them, staring out of the shade and cold into the sunlight, their expressions a study in despair.

A waxed midnight-blue four-door car was parked in front of the building, the driver sleeping with his slug cap pulled over his eyes. Hackberry's jitney pulled in behind. Hackberry took a ten-dollar bill from his wallet. He tore it in half and handed one half to the driver.

"If I don't come out in fifteen minutes, come in and get me. I'm often forgetful about the time."

"The kids fill garbage cans with water and throw them off the roofs. It's like getting hit with a piano. This street is called 'Micks and Spicks Avenue.' You ever hear the expression 'You can lead an Irishman to water, but you can't make him take a bath'?"

"I'm Irish."

"Sorry."

"You are. How about I pay you now?" Hackberry said, dropping several bills through the window on the seat, taking back the torn half of the ten, no longer even aware of the driver's presence.

Thirty feet away, a handsome woman wearing a riding dress with a lace hem and boots spotted with mud had just emerged from the entrance of the building. Hackberry walked toward her. "What are you doing here, Miz DeMolay?"

"Conducting business. You need to go home, Mr. Holland."

"That's what people in the saloon used to tell me."

"Get out of here."

"The man inside tried to disfigure your face. I don't understand why you're here. Are you trying to he'p me?"

"Please go, sir. Now."

"I'm not going anywhere. Where is Andre?"

"That's not your concern." She glanced at a silhouette in an upstairs window. "Get out of my way."

He stepped aside. When he reached to open the back door of the car for her, she slapped his hand. "Get away from me. I don't want to see you again. You're nothing but trouble. You're ignorant and uneducated and willful. You're everything you disdain in others."

She slammed the car door behind her and turned her face away as the driver started the engine and pulled from the curb, honking at the children in the street.

THE DOWNSTAIRS OF the building had a long hallway with offices in it that contained nothing but stacked furniture and crates of canned food with Oriental printing. Hackberry walked up the stairs and saw

Arnold Beckman behind a desk in a cluttered office, a ledger book spread in front of him, paper cuffs on his forearms to prevent ink spills from getting on his skin or clothes.

"Nice building you have. What's the rent, a dollar a week?" Hackberry said.

Beckman lifted his head, smiling, his silvery-blond hair hooked behind his ears. There was a bandage on his chin and one on his forehead. "My warehouse is one block away. You had a little spat outside with the Great Whore of Babylon?"

"No need for rough language."

"I forgot. Beatrice is one of the vestal virgins."

Hackberry gazed around the office. "No painting of Custer at the Last Stand?"

"You're an admirer?"

"I suspect he was a pretentious asswipe."

"You're quite the conundrum."

"You got my boy. What do I have to do to get him back?"

Beckman put down his pen and knitted his fingers together. "You've lost me."

"I'll give you the cup and the candlesticks, too. I spent the coins and the currency. That's everything I took from the hearse."

"I'll speak to Beatrice about this. Maybe she'll understand what you're talking about."

"Beatrice DeMolay is your friend?"

"Of course she's a friend."

Hackberry tried to refocus his concentration. "I'm the one with the cup. No one else knows where it's at."

"Would you like a drink?" Beckman said, opening a bottom desk drawer.

"Deal with me. I keep my word. What do you have to lose?"

Beckman set two chrome-plated shot glasses on the desk blotter and squeaked the cork from the neck of a whiskey bottle. "I think you're unsettled by the fact that Beatrice and I have a long-term relationship," he said, pouring. "When she was younger, she was quite a piece. She probably told you she made her fortune from the oil discovery at Goose Creek Bay. Do you really believe that?"

"I don't like the way you're talking about her."

"She's been a prostitute since she was fifteen. How did she suddenly grow into a geologist?"

"I'm here about my boy, not Miz DeMolay."

"Take your drink. I love bourbon on ice with a sprig of mint and a teaspoon of sugar, but this is all I have on hand. Do you realize you're perspiring?"

"Where's Maggie?"

"Doing odds and ends. Do you think she's going to help you? Mr. Holland, you have to be the most naive man I've ever met."

"I'll leave the cup in a neutral place. Your people can leave my boy at a hospital."

"You stole from me, and you're going to pay for it, on my terms."

"Do you have a son?"

"I have sons and daughters all over the world."

"Miz DeMolay said you're in a medieval painting she saw in Paris. I didn't believe her."

"You do now?"

"I wonder if maybe you're the genuine article."

"What is the genuine article?"

"The one everybody is afraid of seeing. The one that's got the body of a goat."

Beckman laughed. "You probably know I had an encounter with your common-law wife. What's-her-name? Ruby? That's what I call a woman. A shame you put her in the mix."

"Repeat that?"

Beckman drank his shot glass empty and set it on the blotter. He opened the cover on his watch and looked at the time. "If I were you, I'd toggle back to my hotel."

THE SUN HAD gone behind the clouds unexpectedly. A moment later, just as the telephone rang on Ruby's nightstand, rain began clicking on the French doors that opened on her balcony, glasslike pieces of hail bouncing on the rail. A thunderous boom shook the room. She picked up the receiver.

"This is the front desk, Miss Dansen. A colored man just delivered a message for you," the clerk said.

"I can hardly hear you. A message from a colored man?"

"No, the colored man delivered the message. He said it was from your son."

"Stop him."

"He's already gone."

"Send the message up. No, I'll come down."

In the elevator she had to press her hand against her chest in order to breathe correctly, to keep her balance, to stop her head from floating away. When she stepped into the lobby, the floor seemed to tilt, the potted palms and marble columns to break into molecules. Outside, sheets of rain slapped against the front of the hotel and whipped the awning over the entrance. "I'm Miss Dansen. Which direction did the colored man go?" she said.

"I didn't notice, ma'am," the desk clerk replied. He took an envelope out of her key box and handed it to her. The message was in pencil, the lettering full of ripples, as though written by an unsteady hand. It read:

> Dear Mother,
>
> Trust the man of color who brought this. He is as brave and good as the men I commanded on the Marne. I am four blocks away at the end of the alley. I am unable to move or get help. Please come.
>
> Love,
>
> *Ishmael*

There was a map drawn at the bottom of the notepaper. She went to the lobby window and looked at the rain swirling out of the sky. A hundred questions pounded inside her head. Where was Hackberry? How could Ishmael know where she was staying? Did he overhear his captors talking? Was the colored man the Haitian who had driven Hackberry from Kerrville to San Antonio? If the note was a fraud, how did the hoaxer know of Ishmael's affection for his troops? Was Maggie Bassett involved? Or was this the miracle she had prayed for?

"Tell the doorman to flag a jitney for me," she told the clerk.

She went upstairs and put on her coat and her sweater and a long coat and a hat that had a four-inch pin with a purple glass knob shaped like a lily.

Don't go by yourself, a voice said.

And do what? Wait on Hack? she answered herself. *Or call the police officers who kidnapped Ishmael from the clinic?*

A tree of lightning burst in the clouds as she ran for the open door of the jitney, a newspaper over her head.

HACKBERRY COULDN'T BELIEVE the change in the weather when he came out of Beckman's building. The sky was dark, the sidewalks spotting with raindrops, thunder echoing like cannon beyond the hills. He wondered if it signaled a change in his life, the deliverance that had been denied him the day he led a stolen horse up the incline to Beatrice DeMolay's brothel in Old Mexico.

On the corner, the two black prostitutes had stepped beneath an overhang. He walked toward them and touched the brim of his hat. "I wonder if you ladies could tell me where I can hire a taxi."

"On the main street, maybe," one said. "They ain't none down here."

"It's fixing to cut loose," he said, squinting at the sky.

"The crib is up the alley. If you got the money, we got the time," said the same woman. "Ain't no rain in there."

"I appreciate the offer, but I have someone waiting on me. You know Mr. Beckman very well?"

Both women looked straight ahead, the wind ruffling their hair, their faces impassive, as smooth and dark as chocolate.

"I hear he's rough on working girls," Hackberry said.

"You ain't heard it from us," said the same woman.

"I heard he hangs them up and beats them with his fists. Mostly Mexican girls. I suspect some black ones, too."

"Why you telling us that?"

"Maybe you can do a good deed. Stop another girl from getting hurt."

The spokeswoman for the two looked at the clouds. She was missing a front tooth; a scar like a piece of white string ran horizontally through one eye. "My charge for good deeds is ten dol'ars," she said.

He took a gold piece from his pocket and opened his palm so she could see it.

"He brung a colored girl to a basement. Not in this part of town. I ain't said who brung her. I just said 'he' brung her. He left her alone and she got out a window. She came back here to get her pimp, and the two of them took off, traveling light."

"What's her name? Where did she go?"

The woman took the gold piece from Hackberry's hand. "Don't know. Don't care."

"Where's the basement?"

"Don't know that, either."

"Beckman has my son."

She put the gold piece in her purse and showed no reaction.

"I'm talking about my son," he said.

The woman seemed to be drifting off to sleep. Hackberry looked back at the entrance to Beckman's building and at the broken wood crates stacked on the sidewalk for pickup. "You ever see any Chinamen down here?"

"They don't kill nobody," the woman said, opening her eyes.

"I don't follow you."

"We know who you are. You the one killed Eddy Diamond."

"I didn't mean to."

"You done it just the same."

"Maybe it was more complicated than you think."

"You want some jelly roll, baby? If not, beat feet. Ain't nothing free."

He began walking toward the main street of the brothel district, his head bent against the wind, the raindrops cold and hard as bird shot.

THE SIDEWALKS WERE empty, the gutters running fast, when she stepped out of the jitney in front of an alleyway that yawned like a ravenous mouth. Ruby heard the streetcar clang behind her, then the sound of its wheels diminishing on the tracks. The alleyway was brick-paved, channeled with runoff in the center, lined on either side with trash cans and wet paper bags splitting with garbage. At the far end was a green wood door with a rope for a handle. She began walking toward it.

Above, rainwater was sluicing off the roofs and twirling down on her head, running into her eyes. She looked over her shoulder, hoping to see someone on the sidewalk, perhaps a happy group of soldiers on pass from the army base. A vagabond stared back at her, his clothes as soaked as tissue paper. He walked away.

The door was ajar. She cupped her hand around the rope that served as a handle. "Ishmael?" she said.

The only sound she heard was a strip of gutter swinging from an eave high above. She pulled back the door, scraping it across a concrete bib. There was a glow from another door down a hallway. The interior of the room smelled of malt and mold and wood barrels.

"Ishmael?" she repeated.

As her eyes adjusted, she saw the back of a wheelchair and a figure sitting in it, wearing a tall-crowned, wide-brimmed hat, a blanket draped over the shoulders. "Oh, Ishmael," she said, running toward the wheelchair.

The door slammed shut behind her; a man stepped out of the shadows and locked it with a steel bolt. He wore a goatee and had a triangular face and a weak mouth and hands with long fingers that made her think of an amphibian.

"You're sure a dumb bitch," he said.

He hit her in the middle of the face with his fist, knocking her into the wheelchair. A manikin with hinges on the arms and legs toppled from the wheelchair onto the floor. Ruby stared up at the man. He wore steel-toed boots and canvas pants and a wide belt with an antler-handled knife on it. "My name is Jessie. I'm gonna teach you how to yodel."

She pushed herself on her hands against a barrel, her hat crooked on her head. "Where's my son?"

"I'll take you to him. You're gonna have to do me a favor first. You're gonna be a good girl. You know what being a good girl means, don't you?" He stepped closer to her. "Don't look at the door. There ain't no cavalry coming. You're in the hands of the J Boys. I'm the gentle one. You don't want to meet Jim or Jack or Jeff. They don't got healthy urges."

His trouser cuffs and the tops of his boots were bluish green, smeared with a substance that looked like clay.

"Don't hit me again," she said.

"I wouldn't dream of it, darlin'."

"Help me up, please."

"I think you're doing fine right there."

"When will you take me to see Ishmael?"

"Soon as we finish with the favor I mentioned."

"It was you who wrote the note?"

"Maybe your son wrote it."

"My son wouldn't lure me here."

"You cain't tell what a man will do when his life is in danger, war hero or not." He lowered his hand to his belt and hooked his thumb in it, his fingers hanging below the buckle. He smiled at her almost kindly.

"I don't think I can do what you're asking me to," she said.

"Sure you can. You know, you're cute when you say it like that. Come on, hon. Time's a-wasting. Let's get with it."

"I hurt my back. You have to help me up. I'll undress."

"It's all right if you try to buy time. They all do. But you're not leaving here until the right things happen. That's the way it is."

"I understand."

"That's a good girl. Now get them bloomers off."

She raised her arms to him and waited. He grasped her by the wrists and pulled her to her feet. He was grinning, his teeth like kernels of corn, his breath rife with the smells of nicotine and fish. "You're quite the little heifer."

She pulled the pin from her hat, gripping the glass knob tightly in her palm, and drove the point into his mouth. He gagged and tried to push her away, but she drove the point deeper, past his teeth into the cheek, scraping bone, piercing the skin behind the jaw, the glass knob wedging against the roof of his mouth.

"Where is he? Tell me where my son is," she said, kicking his shins, flailing at his head with her fists.

Whatever he tried to say was lost in the blood clogging his throat. She leaned down to pick up a loose brick and heard him grunt as he pulled the hat pin from his mouth. She lifted the brick above her shoulder and hit him just below the eye, caving in the cheekbone.

But he wasn't done. He ran at her with his full weight, swinging his fists, and knocked her to the floor again. A moment later, he was out the door and running down the alleyway into the storm. The manikin lay beside Ruby, its face turned toward her, as glossy and smooth and eyeless as a darning sock.

Chapter 32

Ruby sat on the side of the bed in her hotel room and told Hackberry everything that had happened behind the door in the alleyway. When she finished, he sat beside her and put his arm over her shoulder. "You didn't want to wait on me?" he said.

"I didn't know when you'd be back," she replied.

"His name was Jessie? And you've never seen him?"

"Would the police have a photograph of him?"

"It's unlikely. A man like Beckman doesn't hire known criminals. Or he brings them in from somewhere else and then gets rid of them."

"What do we do now, Hack?"

"I see only two choices. Maybe they're not the best, but I don't know a third one."

"What are they?" she asked.

Through the window, the sky seemed unrelenting in its darkness, as though neither the moon nor the sun would ever be more than a vaporous smudge.

"I want to use the telephone in my room," he said.

"Use it here."

"I need to have a conversation of a kind I've never had."

———

BACK IN HIS room, he asked the switchboard operator to dial Beatrice DeMolay's number. She picked up the phone immediately. "Mr. Holland?"

"How'd you know it was me?"

"You want to know why I talked to you so angrily outside Arnold Beckman's office."

"It crossed my mind."

"I'm entering into a business arrangement with him. You need to stay out of it," she said.

"I think you let me down."

"Do you, now?"

"Call it what you like, Miss B. I had a world of respect for you. What the hell are you doing?"

"What gives you the right to ask me that?"

"You've got a point. So I won't. That's not why I called, anyway. I need your man Andre."

"Boy, if you don't have nerve."

"*I* have nerve? You were Ishmael's friend. I thought you were mine, too. Maybe you have a reason for being with Beckman. But seeing you there was hard to swallow."

"What do you want Andre for?"

"He offered to he'p me. He's the only one."

"Help you in what way?"

"Ask him. Or don't. You can hang up the telephone if you like. Ishmael's mother was attacked by one of Beckman's men. He wanted to violate her as well, except she shoved a hat pin halfway down his throat."

He waited and watched the rain sliding down the windows, the electricity flickering through the heavens. He wondered if the latter indicated a sign and decided it did not.

"I'll send him over," she said. "He's driving my new motorcar. As you are aware, my REO is undergoing massive repairs."

"I hope they do a good job on that," he replied. "I hear there are some right good mechanics here'bouts."

"Good-bye, Mr. Holland. You never fail to distinguish yourself. I thought I had met every kind of man. I didn't realize how vain I was."

Before he could reply, she hung up.

He called Willard Posey in Kerrville. "It's Hack. I need Deputy Pickins to bring a certain item to my hotel room in San Antonio."

"The Kerr County Sheriff's Department is running a delivery service to San Antonio?"

"Don't be light about this."

"How could I be light about it? Are you talking about the item I think you're talking about? I cain't take any more of this craziness, Hack."

"I think that cup is the real thing."

"What are you going to do with it?"

"What do you care?"

"One of two things is going on here," Willard said. "Either you've lost your mind, or you have in your possession an object a baptized person is going to have to think very seriously about."

"I'm not sure what I'm going to do. But if I don't do something pretty soon, I'm going to lose my boy. What would you do in my stead? He's in the hands of people who are worse than the convicts in Huntsville."

"You never ease up, Hack. You could squeeze blood from a rock."

"Get off the pot."

"I won't forget that."

"I hope you don't," Hackberry said.

"Tell me where the cup is and give me the directions to where you're at."

A HALF HOUR LATER, a different desk clerk called Hackberry's room. "There's a peculiar nigger down here. He says you told him to come to the hotel."

"What's his name?"

"He didn't give it."

"Then ask him."

The clerk went away from the phone and came back. "He says his name is Andre."

"Send him up."

"We cain't do that, sir."

Hackberry took the elevator down to the lobby. Andre was standing by the side door, his hat in his hand, water dripping off his coat on the marble floor. Hackberry went to the desk. "I need the use of your office."

"The office is restricted to employees," the clerk said.

He was sorting the mail and didn't look up when he spoke. Hackberry stared at him, but the clerk didn't notice. He was tall and had slicked hair and a high, shiny forehead and wore a silver and red necktie and a white shirt with garters on the sleeves.

"This man is my friend and associate," Hackberry said. "I don't like the way you've treated him. We'll be using your office. If you don't like it, call the owners. In the meantime, don't disturb us."

He motioned for Andre to follow him into the office and closed the door behind them. The desk clerk was staring at them through the glass, his jaw flexing. Hackberry pointed a finger as he would a pistol. The clerk began stuffing mail into the key boxes, glancing back over his shoulder.

"You are always very candid in your dealings with people, Mr. Holland," Andre said. "I'm not sure that is necessarily wise."

"Rude pipsqueaks are rude pipsqueaks. So you treat them as pipsqueaks. The police knocked you around?"

"They have done much worse to others. Miss Beatrice said I should talk with you. She also said you might make unreasonable demands of me and that I must use my own judgment in dealing with you."

"She tell you anything else?"

"She said you have concrete for brains."

"I saw her at Arnold Beckman's office in the brothel district. Another man was driving her."

"She knows what I think of Mr. Beckman. My feelings about him are not positive ones."

"If a rusty drainpipe could talk, I know what it would sound like," Hackberry said.

"I told you about the men who abducted my children and the fate that was theirs as a result," Andre said. He had not sat down. He

wiped the dampness from his face with a handkerchief. "I told you how I took these wicked men into the jungle at night and by dawn had relieved them of the evil presences blocking the light from their eyes. I think you want to know the details of an event that should be left in the jungle, except you are afraid to ask."

"What you tell me is up to you," Hackberry said.

"The trees and the foliage do not have eyes or ears, but men do. People in my village heard the sounds that came out of the jungle that night. Later, some of the villagers would not look into my eyes when we passed on the street. They no longer wanted to be my friend or my neighbor. They were ashamed that I had ever been a priest in their church. I do not want that to happen to us, Mr. Holland. I do not want to lose you as my friend."

"Would you be willing to do to Beckman the same things you did to your children's kidnappers?" Hackberry said.

"That is not an honest question."

"I don't *comprendo*."

"The question is whether *you* are willing to do these things, Mr. Holland. I think you are not. And for that reason, I cannot do them for you."

"I'll do what it takes to get my son back."

"You will not be the same later."

"I fired my revolver into a cattle car loaded with Mexican peasants, including women and children."

"You did this deliberately?"

"No, I fired inside the smoke and dust. Then I saw what I had done. I wouldn't deliberately kill a woman or a child."

"That is the difference between us. That is why my voice is the way it is. On the night I delivered up these men from their evil deeds, I felt a bird fly out of my breast. It was as white as snow, and it glided over the ocean and died inside the darkness, and I was not the same when the sun rose in the morning."

"Do you want Beckman to end up with the cup?" Hackberry said. Andre didn't reply.

"What are you looking at?" Hackberry said.

"We have made an enemy we did not need," Andre replied.

Hackberry turned around. The desk clerk was on the telephone, his back to them, hunched over, the receiver held tightly against his ear, as though his posture could hide the nature of his conversation.

"Maybe he's calling his wife," Hackberry said.

"Evil men are all born of the same seed and carry it with them wherever they go," Andre said. "That is why many of them resemble gargoyles."

"You'll never make a humanist, Andre."

FROM HIS WINDOW, Hackberry saw Deputy Darl Pickins park a Kerr County Sheriff's Department motorcar in front of the hotel and run inside, an object wrapped in a slicker held against his chest. In less than two minutes, he was at Hackberry's door, out of breath.

"You must have put the spurs to it," Hackberry said.

"Elevator was broke."

"I meant between here and Kerrville."

"I went to the cave like Sheriff Posey said and—"

Hackberry reached through the doorway and pulled Darl inside. "We don't need to be advertising our business."

"The sheriff give me that sense. Where you want me to put it?"

"On the bed is fine."

"Can you tell me what it is?"

"Maybe I better not."

"Your pistol and your bowie knife are on the bed, Mr. Holland. I also heard some of what the sheriff said to you on the telephone. I'm off duty today."

"I don't think you can he'p on this one."

"I ain't stupid, sir. Sheriff Posey don't get upset often. You got to him. Has this got something to do with the church?"

"Indirectly, I guess. Which church you mean?"

"For me, one is just the same as the other. If we're Christians, ain't we supposed to he'p out each other?"

Hackberry wasn't listening. "It was you wrapped it with twine?"

"I didn't want it to fall loose."

"You didn't look inside?"

"I wouldn't do that. Not without asking."

Hackberry opened his pocketknife and cut the twine. He lifted the cup from the bed and placed it on the nightstand, under a lamp.

"What is it?" Darl said.

"Probably depends on who you talk to. The gold and the jewels are most likely from medieval times. The two onyx goblets fused together might go back a bit farther."

"What are we talking about here, Mr. Holland?"

"A lady who used to run a brothel and a Haitian who was a pagan priest say it was used by Jesus at the Last Supper. I found it in a hearse that was carrying a load of ordnance down in Mexico. That was right before I burned the hearse. The ordnance belonged to Arnold Beckman."

Darl was staring at the two goblets, fused end to end, one acting as the base. "So the gold cup set in the top was drank out of by Jesus?"

"I don't think a carpenter would be using gold dishware. The onyx cup is another matter."

"This makes me feel a little uneasy, Mr. Holland."

"Why?"

"It's not exactly your ordinary day-to-day experience," Darl replied.

"Beckman has got his hands on my son."

"That's why you've got your revolver and bowie knife and ammunition laid out on the bed?"

"I wish it was that simple."

"How'd Mr. Beckman get holt of your son?"

"My ex-wife betrayed me."

"The one people say was hooked up with the Hole-in-the-Wall Gang?"

"That's the lady."

"Sounds to me like her butt ought to be sitting in a jail cell."

A strand of Darl's red hair was hanging in his face; his thin frame and wide shoulders had the angularity and stiffness of coat hangers. The blue kerchief tied around his neck was embroidered with tiny white stars.

"I changed my mind," Hackberry said.

"Sir?"

"If you don't mind, I'd like for you to hang around."

MAGGIE PACED THE floor in her living room, her nails biting into her palms, a habit she couldn't rid herself of any more than she could get the cold out of her bones. Dr. Romulus Atwood, who had actually been to veterinary school, had told her that a thyroid disorder was responsible for her subnormal body temperature, and it could most likely be cured by the mineral baths at Hot Springs, Arkansas, a resort for criminals of every stripe. Once they arrived there, he set about fleecing anyone he could at the card tables, using her as his shill.

And that was what she had been, a shill for everyone: pimps, madams, opium den operators, cardsharps, and the worst of the lot, the mercenary contractors who sent passenger-car loads of gunmen to kill and terrorize the sodbusters during the Johnson County War. And now an international arms dealer. Top that.

She put another log in the fireplace. When it didn't catch right away, she jabbed it with the poker and stacked another one on top of the first and poked at the green bark on both of them, not raising the temperature one degree.

When would it stop raining? She could not remember seeing a darker day. The sky was black upon black, relieved only by the fog rising from the river or a silvery quivering in the clouds that briefly illuminated the countryside, like the flickering scenes of a newsreel filmed in the trenches.

She mustn't think of the trenches or the war, she thought. That was all she had heard about for years. First it was the sinking of the passenger ships by the submarines, the stories about the survivors crawling like lines of ants along the hull, slipping helplessly into space, finally succumbing to the coldness of the depths. Then there were the photos of the disfigured, the amputees, and those who sported glass eyes and prosthetic faces so others would not see what they really looked like. War was bad. Who could argue with that? Why did everybody have to keep talking about it?

But her depression and angst and guilt were not about the war or having to hear about it. She wadded up more paper and stuffed it between the logs, trying to shut down her thoughts before they got out of hand. Then she gave up and allowed herself a moment of clarity, the kind she usually avoided, and thought about the telegram and letter from Ruby Dansen to Hackberry that she had burned in the fireplace at their home on the Guadalupe.

With forethought and design, she had destroyed any chance of Hackberry and Ruby reuniting; she had inculcated suspicion and animosity in each of them that had lasted for years. She had created a masterpiece of deceit that had ruined a large part of their lives.

She stared wanly out the window at the hills. She could see bare trees silhouetted against the sky, like stick figures hooked together in a medieval painting depicting doomsday. No, she mustn't think like that. As bad as her deeds were, they were understandable. She was fighting to save her home. She was Hackberry's wife; Ruby Dansen was not. What woman wouldn't do the same? Who were they to judge her?

The answer was no one. And that was because no one else knew what she had done.

The thought was not a comforting one. By the river, she witnessed a phenomenon she had heard of but never seen. A streak of lightning struck a hill, and instead of disappearing inside the darkness with a clap of thunder, it rolled in a yellow ball across a meadow and exploded at the base of a tree with the rippling brilliance of a Klansman setting fire to a kerosene-soaked cross, burning brightly in the great blackness that seemed to cover the land.

She stepped back from the window, swallowing, waiting for the thunder. But none came. Instead, a motorcar pulled up in front, one wheel sinking into her lawn, and two men got out, grinning, even though the rain was blowing in their faces. She felt her stomach curdle and her buttocks constrict.

THEY COMPRISED HALF of the group Arnold referred to as his J Boys. What were their names? It didn't matter. They represented a group that had been poured into a single mold from the same mix, like primeval ooze that had been separated from the rest of the gene pool and couldn't be disposed of in any other fashion.

She opened the door, the wind blowing inside. "What are you doing here?" she said.

"Mr. Beckman wants you protected," one of them said.

"From what?"

"Someone who might hurt you. Like they done to Jessie."

"I can't begin to understand your English."

"He got a hat pin rammed in his mouth and out his cheek. Right now he's spitting blood and whiskey in a pail. He's not having a lot of laughs about it. We'll just step inside, if you don't mind."

"I do mind."

"Sorry, ma'am, it's what Mr. Beckman says. You have a right nice place here."

Then they were inside, one of them pushing the door shut, their eyes roaming the walls and framed pictures and paintings and bookcases and mantel and furniture, everything that was hers, that told her who she was.

"Want us to take off our shoes?"

She didn't answer. She stared at them, her thoughts concealed. *Don't fight or argue with them. Don't play on their terms.*

"Do you like working for Arnold?" she asked.

"Mr. Beckman? It's all right."

"Are you afraid of him?"

"He don't hire men that's afraid."

"That's what I thought," she said. "Do you want a drink?"

"We're not supposed to do it on the job. But in this kind of weather?"

"That's a good attitude. Sit down at the kitchen table."

"We won't argue," the second man said. Unlike his friend, he had the upper body of a hod carrier and walked with a slouch, the way recidivist convicts did, and smelled of earth and damp wool. His work boots were smeared with bluish-green clay. "I better take them off."

"The cleaning lady is coming tomorrow," she said.

"I could tell you was looking at them."

"She's a thinker," his friend said. "Right, Miss Maggie? That's what Mr. Beckman says. You're always thinking."

That's right, imbecile. That's why getting even is so much fun. A little planning, a little application of superior intelligence, and people like me turn people like you into weapons and do damage that gets worse by the day. I hope you enjoy the ride, you stupid shit.

"Would you like wine or bourbon?" she said.

"How about both?" the man in work boots said. "That's what winos call 'wine spodiotti.'"

"Maybe I can freshen up and join you," she said.

"There's nothing wrong with that. I'm Jim," the first man said. "This here is Jack. You got to watch Jack. He's bit randy. Just kidding."

"I think I can handle you fellows."

"Ma'am?" Jim said. He had removed his hat when he entered the house, revealing a pointy bald pate combed over with hair that resembled mop string.

"You think I'll be up to it?" she said. "Come on, tell me. I'm not shy."

The two men were looking across the table at each other. "Who are we to comment on a lady such as yourself?" Jim said.

"I'll be right back. Don't go anywhere."

"You can count on it," said Jack, wiping his nose on his wrist.

She went into her bedroom and closed and locked the door, easing the bolt into place as softly as possible. She undressed and shook out her hair and put on a pair of eggplant-colored high heels, decorated with a steel-cut bronze-bead design, and turned sideways in the mirror, running her fingers along the flatness of her stomach, letting them trail off her appendix scar.

Want to play, boys? Want to see what it's like to stick your pathetic penises in the light socket?

She took a nickel-plated .32-caliber revolver from her dresser, then walked naked to the door and unlocked it, snapping the bolt loudly. She raised her left arm against the jamb and leaned on it, her right hand holding the revolver behind her hip. "See anything you like?"

They stared, openmouthed, obviously unable to assimilate what they were seeing.

"You're not bothered by the scar on my tummy, are you?" she said.

"No, ma'am," Jim said.

"Are you boys hungry?"

"Yes, ma'am," Jim said.

"How about you, Jack?"

"I wouldn't mind."

"You don't sound very enthusiastic," she said.

"Long as it's me first," Jack said.

Jim looked at him. "Where you get off with that?"

"I got my standards," Jack said.

"Will y'all tell Arnold?"

Jim made a cross over his heart. "You got our word."

"I thought you might say that."

She placed her left hand behind her neck and rotated her head. "I get such a crick back there. Can you take it out for me?"

"In ways you wouldn't believe, lady," Jack said.

"You say you have your standards?" she said, her gaze not meeting his.

"I don't take sloppy seconds."

"Stand up for me," she said. "Both of you."

"That may not be easy to do at the moment," Jim said, grinning.

"I have my standards, too. Let's have a look at you."

"What's the joke?" Jim asked.

"I just want to see if your expectations are rising. It's a vanity of mine. You're sure you're not going to tell Arnold about this?"

"You got our word," Jim said.

"Come on, big boy. Stand up."

They rose from their chairs, hunched slightly forward, waiting, their fingers touching the tabletop. She brought the revolver from behind her hip and pointed it at them.

"Now get your worthless asses out of here," she said.

Both men averted their eyes from the muzzle.

"You're gonna regret this," Jim said, breathing heavily.

Maggie lowered the pistol barrel slightly. "Say one more word and I'll shoot your dick off."

They edged through the living room, their hands in front of them, as though pushing back the air. Then they skittered sideways like crabs out the door and ran for their motorcar. She locked the door after them and went back into the bedroom and called Arnold Beckman's office, still in the nude. She heard the motorcar drive away.

Beckman picked up the telephone. "Beatrice?"

"No, it's Maggie, you bastard. You're dealing with Beatrice DeMolay?"

"She's putting together a big shipment of Mausers for some friends in South America."

"I give a fuck about your business deals after you sent these two animals to rape me?"

"Sent *whom* to rape you?"

"Jim and Jack. They didn't give their last names. They were too busy tearing off my clothes."

"Are you crazy?"

"I just chased them out the door at gunpoint. If I hadn't gotten to my pistol, I would have been raped. Why would you do such a thing to me, Arnold? I can't believe you'd do that." She began to cry into the receiver.

"I don't know what's going on here. They wouldn't dare. They know I'd have them ripped apart. With machines and chains, joint and seam."

"You think I made it up. They were going to sodomize me. They were describing what they were going to do to me. In detail."

"Stop crying. I know you, Maggie. You could lie the paint off a battleship."

"Why would I lie? The thought of them touching me makes me sick to my stomach."

"You're up to something."

"You cheap motherfucker. I hate you. I know we've both done loathsome things in our lives, but I didn't believe you were capable of this."

"I'll talk to them."

"You'll *talk* to them? I have their scratches all over me. I can feel their breath on my skin. The one named Jack put his tongue on my appendix scar. Ask him, you son of a bitch, and see what he says."

Then she hung up and began drawing her nails down her breasts and arms and shoulders and thighs, her eyes closed, her chin lifted, as though she were at prayer or offering up a sacrifice on an altar dedicated solely to her.

Chapter
33

ISHMAEL LAY ON his side on the cot, his eyes still taped, the cool, damp, moldy odor of stone surrounding him, comforting and restorative in its way, a touch of a netherworld that contained no pain. Another blessing had come to him, one he had not anticipated. Either through fear or stress or physical exhaustion, or maybe surrender to his fate, his body seemed purged of the withdrawal symptoms that were the plague of every intravenous addict. The nausea and night sweats were gone, and so were the flashes of light behind the eyes, the heart palpitations, the shortness of breath, the vertigo, the ache in the joints and the fire in the connective tissue, the premonitions of doom, the conviction that a fissure was opening under one's feet.

Maybe all these things would return. But at the moment, they were gone, and he breathed the smell of the stone that reminded him of the cave across the river from his father's ranch and a time in his life when spring was eternal and bluebonnets and Indian paintbrush covered the riverside. Something else had occurred that he could not explain, a dream or a moment on the edge of sleep that he associated with hope and a belief that he was not alone, no matter the degree of adversity imposed upon him.

During the rainstorm, he had drifted off, and inside the darkness, he saw himself as a little boy standing in front of a hill that was struck by lightning. But the lightning did not disappear with the strike. It gathered into a churning ball and rolled up a grassy slope and exploded on a tree that was cruciform in shape, setting it afire. The radiance it gave off was as bright as liquid gold and so intense it made his eyes water. Then he saw his father walk into the light and kneel in the grass and gather his son in his arms.

When Ishmael woke, he didn't know where he was. "Big Bud?" he said to the darkness.

"Who?" Jeff replied.

"Didn't mean to bother you," Ishmael replied.

"Bother *me*? You're the one with the problem, kid."

That was no longer the case. The man named Jessie had gone away, then had returned to the basement, hardly able to speak, making gargling sounds and spitting into a tin bucket.

"What the hell happened to you?" Jeff said.

"She rammed a fucking hat pin down my throat, that's what."

"Who did?"

"That crazy Dansen bitch."

"Why did you let her do that?"

"*Let* her? You think I *let* her? I swallowed a pint of blood. I'm lucky she didn't put out my eyes."

"You let her get away?"

"What's with you? Are you listening? Have you ever got stabbed through the mouth? She tried to pack a hat pin down my throat. It had a knob on it big as a walnut."

"You don't look so bad. Quit whining."

"*Whining*? You said *whining*?"

"She saw your face?"

Jessie gargled and spat again. Ishmael could smell whiskey and hear it slosh in the bottle.

"It was dark in the room," Jessie said. "She couldn't see my face. I'm sure of it. I knocked her on her ass, too."

"What's Mr. Beckman say?"

"Nothing. He didn't say nothing."

"Sounds like you messed up proper. Been good knowing you, Jess."

Jessie gargled and spat again, his throat choking up. "You backstabbing son of a bitch."

Ishmael closed his eyes behind the cotton pads, the animus of the two men no longer his concern, the image of his father embracing him amid the green softness of the hillside as real as the cool air he breathed into his lungs.

DURING HIS CAPTIVITY, he had invented games to occupy his mind, speculating on the great mysteries that had no solutions, speaking to dead comrades-in-arms, revisiting his lifelong fascination with anthropology and history. By listening to the footfalls and voices of his captors, and the shutting and opening of doors, he knew the basement room he occupied was at the end of a corridor, one that had a stone or brick floor. No, it wasn't a corridor. It was a tunnel with a trapdoor at the far end, one made out of perhaps oak and steel that fell heavily from a ceiling with enough force to jar the floor. The tunnel smelled of lichen and water seepage. It smelled of the tomb, or a cave deep inside the mists of Avalon, the kind to which mankind continually returned in one way or another. The fascination with the netherworld, the spirits that groaned inside the trunks of trees, the sword frozen in the rock, the hunters chasing the stag across the heavens, all of these things were less about magic than testimony to the glory of creation. It was not coincidence that the walls of the great catacombs of Europe were stacked with row upon row of grinning skulls, as though they had come home and joined a party in progress that no one else saw.

Shortly after Jessie's falling-out with Jeff, the sound of the trapdoor striking the floor reverberated down the tunnel, followed by footsteps hammering down steps or a ladder, then the voice of Arnold Beckman shouting, "Get down there, you pair of jackasses, and clean the toilet and the grease trap and mop the floors, and stay there until I get to the bottom of this!"

"Sir, that woman is lying. She come out of the bedroom in the nude," another voice said.

"I understand perfectly. You're such a debonair and handsome pair that an educated woman can't keep her clothes on while she's around you?"

"No, sir. What I mean is she showed us the scar on her stomach. That's how come we knew about it. We thought maybe this was something she does to people, like a nymphomaniac carrying on, and you was fixing to tell us not to worry about it, maybe you was just playing a big joke or something. Jesus Christ, Mr. Beckman."

"A joke? She says you licked her scar," Beckman said.

"Whores lie," said Jack. He didn't fit with the others. He was more aggressive, surly, the kind of man who enjoyed fighting with his fists and breaking things.

"*You* don't get to call her a whore," Beckman said.

"Okay, she's not a whore," Jack said. "She just acts like one. I told her I didn't like sloppy seconds. It set her off. Whores like to put on airs. But she's not a whore, so this don't apply to her."

"You said that to Maggie Bassett?" Beckman asked.

"Who cares what I said? The cunt is lying."

"What did you say?"

"You sent us to watch her. That's what we done," Jack said. "Except she snookered all of us. She got Jim and me on the bone, then run us out of her house with a pistol and took you over the hurdles. That don't make me feel too good. She must be one great piece of ass."

"Wait here a minute," Beckman said.

"Forget it," Jack said. "I was at Saint-Mihiel. I knew I shouldn't have signed on with a Hun. I formally resign and now salute you with both my buttocks. Here, kiss my West Texas ass."

A silence followed that was so intense, Ishmael's eardrums were creaking. Then he heard Beckman's voice again: "Pull your pants up and look at me."

"What for?" Jack replied.

"This."

The blast must have been from a shotgun, probably a twelve-gauge. Ishmael heard the pellets bounce off the stone and scatter along the tunnel. He also heard a scream like that of a man who'd had his eyes gouged out, then the *kla-klatch* of the empty casing being ejected and another shell being pumped into the chamber. Someone, probably Beckman, was now descending a set of wood steps, his weight balanced, taking each step in measured fashion, the shotgun probably held in one hand.

"Mr. Beckman, I didn't say nothing bad about the lady," Jim said. "She's got her side of the story. I ain't criticizing her for it. What I told you is what I saw and what I heard."

"Shut up."

"Sir, what are you fixing to do?"

"I'm deciding."

"Cain't you give him a chance?"

"You want to trade places with him?"

"No, sir."

"A shocking revelation. Can you hear me, Jack?" Beckman said. "Don't play possum on us. Look up here. You won't have to worry about boners anymore. How do you like this?"

There was another blast from the shotgun. This time Ishmael could smell the burned powder.

"Stop trembling and clean this up," Beckman said. "Get the others to help you."

"Where are we supposed to take him?"

"Cut him up and put him in the dump."

"Sir, what about the soldier?"

"What about him?"

"He could hear all this."

"Your keen sense of perception always leaves me in awe."

Ishmael wasn't sure if he was alone in the basement. He had heard no sound in his proximity since he was awakened by the trapdoor dropping into the tunnel. He twisted his body on the cot, his wrists manacled to the leather belt, then slowly drew up his knees until they touched the wood poles along the edge of the canvas. Could he roll onto the floor and stand erect? Could he find the wall without falling, and rub the tape and cotton pads from his eyes?

"Don't be having those kinds of thoughts, kid," Jeff said, not more than two feet from him. "They'll get you in a whole lot of trouble."

"Address me as 'kid' again, and you'll have troubles of your own," Ishmael said. "Ever have your butt kicked by a blindfolded gimp?"

Dᴀʀʟ ᴘɪᴄᴋɪɴꜱ ꜱᴛᴏᴘᴘᴇᴅ the Kerr County Sheriff's Department motorcar in front of Maggie Bassett's house. The rain was puddling on the lawn, the sky black except for an occasional igneous pool that flared and disappeared like a yellow lake draining into the dark.

Andre was sitting in the front with Darl, Hackberry in back.

"Want us to wait out here?" Darl said.

"If you wouldn't mind," Hackberry said. "Maggie is not given to predictability or protocol."

Darl nodded as though he understood, which he obviously did not. "Can you tell me exactly what we're doing here, Mr. Holland?"

"I didn't tell you why because I don't know myself. I was married to the woman for years and never had any idea who I was living with. It was like waking up every day with a stranger in my bed. I won't get into the conjugal side of things."

Darl squeezed his eyes shut as though he had a headache. "We're here for reasons we have no understanding of?"

"Exactly."

"That doesn't make real good sense, sir."

"Put it this way: Maggie Bassett is the most dishonest and manipulative human being I have ever known. She could sell hot-water radiators to the devil and snow to Eskimos. You said maybe she should be sitting in a jail cell. That's one place Maggie has never been. I wonder what she'll have to say if she thinks she's going there."

"That's pretty slick," Darl said. "So we wait out here while you go in, and she looks out the window at a car from the sheriff's department and has to study on her prospects?"

"You've got your hand on it."

"Was she really tied up with the Sundance Kid and Butch Cassidy? They was pretty mangy, wasn't they?"

"Thanks for that reminder, Darl. I'll be back out soon."

"Anything you want us to do in the meantime?"

"Wait in the car. When you see me come out of the house, that will mean it's time for us to leave and go somewhere else."

"I got it," Darl said.

Hackberry knocked on the door. He wasn't prepared for what he saw when he opened it. She was wearing a white cotton nightdress, unbuttoned at the top, so gauzy it was almost transparent, her face and shoulders and chest crosshatched with scratches and welts, as though she had been clawed by a rosebush.

"Excuse my appearance," she said. "I just got out of the shower. I'm trying to clean up the house now."

He removed his hat and looked away from her and then back at her face. Some of the scratches on her chest had bled through the nightdress. "Who did this to you?"

She closed the door behind him and walked into the living room. Through the kitchen door, he could see a mop and a broom and cleaning rags and a bucket of soapy water. The living room rug was printed with mud or clay.

"Arnold sent his men over," she said. "Two of them. Maybe you've met them."

"I don't need to meet them. They attacked you?"

"I've already talked with Arnold. I thought you were the police. I thought he might have called them."

"Did they rape you, Maggie?"

"I'm taking care of things. I don't need any help. Why are you here?"

"Why do you think? My son's time is probably running out. You have to tell me what you know."

"You think I'm privy to all of Arnold's secrets. I'm not. He owns property all over Texas. Ishmael could be anywhere."

"Give me something. Anything. Even if it seems unimportant."

Then a phenomenon took place in her eyes that he had seen before but had never been able to deal with. They became impenetrable, the pupils reduced to dots, the irises made up of tiny green and black and blue pinpoints that yielded no emotion, no message or signal or content of any kind. It was a look men could not disengage from; at the same time, it made them wonder why they had ever gotten involved with her.

"What is it?" he asked.

"I need to tell you something. I've never told this to anyone else."

"Say it."

"When you tried to make up to Ruby years ago, when she was living in Denver, she wrote you back and telegrammed you. I read the messages and destroyed them. You thought she didn't want you back. It wasn't true, but I made you believe it was."

"I have a hard time accepting that, Maggie."

"It's what happened. You want coffee? I have some on the stove."

"No, I don't want coffee. Why did you do that?"

"It seemed like the right thing at the time. I was your wife, she wasn't. I ruined a large part of y'all's lives, particularly Ishmael's. You have bad judgment when it comes to women, Hack. Except for Ruby. I have to give it to her."

He looked at the blood stippled on her dress, the scratches next to her eyes. "If I had taken care of my obligations and been more a decent man, we wouldn't have these problems. It's not your fault."

"Watch out for the DeMolay woman. She's in business with Arnold. They're shipping German rifles to South America."

"I didn't think she'd do something like that."

"You think you're a dissolute drunk. The truth is, you're a rube. I'm not doing well with this. Get out of here, Hack."

"Doing well with what? The attack? Your feelings?"

"It could have been different. I did it my way, and now I get to live with it. So long, Big Bud. Look me up if Ruby throws you out."

Those were the last words he ever heard from the lips of Maggie Bassett.

He got into the backseat of the car and sat with his hands on his knees, his face empty, rain dripping off his hat brim. Andre turned in the front seat and looked at him; Darl was at the wheel, watching him in the rearview mirror.

"A couple of Beckman's men were here," Hackberry said. "She's not in real good shape right now."

"What'd they do?" Darl said.

"Somebody marked her up. She says it was Beckman's people."

"You don't believe her?" Darl asked.

"I think if they'd tried, they'd be dead. Andre, is Miss Beatrice cutting an arms deal with Beckman?"

"I do not ask about her business matters or her personal life, Mr. Holland."

"You don't need to ask. You see and hear everything," Hackberry said. "You put me in mind of a giant pterodactyl flying over the landscape."

"A what?"

"What was she doing in Beckman's office?" Hackberry said. "Why would she be with a man of his kind? I can abide anything in human beings except treachery."

"It is not good to talk of her this way, Mr. Holland."

"I do so only because I put my faith in her," Hackberry said, his voice rising. "I misplaced it."

"You are in an emotional state right now," Andre said. "It is better you review your words before you speak them."

"It's better I don't hold conversations with pterodactyls. I'm going to give it to him."

Darl turned around. "You're gonna give the cup Jesus drunk from to a fellow like that? That ain't right, Mr. Holland."

"In a public place, where everyone will know he has it. He'll be forced to return it to wherever it came from. He'll no longer have any reason to hold my son."

"You're deceiving yourself, Mr. Holland," Andre said. "Do not do this. You know better. Do not give yourself over to foolish thinking. If you give the cup to this man, you will never forgive yourself. Nor will I."

"Did torturing and killing those men in Haiti get your children back?" Hackberry said.

"No, it did not. But it purged the world of men who had no right to live. Also, no other child had to suffer at their hands."

"Take me to Beckman's office."

"Where is the cup?" Andre said.

"In a place nobody is going to find it."

"You are acting in a willful and stubborn fashion, Mr. Holland. There is only one alternative for us. I do not want the young deputy to hear this. You know what we must do. There are instances when we have to put aside the restraints of mercy."

"You're right, Andre, I don't want to hear this," Darl said. "And as a deputy sheriff of Kerr County, I'd damn well better not."

"I think Darl means it, Andre," Hackberry said.

"Where is the cup?" Andre said.

"In the kind of place it should be. In a place the original owner would probably be happy to see it."

"You've been told you were chosen," Andre said. "But you have never asked what you were chosen for. Do you think you were chosen only to protect the cup? There are many who could have done that."

"Those words were spoken to me in a dream," Hackberry said. "The only person I told of this dream was Miss Beatrice. Did she tell you about it?"

"No, she did not. She is not one who breaks confidences."

"Then how did you know?"

"I know little and am not worthy to speak on these things. So I will do as you say and not speak on these matters again."

"Don't get your feathers ruffled," Hackberry said. "I value your advice."

Andre made no reply. They drove to the office of Arnold Beckman.

Chapter
34

THE ASIAN SECRETARY said he was eating with friends at a steak house not far from the Alamo. Hackberry nodded and looked through the front window at the sky. "You ever see weather worse than this?" he asked.

"No, it is very bad. It is flooding the property," she said.

"You ever meet my son, Ishmael?"

"I have heard Mr. Beckman speak of him, but I do not know him."

"I cain't find him anywhere. I was hoping Mr. Beckman could he'p me. With all his resources and such."

"I am sure he would be happy to."

"My boy was hurt in France and gets confused about where he is. He had the notion he was going to work for Mr. Beckman. Sometimes I wonder if he wandered into one of Mr. Beckman's warehouses or storage places and got himself locked in."

"I will make a note of this. But I don't think that is likely. The employees would have told us."

"Maybe he wandered off to a hunting or fishing camp or a boathouse. I bet your boss has a mess of them."

"No, Mr. Beckman is not a hunter or fisherman or sportsman. His interest is history. He wanted to buy the Spanish mission by the river, but the owners would not sell it. Mr. Beckman was very disappointed."

"Why would he want a run-down mission?"

"Possibly to restore it. This is a very historical area. He and my grandfather do many civic-oriented works. Did you know this site was once a prison?"

"No, I didn't."

"Ask Mr. Beckman about it."

"I might do that," Hackberry said.

Darl parked in front of the restaurant, cut the engine, and got out, his slicker blowing in the wind. Hackberry stepped up on the curb and stood beside him. From where they stood, they could see both the Alamo and the upper stories of the Crockett Hotel, the windows lit against a black sky. The window of the restaurant was painted with the words CHOPS*STEAKS*FISH, steam or fog running down the glass. The rain was driving almost sideways in the street, the sewer grates clogged with flotsam.

Andre had not gotten out of the car. Hackberry tapped on his window. "Let's go."

Andre rolled down the glass. "People of color are not allowed here."

"They just had a change in policy. Now get out."

Andre stepped out on the sidewalk, his bare head beading with rain. "I'm beginning to understand why you do not have many friends, Mr. Holland."

"Why is that?"

"It is very dangerous," Andre replied.

Hackberry opened the restaurant door and walked in first. The interior was warm and brightly lit, the tables crowded, the walls lined with framed photos of cattle drives and drovers gathered around campfires and buffalo hunters posing with cap-and-ball weapons and squaws whose faces had been cut for infidelity. Hackberry wondered how many of them he had known and how many lay in unmarked graves.

It took about thirty seconds for everyone in the restaurant to take notice of Andre. The maître d' came from the back in a tuxedo, walking quickly, his menus tucked under his arm. "Sir, we cain't serve Negroes here."

"I'm looking for Arnold Beckman. We're not asking to be served," Hackberry said.

"This man cannot come in here. Unless you're an officer of the law, we do not allow firearms in the restaurant, either."

"If you'll notice, it's in full view. That means I'm in compliance with the law. Tell me where Arnold Beckman is, or I can just whip a knot on your head. Which would you prefer?"

The maître d's face was white, his finger unsteady as he pointed to a back room.

"Thank you," Hackberry said.

None of the people at the tables lifted their eyes until Hackberry and Darl and Andre had walked past them. Then they spoke only in whispers.

Beckman was seated at the head of a table with several other men in a private room. On the wall was a painting of a reclining nude. Beckman had a piece of meat pouched in his jaw as tight as a golf ball; he was speaking to an Asian man next to him, his eyes never registering Hackberry's or Andre's or Darl's presence.

"Are you feeding my boy the way you feed yourself?" Hackberry said. "Steak and spuds and fried maters and buttermilk biscuits and a bowl of sausage gravy on the side? You treat my boy as good as your own self?"

Beckman wiped his mouth with a napkin tied in a bib over his shirt. "As usual, you don't make very much sense, Mr. Holland. But I've got to hand it to you. You bring a nigger into a white man's chophouse? They must have shit their pants out there."

"You want to talk here or in back or outside?"

"I don't want to talk with you anywhere, thank you very much."

"I'm going to bring you what you want."

Beckman shook his head as though bewildered. "Gentlemen, I'll be right back. This man is a former Texas Ranger, and I treat him as such. Perhaps after our talk, he'll join us for a drink. You will, won't you, Mr. Holland?"

Hackberry didn't answer. He looked into the face of each man at the table, one at a time, and in turn each looked away or lowered his eyes. Beckman walked into a hallway in back. "What kind of besotted idea have you come up with now?"

"I'll give you the cup in a public place, in front of others."

"I see. That's brilliant. So I'll have to return it to the original owners and release your boy at the same time? Do you think I'm simpleminded?"

"I wouldn't know."

"You're an idiot, Holland. I have complete power over you. If you hurt me—or, even worse for you, if you kill me—your son will starve to death. Consider this image for just a moment: Buried alive in a box, able to hear people who can't hear him, dependent on others for his next sip of water or morsel of food or breath of air. Think of him listening to the footfalls above his head while his thirst and hunger and fear grow by the minute and his screams remain unheard. You've come to *bargain*? Before I'm done, you'll beg."

"I tried."

"Is your speech encrypted? Am I supposed to extrapolate great meaning from that?"

"There's a Rubicon I never went across. I guess that's where I'm at now."

"Collect your nigger and that boy with him, and go back where you belong: a soup kitchen for bummers, a dollar-a-throw crib, the kind of place you'll end up one day, regardless of what happens to me."

"Maggie Bassett ran me off in the same way. I guess it's not my day. Did you know you got something sticky on your boot? I'd say it was blood."

Hackberry left Beckman staring at him, and went back outside with Darl and Andre, and got into the backseat of the motorcar. The rain had slackened, and people with umbrellas were walking to their cars or into bars and cafés, laughing, glancing at the sky, as though they had been spared an impending disaster. There was a silvery glow in the clouds; even the thunder seemed to have receded over the edge of the world.

"Where to?" Darl said.

"I thought I saw blood on Beckman's foot."

"Whose do you reckon it is?"

"I missed something at Maggie Bassett's this afternoon. Beckman's men tracked up her house. They had either green clay or horse manure on their shoes. Ruby said the man she stuck a hat pin in had green stains on his trouser cuffs."

Andre turned around. "There's green clay down by the river. I saw it behind the Spanish ruins, down by the river."

Hackberry gazed at the clouds. "I never saw the moon rise this early. I never saw it rise in a rainstorm, either. I don't think the world will end by fire. I think the stars will fall out of the heavens, and all the natural laws will go out the window. I think this is how the sky will look on the day the world ends."

Darl and Andre looked at each other but kept their thoughts to themselves.

BACK AT THE hotel, Hackberry knocked on Ruby's door. "I need to tell you a few things," he said. "I don't have long."

"Where have you been?" she said.

"At Maggie's place. I also talked with Beckman." He went to the window and looked down in the street where Darl had parked the motorcar. He could see the green arbor in the center of the plaza and, through the fog and trees, the shiny glimmer of the wooden carousel horses. He looked back at Ruby. "Maggie owned up. She destroyed the telegrams and messages you sent me from Denver. All these years I thought you didn't want me back."

Ruby stared out the window. "I guess I wanted to think better of her."

"Maggie has her moments. Give the devil her due."

"You sound like you admire her."

"I admire her because she possesses some of the qualities you have in abundance, Ruby."

"What are the other things you wanted to tell me?"

"I'm going to get the cup, then I'm going to Beckman's. I'm either coming back with Ishmael or I'm not coming back. I may do some things today I've never done before, but I'll do them if I have to."

"What did Beckman say about Ishmael?"

"He made threats."

"What kind?"

"He's a coward. He tries to transfer his fear to others."

"What kind of threats?"

"If I kill him, Ishmael will be left to death by starvation and thirst."

"I want to go with you."

He squeezed her hand. "Stay here. We can be a family again. I mean, if it's what you want."

"You're going to beat it out of him? That's why the Haitian is with you?"

"Sometimes it's not good to look around the corner in your own mind. Sometimes you have to let things happen," he said.

"I don't care what you do to him. No matter how this works out, I think I'm going to kill Arnold Beckman."

"You're not the killing kind, Ruby."

"You're wrong," she said. "I feel very strange. For the first time in my life, I understand the violence that has always lived in you. I'm going with you."

But he was out the door before she was finished speaking.

HACKBERRY CROSSED THE street to the park, without stopping at the motorcar where Darl and Andre were waiting for him. He followed a concrete walkway through the trees, past a set of swings and seesaws and a wading pool crosshatched with floating leaves. Someone had tried to cover the carousel with canvas, but it had pulled loose and was flapping in the wind. He stepped up on the floor and worked his way through the wooden horses and the ornate pewlike benches to the center of the carousel and the panel behind which he had hidden the cup. The mirrors on the panels were oblong and wavy and reflected his image as though it had been scissored into parts, and he wondered if he was not one man but many, and he wondered if this was not the reflection every man experienced at the close of his life. The last chapter, even the last page in the book describing one's days, did not give unity or understanding to one's life; at best, the narrative sorted out the chaff and allowed a man to step over a line with a lighter load and mount a fresh horse for a journey that hopefully had no end.

At least that was what he wanted to believe.

He pulled away the panel and lifted the cup from inside. He had rewrapped it in the slicker Darl had brought it in and retied the twine. He put his fingers between the rubberized folds and touched the rim of the cup, his eyes closing. *Here we go, Lord. He'p me take it to them. And you know what I mean by "it."*

To his dying days, with his hand on the Testament, he would swear he heard a voice that rang as clear as a spoon striking a crystal glass. The cheat was he didn't know what the words meant, as simple as they were: *Are you sure about that, partner?*

For what shall it profit a man if he gains the world and never figures out a solitary thing coming down the pike?

Iᴤʜᴍᴀᴇʟ ʟᴀʏ ɪɴ the darkness, both hands manacled to an iron ring in the wall, and listened to the sounds coming from the tunnel. He could hear two men talking while they pulled a heavy weight across a hard surface, and he suspected they were removing the body of the man Beckman had killed with a shotgun. He also heard the sounds of mops and pails, and water being sloshed against a wall or the floor of the tunnel, and later, the sound of someone laboring with a saw, pausing to retch and then curse under his breath.

Hope was the light that allowed man to prevail in the worst of circumstances. But it also could become the narcotic of the self-deluded and the naive. How did a man know when it was his time? The answer was simple. There comes a moment when you no longer resist the inevitable and you accept the fact that billions have preceded you and that your death is not more important than theirs. That's when you know the hands on the clock have frozen on the hour and the minute and the second that were appointed as your time, and nothing you do will restart them. That's how you know now and forever that your time has not only come but has already ended, and oddly enough, the realization is not all bad.

Ishmael wondered how they would do it to him. Since they

bore him no personal grudge, they would probably carry out his execution in a pragmatic fashion, one that would make the least work for them. In all probability, they would use guile rather than force in his final moments. They would tell him they were taking him to a more comfortable setting, perhaps a hospital. Or they would remove the pads from his eyes and offer him wine and a hot meal. While he sat at a table or in the passenger seat of a motorcar, a bullet would be fired into the back of his skull.

Acceptance of his fate did not mean he should be passive about it. For just a moment, as though he were looking through a third eye in his forehead, he saw a medieval fortress on the shores of Malta and Crusader knights in chainmail and white tunics with red Templar crosses, surrounded by their Saracen enemies. Their death was a foregone conclusion, but rather than surrender, they executed their prisoners and used catapults to fling the decapitated heads over the walls into the Saracen line and went down to the last man, their swords ringing.

Could he be as brave and defiant as they? He had gone across no-man's-land into gas and machine guns and flamethrowers and rounds the size of boulders fired from railroad mortars, but he had been armed, and his brothers-in-arms had been at his side. Was there any challenge greater than remaining resolute while you stood unarmed and waited for your enemies to take your life and bury you in a place where no one would find you, knowing in advance that your last words would never be heard and the deed would probably never be punished?

Big Bud had to be out there somewhere, all six feet eight inches of him, armed and dangerous and capable of sowing destruction over an entire landscape, as he had probably done behind Beatrice DeMolay's brothel down in Mexico. Could Ishmael's thoughts reach his father? Did each see the other in his dreams? Did those Crusader knights at Malta have the same feelings as they awaited the final assault of the Saracens, their agony written on the glittering blue emptiness of the Mediterranean?

Ishmael heard footsteps in the tunnel, echoing off the walls, coming closer, splashing through a pool of water, a metal instrument scraping against stone. Then the sounds stopped. A moment later, a man was urinating loudly in the toilet cubicle. When he finished, he pulled the chain on the box tank high up on the wall, and a few seconds later, he was standing within inches of Ishmael's face.

"Who are you?" Ishmael said.

"It's just me."

"Jeff?"

"One and the same. I got good news for you. I'm fixing a hot meal for you, too."

"I'm not hungry."

Jeff picked up Ishmael's feet and cut the rope that bound his ankles. "Believe me, you'll develop an appetite. I can rustle up a pan of brains and eggs that'll break your heart. Come on, boy, rise and shine. Let's get you out of this damn hole in the ground."

Chapter 35

Ruby's heart leaped when she heard the knock on her hotel door. *Oh, please, please, please let it be Ishmael and Hack,* she prayed. She could almost see through the wood door, both of them grinning, standing side by side, their bodies filling the doorway, the men who had been the center of her life and the only real family she had ever had. She threw open the door.

The woman standing in front of her did not smile. She wore a dark purple velvet dress and a straw hat with a pale blue ribbon and veils wrapped around the crown. She was holding a dome-shaped package wrapped in white butcher paper. Had it possessed an odor, Ruby would have thought it a Thanksgiving turkey.

"I'm Beatrice DeMolay, Miss Dansen," the woman said. "Perhaps Hackberry has spoken of me."

"I know who you are, all right," Ruby replied. "I know how you made your money, too."

"I have something for Hackberry. I went to his room, but he wasn't there. I sent my driver to protect him, but Andre hasn't called. I'm a bit worried."

"We don't need you to worry about us."

"Evidently, you don't approve of me," Beatrice DeMolay said.

"I've known the young girls who end up in the kinds of places you operate."

403

"And where would they be if my places hadn't been there?"

"Peddle your justifications somewhere else, please."

"Where is Mr. Holland?"

"None of your business."

"It *is* my business, Miss Dansen. Mr. Holland was born in another era and thinks the old ways still work. As a consequence, his enemies use his virtues against him. Where is he?"

"He was going to Arnold Beckman's."

Beatrice DeMolay's eyes were recessed, the color of coal; the bones in her face seemed to harden inside her skin. "I knew he would do it. I also knew that no one around him would try to stop him."

"Why didn't *you*?" Ruby said.

"Because I entered into a situation that is very complicated and could send me to prison. I'm not going to discuss this with you in the hallway. I'm also a bit tired of dealing with the indignation of people I'm trying to help."

Ruby hesitated. "I don't trust you."

"Then I'm going."

"No, come in," Ruby said, stepping aside.

Beatrice DeMolay walked past her to the window and looked down into the street. "You need to be aware of some things, Miss Dansen. The desk clerk downstairs works for Beckman. So do some of the police officials. There is hardly anything in this city that Beckman doesn't control. He also owns United States senators and congressmen and state attorneys and the wardens of penitentiaries. The only thing that can undo him is to use his own corrupt system against him. What is Mr. Holland planning to do at Beckman's?"

"Whatever it takes."

"That is really stupid. He's undoing everything I've done."

"What is it you've done? I don't see it. All I see is an angry woman who's been a lifelong tool of capitalists."

"I convinced Beckman to make a large sale of weaponry to a consortium in Argentina. He signed all the documents. What he doesn't know is that the weapons are being purchased for Communists in Indochina. This puts him in violation of the Sedition Act. If he

doesn't go to prison, he will spend years in court. In the meantime, most of his assets will be seized or frozen, including his warehouses."

Ruby felt sick. "Why didn't you tell us?"

"What do you think I'm doing now?"

"What's that in your hands?"

Beatrice DeMolay set the package on the writing table and tore off the butcher paper. Encased in domed glass was a painting of a pinkish-orange sunrise, with cherubs sitting on each of the sun's rays. "This is how the House of the Rising Sun in New Orleans came by its name. I thought Mr. Holland might like it."

"Why would he want something from a bordello?"

"I had it with me in Mexico when he and I first met. I treated him shabbily. I had no idea what a brave and kind man he was. I also learned that he suffered gravely because of his accidental shooting of innocent people in a boxcar."

Ruby could hear the rain ticking on the balcony, the latched French doors straining against the wind. "Do you have a motorcar?"

THE ROAD WAS washed out in two places, the countryside shrouded in mist. Darl cut the headlights on the car a hundred yards before they reached the poplar trees lining the road in front of Beckman's building, which was dark. They could see the Spanish ruins down by the river, the crumbling walls and bell tower flickering when the remnants of the storm flared overhead. Darl parked on the road, in the shadow of the trees, but didn't turn off the engine.

"Where exactly did you see the green clay?" Hackberry said to Andre.

"Behind the mission, where a coulee runs down to the river."

"Why would they be in the mission?" Hackberry said.

"I only know that this is cursed ground."

"The mission grounds are cursed?"

"No, the ground we stand on is," Andre replied. "It was a barracoon."

"What's a barracoon?" Darl said.

"A holding place used by slavers," Andre said.

"I never heard of a barracoon here'bouts," Hackberry said.

"Maybe because you did not want to hear about it," Andre said.

"You ever read Cotton Mather, Andre? You should. If ever a colored man inherited Mather's great talents, it's you."

"What do you want to do, Mr. Holland?" Darl asked, twisting around in the seat.

"Turn on to the property and cut the engine."

"They'll see us."

"Never tether your horse where you cain't get to it."

"Here we go," Darl said. He angled the car up the driveway and stopped. There was no movement or show of light inside the house. Darl turned off the engine. "What about the cup?" he said.

"It stays in the car," Hackberry said.

"This don't feel right."

"What doesn't?" Hackberry said.

"Everything. What if we don't make it out of here and these guys get the cup? What do you aim to do with that bowie knife?"

"Cut off Beckman's fingers and make him eat them one at a time."

Darl's face went white.

"That's a joke," Hackberry said. "Trust me, everything will be all right. Let's get out of the car and find out where they've got my boy."

"I don't believe you," Darl said, opening the door. "Look yonder. There's a red light shining through that mission. What have we got ourselves into, Mr. Holland?"

"JUST PUT ONE foot after another," Jeff said, leading Ishmael along a stone wall, his eyes still taped. "Now turn left into this little room. There you go, buddy. Sit down in the chair. Let's take off those eye pads so we can talk while I fix some grub. Well, lookie there."

"Look at what?" Ishmael said.

Jeff pulled the adhesive tape from Ishmael's brow and cheeks and the bridge of his nose and lifted the pads from his eyes. "See? It's kind of like the Northern Lights. Nature doesn't follow its own rules sometimes. Here, stand up and take a look."

"Can you take off the manacles?"

"That's up to Mr. Beckman. Stand up."

There was one window in the room, ground-level and narrow, like a slit in a machine-gun bunker. Ishmael could see a massive bank of black clouds in the west and, at the bottom of the sky, a red ember burning inside a blue patch behind the Spanish ruins.

"It'll go away directly," Jeff said. "Those kinds of sunsets give me the willies. I cain't tell you exactly why. They put me in mind of my father for some reason. He'd start preaching while he was whaling the tar out of us. I flat hated that son of a bitch. Even after one of my brothers pushed him off a cliff, I'd dream about him and have these funny feelings, like time had run out and the whole earth was fixing to be consumed in a fire. Know what I mean?"

"No, not at all."

"You probably had a different kind of upbringing. Why you got that look on your face?"

"I didn't know what you looked like."

The walls were plastered and painted white. A wood cookstove stood in one corner, a tin pipe leading up through the ceiling. Jeff began stuffing kindling and newspaper into the hob. His beard was rust-colored and as stiff as wire, his eyes many-faceted, undefinable, as impervious as agate.

"When are you going to do it, Jeff?" Ishmael said.

"Do what?" Jeff said, concentrating on his work, a grin at the corner of his mouth.

"Kill me."

"I wouldn't do that. I like you."

"You're full of it, bub."

"Wish you wouldn't talk to me like that."

"My father will hang your hide on a nail."

Jeff swung his fist backward across Ishmael's face, knocking him into the chair, Ishmael's wrists hooked to the leather restraining belt. Jeff opened and closed his hand and shook it in the air, as though slinging water off his fingers. "Sorry about that. I got triggers in me people shouldn't mess with. You all right?"

"No."

"It's the breaks of the game, kid. None of this is personal. We each got a job. One guy wins, one guys loses. Down the track everybody ends up in the same place, with a shovel-load of dirt raining down in his face."

"I've already done that. On the Marne, buried alive. I told you about calling me 'kid.' Jeff, I hate to tell you this, but you piss me off."

Jeff struck a match and dropped it in the hob. He tried to fan the kindling alight, then gave up and closed the hob and watched a single puff of white smoke rise from one of the stove lids. "Let's go."

"Where to?"

"Back to your cot and the blindfold. On your feet."

Ishmael bent forward, his head hanging down, his arms stretched behind him. "I don't think I can do it."

"Get up!" Jeff said, grabbing Ishmael under one arm. "Did you hear me? You get your goddamn ass out of that chair."

Ishmael ran his body into Jeff's and knocked him on the floor, then kicked him in the face, breaking his lips against his teeth. Then he stomped Jeff's head with the sole of his shoe, again and again, bouncing it off the bricks, until Jeff's eyes rolled. Ishmael fell back against the wall, the room spinning, his legs aflame. Outside, thousands of tree frogs were singing. He heard the trapdoor drop heavily from the ceiling in the tunnel and smack against solid stone, shaking the walls in the room.

"Jeff, get up here! Bring the Lewis!" Arnold Beckman shouted.

HACKBERRY GOT OUT of the motorcar first and went through the breezeway to the back of the building and cut the telephone wires with his bowie knife. With the butt of the knife, he broke out a pane in the French doors on Beckman's office and unlocked the dead bolt and stepped inside, over the broken glass. Darl and Andre followed.

Hackberry pulled his revolver and worked his way through the furniture to a door in the rear wall and turned the handle slowly and let the door swing back on its own. The room was too dark for him to see inside, but he was sure he heard someone go out another door and slam it behind him. He was sweating inside his clothes now. Even though the air outside was almost wintry, the room seemed as hot as a closed barn in July, the air pressurized, the walls damp, the silence like fingernails on a blackboard.

He felt Andre bump against him. They had made a mistake. They had gone in together and bunched up in the process. His father had been with the Fourth Texas at Petersburg and seen the Yankees, many of them black, pour into the breach known as the Crater, piling on top of one another, slipping helplessly down the clay slopes into the mire, while the Confederates regrouped and slaughtered them en masse. Hackberry turned around and motioned Andre and Darl out the door. "Go around back," he whispered. "Three minutes from now, break a window. With something big. A brick."

"Why?" Andre said.

"Do it," Hackberry said, pressing his hand against Andre's shoulder, feeling the man's body tense. "We don't herd up. Three minutes."

Andre nodded, and he and Darl went back out the door into Beckman's office. Hackberry felt his way through the room, tripping on a table that had a typewriter on it. He pulled open the door to the next room. There was no glimmer of electricity in the clouds, no moonrise, no red spark at the bottom of the sky, no sound of tree frogs drumming, nothing but darkness and a heady, sweet odor that made him think of San Francisco and Chinamen and alleyways that led to subterranean dens.

You make a dollar where you can, don't you, Mr. Beckman? he thought.

But his discussion was a distraction and a luxury he couldn't afford. He had no way of knowing how many men were in the building or if his son was there or somewhere else. Worse, he didn't know if Ishmael was even alive. David had cried out, *Absalom, Absalom, my son Absalom, would God I had died for thee.* But Absalom was a traitor unto his father, and Ishmael was nothing of the sort. Ishmael had been cast out, betrayed by Hackberry, left to grow up in poverty while his father lived on a magnificent ranch on the Guadalupe in the arms of a Jezebel. How does a man rid himself of memories like those? Answer: He doesn't.

Hackberry realized his palm was sweating on the grips of the

Peacemaker. *Think,* he told himself. *Don't mess this one up. Pay any price, sustain any injury, any disfigurement, eat your pain, willingly give your life without regret, get your son back, and if you cannot get him back, make the men who did this suffer the torment of the damned.*

He was breathing so hard that he was starting to hyperventilate. He felt along the line of stacked boxes and found a knob on the next door. As he eased it open, he looked into the face of a man almost his height, wearing a coat and a broad-brimmed slouch hat, a man with wide shoulders and a white shirt and an odor like sweat and detergent that had dried in his clothes. Hackberry swung the barrel and cylinder of the Colt .45 across the side of the man's head, then hit him again, this time raking it across his nose. The man went down hard, trying to hold on to Hackberry's slicker. Hackberry kicked at him and heard him cry out as he struck a piece of furniture in the dark.

Hackberry knelt beside him and felt for his face, then inserted the point of his bowie knife in one of the man's nostrils. "Where's Ishmael Holland?" he said. "Where is my son?"

The man on the floor didn't respond.

"I'll make a slit-nose out of you," Hackberry said. "The way the Indians did it. You'll never want to look in a mirror again." He pushed the knife deeper. The tall man didn't move. Hackberry set down the knife and grabbed him by the shirt and shook him. "Did you hear me?"

He fished in his coat pocket for a box of matches and scratched one across the striker and held it aloft. One of the man's eyes was almost shut; the other had eight-balled. A single rivulet of blood ran from a triangular-shaped wound in his temple where he had probably struck the corner of a desk. Hackberry had seen the man's face before. It belonged to one of the three who had put Ishmael in the geek cage at the carnival. Hackberry dropped the dead match on the man's face.

He got to his feet and walked to the next door. It was partially open, and he could see light glowing from under a rug on the floor. He stood outside the door with his back against the wall, the Colt Peacemaker hanging from his hand. "Can you hear me, Beckman?"

Hackberry's breath was coming hard in his chest, his eyes stinging with moisture, his nose itching miserably. He counted to five and felt his heart quiet, his breathing slow. "Your telephone lines are cut. We have all your exits covered. We control the access to your road. If the right things don't happen here, I'll set fire to the building and make sure you don't get out. You don't have to speak. If you're hearing me, just tap twice on a hard surface."

In the silence that followed, Hackberry pulled off his slicker as quietly as he could. "Turn to stone? I figured as much," he said. "For a rich man, you don't seem to have much smarts. Like maybe you were taking a leak behind a cloud when God passed out the brains. You're going to give my boy back or you're going to die, and maybe in pieces. I've got a Haitian out there who scares the doo-doo out of me."

There was no reply.

Hackberry felt for a lamp on a desk and pushed the door open with his boot and threw the lamp into the room. He heard the lamp break apart.

"I guess I'll have to come in after you," he said. "I hate to do that. You don't want to catch a ball from a Peacemaker. How about it? Let's shut this whole business down and get a drink."

He thought he could hear sounds under the floor, a door opening and shutting, a muffled voice. He hung his slicker on the tip of his pistol and extended it past the opening in the door, rustling its folds. Three rounds popped in the darkness like small firecrackers, from either a .22 or a .32, flapping the slicker. Just as Hackberry jumped back from the frame, flinging the slicker off his gun barrel, someone kicked the door shut and bolted it, and he realized there was more than one man in the room. Maybe the whole building was a beehive.

Then he heard a sound like a great mechanical weight crashing loose from its fastenings and slamming into a hard surface beneath the building, shaking the walls. Someone shouted down a stairway. He tried to picture what was happening but couldn't.

He looked back over his shoulder through the series of doors he had opened, and saw that the moon had broken out of the clouds and was shining on the front yard and the motorcar. He worked his way back toward Beckman's office and thought he saw Darl in the shadows of the live oak, trying to position himself, aiming one of his blue-black double-action revolvers. What or whom had he seen?

Hackberry had not anticipated the next few moments. But neither had the young men of Europe and Great Britain the first time they went over the top and charged into an invention that operated as efficiently and thoroughly as a scythe cutting wheat, nubbing it down to the dirt with one clean sweep.

THE FIRST BURSTS came from a downstairs window, the tracer rounds floating like strips of molten steel across the landscape. But either the angle was bad or the shooter's position was vulnerable or the shooter decided to take the high ground and command the entire area. Hackberry heard him run up a stairway and cross the floor and begin firing from a window in front, the rounds whanging into the motorcar, blowing the glass out of the windows and headlights, stenciling the radiator, exploding the tires on the rims. When the shooter released the trigger, the motorcar was pocked with holes as bright as newly minted quarters.

Hackberry pressed his back against the side wall of Beckman's office and tried to see around the window frame. Had Andre and Darl taken cover behind the motorcar or inside it? Were they wounded or dead? The shooter began firing again from a window that was not directly overhead but somewhere close to it, the empty casings bouncing and rolling across the floor. He was obviously trying to divide his fire between the live oak and the motorcar, the tracer rounds burning inside the tree trunk. The rate of fire was too rapid and too long to be a Browning. It had to be a Lewis. What was the rate of fire? Five hundred rounds a minute? Hackberry couldn't remember. Where were Darl and Andre? And what about the cup? Had it been blown apart after almost two thousand years of wandering?

He moved across Beckman's office and positioned himself against the side wall, staring up at the ceiling, holding the Colt with both hands, the hammer cocked. When the shooter let off his next burst,

Hackberry began shooting through the floor, cocking the hammer with his thumb as fast as he could, the recoil jerking both his elbows like a jackhammer. Plaster and paint and bits of wood drifted down into his face; his right ear felt like cement had been poured in it.

He shucked his spent shells out of the cylinder with the ejector rod and reloaded. There was no sound from upstairs. He went to the outside door and pushed it open with his foot. He saw Darl under the live oak, a .38 revolver in each hand. Andre was nowhere in sight. How many feet was it to the motorcar? Maybe seventy. The night air was as dank as a cistern, the oak tree dripping, the moon little more than vapor, the blue patch on the horizon now purple with rain. A cup was just a cup. It was made of smelted minerals or carved stone. You didn't lose your life for a drinking vessel. The Creator would not require that of him. But what if Andre had gone after it and lost his life? Could Hackberry do less? What was the value of honor if it could be negotiated? What value was life if you surrendered your beliefs in order to sustain it? *Make your choice, Holland,* he told himself. *Take the easy way, then see how you like living with it.*

He who dies this year is quit for the next, he thought. He opened the French doors. "Pour it on, Darl!"

"Yes, sir, you got it!" Darl said.

Darl began firing with both revolvers at the shooter's window. Hackberry ran for the motorcar. He heard one burst from the machine gun and saw the rounds blow leaves out of the branches and chew into the trunk; he saw the streaks of flame from Darl's revolvers and heard the rounds smack against the building and break glass above his head. He felt shards of glass hit his hat and shoulders; his face was sweaty and cold at the same time, his breath as ragged as a broken razor blade in his windpipe. Then he was out of the building's lee, in the open and within the shooter's angle of fire.

The Lewis was momentarily silent, then the shooter shifted his position, forcing Darl to shift his, and zeroed in on Hackberry.

Hackberry saw the rounds hitting the ground in front of him and realized the shooter was leading him, now in full command of the situation, the burst of .303 rounds almost seamless. Hackberry had no cover. He leaped over a garden hose, a broken ceramic pot that contained a root-bound Spanish dagger plant, and splashed through puddles of water thick with yellow and black leaves. A spray of rounds hit the motorcar's bumper and tore the headlights out of their sockets, and in an instant, the back of Hackberry's head felt as bare and cold and soggy with sweat as that of a French convict waiting for the guillotine's blade to roar down on his neck.

So this is how it ends, he thought. *One more burst from the Lewis and your back will be tunneled with holes, your breath ripped from your lungs, your brainpan emptied on your shirt. All of it for naught.*

Except it didn't happen. The upstairs went silent. Hackberry turned and fired his Colt at the window. The sky flickered with electricity, and he saw the aluminum cooling tube of the Lewis and the flash suppressor on the barrel and the pistol-grip stock and the ammunition drum and the hand of the shooter frantically trying to clear the bolt.

The Lewis had jammed, even though Lewis guns never jammed, even in sandstorms or when they were caked with mud or snow or had been fired so long the rifling was eaten out and the barrel was so hot it was almost translucent.

Hackberry dove into the back of the motorcar while Darl opened up on the shooter again. Hackberry grabbed the cup, still bundled in the slicker, and ran for the far side of the building, where he saw Andre waiting for him, smiling ear to ear, blood leaking from a rip in his trousers across the top of his thigh.

Behind him, the motorcar erupted in flame.

Chapter
36

"Y<small>OU RETRIEVED THE</small> cup," Andre said. "In spite of the machine-gun fire you had to run through. Miss Beatrice said you would not fail us."

"I didn't get the sense she was all that confident," Hackberry said. He was holding the cup under his arm, looking up at the windows on the second story. "How bad is your leg?"

"The wound is clean. I have no broken bones. There is no bullet inside. It is a nice night. I feel very happy."

"How many men do you think are inside?" Hackberry said. He could see Darl reloading his revolvers behind the live oak.

"I have seen two in the upstairs windows and three downstairs. Briefly, I saw lights in a basement window that was half-buried in the earth."

"Tell me about this barracoon."

"The slaves were brought up the river after their importation was banned. A great deal of money was made on the sale of these poor souls. Your hero James Bowie was one of those who defied the ban and became rich off my people's suffering."

"We're going to leave Darl out front. You and I will go through the back. I'm going to ask him to give you one of his revolvers."

"I don't know how to use one. I do not like firearms."

"Bad time to tell me."

415

Andre held out his hands. "Do you know what these have done? Where they have been?"

"We may not come out of this building, Andre. You know that, don't you?"

"Look at the night, hear the rumbling like horses' hooves in the clouds. Smell the river and the odor that is like fish. There are worse places to die."

"You want to carry the cup?"

"No, it is yours. I was never meant to have it."

"That's the last talk of that kind I want to hear," Hackberry said.

"The machine gun jammed. Is that coincidence?"

"I don't know. Neither do you."

Darl finished loading his revolvers and moved from the live oak's shadow to the corner of the building and tried to give one of the revolvers to Andre.

"As I have explained to Mr. Holland, I do not want one," Andre said.

Darl looked at Hackberry, who said, "It's his choice. Stay out here unless there's shooting inside the building. If it starts, come in through the front and shoot anything wearing pants, except Andre and me and my boy, who looks a lot like me."

"That don't sound good, Mr. Holland."

"Darl, would you stop examining every word I use? You have to think in a metaphorical fashion. Got it?"

"Yes, I have absolutely got it. Want me to go for he'p if y'all don't come out?" Darl said.

"No, burn the place," Hackberry replied.

"That's not a metaphor?" Darl asked.

"It's a literal statement."

"Burn it down? That's what you're saying?"

"Who wants to be a good loser?" Hackberry said.

"They must have done it a lot different in your day."

"I'm about to hit you, Darl."

ISHMAEL STOOD IN the doorway of the room with the plastered walls and the wood cookstove. Jeff lay on the floor, his tongue blue, his eyes like drops of mercury. The manacles on Ishmael's wrists were old-style, connected with a length of chain that was threaded through the steel rings on the restraint belt, and the rings on the belt were placed so his fingers could not reach the buckle. To get the key off Jeff's body—if he carried one—Ishmael would have to get to his knees and try to search Jeff's pockets with almost no mobility in his hands, all the while dealing with the pain in his legs. In the meantime, Beckman might be coming down the tunnel while Ishmael wasted time trying to figure his way out of an impossible problem.

He went out the door and turned right, back toward the basement and the half-sunken window that gave onto low hills and the Spanish ruins near the river.

Where are you, Big Bud? My legs are weak, my race almost done, whether I agree that this is the end of the line or not.

Then he realized that he was no longer rational and had returned to the Marne and the cacophony of no-man's-land and the frame of reference that, once branded on the unconscious, could never be removed from one's memory. The admonitions were many: *Don't silhouette on a ridge. Get rid of civilian jewelry. Turn into a stick and look at the ground when trip flares pop overhead. Remove your officer's bars. Don't be the third man on the match unless you want to eat a sniper's round. Zigzag and never run in a straight line. Tape your gear on patrol and don't let Fritz hear you clink. If you're about to be overrun, throw away the souvenir belt buckle, the pornographic pictures of dollhouse girls, the machine pistol that sold for fifty dollars in Paris, the warm German greatcoat that means an immediate death sentence.*

What did all this wisdom mean? Nothing. They were killed just the same, often by shells fired from guns fifteen miles away.

Was he losing his mind? Probably. But the sane man accepted the world and, in so doing, became part of it; the irrational and unbalanced man rejected and overcame it, and it was from him that others learned. Ishmael thought he heard machine-gun fire but couldn't be sure, any more than he could be sure about the sounds of footsteps across wood floors overhead and the jiggling of electric bulbs on the tunnel roof that created multiple shadows on the walls.

Then he heard a new sound, one that was different from the rest, like mountain-climbing cleats scraping on stone, clicking methodically toward him.

He entered the basement. Maybe there was a door that opened on a stairwell. Or maybe he could climb onto a chair or a stool and knock the glass out of the window. He heard a single shot, one that was high-powered, followed by a man's scream. Then the entire building was silent, except for the clicking of cleats or hobnailed boots on the stone.

HACKBERRY AND ANDRE found a service door at the rear of the building. The door was made of oak and dead-bolted in at least two places, the knob key-locked, the small glass panes overlaid with iron grillework.

"There's a window on the other side of the building," Hackberry said. "You may have to lift me up."

"Why not go through the door?" Andre replied.

"Because it might as well be made of steel."

"Stand back, please," Andre said.

"What are you doing?"

Andre didn't reply. He balanced himself on his injured leg and drove his good one into the door, cracking one of the panels. Then he began cracking one panel after another. He gripped the grille and tore it out of the frame as though ripping apart a packing crate. He reached inside and unlocked the dead bolts and kicked what was left of the door onto the floor. "There," he said. He stepped back to let Hackberry walk in first.

"They know we're inside, Andre. Legally, they can kill both of us. Stay behind me."

"Should you have brought the cup, Mr. Holland? What if we die here? What will happen to it?"

"I got enough on my mind. If you please, don't add to my grief."

"How is it that I am adding to your grief?"

Hackberry closed his eyes and opened them again, as though falling down an elevator shaft.

They walked down a carpeted, unlit corridor and went up a half flight of stairs to what was probably the first floor. Through an open door, Hackberry could see a room in which the rug had been rolled back and a trapdoor opened to a lower level, and he realized it was the same room he had glimpsed earlier, the one where a pale square of light had radiated from the floor. His pistol was holstered, the twine-wrapped, bundled slicker hanging from his left hand. He turned and touched his finger to his lips and let Andre descend the stairs first while he kept his eyes on the door that faced the front of the building. The trapdoor and the springs and the steps screeched with Andre's weight.

The man who came through the door may or may not have heard the noise. He held a cut-down pump shotgun with a stock that had been wood-rasped down to a pistol grip. His face was as blank as a pie pan, his eyes cavernous. Hackberry drew the Peacemaker and cocked the hammer in the same motion and fired only one round. The room was small, and the sound of the discharge left his right ear ringing. The round tore through the man's shoulder and splattered the doorjamb. He crumpled to his knees, his hand pressed to his wound, his fingers glistening. Hackberry went down the steps into a tunnel, the smell rising up like the odor of a storm sewer. He picked up the trapdoor with both hands and pushed it up until the springs carried it the rest of the way, slamming it shut.

Two men came around a bend in the tunnel, their boots and trouser cuffs dark with water. One of them carried a baseball bat. The other man looked like a Mexican or an Indian and wore black braids and a long-sleeved blue cotton shirt with a shoulder holster strapped across it, the butt of a German machine pistol sticking out of the holster.

"We just want to talk," the white man said.

The man in braids was more ambitious. His teeth were white against his dark skin, his face lit with the same malevolence Hackberry had seen in the faces of the Mexican soldiers he had shot behind Beatrice DeMolay's brothel in Mexico. The man had just touched the grips of the machine pistol when Hackberry hit him with the butt of the Peacemaker, then clubbed him again and kicked his head into the wall.

Andre ripped the bat away from the white man and slung it down the tunnel, then pinned him against the wall by the throat. "Where is Mr. Holland's son?"

Spittle was draining off the man's chin. He stabbed his finger at the air, toward the far end of the tunnel. Andre grabbed him by the shirt and coat and swung him in a circle, as he would a sack of feed, then slammed him into the wall. "Do not move. Do not talk. Do not think until I come back and give you permission."

"He's unconscious," Hackberry said.

"Sometimes they are bluffing. I will make sure."

"He's done. Now slow your motor down," Hackberry said, pulling the machine pistol from the shoulder holster of the man with braids.

Hackberry looked down the tunnel and saw a pool of water, one that was dull green, the light from an adjacent room reflecting on its surface. There was a bend in the tunnel, and he could not see inside the room. He handed the machine pistol to Andre. "Don't argue with me. If we get into serious trouble, push this little button and pull the trigger. It'll do the rest."

WHAT ARE THE *limits of courage?* Ishmael wondered. Certainly they existed. There were moments and situations for which no one had a cure. On a battlefield, a soldier died in hot blood. He also died with his comrades at his side, in Ishmael's case with the men of color he had come to love. To have to choose between honor and duty and irreparable suffering at the hands of a sadist was another matter.

Could he do it? He would have traded the worst artillery barrage the Germans could throw for the situation he was now in, his wrists manacled to his sides, sitting on his buttocks, the walls of the room sweating with humidity, Beckman squatting next to him in alpine climbing boots, pressing the tip of a screwdriver just below Ishmael's right eye.

"That's a good boy," Beckman whispered. "Daddy will be here in a minute. Who knows? By the end of the evening, you might be back in the arms of Her Majesty Maggie Bassett. Have you ever tried to count up the many ways she's fucked you?"

There was a sound like someone stepping in a pool of water down the tunnel. Beckman stopped talking and stared at the door, listening. He leaned close to Ishmael's ear, his breath like a line of wet ants crawling across Ishmael's skin. "Not a peep, sweet boy."

Beckman again pressed the tip of the screwdriver just below Ishmael's eye. *He won't do it,* Ishmael thought. There were some things no man would do. Then he remembered what he had seen Legionnaires do when they captured a German carrying a sawtooth bayonet. Beckman began to breathe more heavily, working his knee into Ishmael's ribs, knotting Ishmael's hair in his fingers for better purchase.

Ishmael now had no doubt Beckman was going to blind him. And he would enjoy every second of it, in spite of the price he might pay.

Ishmael squeezed both eyes shut, his vulnerable eye watering uncontrollably. "Don't come in, Big Bud!" he shouted.

Then he tried to bury his head between his knees while Beckman hit him again and again in the head with the butt of the screwdriver, his face twisted like an angry child's.

HACKBERRY STEPPED THROUGH the doorway, the Peacemaker held at an upward angle. Beckman was standing above Ishmael, a small nickel-plated revolver pointed into the top of his skull. "Do you believe I will shoot your son, Mr. Holland?"

"Yes, sir, I truly do."

"Your weapons. First you, then the nigger."

Hackberry leaned down and laid his Peacemaker on the floor. Andre set the machine pistol next to it. Beckman screwed the small revolver into Ishmael's neck.

"What did you do to my son?" Hackberry asked.

"Nothing. I took care of him. Which you didn't." Beckman's gaze wandered to the bundle hanging from Hackberry's left hand. "Did you bring me something?"

"I guess that's the way it worked out." Hackberry looked at Jeff, on the floor, his face turned toward the wall. "What's wrong with him?"

"I asked him to cook your son breakfast. He must not like brains and eggs. Is that my artifact you have there?"

"What about it?"

"It's my artifact."

"It's not an artifact. It's a cup that has special meaning for many people. I don't think it was ever yours."

"You stole it from me. Along with my candleholders and some rare coins. Where are they?"

"I don't remember."

"Do you want your son to live?"

"Yes, sir."

"Then give me my artifact."

"Take it."

"No, set it down. Then remove the string and unwrap the cup from the raincoat. Also tell your nigger to stop looking me directly in the face."

"You shouldn't call him by that name."

"The term is a mispronunciation of the word 'Niger,' as in Niger Valley. That's where many of the slaves came from. Tell him to stop staring in my face. I won't abide insolence."

"You're looking at *him*, Beckman, not the other way around. Does Andre bother you for some reason?"

"Unwrap my artifact."

Hackberry did as he was told and set the cup on top of the stove. He could smell the odor of ash and partially burned newspaper under the stove lids. Beckman stared at the jewel-encrusted gold bands and the gold inlay inside the onyx cup. His expression bordered on the lascivious.

"Tell your darky to step back," Beckman said.

"You tell him."

"Do you remember where you saw me before, Mr. Beckman?" Andre said.

"In the restaurant. You're Beatrice DeMolay's driver."

"Before that," Andre said.

"No, I never saw you until today."

"Many, many years ago," Andre said. "Two men were tied to a stake."

"You save that rot for the gullible and the naive."

"Look into my eyes and tell me what you see there," Andre said.

"You'll have a dead nigger on the floor unless you shut him up," Beckman said.

"I think you've got a problem, Beckman. It's not Andre, and it's not me. So what is it?"

"Hand me the cup," Beckman said.

"Pick it up yourself, you son of a bitch."

"Step back, the pair of you," Beckman said. He inched forward, the revolver still aimed at the crown of Ishmael's head, his other hand reaching for the cup. He wet his lips, the blood draining from around his mouth. He closed his hand around the cup's gold framework, gingerly, like someone entering water that was too cold or too hot. Then his face blanched; he dropped the cup into the middle of the slicker's rubberized folds.

He stared at his hand as though it were stricken or had been severed from the rest of his body. He had lost all concentration and dropped the revolver to the floor. Hackberry picked up his Peacemaker and pointed it at him, then realized he had no need for his firearm.

"It burned me," Beckman said. "It was heated by the stove. That's why you put it there."

Hackberry let his hand hover over a stove lid, then placed his hand on it. "There's no heat."

"You're lying."

"Why would I lie? Here, I'll press your face down on it," Hackberry said.

Beckman's mouth twitched.

"I'm kidding," Hackberry said. He reached down and helped his son to his feet. "Let's get those manacles off you. Somebody might think you're a convict, old pal of mine."

"I saw you in a dream, Big Bud."

Beckman had backed against the wall, holding his right wrist. "I'm so glad we're all reunited here," he said. "But here's the reality,

Mr. Holland. You've invaded my home. You've either wounded or killed people here. We were keeping your son to cure him of his addictions. You're a drunkard and have no credibility."

"Andre, I think I would really like to go ahead and kill this man," Hackberry said. "What do you think about it?"

"That is not necessary," Andre replied. "It will get him."

"Somebody else said that to me," Hackberry replied. "A man in the desert, down in Mexico. What is 'it'?"

"'It' is it. You'll see. Look at Mr. Beckman. Have you ever seen greater fear in a man's eyes?"

But Hackberry Holland was no longer interested in linguistic nuances or metaphysical mysteries. As he and Andre walked out into the night, each of them holding one of Ishmael's arms over his shoulder, they heard a screeching sound like a corrugated roof being ripped in half.

They rounded the front of the building and saw Willard Posey getting out of his motorcar, the one whose entire roof had been hacksawed off the car body.

"Glad you dropped by," Hackberry said.

"Don't get the wrong idea," Willard said. "I think you ought to be locked up in an asylum."

A second motorcar pulled off the road. Ruby Dansen and Beatrice DeMolay got out, the headlamps flooding the yard, burning away the shadows, creating a white radiance on the faces of Darl Pickins and Hackberry and Andre and Willard and Ishmael and Beatrice and Ruby, as though indeed they were children of light and not merely a human extension of an ancient metaphor.

Epilogue

Six months later, on a fine spring day in Pacific Palisades, California, a woman wearing a lavender and silver dress and red velvet boots and a wide, stiff-brimmed black hat with a veil stepped off a passenger train onto the station platform and waited for the baggage handlers or porters or jitney drivers to approach her, as though their collective attention were her obvious due.

Her elegance, her posture, and her regal bearing made onlookers assume that she was another member of the motion picture studio and burgeoning actors' community not far away.

Later, police investigators would discover that nobody in the film community knew who she was or where she came from. The driver of the cab she hired thought it strange that her first destination was a hardware and building-supply store. Her second destination, as everyone learned, was the home of the millionaire Arnold Beckman. It was only natural that a man like Mr. Beckman, an international soldier of fortune who had been at Flanders fields and Gallipoli, would have a guest like the mysterious lady swathed in a veil.

His home was created in the style of a Roman villa, on a hilltop overlooking the ocean, with fluted pillars and airy terraces and colonnades above the walkways and reflecting pools dotted with floating flowers and bougainvillea and orange trumpet vine dangling from the latticework. The cabdriver was particularly struck by the woman's gentility. When he told her in his embarrassment that he didn't have enough change to break the fifty-dollar bill she gave him, she closed his hand on the bill and told him to keep it all. He also said she winked at him before she walked away.

ARNOLD BECKMAN WAS obviously overjoyed when he opened the door. "Maggie, Maggie, Maggie," he said, spreading his arms wide, ushering her in, speaking so rapidly that his bottom lip was flecked with spittle. He was witty and gracious, humble and without bitterness, even about his legal troubles in Texas. "If I had it to do over, I suppose I would handle a few things differently," he said as he gave her a tour of the grounds. "On balance, things have worked out exceptionally well. Americans love public contrition. No matter how many times a real bastard sticks it to them, they welcome the sod back home. Attorneys are also a marvelous invention. I send a check, fix a drink, and watch the sun set on the Pacific Ocean."

He was standing on a precipice at the edge of his property, sand and black rocks and pounding surf far below. He lifted a hand as though indicating all the potential of the future, perhaps an empire that lay beyond the horizon. "What do you think of my digs?"

"Can you find a place for me out here?" she asked.

"I'll make you a partner. You'll be popping the whip over the whole studio. I'm so happy you've put our little tiffs behind us. You have, haven't you?" Before she could reply, he caught the attention of his manservant. "Fix brunch for us, Walter. Also sweep the leaves off the patio and lower the sunscreens for Miss Bassett. We'll be eating on the glass table."

"How many places shall I set, sir?"

"How many people do you see here, Walter?" Beckman said. He turned his attention back to her. "Remember what I said about Venus rising? I'd love to see you in the surf at eveningtide, with the sun behind you like an enormous, succulent orange."

"I'm a bit tired, Arnold. Do you mind if I take a hot bath and a little nap afterward?"

"You don't have to convince me about the restorative value of a good soak. Gad, I'm glad you're here. Tell me, do you see your former husband?"

"I think he's had quite enough of me."

"How about the war hero?"

"Ishmael is reading for the law," she said. "I think you already know these things."

"Just checking up," he said.

Checking up on whom? she thought.

His eyes roved over her person. "I turn to water when I look at you."

"You've always been a dear," she said. "I knew you wouldn't let me down now. It's beautiful here on the promontory, but I really need a bath."

"After we eat."

"I had a bite on the train. I just want a bath."

"You need to keep up your strength. I know what's best for my girl."

She slept the entire afternoon and woke refreshed and happy, combing back her hair with her fingers, stretching in front of a window that gave on to palm trees and an ocean aglitter with the sunset. What had Arnold said of her? She was Venus rising from the surf? Was he mocking her again, as he had in San Antonio? Fannie Porter had advised the girls that the key to success in business lay in a short memory and shallow feelings. *What dreck,* Maggie had thought at the time. Upon reflection, she'd revised her opinion of Miss Porter's admonition to: *It's not just dreck. Anyone who makes a statement like that is either lying or a sap and deserves to get reamed with a telephone pole.*

After a candlelight supper on the terrace, she drank coffee while Arnold drank brandy, and kept him up as late as possible. Then they played gin rummy and walked on the beach and ended up at the amusement pier, where she made him take her on the rides until it closed for the night.

"You're inexhaustible," he said. "I can't keep up with you. I must go to sleep."

"Let's walk out on the rocks," she replied. "Please. Look at the breakers. I love California."

"Would that you were mine, Maggie."

"Maybe I will be. Someday."

"Ah, the caveat," he said. "But if there were no caveat, you wouldn't be Maggie."

At eight-thirty the next morning, she went into his bedroom and shook him awake.

"My God, woman, have you lost your mind? What time is it?" he said.

"I fixed you a fine breakfast."

"That's what I have a cook for."

"Not today."

"What?"

"I sent him home. The other servants as well."

"What are you doing?"

"I'd like us to be together. I'd like to talk about some motion picture ideas I have. Sundance and Butch didn't die in South America."

"Oh, this will shake the foundations of modern history."

"I think it's an important story," she said.

"Nobody is going to see a film about a couple of ignorant Wyoming hayseeds."

"All right, the truth is, I want to be alone with you." She let her gaze drift out the window to the ocean.

He looked sideways. "Be alone with me for what reason?"

"Use your imagination."

"You're serious?"

"Do I have to write it on the wall?"

He propped himself up and pulled back the covers, patting the mattress.

"No, I'm going to put breakfast on the table while you take a bath," she said.

"I bathed last night."

"You could use another one. A shave as well."

He rubbed the stubble on his jaw. "Whatever makes you happy."

She went into the kitchen and scraped pots and skillets on the stove until she heard the water running in the master bathroom. Then she called the hardware and building-supply store. "This is Mrs. Levy. I have an order on hold. I'd like you to deliver it now. Do you know where Mr. Arnold Beckman's residence is? Would you set it on the back steps, please? You're so kind."

She set the table, making noise with the plates and knives and forks and crystal glasses, then brought coffee on a silver service to Arnold's bathroom. He had just finished shaving and was seated in the tub, hot water pouring out of the gold-plated faucet, a bottle of bubble bath resting sideways in the soap dish.

"I fixed you café au lait, the way they do it in New Orleans," she said.

"How much did I drink last night?" he said, taking the cup from the tray.

"You were a bit on the grog. It wasn't a problem." She glanced at the surface of the bathwater. "You're showing. Let's put a little more bubbly in."

"Why should one be ashamed of his or her endowment? Hop in. The water is fine."

When she didn't answer, he drank his cup empty and held it out for a refill. "You wouldn't try to put one over on me, would you, Maggie?"

"If that's what you think, I'll go."

"You're a practical woman. You have to look out for yourself. There's nothing wrong with that."

"I need a job. There are a lot of things I do well. Your strongest attributes are your confidence and your personal strength, Arnold. That's what every woman wants in a man, even though she may not admit it. No man should ever underestimate a woman's secret need."

"Are you broke?"

"No. Do I want more money than I have? Guess."

He smiled and scratched the corner of his eye. His skin was bronze and running with sweat, his knife scars as slick as snakes. "Wash my stomach?"

"Wash it yourself. And stop acting like an adolescent."

"That's my girl."

She rolled a towel into a pad and placed it on the back rim of the tub. "Lean back and close your eyes."

"What did I drink at the amusement pier?"

"A champagne cocktail or two. Or maybe three."

"I must have had ten," he said. "My head is hammering."

She soaked a washcloth in hot water and squeezed it dry, then placed it over his eyes. Through the window curtains, she saw a delivery vehicle pull to a stop behind the house. The surface of the bathwater was covered with foam and iridescent bubbles. "There's a telephone repair vehicle outside. I'll be right back. Take a nap. Just don't slip under the water."

"Hurry up. I'm developing a male problem that could use some attention."

"Make a wish list while I'm gone," she replied.

She retrieved the delivery from the back steps and went into the kitchen and began pouring the devil's brew into two large buckets. She picked up each bucket by the bail and carried them into the bathroom, setting them down heavily, blowing a lock of hair out of her face. "Close your eyes tight. I'm going to rinse you off."

She poured the buckets over him, his silvery-blond hair pasting to his skin.

"You're always full of mystery," he said. "Did you read mysteries as a child, Sherlock Holmes and that kind of thing?"

"I read Shakespeare. My favorite character was Lady Macbeth."

"As a role model?"

"If you only knew, darling Arnold. How do you feel?"

"Not too well. My eyes are burning."

"Move your hands."

He stared at the froth on the surface of the water. She saw both fear and a terrible sense of realization climb into his face.

"Try your legs," she said.

"What's happening to me? What did you do?"

"It's a concoction used by the Indians in South America. Guess the name of the Wyoming hayseed who originally told me about it."

"What did you pour on me?"

"If you had a sense of smell, you would detect the odor of naphtha, coal oil, paint thinner, and a pound of wax crystals."

"Wax?"

"For adhesive purposes."

She couldn't tell if the collapse of his facial muscles was caused by his stupefaction or the toxic mix of depressants she had been feeding him since the previous night.

"You win," he said. "Call a physician. I'll give you half of everything I have."

"That's not necessary. During the night I took your ledger books from your desk, your bank account numbers in Switzerland, your jewelry, and a stack of bearer bonds. Did you know you left your safe open? I haven't had time to count the cash, but I think it's quite a bit."

She picked up one of the buckets and began pouring a trail out the door. He had slipped lower in the bathwater and was cursing her incoherently, his head bobbing like a coconut on a frothy sea.

She looked up and silently mouthed, "Ta-ta," then continued backward with the bucket into the kitchen. She lit a solitary candle on the breakfast table, blew out the match, opened the oven door, and turned on the gas.

With a big carpet bag hitched over her shoulder, she shut the front door behind her and walked down the hill toward the ocean.

Fifteen minutes later, an explosion blew glass and flame out of the windows, but a secondary explosion, far more powerful, leveled the building and caused the reflecting pools to boil. Some said Beckman had stored ordnance for his motion pictures in the basement. Others said a gas line had exploded under the house. The fact that his body parts rained down all over the neighborhood was a subject of jokes for perhaps a week. Otherwise, his passing seemed to be noted only by the seagulls perched on the debris in the lawn, and looters who carried off souvenirs. His memorial service, arranged by a business agent, was unattended, even by the business agent.

IN THE SAME month, a related event took place deep down in rural Mexico, although it commanded no newspaper space or study

by historians. An ornate open touring car with two people in it
and an engine that sounded like a dollar watch ticking out of
control wended its way through round-topped hills that resembled
ant mounds and outcroppings of volcanic slag and dry washes
surrounded by the carcasses of dead animals. When the touring car
reached a riverbed that had shrunk from its banks into a thin red
stream that glistened as brightly as blood in the sunrise, Hackberry
and Mrs. Ruby Holland got out and crossed a wooden bridge lashed
together with rope and leather thongs.

They walked up a sandy trail bordered by cactus that bloomed
with yellow and red flowers, and entered a grove of cottonwoods
swelling with wind, and continued on to a village that had no name
and whose indigenous people knew nothing of the outside world or
the one from which they had probably descended.

The dirt streets had not changed, nor the lay of the mud buildings or
the jail or the cantina or the outbuildings constructed of discarded slat
board. The only differences Hackberry could see in the village since his
visit in 1916 were the increase in bullet holes and the expansion of the
cemetery, whose sticklike crosses stretched up a hillside.

Hackberry was wearing a powder-blue coat and a new Stetson
and shined boots and dark trousers and a snap-button shirt that
crinkled with light. He was not carrying a firearm, only a drawstring
bag he had thrown over his shoulder. An old man in sandals and
baggy pants tied with rope was sweeping off the line of flat stones
that served as a walkway into the mud-walled church where
Hackberry had awakened and been fed and cared for and armed
with a hatchet three years ago.

"*¿Dónde está el sacerdote?*" Hackberry asked.

"*¿Qué sacerdote?*"

"*Es* Maryknoll."

The man stopped sweeping. His eyes were blue and rheumy, his
cheeks covered with white whiskers. "*Con los muertos.*"

"*¿Está muerto?*"

The man with the broom pointed at the cemetery on the hillside.
"No, *él está limpiando las tumbas.*"

Hackberry put his arm over Ruby's shoulders and walked up

the incline behind the church. The Maryknoll missionary cleaning the graves looked up from his work, the sun in his eyes, obviously unable to see the two figures approaching him.

"Remember me?" Hackberry said.

The missionary shaded his eyes. "Mr. Holland, the Texas Ranger."

"This is my wife, Miss Ruby."

"How do you do, Father? I'm a great admirer of the Maryknolls," she said. "One big union."

He didn't seem to make the association.

"Who shot up the place?" Hackberry asked.

"Everyone."

"We won't take up your time, Padre," Hackberry said. "I brought you something I didn't quite know what to do with."

He swung the tote bag off his shoulder and handed it to the missionary. The weight of the object inside made a hard rectangular outline against the cloth.

"What is it?"

"Good question. I suspect it may have wandered two thousand years to arrive here. Or maybe not. I've yet to depuzzle it."

"I don't think I've heard that one before. If I remember correctly, you suffered a serious head injury. Are you all right, sir?"

"You gave me a hatchet I told you I was going to split wood with. I'm afraid I used it for other purposes. That's bothered me a little bit."

"Mr. Holland, what is in this bag?"

"The most evil man I ever met tried to get holt of it and hide it from the rest of the human race. For that reason alone, I think it's probably the real deal. I saw a mess of children playing out in the street. I think the man who drank from this cup would like to see it here."

Hackberry tipped his hat, and he and Ruby said good-bye and walked to their vehicle and drove away, the dust billowing in yellow clouds across the sun, filling the sky with the threat of a storm or monsoon that would bring new life to the land, reminiscent of the time when he was fifteen and flying hell-for-breakfast across the Cimarron, Indian arrows embedded up to the shaft in the leather mail pouches slung on his back.

ACKNOWLEDGMENTS

I would like to thank my editor, Sarah Knight, and my copy editor, E. Beth Thomas, and my daughter, Pamala Burke, for their invaluable help on this manuscript. I would also like to express my appreciation to my publishers, Carolyn Reidy and Jonathan Karp, and my publisher at Pocket Books, Louise Burke, and my editor at Pocket, Abby Zidle, and the art director, Jackie Seow, and the production editor at Simon & Schuster, Kathleen Rizzo, and all the production and marketing and publicity team for the loyal support they have given my work over the many years.

ABOUT THE AUTHOR

Born in Houston, Texas, in 1936, James Lee Burke grew up on the Texas-Louisiana Gulf Coast. He attended Southwestern Louisiana Institute and later received a BA and an MA in English from the University of Missouri in 1958 and 1960, respectively. Over the years, he worked as a landman for the Sinclair Oil Company, pipe liner, land surveyor, newspaper reporter, college English professor, social worker on skid row in Los Angeles, clerk for the Louisiana Employment Service, and instructor in the U.S. Job Corps. He and his wife, Pearl, met in graduate school and have been married fifty-five years; they have four children.

Burke is the author of thirty-four novels, including twenty in the Dave Robicheaux series, and two collections of short stories. His work has twice been awarded an Edgar for Best Crime Novel of the Year; in 2009 the Mystery Writers of America named him a Grand Master. He has also been a recipient of Bread Loaf and Guggenheim fellowships and an NEA grant. Three of his novels (*Heaven's Prisoners, Two for Texas,* and *In the Electric Mist with Confederate Dead*) have been made into motion pictures. His short stories have been published in *The Atlantic Monthly, New Stories from the South, The Best American Short Stories, The Antioch Review, The Southern Review,* and *The Kenyon Review.* His novel *The Lost Get-Back Boogie* was rejected 111 times over a period of nine years and, upon its publication by Louisiana State University Press in 1986, was nominated for a Pulitzer Prize.

He and Pearl live in Missoula, Montana.